AWARDS FOR THE SPARKS

National Silver Award Winner For Best Young Adult Fiction 2015
and Gold Award For Best Young Adult Book in Florida 2015
FLORIDA AUTHOR'S AND PUBLISHERS ASSOCIATION

Bronze International Moonbeam Award and
Indie Fab Award for Best Young Author

Silver award at the Florida Book Festival

HONORABLE MENTIONS:
- International London Book Festival
- Midwest Book Festival
- Hollywood Book Festival
- Southern California Book Festival
- New England Book Festival

PRAISE FOR THE SPARKS

"A crackling read. Feud: The Sparks builds a vivid world that is at once otherworldly and relatable. Characters spring from the page in a deft twist on mythology that belies Kyle Prue's young age. He's a voice to be heard."
SCOTT BOWLES, USA TODAY

"5 Stars!!…This is a great story. I got sucked in…Kyle Prue is a young author but he is one that you don't want miss. His writing just draws you in and keeps you wanting more. This is a great story that is well developed and very descriptive. I will be making sure to keep my eyes out for all of his books."
J BRONDER BOOK REVIEWS

"Great ready for a great adventure!…A full bodied world with characters that will hold you tight in tension as they fight their battles…I am very impressed with this young man's writing. It's smooth, flows well, and he's a great storyteller."
JO ANN HAKOLA, BOOK FAERIE

"Kyle Prue is a highly talented young writer with an extreme amount of potential… Prue does a fantastic job of keeping the somewhat large cast of characters clearly organized and distinct, which is highly impressive…The pacing of the story was perfect—the book kept me turning pages and seemed to fly by in no time. Kyle Prue is an author to watch."
MARY RUTH PURSSELLEY, THE WRITER'S LAIR

"Kyle Prue creates a well developed fantasy world for this trilogy… Prue is a talented writer and storyteller-who knows his audience…keeps the book fun and interesting for adults and young adults alike…Do not let the author's young age discourage you from reading this book-it is more than worth your time."
ANGELA THOMPSON, A MAMA'S CORNER OF THE WORLD

"Have you read any amazing books written by a high school senior lately? Now, I can say that I have had such an experience. Filled with fast-paced action, debuting his first book of an eagerly anticipated trilogy, he creates an intricate fantasy world that delights and grasps readers from the beginning straight through until the end. Introducing himself as a young author with an extensive command of the literary world, Kyle Prue should proudly add accomplished author of The Sparks to his list of achievements."
NIECYISMS AND NESTLINGS

THE
SPARKS

BOOK 1 OF THE FEUD TRILOGY

KYLE PRUE

Cartwright Publishing, Naples, Florida

Paperback ISBN: 978-0-9994449-1-7

Cover design by Ashley Ruggirello www.CardboardMonet.com
Interior formatting by Ashley Ruggirello, www.CardboardMonet.com

Library of Congress Control Number: 2014951949
The Sparks / Kyle Prue

Printed in the U.S.A.

This is a work of fiction. All characters, organizations, and events portrayed in this novel are either products of
the author's imagination or are used fictitiously.

DEDICATION

For Seacrest Country Day School
It truly was a magical journey.

In memory of Drew Harrison
I never would have had the courage to express my
creativity if I hadn't met you.

CHARACTERS

THE VAPROS FAMILY
- Neil Vapros
- Rhys Vapros
- Jennifer Vapros
- Victoria Vapros
- Sir Vapros

THE TAURLUM FAMILY
- Darius Taurlum
- Michael Taurlum

THE CELERIUS FAMILY
- Lilly Celerius
- Anthony Celerius
- Lady Celerius
- Sir Celerius
- Thomas Celerius
- Jonathan

THE EMPIRE
- The Emperor
- Saewulf
- Carlin Filus
- The Empress
- Virgil Servatus
- Quintus
- Captain of the Guard

CITIZENS OF ALTRYON
- Bianca Blackmore
- Robert Tanner
- Anastasia
- Alfred the Bartender
- Bill the Bartender
- The Pig
- Ainsley Bovick

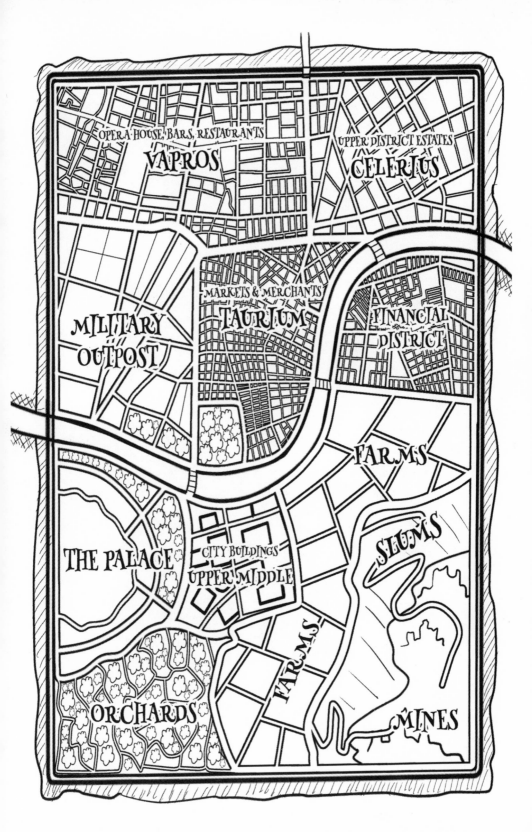

PART ONE

THE FAMILIES

Vox Populi Vox Dei
The Voice of the People is the Voice of God

Chapter One

TAURLUM MANSION
NEIL VAPROS

SLIDE THE KNIFE BETWEEN THE THIRD AND FOURTH RIB.

Neil's father's words rang in his ears as he pulled his dark, ornate hood over his head and raised his cloth mask to cover his mouth and nose. He knew all Taurlum had several weak spots on their bodies, but only one was vulnerable enough to cause an instant kill. All he needed to do was thrust his knife directly between the ribs (*the third and fourth ribs*, he reminded himself) and straight through the heart. Neil's father had taught him this trick on his tenth birthday. It had been one of the more pleasant ones.

He spent a moment adjusting his mask, making sure his face would remain concealed. Not that it really mattered; during the middle of the day, the mask would do little to camouflage him. Any Taurlum would spot a Vapros like him from a mile away. The disguise had been given to him mostly for the sake of preserving his identity. Nobody needed to know which Vapros boy had made the kill.

Neil ran his finger over the hilt of the knife. His father had presented it to him upon completion of his assassin's training. Engraved in the handle was the Vapros family crest. The background of the crest was purple and black, with a raven embedded in the center. The Raven was the family nickname, as the black-haired, green-eyed descendants seemed to favor their swift, calculating animal mascot. The raven was known as the bringer of death: an appropriate symbol for the trained assassin. The family motto was inscribed along the bottom: Victory Lies Within the Ashes. Neil loved his knife; it made him feel like a real assassin.

Neil craved the assassin's glory but knew in his gut that he desperately needed another assassin to assist in this mission. Two stealthy ravens against a Taurlum bull was still a risk, but they would have the element of surprise on their side. Alone it was a certain death mission, but his father's orders were clear. Neil was desperately alone.

Making it into the giant Taurlum mansion had been easy. Navigating its giant corridors would be harder. Neil glanced carefully around the marble corner. A single guard stood watch. The man wore simple plated armor with red and gold war paint but had removed his helmet to reveal his entire head. *Not a Taurlum*, Neil thought. The guard lacked the golden blonde hair shared by every direct descendant of the Taurlum line; therefore, this man was not worth his time or effort. Neil squinted in concentration, and then threw all his energy into dematerializing. He reformed a split second later on the other side of the corridor. The guard continued watching the hallway and never noticed Neil materialize just behind him. As silently as he could, the Vapros boy made his way down the hallway toward the communal baths where his target would be waiting.

A Taurlum family crest hung above the door to the bathhouse. Its colors were the same gold and scarlet that covered the uniforms of the Taurlum guards who roughed up villagers in the market. A proud-looking bull stood in the center of the crest, eyes narrowed, as if challenging all who dared to oppose the name of the "great Taurlum." At the thought of eliminating his first Taurlum man, Neil's heart began to quicken, jump-started by adrenaline. He reached for his crossbow and fired a bolt directly into the bull's pretentious forehead. Then he opened the door and dematerialized as quickly as he could.

He reappeared behind a marble pillar a few feet away from the entrance. The inside of the Taurlum mansion was lavishly decorated with red and gold, from long velvet banners to giant tapestries depicting the family's crest. The manor itself stood in the center of the marketplace so that all the merchants affiliated with the Taurlum could get home quickly if the mighty Vapros warriors showed up. Even though Neil was disgusted at the opulence of the mansion, he couldn't help but admire how impressive it was. The entirety of the Taurlum mansion was made of polished marble to accommodate the great weight of its residents. A marvel like this had never been built before and was quite a change from the wooden and brick buildings that filled the city.

A door on the opposite wall opened. Neil risked a glance around his pillar. Two towheaded men wearing red and gold swimwear came into the bathhouse. Neil resisted the urge to snort. They never missed a chance to bear their family colors and boast of their "superior lineage." The two Taurlum were young, one looked to be Neil's age, the other a few years older, and they were unarmed. But their skin, Neil knew, was hard to pierce. The boys might as well have been made of iron.

Neil glanced around the corner to look at their swimwear. He had never seen anything like it. Most people in Altryon didn't have the money or opportunity to swim for fun, but when they did, their swimwear covered their chests along with their legs. These boys wore nothing except what appeared to be swim shorts. This was most likely because they wanted to show off as many muscles as possible. The taller one chatted loudly and easily to his companion. Neil dared to relax. They didn't suspect he was here. The shorter Taurlum was quieter, but the proud, almost cocky way he held himself when he walked made Neil roll his eyes.

"So," the taller boy was saying as he walked into Neil's line of vision. The Vapros boy held his breath. "Did you hear about the Pig?" Neil recognized this boy now: Michael Taurlum, known as "the Nose" among the villagers because of his prominent snout. He wore a gold ring on every finger, and the multitudes of bracelets adorning his arms clinked loudly. Any normal man would struggle to carry all that jewelry, but Michael's skin bore the weight easily. His droopy, yet unsettlingly alert eyes were fixed on his Taurlum companion and he had a thin, blonde beard growing on his iron jaw. He didn't see the Vapros enemy behind the pillar, which was incredibly fortunate for Neil. Michael wasn't well known for his mercy.

The younger, clean-shaven boy sank into the warm bath water. "The Pig?" he asked, raising an eyebrow.

Michael climbed into the bath beside him, not bothering to remove his jewelry. "Come on, Darius, learn the damn city." His voice was louder and bolder than his brother's. It was almost as if he wanted the entire city to hear him, and to hear him clearly. It made Neil want to shoot him on the spot. Patience, he reminded himself. He couldn't make his move yet. If these two realized he was here, he would not only fail his mission, he would probably also be killed, or worse, held for ransom. Even if his family paid the ransom to get him back, Neil's cover would be blown and he would be forced to spend the rest of his days working as a socialite. That was not the life he'd been working toward for all these years. He was trained to be an assassin. He could not mess this up. Failure would not be tolerated.

"The Pig is the guy who owns the mask shop in the market," the Nose was explaining to the one called Darius. Neil focused his energy and rematerialized behind another pillar a little farther away from the boys.

Darius cocked his head. "And why is he called the Pig?"

Michael waded into deeper water and smiled. "Because he's a pig," he chuckled. "And because he's famous for forcing himself on women."

Darius's mouth stretched into a grin. "You shouldn't be talking. You're kind of famous for that, too."

Michael's smile quickly turned to a frown. Behind the pillar, Neil nearly laughed out loud. This Darius wasn't afraid to speak his mind. From across the room, he heard the men continuing with their conversation, but he couldn't stay to listen. There was a mission at hand.

He rematerialized behind a new pillar, edging his way closer to the other side of the room where the door to the next room was waiting. Coming to the baths had been a waste of time; neither Darius nor the Nose was his target. Neil could still hardly believe his father had chosen him for this critical mission. His target was the Taurlum grandfather, the titular head of the Taurlum family. The Vapros controlled the nightlife district and the production and distribution of ale. The Taurlum controlled the markets. But in an unexpected power play, the Taurlum were attempting to corner the market on barley, wheat, and hops, buying up the ingredients needed to produce the Vapros ale. This assassination was in direct retaliation for this ill-advised maneuver.

Neil dematerialized again, and then again, and then stopped short; he was out of pillars. Nothing but empty space stood between him and the door, but it was too far. He wasn't strong enough to rematerialize that far away. Neil felt his heart begin to pound and he ran his hand through his raven hair angrily. He was stuck.

He considered his options. He could try to make a run for it. Darius was sitting with his back to the exit, but the Nose wouldn't sit still. If he turned at just the wrong time, he would spot the Vapros boy. Neil pulled his knife from its sheath. It had been specially curved so that it could slip in between a man's ribs. However, that tactic would prove ineffective against a Taurlum, unless Neil was perfectly precise. The only way to kill a Taurlum was to press the knife into a pressure point. Once the knife pierced the skin there, and the Taurlum started to bleed, he was as easy to kill as any other mortal. It wouldn't be so hard to sneak up behind Darius and stab him, and then it was just a matter of Michael. The Vapros loved to tell stories about how much of a brutish monster he was in combat. Michael also had the added advantage of his massive size. Neil estimated that he stood at nearly six-and-a-half feet tall, and every inch of his body was composed of hard muscle. Darius was smaller and leaner, but Neil didn't let that fool him. Darius was lean, but he had an athlete's hard body and definitely wouldn't go down without a fight. If Neil could only strike down Michael first somehow....

Suddenly, the door Neil had come through burst open, and a guard came running into the bathhouse. "Sirs!" he cried. "We have reason to believe there is an assassin in the house!"

Neil almost dropped his knife. Michael leaped out of the pool, bracelets clanging obnoxiously against each other. The other boy didn't move. "What makes you think there's someone in the house?" asked Darius with a raised eyebrow.

"There was a crossbow bolt fired into the Taurlum seal over the door to this very room," the guard said nervously. "A Vapros weapon, from the looks of it. We are on high alert. Either one of you could be the target."

Neil shoved a hand through his hair and cursed his own arrogance. He slid the curved knife back into its sheath and planned his next move. Fighting had seemed like a good idea when it was only two boys in a bath, but now he had lost the element of surprise.

On the other side of the room, Michael scoffed, "I fear no assassin. I am going to go get my hammer and then I am going to find him and use his insides to decorate the floor."

Darius stepped out of the bath and put a restraining hand on the Nose's shoulder. "Settle down, Michael. The guards will take care of this. Any assassin stupid enough to fire a bolt into our crest is not stealthy enough to stay hidden for long."

Darius and Michael left the bathhouse together, leaving puddles in their wakes. Now, only the lone guard remained. Neil waited as patiently as he could but the man didn't seem to have any intention of leaving. Neil took a breath and tried to still his hammering heart. He had never actually killed a man before. Carefully, Neil raised his crossbow and fired a bolt into the back of the guard's head. The guard let out a surprised gasp as he began to fall. Neil materialized behind him and grabbed the back of his neck before he hit the ground. As he held onto the lifeless body he began to gather all his energy and then with a strong exhale, he released it. The guard's body instantly dissolved into ash—clothes, weapons, and all. Every fiber of his being was cremated in less than a second. The ability to dissolve his enemies into ash was a useful one, but for Neil, it only worked on bodies that were already dead, and it would be ineffective as a tool in the coming assassination.

Neil doubted anyone would notice the ash on the ground until he had already completed his mission, but he kicked through what was left of the guard for good measure. A pang of guilt began to arise in his chest and he clutched his stomach. He felt his face grow warm and for a moment, he was sure he would faint. He very quickly found himself vomiting onto the marble floor. He took a deep breath and approached the pool. With cupped hands, he brought some water to his mouth. He swirled it around and then spat it out. *Don't feel guilty*, he told himself. *Any guard who decided to work for a prominent family like the Taurlum understood the risks*. He started toward the door, but fatigue and shortness of breath made him pause and double over. Materializing took an inordinate amount of energy. He had been stupid to use his powers so often in such a short amount of time. He stumbled to one of the pillars and leaned against it as he tried to stay conscious. A full minute passed before he felt well enough to stand, and as he made his way to the exit, he promised himself not to materialize again unless it was absolutely necessary.

The exit took him to the bottom of a giant spiral staircase. He climbed the steps with as much vigor as he could muster in his weakened state, panting a little from the effort. By the time he reached the top stair, he was gasping for breath. Before him stood a giant door which stretched up to over three times his height. Why was everything in this house so tall? It was as if the Taurlum mansion was built for a community of elephants, instead of men who just happened to have tough skin.

The door didn't have a handle. Neil threw himself against the wood with all his force, but it held fast, and with a sinking heart, he realized someone with the strength of a Taurlum warrior designed the door. No one without such strength would be able to push it open. Not for the first time in his life, he wished it were possible to materialize through walls.

As Neil backtracked a few steps to try throwing himself against the door again, it was pulled open with a staggering amount of force from the opposite side. The Vapros assassin found himself face to face with a familiar pair of Taurlum brothers, now armor-clad and holding weapons. "Got him," the Nose said to Darius, brandishing a hammer high above his head. Neil forgot every bit of his training and made a run for it.

In spite of promising himself not to, Neil materialized behind the two brothers and bolted into a circular room filled with armor and weapons. He gasped as he entered and realized this was a dead end. He didn't have the energy to materialize again. The two Taurlum turned to face him, amusement spreading across their faces. Michael stood back and watched as Darius began to walk forward to confront Neil. "Remove your hood, Vapros," he commanded.

Neil pulled away his hood and mask to reveal his face for the two young men. Michael seemed slightly surprised by his age, but Darius held his icy composure. Neil was finally able to see Darius up close. He had wavy golden hair and something in his blue eyes that was almost intelligent. Neil quickly decided that Darius's eyes didn't show wisdom but more of an ironclad determination. Unlike Michael, he didn't wear any jewelry. It was as if his entire outfit had been designed to be practical and battle efficient. This didn't stop Neil from noticing the blood smeared on his armored chest. Neil was ready to bet that it wasn't his. "Who are you here to kill?" Darius asked, advancing slowly. Neil backed away until he was pressed up against a giant floor-to-ceiling stained glass window. He glanced over his shoulder. The window would be easy to shatter, but a fall from this height was risky.

"The oldest Taurlum," Neil answered finally. "Your grandfather probably. I haven't exactly looked at your family tree recently."

Darius narrowed his eyes. Neil braced himself for a deathblow. "You're kind of an idiot, aren't you?" the Taurlum boy said, a hint of laughter in his eyes.

This question caught Neil off guard. "Not exactly. I'm just unlucky. Why?"

"Look at you!" he laughed. "You've run right into a dead end. You aren't even remotely in the right part of the house, if you're looking for my grandfather. Was that your intention?"

Neil tried to stand up straight as he responded sarcastically, "Well, if you could point me to the right part of the house I'd be on my way."

Michael exhaled heavily through his oversized nose and rubbed his bearded face leisurely. "On with it, Darius. I want to continue my swim."

As Darius took a step closer to his target, Neil realized he might have stalled long enough to gain back sufficient energy for one last escape. He concentrated his energy and prepared to materialize somewhere near the door. Darius realized what Neil was doing too soon, and before Neil could disappear, the Taurlum had planted his right foot against Neil's chest and kicked him straight through the window.

As Neil fell, he used the last of his energy to rematerialize slightly closer to the ground. He hit it chest first with a thud. Neil groaned as he tried to get up. His breastplate was horribly dented and his mouth tasted of blood. He slowly made it to his hands and knees and realized he was facing the markets. The massive city wall loomed in the distance, shrouded by a thin fog.

He rolled around and tilted his head back to glare up at the window. He made eye contact with Darius, who now held a mammoth war hammer. A small smile played around the Taurlum's lips as he raised the weapon above his head. Neil realized what was going to happen just in time. The hammer hit the ground with such force that it tore apart the bricks where Neil had been lying a moment before.

"Is that the best you can do?" Neil shouted. Darius scowled and stepped straight out of the broken window. He plummeted to the ground (as did Neil's jaw) and landed so hard that the cobblestone street beneath him shattered and sent up a cloud of dust. He rose from the rubble, dusted himself off, and swaggered over to Neil. "If you value your life," he said, pulling the massive hammer from the ground, "you should run."

A group of villagers had come running when they saw the boy thrown from the third story window of the Taurlum mansion, but as Darius advanced on Neil they turned to flee. The citizens of Altryon knew what happened when members of opposing houses came across one another. Better to get as far away from the coming brawl as possible.

Neil met Darius's icy gaze and tore away his dented breastplate. For an instant, he considered fighting. Darius raised a challenging eyebrow and stretched out his arms threateningly. Neil took a step forward, threw his breastplate to the ground, and turned tail to run for his life. Darius smiled and waited a few seconds to give Neil a decent head start. Then, hoisting the hammer above his head, he let out a roar and chased after the terrified Vapros would-be assassin.

Chapter Two

CELERIUS ESTATE
LILLY CELERIUS

LILLY CELERIUS FROWNED AT HERSELF IN THE MIRROR AND DECIDED THAT being seventeen years old looked exactly the same as being sixteen. She lifted a comb and pushed it through her lengthy auburn hair, then gently guided the stray strands into place with her fingertips. She passed her palm down the front of her military coat, checking to make sure each button was still fastened, and then reached up to dab away a bit of smudged lipstick from the corner of her thin lips. She had wide mahogany eyes and well-defined cheekbones. These were common Celerius traits that she wore with pride. She nearly always looked presentable, but this was a special occasion. Nothing could be out of place—not today.

The door to her bedroom opened quietly, and Jonathan came inside. Lilly didn't bother to turn around. She looked his reflection up and down in the mirror. "Yes?"

The servant bowed, then stood at attention like a loyal guard dog. "Are you ready, Miss?"

More ready than you are, she thought, sighing. Jonathan's black hair hung down over his forehead, unkempt and far longer than a servant's hair was supposed to be. His royal blue coat, which had clearly been made for a much taller man, dangled past his ankles. The coat, Lilly knew, had been a gift to Jonathan from her father, and the former wore it proudly almost every day, in spite of the fact that he appeared to be drowning in it. "Let's go," she said, giving her hair a final pat. She hesitated for a quick second to readjust Jonathan's collar for him.

Jonathan bowed again, gestured to the door and answered, "After you."

She exited briskly and he trotted after her, stumbling slightly as he hurried to keep up. The poor man had never made it past five feet tall and he had to maintain a steady jog to stay next to his mistress. "When was the last time you saw General Anthony?" he asked, trying to sound serious in spite of his hurried pace.

Lilly rolled her eyes and sighed audibly, but slowed her steps. "It's been weeks, understandably. He's the busiest man in the entire realm." Anthony was the General of the Imperial Army.

"At least he made time to see you on your birthday," Jonathon said.

"Yes." From the corner of her eye, she saw Jonathan give a little sigh of contentment, which angered her, until she realized his relief was probably in response to her slowing down rather than her brother's absence.

The Celerius estate was vast and their manor lavishly decorated. Each wall was adorned with their blue and gold colors, and decades worth of medals and weapons hung side by side. These were their trophies. Lilly paused for a moment to admire the crest positioned on the wall at the top of the staircase on the second floor. A downward facing sword above a golden banner was all the Celerius family needed to prove their worth to passers-by. The embroidered letters read, "Highest Honor." Lilly stared at it and straightened her coat with a quick pull. Jonathan fixed his posture and tried to do the same.

They proceeded toward the grand staircase that led to the front entryway of the Celerius estate. As they descended the long flight of steps, Jonathan comically reached around to hold the back of his jacket to keep it from dragging on the ground like a wedding train. Lilly would have laughed if things weren't so important today.

"Have you heard the rumors?" Jonathan asked.

Lilly stopped walking. She turned her head slowly and looked down at him, "About Anthony?" Jonathan gulped and nodded as he tried desperately not to meet her icy stare. "Yes, Jonathan," she said, "I've heard the rumors. They are nothing more than Vapros lies and deceit."

Jonathan smiled weakly but Lilly didn't lift her glare. Although one would normally associate such large brown eyes with warmth and kindness, Lilly's eyes could practically freeze time with their intensity. He tried not to squirm in discomfort. Finally, she started walking again, and he closed his eyes and let out a breath he didn't remember holding before tripping after her.

As they exited the house and stepped onto the gravel road, Lilly gazed across the distant fields that comprised her family's estate. Jonathan offered a hand to help her into the carriage, but she ignored it and climbed aboard herself. "Miss," the driver said, turning in his seat to face her, "we can't get to the military outpost without crossing through the marketplace or the nightlife district." Jonathan grunted a little as he struggled to climb into the carriage. "So it's either Taurlum territory or Vapros territory."

Jonathan opened his mouth. "I think we should—"

"Marketplace," Lilly decided firmly. "It's closer, and if we are attacked, we will have an easier time fighting off one bull rather than ten ravens." The Vapros usually travelled in teams and the Taurlum tended to operate alone. Lilly wasn't particularly worried though; it had been a few months since the last physical brawl between families. Even if a Taurlum saw her carriage in the markets it was doubtful that he would attack, unless of course, it was that idiot Michael Taurlum.

"That's what I was going to say," Jonathan muttered, settling himself into the seat opposite his mistress. The driver clucked to the prized Celerius horses and they sprang forward, seamlessly pulling the carriage down the road with a smooth, steady haste. Despite how quickly they reached the city district, Lilly knew that this journey would take her all day. The city of Altryon was twenty-five square miles across and they were travelling across half of it. There were roughly two million people living outside the slums and a population that large didn't exactly make it easy to navigate. Lilly stared absently out the window at the glorious stone walls of the bank where her family stored their endless funds. Selling weapons had proven to be a lucrative business. She could see the great wall of Altryon in the distance and her subtle smile turned into a frown. Everyone in the city was assured daily that it was to protect them from the savages outside the wall, but as a member of the Celerius family she was frequently treated to smaller bits and pieces of information about the alleged "wasteland" beyond the walls. Sometimes when she stared upon its vastness it didn't make her feel safe. It made her feel suffocated.

"I think we're almost to the markets," said Jonathan quietly. "Hopefully everything goes all right."

Lilly didn't appear to hear him. The carriage began to bounce up and down furiously. Jonathan was nearly thrown from his seat. Lilly closed her hands into fists at her sides. "Why are there so many potholes?" she asked through gritted teeth.

Jonathan chuckled a little, but stopped when Lilly turned her glare toward him. "This is Taurlum territory," he said. "There are bound to be a few holes in the road." Suddenly the carriage came to a halt. Lilly's annoyed expression turned to one of fear. She shared a knowing look with Jonathan and they both reached for the door simultaneously.

As Lilly stepped out onto the street, she realized how very out of place she looked here. Her military coat and dress were both a bright royal blue, a color nobody else seemed to be wearing. The crowds of villagers were clad in darker colors, the fabrics stained with sweat and hard work.

It was never difficult to determine someone's social class; all that was needed was a quick look at their clothes. A large mob had gathered in the streets, blocking the carriage. Lilly looked at Jonathan expectantly, waiting for her servant to order the crowd to move, but he seemed too terrified to speak. She scowled and approached the nearest merchant, checking first to make sure he wasn't blonde. "You," she said flatly.

The villager jumped and stared up at her as he wiped his hands on his stained apron. "Me?"

"Why is the road blocked?" She phrased her sentence the way her father always did; it was an order, not a question. That was the best way to command respect.

The commoner looked at her coat instead of her face as he answered. "Darius Taurlum caught some Vapros kid in his house. He's about to kill him."

Lilly suppressed a smile; it was always satisfying to see her two worst enemies fighting it out. "An execution?" she inquired.

"Not yet. Darius is still chasing him, but he doesn't play around. The kid will be dead before lunch."

Lilly smiled and said, "Thank you, sir."

She glanced back at the carriage and realized that it would take some time to turn around. This made her nervous; the Celerius weren't exactly beloved in the working parts of Altryon. The Celerius estate was on the eastern edge of the city, past the Imperial Palace and the nightlife district. Most people from the working class wouldn't have any reason to venture so far east. Lilly hardly ever journeyed out past the protective gates of the family estate, unless she was accompanying her father on business or to visit other nobles in the area. However, her desperate need to see Anthony had led her to pass through the working class area and the markets on her way to the military base on the northwest edge of the city.

She stood, her face hard, as her driver and Jonathan struggled to redirect the carriage. She could hear a few men in the crowd whispering as they noticed her, but she forced herself not to betray any emotion. "Hello, lovely," called a large, sweaty man, as he broke away from the crowd. "I like that coat of yours."

"Then you should understand what it represents," she said calmly, wrapping her fingers around the handle of her sheathed sword.

The man growled and wiped his forehead with a massive hand, leaving a trail of soot behind. He looked strong. Lilly guessed he was a blacksmith. "You've got quite a mouth," he said, advancing toward her, "and I'm not sure I like your tone."

Lilly took a quick glance at the carriage. Jonathan and the driver were arguing about something and didn't seem to notice her new friend. "Leave me alone," she snarled, as he took another step. "That's your one and only warning."

The man noticed how tightly she was gripping her sword. He snickered. "I've heard a lot about your family, girlie," he taunted. "You're supposed to be quick. But I'm the strongest and quickest in the market. What do you say to that?"

"I'm a lot more than just quick," she fired back. "Do you require a demonstration?"

Jonathan had finally noticed Lilly was in danger. "Miss?" he asked as he trotted over to her. "We should be going."

The blacksmith glared at him. "Take a walk, slave," he growled. "Me and your master are just getting acquainted."

As inconspicuously as she could, Lilly began to remove her sword from its sheath. Her adversary saw the blade catch the sun and quickly pulled a knife out from a holster on his hip.

Lilly didn't appear to be fazed. "Last chance," she said calmly.

They had attracted the attention of a few villagers who gathered around to gawk at the confrontation, but Lilly only had eyes for the blacksmith. "You sure you want to do this, woman?" he asked. "If you engage me in a duel, I'm sure it's completely legal for me to cut you up. Even if you are a lady."

"Ah." She cocked her head and a reminiscent smile crept across her face. "So you underestimate me because I'm a woman." She let the blade slowly slice through the air. "That's a mistake."

He took a moment to size her up. He was around six feet tall and had a large weight advantage over her. With a glint in his eye, he lunged forward with his knife.

She evaded him easily, leaving him to slice nothing but air. He recovered somewhat gracefully, pivoting on his heel to face her. He lunged again, faster this time, but still managed to hit nothing. He swung wildly at her outstretched arm and, to his relief, made contact. His knife nicked her hand and a stream of blood fell to the street. He grinned and took a step backwards. "What now, love?" he asked, arms spread wide.

She held up her hand so that her adversary could see it. Before his very eyes, her skin reformed around the wound and left her with nothing but a quickly fading scar. "Now," she said, slashing across his neck with her sword, "you yield."

His hand flew to his throat. Blood dripped between his fingers and puddled onto his toes. It was nothing but a small cut along his throat; Lilly knew it was not enough to truly hurt him, but enough to make him scared. It would have been easy for her to extend a bit more and decapitate him, and he knew it. He dropped his knife, cursing, and retreated into the crowd.

Jonathan was trying not to beam. "Back to the carriage, Miss?" he asked.

She sheathed her sword, eyes still on the place where the assailant had disappeared, and led the way back to her awaiting carriage. "Apparently the road is blocked because of a fight. Taurlum against Vapros," she explained upon re-entering the carriage.

Jonathan grinned. "So I guess we don't have to worry about being ambushed," he concluded. "Our enemies are busy killing each other."

Lilly gave Jonathan a rare smile as the driver directed the horses down an alternate route. Every street in the marketplace was Taurlum territory, but villagers and merchants, neutral commoners who held no grudge against the Celerius house, frequented the back alleys. Nobody tried to stop the carriage again.

When they finally reached the military establishment, the soldiers on patrol waved them through the giant gates and directed the carriage to the stables where the horses could rest. Jonathan insisted on leading Lilly inside, and even though she knew the military base backwards and forwards, she humored her diminutive servant and allowed him to accompany her to her brother's quarters. Lilly had grown up playing in these hallways, as Anthony would often let her tag along on quiet days when he worked in his office, catching up on paperwork.

The small office was empty. "Where do you think he is?" Jonathan asked with concern.

"He's just late," Lilly reassured him, sinking carefully in a high-backed chair. "He's busy. He'll be here. He's expecting me."

It wasn't long before the door opened to reveal Anthony Celerius. Lilly rose automatically as he entered the room, her eyes sparkling but her face arranged in a respectful countenance. Her brother was a large man, and when they were younger he used to hoist her up on his shoulders and gallop around the estate like a pony. Those days were long gone. His broad body was clad in shining armor, probably polished just this morning, and a royal blue cape was draped over one shoulder and connected with a gold brooch that bore their family crest.

Lilly's eyes widened as she took a closer look at his face. Anthony once had an iron jaw and long auburn hair, but now his once-youthful face was marred with premature wrinkles and his hair was covered in streaks of grey. Being the youngest general in the history of Altryon was clearly taking its toll. "Anthony," she whispered, dropping a curtsy.

He smiled. Lilly was relieved to see it made him look younger. "Lilly, happy birthday, darling girl." He came forward, armor clanking, and wrapped her in a bear hug. She allowed herself to grin. "We will speak in the war room," he said, releasing her and nodding to

Jonathan, who had bowed so low that he was having trouble standing up again.

They followed him down a hallway into the renowned war room. Anthony pushed through the door, chatting easily, as if he did not realize how exhausted he looked now. "You remember Carlin Filus," he said, gesturing to the corner where Anthony's second in command stood at attention.

Carlin offered the trio a smile, bearing crooked teeth so different from Anthony's perfect, pearly whites. Lilly suppressed a shudder. Carlin and his smug smile had always unsettled her; he looked like he knew something she didn't. He slid his palm over his brown military-length hair and came forward. "Lilly Celerius," he grinned, reaching for her hand. She held her breath and offered it to him. "It has been too long. How are you on this fine day?"

She was close enough to see the stubble lining his cheeks. He had gained a fair amount of battle scars during his time as a warrior; most noticeable was a deep cut on the upper right side of his lip that made him look like he was permanently scowling. "I am well, thank you," she replied carefully. He pulled her hand to his lips and kissed it formally, his dark brown eyes not leaving hers. It was almost as if he were telling her something silently with his eyes, that he had a terrible secret that he wasn't willing to disclose. Lilly felt the hairs rise on the back of her neck. Then, with a bow to Anthony, he brushed past Jonathan and hurried from the war room, red cloak billowing behind him.

Lilly shivered once he was out of sight. "He's terrible," she said to Anthony, wiping the back of her hand on her dress.

Anthony moved to close the door. "You don't know the half of it," he muttered as he sank into one of the large chairs. Lilly took the chair opposite his, leaving Jonathan to stand awkwardly by the door. "I assume you've heard the rumors?"

Lilly nodded. Anthony flicked his eyes to his sister's servant. "Jonathan," he said, not unkindly, "leave us."

Jonathan looked mildly offended. "Miss?" he asked, looking at his mistress with wide eyes.

"It's all right, Jonathan," she said, and he went, head hanging down like a kicked puppy. As the door closed behind him, Lilly abandoned her perfect posture and leaned toward Anthony intently. "Are they true?" she asked urgently. "The rumors? Jonathan can be trusted, you know."

Anthony shook his head and replied, "Not with this." He rose and retrieved a bottle of gin from the other side of the room. With a heavy sigh he sat back down and poured himself a glass. "There's something very important we need to discuss." She saw him slide a hand over one of his eyes and she realized he had brushed away a tear. "But before we begin, understand that I love you very much, Lilly."

She blinked and said, "Begin what?"

"Our last conversation," he whispered as he took a sip of his drink.

Chapter Three

THE MARKETS
NEIL VAPROS

NEIL DIDN'T KNOW ALTRYON'S MARKETS AS WELL AS HE KNEW OTHER parts of the city, but he knew a few key things. For instance, half the market was divided into stalls for farmers and other small businesses, and the other half was dedicated to large stone stores that sold luxury goods. Most of the buildings in Altryon were several stories high. This was due to the fact that the city was walled and needed to accommodate its rising population. This information, however, did not help him make a decision about which way to run for his life.

Just as Neil began to gain a lead on his pursuer, the hammer soared within an inch of his head and embedded itself in the wall of a clothing shop. He ducked into an alley, clutching at his chest as he ran. He couldn't take much more of this. The physical exertion was wreaking havoc on his body. Every muscle screamed at him to stop running, to take a break, but Neil couldn't risk stopping.

As he hurtled down the alley, lungs burning, he remembered something his father had told him the very first time he'd collapsed after overusing his powers: "You'll get older and stronger, and so will your powers. Someday, materializing will feel like nothing."

Easy for him to say, Neil thought, pushing his raven hair back off his forehead. Neil's father was the strongest Vapros alive. He had pushed his abilities past every limit imaginable. He could turn his entire body into smoke, envelop live men, and turn their bodies to ash. Moreover, he could accomplish it without even breaking a sweat.

As Neil neared the end of the alley, he allowed himself a quick glance over his shoulder. The alley was empty. Darius wasn't following him; Neil either lost him, or the brute had given up altogether. Nearly crying from relief, Neil let himself stop running. He was safe. It was over.

For a few blissful moments, the alley was silent other than Neil's heavy breathing. Then the sound of heavy footfalls came within earshot, and Neil cursed and raised his crossbow. As Darius rounded the corner, Neil fired a bolt; the weapon hit Darius's forehead and broke, not even putting a dent in the Taurlum's skin. Darius didn't even seem to notice. Neil sprinted down the alley. "You can't run forever!" Darius shouted after him.

Neil was about to collapse. "If you would hold still and let me shoot you, I wouldn't have to!" he shouted back over his shoulder.

Darius roared as he charged after him. Neil loaded another bolt and fired. It sailed harmlessly over Darius's head. Cursing, Neil rounded a corner and tore down a new street, heading for the square. Darius was gaining, but if he could make it to the busiest part of the marketplace, maybe he could blend in with the throngs of villagers.

Neil had almost reached the square when he was yanked off his feet and into the air. Darius let out a scream of triumph and threw him to the side, sending him flying into the wall of a nearby store. Darius held his hammer high, posing dramatically for the crowd that had gathered to witness the brawl.

A broad-shouldered man in Imperial armor stepped between the boys. Neil recognized him as the Captain of the Guard. "Taurlum," he ordered, drawing a long sword, "by order of the Emperor, I command you to--- "

Without taking his eyes off his prey, Darius swung his arm and knocked the Captain of the Guard into a wall, where he left a sizable dent. Darius blinked and glanced at his victim, acknowledging the fact that he might have gone too far.

Neil lay on the ground, groaning in pain. Darius sneered down at his victim. "Here's to my family," he said, grinning. "And here's to the end of yours."

Just as he began to swing his hammer down, a silver blur shot through the air and imbedded itself in his neck. A small trickle of blood dripped down onto his shoulder. The impact made Darius jerk his arm to the right, and the hammer hit the ground just shy of Neil's head. Darius's expression changed from savage triumph to one of confusion, and then fear. His precious iron skin had been pierced at a pressure point. He was now just as mortal as everyone else around him.

Neil staggered to his feet, smiling in relief. "Today is not your day, is it, Taurlum?"

Darius ignored him. His hand was against his neck, pulling the silver weapon (a throwing knife, Neil now realized) from his skin. "It was a second ago..." his adversary replied.

"Go home, Darius," Neil said loudly. Darius growled and held the knife tightly in his fist. A few villagers began to whisper nervously.

"I'm still strong," he snarled.

"Yeah," Neil agreed, "but I have backup." He gestured to the knife in Darius's hand.

Darius narrowed his eyes. "Who threw this knife?" he roared, spinning to glare at the crowd. The villagers looked terrified.

Neil was regaining energy fast. "You won't find her over there," he said quietly.

"What?"

"I said, you won't find her there," Neil repeated with more volume.

"I heard you," Darius said angrily.

"You just didn't understand." Neil said. "It doesn't make much sense, does it? Who would have thought, a great Taurlum man like you, bested by a girl?"

Darius blinked. "Bested by a—"

Before he could finish the sentence, an iron bar had collided with his skull. He stumbled two paces closer to Neil with his arms outstretched and then collapsed. As he hit the ground, a girl with shimmering ivory hair stepped out from the shadows, an iron staff held loosely in one hand.

She smiled. "You fight like a girl, Neil," she said calmly, dropping her iron weapon.

The crowd of bystanders, realizing there would be no execution today, began to disperse.

Neil looked the girl up and down. "You dress like a man, Bianca," he countered playfully.

She looked down at herself briefly before meeting his eyes again and asked, "What's wrong with armor?"

Neil grinned. "Most girls who look like you tend to prefer dresses. Besides, isn't leather armor a Celerius thing?"

Bianca said,. "I could wear a dress, I suppose, but I wouldn't want to drive you crazy. You might get distracted and lose another fight."

"I had it covered."

She snorted. "Of course you did."

Bianca was several inches shorter than Neil and had a shapely figure. The noticeable curves were a recent development that Neil expertly pretended not to notice. Her grey eyes always seemed to retain a smile. She had a small smudge of ash on her cheek. Neil could only guess where that had come from. He glanced around at their surroundings. "You should get out of here before more Taurlum show up," he warned. "You know how word spreads around here. They'll be after us both as soon as they hear Darius Taurlum got his ass kicked by a girl from the markets."

Bianca tried to pry her knife from Darius's iron hand but she realized that it wouldn't budge. "Yeah," she muttered, "I probably made some enemies today."

Neil stared down at Darius's body. "Are you gonna kill him?" Bianca asked.

Neil drew his knife. "Yeah," he said quietly.

He approached Darius and pulled his head up by the hair. He felt a familiar dizziness beginning to arise but suppressed it. Bianca watched him with quiet curiosity. Neil sighed and dropped Darius. "No, not with all these witnesses…. he's learned a lesson, I think."

Bianca raised an eyebrow in disbelief. "Whatever you need to tell yourself," she said. "I'm sure we're both going be on the Taurlum's most wanted list after today, anyway."

"True," Neil said and started down an alley. Bianca followed, matching his pace easily. "But things aren't all bad."

"Why not?"

Neil grinned and slung his arm casually over her shoulder. "At least you get to walk down the street on the arm of a handsome Vapros warrior."

Bianca laughed and ducked out of his embrace. "Yes, it's an absolute privilege," she said with a mock curtsy, and then she tossed her hair over her shoulder and skipped down the street ahead of him.

Bianca knew the streets better than anyone else and she led Neil through a twisted back-alley route until they reached the safety of the nightlife district. Neil had dozens of memories just like this one. Since they were children, Bianca always knew how to get where she wanted quickly and she loved to drag Neil along.

Neil slowed as they approached the Vapros house. It wasn't a grand, pretentious building like the Taurlum mansion; in fact, most of the building was underground. The only part visible from the street was a small shack with the Vapros crest etched into the side. The family motto was inscribed on the door: "Victory Lies in the Ashes." Neil put his hand on the iron door as if he meant to open it, then sighed and let it close.

Bianca offered him a sympathetic smile. "He sent you alone. It was practically a suicide mission. He should be happy that you made it home alive."

Neil stared at the ground. "I don't ..." his voice faltered, "I don't think he's going to give a damn."

Bianca squeezed his hand. "Good luck."

He smiled at her weakly. "Please. I don't need luck. No one can resist my apologetic smile."

Bianca turned to leave. "I've seen your apologetic smile," she called over her shoulder. "It needs work."

Neil managed a little smirk in Bianca's direction before he turned and knocked on the heavy iron door.

VICTORY LIES WITHIN
THE ASHES

Chapter Four

VAPROS BUNKER
NEIL VAPROS

As Neil stood in front of the Vapros bunker, a hatch about the size of his torso was opened from the inside. Neil materialized through the hatch and found himself face to face with his younger brother.

Rhys was Neil's opposite in nearly every way. While both shared the Vapros dark hair and green eyes, Rhy's eyes were jade whereas Neil's were emerald like those of his sisters. While Neil was tall and more athletic, Rhys was smaller and more slender than the other siblings. He was a quiet, intelligent type, with hair he kept short and eyes that were constantly darting around. With his innate curiosity, his eyes were constantly wide with fascination.

"How'd you do?" Rhys asked, cocking his head to the side curiously. "The twins and I have been waiting to hear, and—"

Neil brushed past him and started down the narrow staircase. Rhys followed and called after him. "Calm down. I don't think he expected you to be able to do it anyway." Rhys's voice was always soft, but at the same time filled with energy and intelligence.

"Comforting," Neil mocked, stopping to glare back at him and then continuing through the entry hall to one of the corridors that stretched even farther underground.

Rhys kept up, but just barely. "He shouldn't have sent you. Your advanced abilities haven't even developed yet."

"Easy for you to say, Rhys. Maybe Father thinks he can't wait … I may never develop advanced abilities."

Rhys tried to grab Neil's arm, "You can't compare yourself to me. You know it's different. I suffered a major trauma. You said yourself that maybe I got them so early because of that traumatic event."

"This conversation is a traumatic event," Neil said. "And putting people to sleep is not what I'd call 'advanced powers.'"

Rhys caught Neil's shoulder. "Think logically."

"Do you think I can manage it?" Neil asked sarcastically without turning around.

"I've seen how you are with people, Neil. You're charismatic. You're good at talking. You're perfectly cut out to be a socialite. Why are you so desperate to be an assassin?"

Neil finally stopped walking. He ran his fingers through his hair and then met Rhys's eyes and said, "Because socialites aren't impressive. How hard is it to go out and sweet talk people into funding our projects? Not hard at all. Even Jennifer can manage it when she tries, and Jennifer has terrible people skills. Assassins, though—they're rare and powerful— "

"Like Dad?" Rhys interrupted.

"This isn't about Dad."

"Okay." But Rhys didn't look like he believed that.

Neil brushed dirt off his cloak "It doesn't even matter. Dad's going to hate me no matter what I choose to be."

"He doesn't hate you."

"He does. And he has every right. In his mind, I tore our family apart."

Rhys shook his head. "Don't say that," Rhys said. "That wasn't something you could help."

"I want to be an assassin," Neil said through gritted teeth.

"I support you," Rhys said, "but he's going to be hard to convince." He gestured to the door at the end of the hall. "I don't think he'll support you no matter what you say."

Neil closed his eyes. "Thank you," he said slowly as he tapped his brother between the eyes, "for that vote of confidence."

Rhys smiled slightly. "Good luck."

Neil pushed through the door at the end of the hallway and walked into his father's study, shoulders back, head high, just the way he'd been taught. He offered Sir Vapros a little bow.

Sir Vapros sat behind a massive desk that dwarfed nearly everything in the room. After becoming patriarch of the family, he had asked for it to be specially crafted. He shared the common Vapros traits: he was classically handsome, tall with dark hair and vibrant forest green eyes. But he wore an expression so stern that he could silence nearly anyone with a simple look. He was elegantly dressed in evening attire, and his hair was neatly styled. Neil noticed a few new streaks of silver that had appeared at his father's temples, somehow making him look even more distinguished. Yet, Neil knew the polished exterior was a façade; Sir Vapros was a warrior. Underneath his sleeves, Sir Vapros's body was decorated with tattoos.

This was a Vapros tradition: every assassination earned you a ceremony where the patriarch would award you a tattoo representing your most recent kill. The only tattoo visible at the moment was a bloody coin on the back of his right hand. It was new. Neil's sister, Victoria, had told him that it was from killing the head of the Imperial Bank of Altryon. For some unknown reason, the banker suddenly refused to do business with the Vapros establishments stationed around the city. Sir Vapros suspected that the Celerius, with their strong ties to the banking industry, were trying to cripple his businesses in an attempt to expand into the Vapros territory. Sir Vapros had personally gone to "renegotiate" the deal.

Sir Vapros slowly put down the paper he was examining and looked at his son with a deathly calm expression. "I heard what happened in the markets." His voice was cold. Neil hated that his father could make him feel this way, as if he were five years old again and being punished for staying up past his bedtime. "Is it too optimistic of me to ask if you reached your target at all?"

"There were complications," Neil said through a clenched jaw. "I couldn't—"

Sir Vapros raised a hand to silence his son. "You were ejected from the house by Darius Taurlum. You fled instead of fighting."

"He would have killed me," Neil started, but his father interrupted.

"At least you would have died a man!"

Neil felt as if he'd been dunked in icy water. "I'm sorry," he said quietly.

His father didn't appear to hear him and continued. "And after all that, Jennifer tells me you needed help from a commoner. And not just any commoner—that commoner. I've asked you repeatedly to stay away from Bianca Blackmore. Lightborns don't accept help from commoners, Neil." He ran his hand through his straight black hair the same way his son always did. "On top of it all, you had that Taurlum completely at your mercy and you failed to end his life."

Neil felt his heart twist with shame.

Sir Vapros spoke as his eyes drilled into Neil. "Any blood he sheds from this day forward is on your hands."

There were a million things Neil wanted to say, but he settled on, "You had Jennifer spy on me?"

"I didn't. Your sister did it all on her own."

And she didn't even step in to make sure I wasn't killed? Neil wanted to say, but he held his tongue. "Give me one more chance."

Sir Vapros raised an eyebrow and noted, "Not everyone is cut out to be an assassin, son."

"I am," Neil insisted.

Sir Vapros countered, "You're pretty. Become a socialite."

"One more chance," he repeated stubbornly.

"I can't afford to give you one more chance. This is too important. Do I need to remind you who you are, Neil? Who we are?"

"Of course not," Neil said, trying as hard as he could not to sound disrespectful, but he knew that if Sir Vapros got started on the family history, his great passion, there was no stopping him from launching into one of his infamous sermons. It was too late.

"When the savages broke through the doors of the palace in the center of this city, who was there to stop them? Who sat in the throne room waiting to die for Altryon?"

"The first Lightborns. Four brothers: the first Vapros, the first Taurlum and—"

"That'll do." Sir Vapros didn't seem to want to remember that the other families were present for that event. "And who appeared to our ancestor?"

"The glowing man appeared," Neil said unenthusiastically.

"Use his full name. I won't tolerate blasphemy in my house."

"The Man with the Golden Light," Neil amended. "Sorry."

Sir Vapros stood up and begin to pace. "What you don't seem to appreciate is that our powers were given to us by a deity, Neil. That's why the people of Altryon call us Lightborns. We are actually born in the blessing of his light and that's what you seem to be forgetting. The Man with the Golden Light may have bestowed special powers on four families but protecting Altryon is our divine purpose. Not theirs. Ours. We have proven time and time again that we are the only family that can truly protect Altryon. It's not the Taurlum, it's not the Celerius and it's not the family that's already perished. It's us, Neil. It's the Vapros. The people are fickle and might forget all we've done for them, but there are certain gifts we have bestowed that even the most ungrateful men cannot forget. For instance, our ancestors built the wall. No matter where we go in this city, the wall is always visible, reminding us that we are safe. Do you know what's outside the wall, Neil?"

He didn't wait for an answer. "It's crawling with savages who want to come within our paradise and steal it for themselves." Sir Vapros had a faraway look on his face. "But the greatest threat to Altryon has always been inside the wall: the other families.

Sir Vapros drew a long breath. "This feud started before you were born, before any of us were born. It's not ideal. But we still have to protect Altryon and our family. There's no choice. We have to carry out the destiny laid before us by the Man with the Golden Light. It has to be the Vapros, Neil. The other families are inferior to us. They just aren't capable."

Neil felt like screaming but knew better. "But we aren't carrying out the destiny. We aren't in charge anymore. None of us are."

Sir Vapros drummed his fingers along the table. "It's true. An emperor, who was head of the military at the time, took control during the transition period after the people's coup, and now his descendant rules the city. But we're still here. We rule Altryon through other means. We use our wealth, our businesses. We provide the people with jobs. The current emperor might think he holds the power, but I assure you, the real strength is ours."

"I just don't see what our family history has to do with me wanting to be an assassin," Neil said, trying to keep the stubbornness out of his voice.

"If you look back through history, you will see that we only accept the best." Sir Vapros slammed his hand against his desk to emphasize each word. "The Taurlum are a wonderful example of foolishness at its most refined. They force every single child to take up the hammer and become a warrior, and then when they're too old to fight they run those hideous markets. The Celerius all go into banking and arms dealing. Unless they're very special, of course, then they go into the military. We Vapros, we are more . . . efficient. Those who show a talent for blood shed will be assassins for life. The charismatic, gentler ones will be socialites for life. It is my job to know what is best for you. It is my job to know what is best for this family." He looked down at Neil. "You're sixteen. I should have picked a permanent career for you months ago, but you insist on making it difficult. With that charming personality of yours, son, you would make a first rate socialite. Play to your strengths. Do it for Altryon."

"Father," Neil said desperately. "I just need one more chance, a new mission. Give me anyone, I don't care who it is, I'll kill him."

"I cannot be embarrassed again, Neil."

"How can you judge me on this?" Neil said, "This was a suicide mission at the very least!"

Sir Vapros approached Neil silently, with his infamous quiet footsteps. "Don't talk back to me. Do as you're told."

"One last chance," Neil said again, with more force this time. "You can't blame me for what happened to mom, I—"

Suddenly Neil felt a blow to the head. With his cheeks burning and ears ringing, he realized that his father had struck him. This was not exactly uncommon in the Vapros house, but still Neil was somehow surprised. Rage filled him but he did not flinch. He blinked back tears and fixed his posture. He glared at his father who almost looked like he regretted striking his son. "One last chance," Neil begged quietly.

Sir Vapros walked back to his chair and sat down, steepling his fingers in front of his face. Neil thought he caught a glimpse of sadness in his eyes. After what seemed like an endless pause, he said "Okay, one last chance. But do not make me regret this."

"I won't," Neil said exhaling in relief.

Sir Vapros stood up, "Now put on a smile, boy. We're going out tonight—all of us, as a family."

Neil could feel the pain fading and his excitement building. *One last chance.* "Where are we going?" he asked.

Sir Vapros sported a smile of his own. "Tonight, we're going socializing."

Chapter Five

VAPROS BUNKER
NEIL VAPROS

AFTER TAKING A FEW MOMENTS TO SHED HIS ASSASSIN CLOAK AND DON HIS evening clothes, Neil approached the mirror in his bedroom. It was connected to a small dresser nudged into the corner of the minuscule room. The dresser and bunk bed were the only furniture that could fit into a room so small. Neil examined his reflection and hoped the red mark in the shape of his father's hand would soon fade. Neil had an angular face with a strong jawline. His eyes were a distinct emerald green and peeked out from behind his long messy hair. He examined the black locks for a moment and decided to brush them back out of his face. He hoped it would make him look slightly more presentable.

Rhys entered the room briskly and grabbed his own coat. He appeared to be deep in thought, but stopped upon seeing Neil. "You didn't have that mark when you came back today…"

"You know where it came from," said Neil.

Rhys looked at the floor for a moment and nodded.

They ascended the spiral staircase that led to the undersized entryway where his family waited. Everything about the Vapros bunker was specifically designed to be small, and with good reason: no Taurlum invader could charge through these narrow hallways. No Celerius sword could swing down to deliver a deathblow with these low, sloping ceilings. Cramped spaces did nothing to hinder materialization, and so the family had built their dwelling accordingly. Even generations ago, their house had played to their strengths. *Father would have been proud,* Neil thought as he jumped the last few steps and joined the throng of siblings and cousins packed into the foyer.

"Neil!" The cry came from a black-haired beauty. "Neil! Over here!"

Neil threaded his way through the crowd to meet her. "Jennifer," he said to his sister. *Thanks for spying on me,* he added internally. *Thanks for standing by while I almost died.*

Jennifer grinned enthusiastically. It made Neil nervous. "Victoria and I were just talking about you!" Victoria, Neil's sister and Jennifer's twin, reached out to straighten Neil's collar.

"We've been waiting for news about your mission," Jennifer said.

Victoria gave Neil a smile that was much gentler than her twin's maniacal grin. "We already heard some news, actually."

Neil glared at Jennifer. "News travels fast around here, doesn't it?"

Jennifer laughed loudly. "It was too entertaining to keep to myself."

"You didn't have to tell Dad about Bianca," Neil grumbled to Jennifer as she turned to face the entrance to the bunker.

For an instant Neil thought he saw her eyes soften. "Don't socialize with people you're not supposed to, Neil. It never ends well."

"Is everyone ready?" thundered the voice of Sir Vapros before Neil could respond. Sir Vapros opened the hatch at the front of the door and materialized through it. The group followed suit one at a time. They gathered in a circle around Neil's father. He waited until everyone was there and a small grin began to split his face. "Is everyone familiar with Quintus, the emperor's advisor?"

A murmur of consensus went up among the group.

"Tonight, we spread the rumor that Quintus has been visiting the brothels due to his failing marriage."

Neil saw Jennifer smirk. The plan was becoming clearer. Whenever the emperor had an advisor that displeased Sir Vapros, they usually didn't last long. Quintus, for example, was famously anti-Vapros. This was a mission of defamation.

"We also," Sir Vapros continued, "will drop hints that he is battling alcoholism." A grin nearly broke his icy expression. "If any of you finish early, you are encouraged to head down to the Opera House. Tonight's performance is going to be a very special one."

Neil knew all about the new opera because his father had talked of little else for weeks. Apparently, it was finally going to be an "accurate depiction" of the history of the families.

Sir Vapros pointed to the twins. "Jennifer, Victoria, you take the Opera House. Entertain the nobles. Gather information and keep them drinking."

Jennifer pulled her hair back into a tight ponytail and gave her father a nod of affirmation. Neil felt a tiny twinge of jealousy. She looked exactly the way an assassin should look. Despite her delicate facial features, she always had an expression of readiness and intensity. Unlike her socialite twin, she only had the appearance of being slender. Neil knew that the coat hid her well-toned muscle and a multitude of tattoos.

The first tattoo was always given in private and represented the first kill, but the rest were accompanied by a family celebration. Jennifer had been the guest of honor at countless "family dinners." Neil, on the other hand, had never known the honor of such a celebration. She probably had more tattoos than anyone else in the family, aside from Sir Vapros, of course. As the twins began to stroll down the street toward the Opera House, Sir Vapros called after them. "Victoria!" She turned.

"I don't want to hear about your little boyfriend ending up at the Opera House."

She blushed. Jennifer smirked.

"He's not the one I'm asking you to entertain. Do you understand?"

Victoria nodded, lowering her head so her hair fell in a curtain around her face. Jennifer let out a laugh as she grabbed her sister's hand and pulled her down the street.

Sir Vapros turned his attention to Rhys. "There is a masquerade ball near the palace. Go. Meet people. Engage in conversation. Make friends." Rhys smiled as he realized he'd be able to spend the entire night conversing with intellectuals. He trotted down the road toward the mask shops.

One by one, Sir Vapros assigned his family members to different areas of the nightlife district until only Neil was left. He looked down at his son thoughtfully. "Go to the pub near the Opera House," he decided. "Buy a couple of rounds—flirt, boost morale, all that. If you have time, go meet up with Rhys near the end of the night." Neil gave a bow so subtle it could have been a nod and walked away. "And Neil," Sir Vapros called after his son, "do not disappoint me. Once was quite enough for today."

Neil clenched his teeth and materialized onto a roof where he could see the city better. Down below, the older members of his family were heading into restaurants. In the distance, he could barely make out the twins skipping hand in hand toward the Opera House. He began to walk along the rooftops, materializing between buildings when he had to, heading in the general direction of his favorite bar, The Laughing Mask Tavern. His father's voice rang in his ears. *Do not disappoint me. Do not disappoint me. You have one last chance.*

Neil materialized down to the street in front of the bar. He inspected his evening cloak quickly to make sure it was in presentable shape. It was a long, black cloak that lapped near his knees and hugged his sides nicely. It also had a subtle, purple trim to let everyone know who he was. He put on a fake smile and pushed through the double doors with a cry of jubilation. Everyone in the bar turned as he came in, and then echoed his cheer. The girls all sat up a little straighter, and even some of the men improved their postures. They all knew what it meant when a Vapros showed up in a bar—free drinks.

Neil swaggered through the masses of people up to the bartender. "A round for everyone!" he shouted, throwing his hand in the air. The bar erupted into applause. For them, this was a kind gesture, but it was nothing for the Vapros. They owned the bar and they even manufactured the beer. Grinning, Neil scanned the crowd for possible sources of information. If he returned tonight with intriguing gossip, maybe his father would finally realize his worth.

Through the hordes of men chanting tuneless drinking songs, Neil spotted a table of girls giggling and chatting. Women were always good for gossip. In the center table, a group of Imperial soldiers were sitting, laughing, chugging and waving their tankards in Neil's direction. Perfect. The best way to learn new things about the state of the city was from its soldiers. Despite the fact that the punishment for revealing details about military occupation outside the wall was death, Imperial soldiers could still spill little details about what products were coming into the city and what laws were close to being passed. Neil leaned over the counter and grabbed the bartender by his lapels. "Keep their glasses full," he whispered, gesturing over his shoulder at the soldiers.

The bartender smirked knowingly and said, "Soldiers—a wealth of information there. Excellent choice, sir. But are you sure it's not that table you want drinking?" He jerked his head toward the girls in the corner.

Neil grinned, "I don't need booze for that." The bartender nodded in approval. This bartender knew the drill and loved the Vapros like most did. The Vapros kept him employed and provided protection. After Neil returned the nod, he waded through the crowd to the table of women. "Hello, ladies," he said, sweeping a bow. "How are you this fine evening?"

A few of them giggled. One finally spoke up. "We're all doing well. And yourself, Mr. Vapros?"

Neil pulled up a chair. "Can't complain." That was a lie. He, of all people, had every right to spend a great deal of time complaining. His father didn't approve of his dreams. His sister had willingly sold him out, most likely because she saw Neil as a threat to her position as top Vapros assassin. His younger brother's powers had advanced farther than his own, and he'd ruined his family's reputation by running for his life through the markets, until a girl from the streets saved his life. It had not been a good day.

"So," Neil remarked, "how's the city treating you all tonight?"

The girls exchanged a glance and burst out laughing. "We heard it hasn't been very kind to you," one of them said finally.

Neil repressed a groan and tried to fake a smile. "Hey," he said, "I've been through worse."

"Worse than almost dying?" the girl sitting across the table asked.

"I could have killed him if I wanted to," Neil said slowly, making it up as he went along. "But the first thing they teach you in assassin school is that you are only allowed to kill your target. That Taurlum boy wasn't my target. I had to let him chase me." He shrugged. "Call me a pacifist."

The girls, amazingly, bought into his lie. Neil signaled to the bartender to bring more drinks. "So, ladies," he said leaning in, "just out of curiosity, have you all heard about Quintus, the emperor's advisor?"

Chapter Six

CELERIUS ESTATE
LILLY CELERIUS

ACROSS TOWN, THE CARRIAGE RIDE BACK TO THE CELERIUS ESTATE WAS a silent one. Lilly stared blankly ahead, ignoring Jonathan in spite of his best attempts to talk to her. When they pulled up to the main house, she jumped to the ground without waiting for assistance and walked quickly to lock herself in her room. She exhaled slowly and let herself fall onto her neatly made bed, smoothing down minuscule wrinkles in the comforter with her hands. Lilly liked everything to be tidy, cleaning and straightening up provided her with a good distraction from the chaos that followed her everywhere she went.

A knock at the door made Lilly jump. Glancing in the mirror briefly, she smoothed down her hair and rose to admit the visitor. Lady Celerius stood outside the door, cupping her hand around her tight blonde bun to make sure it was still perfectly in place.

"Mother," Lilly said, automatically dropping a curtsy.

Lady Celerius nodded in acknowledgment and came into the room. "Close the door, Lilly," she said. Lilly obeyed. Lady Celerius looked as if she hadn't slept in weeks. The bags under her eyes were too heavy to be concealed by makeup. "What did Anthony tell you?" she asked, skipping over the formalities of small talk.

Lilly stared at the wood of her door, willing herself not to cry. "He says the rumors may be true," she whispered. "His life is in danger. There are changes happening in the Imperial Army—big changes." She took a deep breath. "They're going to execute him."

"No." Lady Celerius sank down on the bed. She did not abandon her perfect posture, but her face grew white. "I was afraid of that."

Lilly didn't reply.

"Why not ask him to step down?" Lady Celerius asked. "Why not just dismiss him?"

Lilly clenched her fists at her sides. "Because they're trying to send a message. They want everyone to see that the families aren't all-powerful. That's what Anthony said."

"I believe in Anthony," Lady Celerius said. "We are very hard to kill. He may have a chance."

Lilly turned to face her mother. "That's not all of it," she said.

Lady Celerius pursed her lips. "What do you mean?"

She took a deep breath. "If Anthony resists—if he fights back at all— the emperor will send his Imperial soldiers here … to kill us. So Anthony . . . he says he isn't going to resist."

Lady Celerius clutched her daughter's bedpost. "But that means …"

Lilly closed her eyes. "He won't risk our lives. He isn't going to fight back. He's going to let them kill him."

Lady Celerius rose and took her daughter's hand. "There is still a chance the rumors aren't true. This could just be more Vapros lies to force us to move against the emperor," she said.

Lilly shook her head. "I think they might be true. So does Anthony," she said, voice cracking. She leaned her head against her mother's shoulder and cried harder than she had in years. "I hope he fights anyway," she choked out between sobs.

Lady Celerius hugged Lilly tightly. "I hope he doesn't have to. We'll discuss this with your father when he returns from his trip tonight. He will never let this happen. If the emperor really wants to send us a signal, we'll send one right back. We'll see him bleeding on his own palace floor."

VICTORY LIES WITHIN THE ASHES

Chapter Seven

THE LAUGHING MASK TAVERN
NEIL VAPROS

NEIL WAS GETTING FRUSTRATED. HE HAD EASILY CONVINCED THE girls at the bar that Quintus was a womanizing alcoholic, demanded all their gossip in return, and bought them so many drinks that most were past offering any more reliable information. Now there was nothing to do but wait for the Imperial soldiers to become intoxicated enough to spill their secrets. He set his chin in his palm, gazing absently at his targets.

"… Captain of the Guard is dead," he heard one of them say above the din of the bar. "… Taurlum injured him … cracked his skull … furious … the emperor says … last straw … Vapros …"

One of the soldiers noticed Neil listening. He nudged his comrades and whispered something that made them all look over at him. Neil waved and crossed the room to meet them. A few girls groaned in displeasure as he departed but most were too intoxicated to notice. He turned his attention back to the soldiers. "How are you gentlemen this evening?" he asked. The soldiers exchanged glances. None of them would meet his eye. "Come on, men. Why so glum?"

One of the soldiers threw back a shot exclaiming, "We're not in the mood to socialize, Vapros."

Neil flashed his famous, charming smile. "What's wrong? Bad day?"

The soldier suddenly became fascinated with his helmet on the table.

Neil tried again. "Must be hard to get comfortable in all that armor. Might that be the cause of your unrest?"

The soldier reddened and looked Neil dead in the eyes. "Listen, Vapros. No offense, but you are literally the last person on this earth I can discuss this with."

Neil raised an eyebrow. "Why?" he asked with genuine curiosity. "Is it something about my family? I'm sure we can handle any complaint you have. Something about the bar?"

The soldier rose to his feet and started toward the door. The others followed. "Thanks for the drinks, kid," muttered one of them.

"Wait." Neil jumped up to follow them, starting to panic. He'd waited all night to pump these men for information. He couldn't let them get away without getting something out of them.

The largest soldier turned around and gave Neil a small half-smile. "Be careful, kid," he said sadly as he walked out the door.

Neil growled and curled his hands into fists. His father was right. He was a disappointment. Those soldiers had been hiding something, something huge, something that concerned his family specifically, and he'd let them get away. He slammed a small sack of coins on the counter for the bartender and started out the door to meet up with his brother. He gave one last wave to the girls before leaving. Maybe Rhys had had better luck tonight. Maybe he'd found his own group of soldiers to question at the masquerade ball . . . or maybe Rhys hadn't thought to question the soldiers, and he, Neil, could swoop in and get the information first.

Neil pulled open the door and stepped back into the bar. "You forget something, Mr. Vapros?" the bartender asked.

A smile was growing across Neil's face. "You don't happen to have a mask I can borrow, do you?"

Chapter Eight

TAURLUM MANSION
DARIUS TAURLUM

DARIUS TAURLUM HAD NEVER ATTENDED THE OPERA. NOT ONLY DID he hate the music, but the operas performed at the Vapros Opera House were basically propaganda discrediting the other families. The most recent featured brutish clans of barbarians running across the stage dressed in red and gold before being vanquished. The allusion didn't escape the clever minds of the rich, and consequently very few Taurlum attended performances there.

Tonight, Darius would be the exception.

The Taurlum boy dug furiously through the armory, searching for suitable armor. He slid a chain mail shirt over his shoulders, wincing as it chafed against the knife wound in his neck. They were going to pay.

Most of the time, members of his family didn't bother with armor. It was unnecessary; their skin was tough enough to prevent injury. In all his seventeen years, Darius had never felt the need to wear the full body armor that protected each of his pressure points. But choosing not to wear all his protective covering had almost cost him his life today, so Darius felt safer with his limbs shielded. He pulled on a breastplate over the chain mail and fastened it tightly. The armor was specifically built for Taurlum warriors, featuring a double layer of metal covering the pressure points. Nothing could touch him now.

Darius smirked a little as he lowered a helmet over his head. The Vapros brat wouldn't be wearing armor. His kind hardly ever did. It was too heavy for them. It slowed the weaklings down. Even the Celerius family was too frail to handle real armor. They had to build their own version out of leather. Only he, a great and powerful Taurlum warrior, was strong enough to protect himself completely. With strength like that, he knew, he could never fail.

The door to the armory heaved open while Darius was selecting a weapon. "I'm going to the market for some tail," said Michael. Darius grunted but didn't look up. "You want to come?"

"I'm going on a mission tonight," Darius replied, weighing a hammer in his hands.

Michael closed the door. "Dad gave you a mission? After what happened today?"

Beneath the helmet, Darius felt his face redden. "I asked him for one."

"Because you're embarrassed," Michael guessed.

Darius clenched his teeth together. "Yes."

"Dad never would have given me a mission if I let a Vapros assassin escape. Maybe back when I used to be the Golden Boy..." Michael rubbed his stubbly chin thoughtfully and then moved to the far edge of the armory. He removed something from a chest and tossed it to Darius, who was still examining the hammers. It bounced

off the back of his armor and hit the floor. "Darius," Michael complained, "pay attention, will you?"

Darius didn't have time for Michael now. He had to focus. He
felt guilty—not that he would ever admit it—about hurting the Captain of the Guard, and if he didn't take time to plan his every move
tonight, he might end up hurting more innocents. He turned to look
at the object that Michael had thrown at him. It was a golden helmet,
much heavier than the simple silver one currently on his head, but
more regal. The finishing touch was the large pair of horns protrud-
ing from the top that would likely give the wearer the appearance of
a bull.

Darius smiled. "Perfect. Thank you." He pulled the golden head-
piece down over his face. Michael gave Darius a cocky grin before
heaving the door open again. Darius could hear him whistling as he
walked down the stairs toward the front door. Darius removed his
cloak from a hook on the wall and draped it over his armored shoulders. He checked his appearance briefly with the reflection in a suit of
armor propped up by the door. He looked like a warrior.

Tonight, the rich nobles of Altryon were going to the opera.
Darius was not.

Darius was going to war.

VICTORY LIES WITHIN
THE ASHES

Chapter Nine

MASQUERADE BALL
NEIL VAPROS

NEIL ENTERED THE LAVISH MASQUERADE BALL SILENTLY AND ASSESSED the crowd, looking for his brother. Rhys wasn't easy to spot. He'd chosen to come to the masquerade dressed as a Taurlum, complete with a red and gold coat to match his mask. If Rhys's hair had been a little better hidden and if he had been a little taller, Neil would probably have been completely fooled. His brother stood among four other men who all seemed overly excited to be talking to one another. Neil wove his way through the waltzing couples and tapped Rhys on the shoulder. "So it looks like I'm not the only one with an ironic mask, huh, brother?"

Rhys peered out from behind his mask, with his jade eyes, and then grinned. Neil had donned a blue mask with gold stars: Celerius colors. "Excellent," he whispered. "Have you met the doctor's guild yet?" he asked in his normal tone, gesturing to the men with whom he'd been conversing.

Neil faked a smile. "I haven't had the pleasure." Neil had never liked doctors. They talked like they were members of a cult. "What's the latest in medical news?"

Rhys began to bounce with excitement. "We have a basic knowledge of where organs are located in the body and how they work."

Neil glanced over Rhys's shoulder, scanning the room for soldiers. "Uh-huh."

"And there's the nervous system, and we've discovered these chemicals that are produced by the brain and they actually control—"

"I hate to cut you off," Neil lied, "but did you manage to tell your friends about Quintus?"

Rhys waved his hand in the air. "Of course I did. So basically these chemicals can control—"

A doctor in a wolf mask had been eavesdropping. "I already knew," he boasted, cutting Rhys off mid-sentence.

"Knew what?" Rhys asked excitedly. "About the chemicals?"

"No," the doctor admitted, "about Quintus."

Rhys and Neil stared. "You knew about Quintus," Neil repeated.

"He's a patient of mine," the doctor informed them. "I've known of his ailments for months."

Rhys and Neil exchanged glances, and Neil tried not to smirk. They both knew the rumors about Quintus's drinking and marital problems were just that: rumors. They were entirely unfounded, just like all the other stories the Vapros family invented and spread around to hurt the reputations of their enemies. Inevitably, someone would pretend to have known about the rumor all along. It was incredible and terrifying to Neil how easy it was for rumors to gain false credibility.

The doctor moved on, and Neil grabbed Rhys by the back of his Taurlum cloak. "Come with me." They wandered away from the group.

"First of all," Neil said, "brilliant costume." Rhys grinned. "Also, this could be nothing, but I talked with some soldiers this evening. They were acting really suspicious."

"Suspicious?"

"They wouldn't talk to me. But I overheard them talking about the Captain of the Guard and it being the last straw. They mentioned the Taurlum and our family. One of them told me to be careful."

Rhys nodded slowly. "I experienced something unusual with an arms dealer about an hour ago. He said he couldn't talk to anyone in my family without jeopardizing some mission."

Neil furrowed his brow. "But you're dressed like a Taurlum."

Rhys's hand flew to his mask as if he'd forgotten. "You're right."

"So whatever's going on with the arms dealer, it affects the Taurlum, too," Neil mused.

Rhys pursed his lips. "Do you think the Celerius are behind it?"

"Maybe," Neil said. "There's a Celerius at the very top of the military. Where's your arms dealer friend? I'm dressed as a Celerius, maybe he'll talk to me."

Rhys shook his head noting, "You don't look like a Celerius at all. You have a blue mask, but look at the rest of your clothes. You're in black and purple. You look just like a Vapros."

Neil said angrily, "Damn. You're right. You're always right."

Rhys shrugged. The brothers sat in silence for a few minutes. "How'd things go with the girls?" Rhys asked.

"How'd you know about the girls?"

"You're Neil Vapros. There are always girls where you're concerned."

Neil smiled to himself. "Yeah, I talked to a few at the bar. All I learned was that Michael Taurlum is as bad as ever. I wish we had a Celerius coat," he said, catching sight of a soldier.

"Neil Vapros," a voice said from just behind them. Rhys turned quickly. Neil didn't bother. He knew that voice almost as well as he knew his own. "Fancy meeting you here."

"Bianca," he said, still not turning around.

"What, you're not even going to look at me?" He could almost hear her pouting. "I even put on a dress and everything." Neil let himself smile as he turned around. She swept a low curtsy. "How are you this fine evening, Mr. Vapros?" she asked, eyes twinkling. But Neil wasn't looking at her eyes.

Neil raised one eyebrow and Bianca saw his mouth twitch as he stared at her dress. Bianca stood in a noticeably extravagant dress, a voluminous ball gown that hugged her torso and then practically exploded into an avalanche of blue ruffles and lace. Neil guessed that she was trying hard to fit in, but the dress was too much, too extravagant for a party like this. She had an expensive-looking pearl necklace and matching pearl earrings. She had pulled her hair up into a twist and little blond strands escaped and hung endearingly along the sides of her face.

Neil pulled a handkerchief from his pocket and leaned over and wiped it across the edge of Bianca's forehead, where a smudge of ash had been overlooked. Bianca's eyes grew wide in surprise.

"What is this?" he asked as he looked at the handkerchief.

"Soot," she replied calmly.

"Why is there soot on your forehead?"

"Burned down a gang member's house," she said as she grabbed a glass of champagne from the table.

"That's hilarious," he chuckled.

"It wasn't a joke."

"And may I ask where you got the dress?"

"This rich-looking girl and I traded clothes."

"Did she want to?" Rhys asked.

"I don't have to answer that," Bianca said with a grin.

"We'll address your crime spree later. But speaking of your dress," Neil said slowly. Rhys gasped and nodded.

"What about it?" Bianca tugged at the sleeves a little.

Neil grinned. "It's blue."

Chapter Ten

VAPROS OPERA HOUSE
DARIUS TAURLUM

Darius Taurlum gained access to the Opera House through the stage door. It was locked from the outside, but he'd pulled it straight out of the wall and walked in hurriedly before anyone noticed. There were probably better, less conspicuous ways of infiltrating, but visions of his impending revenge on the Vapros brat were clouding his thought process.

The backstage area was a maze of tiny hallways crowded with actors, stagehands, and set pieces. Nobody seemed to notice or care that he was there; they all just stepped around him without making eye contact. Looking around, Darius tried to assess the best way to cause chaos during the show. He could smash through the set with his hammer. Or, if he could find a match, he could set the curtain on fire.

A small man in a purple coat grabbed Darius by the arm and began to yank him toward the stage. Darius glared at him. "Your cue is coming up," he said in hushed tones. "Is that a new costume? It looks great."

"You want me to go onstage?" Darius asked, a new plan forming slowly in his mind.

"What do you think we've been rehearsing for? Of course I want you to go onstage! And don't miss your entrance! This isn't amateur hour."

Darius grinned. "Which side of the stage do I enter from again?"

VICTORY LIES WITHIN
THE ASHES

Chapter Eleven

VAPROS OPERA HOUSE
JENNIFER VAPROS

JENNIFER VAPROS WALKED TOWARD THE OPERA HOUSE ARM IN ARM with her twin sister. "Any plans to meet up with you-know-who tonight?" she asked playfully as an usher wearing purple opened the front doors for them.

Victoria blushed. "I don't know what you're talking about."

"Oh, please, Vic," Jennifer said, letting go of her sister to tighten her ponytail.

"Don't tell Dad," Victoria begged.

"Don't meet up with that boy, and I won't have to," her sister fired back. "You have a duty." She started for the grand staircase. Victoria began to follow, but Jennifer stopped her. "I'm going to the second floor. You stay here. We'll meet up at the end of the night."

When Jennifer reached the top of the stairs, she scanned the halls for someone worth talking to. A cluster of giggling girls in large dresses walked by, but Jennifer ignored them. Their brand of gossip wasn't worth the effort. She leisurely approached the nearest balcony and peered out to watch how the opera was proceeding. She remembered that this was her father's latest project: *The Birth of the Saviors.* Her father had overseen its conception over the last few months and had been anxious about how it would go over with the nobles. They never had a problem with lampooning the Taurlum, but this show had a heavier message; it was all about the legend surrounding the manner in which the families received their powers and the beginning of the feud.

From what she could see, they were still very close to the beginning of the story. Four actors stood on the stage: one dressed as a Vapros, one as a Taurlum, one as a Celerius, and one in all black clothing. The lack of design that went into the fourth family was due to the fact that no one actually knew anything about the fourth family. Suddenly a horde of actors in furred clothing stormed the stage; these were the savages. They looked ready to attack the family members, but suddenly the dark and ominous music of battle slowed to a soft and pleasing melody. From the ceiling, a man covered with crystals was lowered by a few discreet wires. A light focused on him and he began to glow, shooting rays of light in every direction. He sang a few verses of blessing. She couldn't quite understand every word, but she got the gist: "Protect Altryon with the gifts I have given you."

This was the Man with the Golden Light. According to the legend, he had given the families their powers so that they could protect Altryon from the savages. The man ascended again into the rafters and the music returned to its rousing battle theme. A complicated fight scene erupted on stage and when finished, the savages and the family member in black lay dead on the ground. Jennifer turned away in disinterest. She knew everything that was about to happen.

She spied a group of rich merchants by the window and allowed herself a slight smile. Perfect.

Jennifer moved like a well-oiled machine. Every action was deliberate and smooth, from complicated fight sequences to simple banter. She was, as her father often reminded Neil, a model assassin. She made a beeline for the merchants, her chest held high and a slight sway in her hips. "Not enjoying the opera, I assume?" she said when they noticed her coming.

One of the merchants nudged his neighbor. "It's a bit trite," he spoke up. "All of the enemy Taurlum' stuff, I mean. We've seen it all before."

"And it's . . . well, it's an opera," the merchant to her right admitted. The others laughed.

Jennifer leaned against the wall, arms folded. "I don't blame you," she said. "I prefer more . . . exciting pastimes." She unfolded her arms and examined her fingernails. "What would you be doing right now if you weren't here?" she asked idly. She could feel their eyes on her. "I know I'd be out on the town, maybe in a bar somewhere or at a party dancing with a handsome stranger." She knew exactly what to say to make them sweat.

"Yeah, a party sounds good," one of the merchants said quickly. "I know there's a masquerade tonight. If you want to get out of here, I can escort you there."

Jennifer smiled coyly. "Now, now, we hardly know each other," she chided. "It wouldn't be proper."

"Neither would dancing with a stranger," he pointed out. Jennifer met his eyes for the first time.

"Touché," she said finally. "I don't believe we've met before."

He bowed. "Clemens."

"Clemens," she repeated. "It's a pleasure."

"I know who you are," a new merchant said before she could introduce herself. "Jennifer Vapros."

She cocked an eyebrow. "My reputation precedes me, I see."

Clemens whistled. "So it is you," he said. "I thought it might be, but I wasn't sure." He looked her up and down. "I guess the rumors are true."

She narrowed her eyes but kept her cool facade. "Oh? And what rumors have you heard about me?"

The merchant countered, "Just that you're the most beautiful girl in Altryon."

Jennifer smirked and felt herself relax. "That honor belongs to my sister, actually."

"Aren't you identical twins?" asked a random merchant. Jennifer ignored him.

"I'm serious." Clemens said as he gave her a small smile. "They say every man who sees you falls in love."

"I've heard more," the first merchant jumped in. "I've heard she's an assassin."

Jennifer whipped her head around to stare at him. "Me?" she said. "An assassin? I'm just a young girl."

"That's right. They say men let their guard down around you. You draw them in, trick them into trusting you, and then kill them. They don't even see it coming."

One of the merchants nudged Clemens. "Be careful, Clem," he joked, "you could be next!"

Jennifer's hand twitched for her knife. Her pulse was quickening. "Not all rumors are true," she said finally. *Hold it together, Jen.*

"She's not an assassin," Clemens said sternly to his companion. "Leave her alone." He took half a step toward her. "So, how about that party?" He offered her his arm.

Jennifer let out a laugh. "With you? I'm flattered, but what would your wife think?"

Clemens looked shocked. The other merchants exchanged glances. "How did you know?" he trailed off.

"Your reputation precedes you as well, merchant," Jen said coldly. She knew she was destroying any chance of getting information out of these men, but she didn't care. This wasn't fun anymore. "I know all of you: Brock, Marques, Edgar." She glared at each one of them as she rattled off their names. "I'm a Vapros. We thrive on knowing everything about everyone."

The merchants looked like they wished they were somewhere else.

Jennifer planted her feet on the ground. "I suggest you all find your way back to your seats and watch the rest of the opera," she said in a low, menacing voice. "Unless you want your darkest secrets spilled over the streets of Altryon." The men, looking terrified, scurried down the hallway.

Jennifer kept a threatening look on her face until they were out of sight, and then leaned against the bar. She took deep breaths until her heart returned to its normal pace. She once again approached the balcony and saw that they were reaching an even more exciting part of the opera. Apparently, the three families had already fallen to infighting. After the families had received their special powers, Altryon had experienced unprecedented prosperity and peace. But as new children were born and their powers advanced, they began to compete over whose powers were better and who was more powerful. Until one day when everything changed and the feud was born. She was always told that the head Taurlum had killed a Vapros child and this started the feud. This was no doubt the message this evening, although she knew the other families disagreed.

Soon more Taurlum would arrive on stage and there would be another fight. Jennifer doubted her father would cover the rest of the story—how the feud had made it impossible for the families to rule as they couldn't pass badly needed laws. How the people had eventually gone on a citywide strike, crippling the economy until the families relinquished power and an emperor was anointed instead. No doubt her father would focus on the Taurlum and their crimes against the Vapros. He'd always loved to say, "The Taurlum drew first blood, but the Vapros will draw last."

Jennifer turned away. She had never been too interested in operas and this one was no different. No longer in the mood to talk to people she didn't know, she darted downstairs to find her sister.

Jennifer quickly found Victoria who was of course with the boy Sir Vapros had warned her about. Jennifer gritted her teeth and watched from afar. Operas might be boring, but Victoria never seemed to care where her father sent her to socialize. Her love always seemed to find her by the end of the night. Even now he was saying something that brought a blush to her cheek. She was shyly grinning back, and playing with a strand of hair. Jennifer gritted her teeth. Victoria was being stupid. Why let some boy turn you into a blushing baby?

Robert wasn't of noble birth. Victoria didn't seem to care in the slightest. She was inching closer to him ever so slightly second after second. She wasn't even trying to be subtle. Jennifer slid behind a nearby corner where she could watch without been seen and still listen to their conversation.

Victoria suppressed a smile. "How do you always know where I'm going to be?"

"I guess," Robert said, eyes dancing.

"Do you?" she asked breathlessly. "Well. You're quite good at guessing."

His face melted into the grin and he started to say something, but a collective gasp from the people in the theater interrupted his train of thought. "Sounds like we're missing something important," he said, furrowing his brow in mock worry.

Victoria played along. "Oh, yes, I've heard this scene is visually outstanding," she said in the snootiest voice she could manage. "It's a shame we aren't in there watching."

Robert was looking at her mouth. "I don't mind, actually," he murmured. "I'm watching something else visually outstanding."

She giggled at that line, and began to lean forward. Jennifer stepped out from around the corner and grabbed Victoria's arm. "Forgotten where you are?" Jennifer asked.

Victoria jumped away from Robert, cheeks burning. "What…" she began.

Robert blushed heavily. "You look lovely tonight, Jennifer."

She glared at him and then back at her sister. "How many times have you been told not to socialize with people like him? This can only end one way, Victoria."

Victoria looked like she was going to cry. "I'm not you, Jen."

"Excuse me?" Jennifer asked.

Before she could unleash her wrath a scream tore through the hall. Victoria and Jennifer shared a wary glance. Robert had already started into one of the boxes that overlooked the stage. The twins didn't hesitate to follow. The scene below them consisted of several actors dressed as Taurlum. One of the actors was taller. He held a comically oversized hammer like the rest, but as he raised it over his head, Jennifer realized it wasn't a prop. Victoria grabbed Robert's hand "We have to tell someone," she hissed. "That's a real Taurlum! We have to—"

She didn't have time to finish her sentence before chaos erupted on the stage.

VICTORY LIES WITHIN
THE ASHES

Chapter Twelve

MASQUERADE BALL
NEIL VAPROS

THE MASQUERADE BALL WAS IN FULL SWING. THE NOISE LEVEL WAS
increasing as the drinks flowed and patrons spoke louder to be heard
above the band. Neil and Bianca crossed the ball slowly. They had
"borrowed" a large blue hat and Neil was tucking her last remaining
strands of hair into it. She was actually starting to look like a Celerius. Hopefully, the arms dealer wouldn't notice that her eyes were
grey instead of deep brown. "All you need to do is gauge his reaction
to seeing you. Act polite. And straighten your spine. The Celerius
don't slouch."

Neil had a customary way of behaving with women. He usually
flashed his charming smile and his voice dropped to a deeper pitch;
he leaned in when he talked and played it as cool as he could. But
when he talked to Bianca it was different; it was almost as if they were
dancing. Information flowed back and forth easily in a rhythm that
had been established over years of communication and friendship.

Neil returned to Rhys's side and they watched from afar as Bianca approached the arms dealer. "I'm confused," Rhys said.

Neil reached for a drink from the table behind them. "It's simple. Bianca is wearing blue. The Celerius family wears blue. The arms dealer will think she's a Celerius and spill the secrets. You're a smart kid. How do you not understand this plan?"

"That's not what I meant," Rhys said indignantly. "I meant I don't understand you two."

"Us two?

"Yes. What is your relationship to her?"

Neil took a long gulp of his drink. "Friends," he said finally. "Just friends." Rhys stared at him skeptically. "You don't look like you believe me," Neil said, thoughtfully watching Bianca across the room.

"It's just …" Rhys paused, "none of my friends have ever toppled titans for me."

Neil smiled briefly. "Don't refer to the Taurlum as titans. We don't need to fuel their egos. That's their job." He set down his drink. "Here she comes."

Bianca had made a beeline for them, her brow furrowed. "He wouldn't talk to me," she said when she was within earshot.

"What?" Neil looked over her shoulder. The arms dealer was nowhere to be seen. "He didn't say anything?"

"He just apologized. He wouldn't stop saying sorry."

"Did he say what he was sorry for?" Rhys prompted.

"No. He wouldn't even look at me."

Rhys frowned. "So the soldiers won't talk to any of the families?"

"Apparently not," Neil remarked as he searched the crowd for the dealer.

"Do you think it's something serious?" Bianca asked.

"I don't know what to think."

"I could try to talk to him as a commoner," she offered. "I'll change out of the dress. I have my armor underneath anyway." She grinned, trying to lighten the mood, but Neil was too lost in thought.

"We have to tell Dad," Rhys said, putting a hand on Neil's shoulder. They started toward the door.

"Wait!" Bianca ran after them. "You're leaving?"

"This can't wait," Rhys told her.

"Don't you want me to come with you? I'm the one who tried to talk to him."

"Sir Vapros won't want to talk to you," Neil said bitterly.

"But Neil!"

"You have to stay here, Bianca," he said sharply. "In case anything happens. You have to … keep watch."

"In case anything happens," she repeated. "You think something bad could happen? And you want me to stay here, to knowingly put myself in harm's way?"

"You have your armor under your dress," Rhys pointed out.

Bianca ignored him. "Neil Vapros, stop walking this instant!"

He didn't stop walking. She finally fell behind. "Fine!" she called after them. "But you owe me! For the second time today!"

He waved over his shoulder absent-mindedly which didn't seem to calm her temper. She huffed and turned to face the people and festivities once again.

⚜

The quickest route back to the Vapros home took them through the center of the nightlife district. Neil and Rhys had to weave between dancing villagers and try to avoid getting hit in the head with mugs of beer. It was slow going. Eventually, Neil ducked into an alley and led his brother to a quieter part of the district. The streets here were deserted; the bars closed early on the outskirts.

"Where are you going?" Rhys asked.

"We'll get there faster this way. There were too many people in the way."

They kept walking in silence. It had rained in this part of town. The streets were full of puddles and a few stray drops still fell from the sky. One of them hit Neil directly on the forehead. He found himself wishing he had his assassin's hood. In the distance, he heard drunken cheers from the part of the district that was still open for business.

"I hate when everything's deserted like this," Rhys mumbled.

"Why?"

"I feel like someone's going to jump out and attack me."

Neil smiled. "This isn't the poor district. Nobody's going to mug you. We're practically princes here. We do own every business you can see." But as he spoke, he reflexively reached for his knife. The villagers of Altryon had become increasingly restless lately. Some of the emperor's policies had left people desperately poor. Year after year, he had relentlessly increased taxes. There were whispers of uprisings. "And why would they attack you, anyway? You're Rhys Vapros. People love your quietness and gentleness. Who could hurt someone as adorable as you?" he mocked quietly. "You'd have more to worry about if you were the emperor."

"I just don't like being out alone this late at night. I don't like the dark. It's an irrational fear. Don't ask me to explain it."

Neil slung his arm over his brother's shoulder. "You aren't alone. You have me—an assassin."

"An assassin in training," Rhys corrected, but he was smiling.

"Same thing," Neil countered as he looked up at the moon.

Neil and Rhys made it to the end of the alley and neared the center of the nightlife district. A large marble fountain stood in the center and the entire square buzzed with activity. Street performers, merchants, and young partygoers brought the street to life. As the two Vapros boys wandered through the crowd, Rhys's eyes scanned the tops of heads. This was a common practice for him. Whenever he entered a new area he was searching for possible threats or unpredictable variables.

"You see that?" Rhys whispered.

It took Neil a moment, but he noticed the grime covered man slipping through the crowds, running his slender fingers across the partygoers as he went. "Pickpocket?" Neil asked.

"Maybe." Rhys said.

"Could it be the big one? The one dad's after?"

"Maybe." Rhys said again.

Neil wrapped his fingers around his knife and glared at the man with unrelenting focus. The second he saw concrete evidence of theft he'd strike. Sir Vapros hated pickpockets in the nightlife district, and one in particular always sought to give him trouble. Neil struggled to remember the lowlife's name.

"I think it's Ainsley Bovick." There was a quiet excitement in Rhys's voice. "The Prince of Pockets."

Neil's fingers twitched. "That's a stupid name," he said even though his adrenaline was running high.

Ainsley was the head of a small gang called the Knights of Night. They were small time and specialized only in pickpocketing, but they spent far too much time in the nightlife district and Sir Vapros had ordered that any discovered be killed. Neil wanted to look over at Rhys but he couldn't take his eyes off of Ainsley. Suddenly he saw the glimmer of a coin as it left a drunken man's pocket and Neil had all the confirmation he needed.

Ainsley weaved through the crowd with outstanding fluidity and Neil remembered that someone had once told him that the Prince of Pockets removed the bones he didn't need to become more nimble. Neil had no time to think of rumors though. He only had time to think of the task at hand. He tracked Ainsley with his eyes and the moment the pickpocket picked up speed, Neil materialized right in front of him.

Neil maneuvered his shoulder so it would land solidly in the man's sternum and Ainsley toppled to the ground gasping for breath. He certainly felt like a man that had bones. Showers of gold and stolen belongings spilled out over the cobblestone street and Ainsley scrambled to reclaim them. Without much effort Neil had his knife out of its sheathe and against the man's neck. "Are you the Prince of Pockets?"

Ainsley grinned, showing two gold teeth and one that looked like a ruby. "I might be. Daddy's favorite assassin?" he asked.

"I might be."

Ainsley laughed loudly and Neil noticed that the entire square had stopped to observe them. Could Neil really slit a man's throat in front of nearly a hundred civilians? Ainsley looked around and realized the predicament. "Do you think your family is respected?" he mused. His voice was impossibly high for a man his age. "I'm just curious. Respect and fear always look so similar from afar."

"Maybe we're both."

Ainsley rubbed a filthy hand over his forehead. "'Billy was a good boy, who was never rude or sad—until he met the Vapros and then everything went bad!'" He was howling loud enough for all of Altryon to hear him.

Neil hated Little Billy rhymes and might have spilled the man's guts just to hear the end of it. "'They took him to their parties, they let him drink their ale. The emperor came—they disappeared—and Billy went to jail.'"

Now it seemed everyone in the square was staring. "I bet every soul in this district has heard the rhyme at least a dozen times." Ainsley taunted. "I wonder, is that how they really think of you? It really is hard to disagree with the simplistic truth of a children's book. I've found most things in Little Billy to be accurate."

"Alright," Neil said, keeping the knife against the pickpocket's skin. "I'll match you one for one. 'Little Billy had never been so poor, he had what his job provided but always wanted more. So he travelled to the richer districts to see what he could steal, he was caught, he was killed, and the crows received a meal.'"

Ainsley snickered. "I like that one."

"I think the 'simplistic truth'" of that rhyme is pretty clear. If you take things that don't belong to you, you end up dead."

"Then do it." Ainsley hissed. "In front of all of these people."

Rhys appeared next to Neil. "This might not be the best idea,." Rhys whispered. "This is quite a crowd."

Neil wanted to respond, but a far-off voice suddenly called his name, "Vapros boys! Over here!"

Neil and Rhys turned to see a preacher standing on the edge of the fountain. Ainsley seized his momentary opportunity and weaved around the blade of the knife. He was into an ally before Neil could even consider going after him. Frustrated, Neil turned his focus back to the preacher. The man gestured grandly to the small crowd surrounding him. "The Man with the Golden Light bestowed his power upon the Vapros. They're the proof! Teleport for us again! Show us your power!"

"Let's get out of here," Neil grumbled.

"Now you're against improving public image? This will be the best press we get tonight." Rhys materialized a few feet away. Neil followed.

"The teachings of the First Church of Enlightenment are proven," the preacher cried. "Centuries ago, the Man with the Golden Light came forth from the heavens and bestowed upon you these divine gifts. And from these gifts, in turn, your feud was sprung." He turned to the boys expectantly.

"I don't want to talk about the feud," Neil said to Rhys.

"Fine," Rhys said, "I'll do it." He positioned himself to face the crowd and spoke clearly, "We were given these powers by the Man with the Golden Light. Our descendants will have them, too. The Man with the Golden Light charged the families with protecting Altryon, and time and time again the Vapros have proven that we are the only ones capable of serving the people. We are the only family that does charity work. We are the only family building things for the people. The other families use their powers for selfish reasons—they monopolize the markets and the banking system. But we Vapros, everything we do, we do for you."

Rhys turned to Neil with a shrug. Before Neil could respond, the preacher boomed defiantly, "No! You were given these gifts for a purpose and you've squandered these blessings in a feud that has lasted for centuries while the people of Altryon suffer from your petty power struggle. You were charged to work together with the other families for the greater good. Instead, you each use these gifts for your own gain while the people suffer under this oppressive regime. Do you boys wear tattoos? Have you inscribed the souls of the dead into your skin? Had we not interrupted would you have spilled the blood of that poor man?"

Neil countered, "Wait! We—" but his words were drowned out by the jeers of the crowd. Rhys grabbed Neil by the arm, and they slipped away down the street as the preacher continued his diatribe. Rhys pulled Neil into The Hideaway, a back alley pub owned by the Vapros family. As they entered the rustic tavern, Rhys locked the door behind him. It was closing time and the bar was empty except for the white haired, weather beaten barkeep wiping down the bar. Rhys and Neil plopped down on stools. "Alfred, we need a minute. Can you stay open for a bit?"

"Of course, Sir Vapros. It is in fact your establishment. Can I get you two something?"

"Yes, can we get some ale?" said Neil. As the barkeep turned away to grab mugs, Neil went off. "What was that? After everything we've done for the people of Altryon, this is the thanks we get? The ungrateful—" Neil was interrupted by the barkeep.

"Your ale, sirs."

"Thank you, Alfred." Neil continued in a more controlled demeanor, recanting the event out loud. "You've run this pub for forty years, Alfred. Are we really that bad?"

For a moment, the innkeeper just looked at the two of them as if contemplating whether or not to respond. After cocking his head and scratching his forehead, Alfred slowly said in his gravelly voice, "It's not a question of being good or bad." This seemed to puzzle and even frustrate Neil. He began to say something as Rhys grabbed his arm.

"Continue," Rhys said to the old man.

"It's not my place, sirs. I should stay quiet."

"No, please continue, Alfred. You know this town better than anyone. After all, you've run this pub forever. If anyone knows the people of Altryon, it's you."

"Well, it's no mystery we are far worse off under the emperor's rule than we were under the rule of the families."

Neil interrupted, "Then what's the problem?"

Rhys once again grabbed Neil's arm. "Let him continue."

Alfred cautiously began again. "Do you even remember what you're feuding about?"

"Sure," Neil retorted in the canned response that had become automatic.

The barkeep stared at Neil for a few seconds. "Well, that's a relief. It would be a shame if all this bloodshed between the families was for nothing. I hope it's for a really good reason, since it is coming at a great cost to the people." Alfred turned and resumed his cleaning.

Rhys stared at Neil. "Do we? Do we really know what this damn feud is about? Cause I sure as hell can't explain it."

Neil opened his mouth, ready to spew the propaganda he had heard his entire life, and then slowly shut it. He ran his hands through his hair, leaned his elbows on the bar, and rested his head in his hands.

Alfred said quietly, "I'm an old man and don't know much, but it seems to me whoever has you upset might have a point. Why were you given these powers? What is your destiny, Sir Vapros?"

Neil didn't have an answer. Alfred shrugged and moved into the back room. "I wonder how Victoria and Jennifer did tonight," Neil said quietly.

"They probably had an even less exciting time than we did." Rhys took a sip of his drink. "Nothing monumental ever happens at the Opera House."

Chapter Thirteen

VAPROS OPERA HOUSE
DARIUS TAURLUM

DARIUS HAD LUMBERED ONSTAGE AFTER THE REST OF THE ACTORS and clumsily joined them as they formed a line. They began to sing a battle anthem. One of the men next to him nudged him when he didn't join in. Snarling, Darius caught a fistful of the actor's shirt and threw him out into the audience. The nobles in the first few rows shrieked; the others began to stand and run for the exit. Darius lifted his hammer and slammed it into the ground, sending splinters of wood in every direction. "This Opera House is closed in the name of the Taurlum family!" he roared, swinging the hammer over his head and down into the stage again. Screams broke out through the audience. "You will not make a mockery of us again!" A Vapros guard charged at him, dagger drawn. Darius pummeled him to death with the hammer.

The Taurlum smashed through pillars and walls as he strolled offstage toward the back exit, only to find it blocked by a familiar figure. "Well, well, well," Jennifer Vapros said, examining her fingernails coolly. "Darius, we meet again."

Darius growled, "Out of my way."

Jennifer smiled savagely and cooed, "I can hear the rumors now: Darius Taurlum, beaten by two girls in one day. I don't think you'd be the Taurlum's 'Golden Boy' anymore."

He lifted his hammer and asked, "Are you sure you want to play this game?"

She raised an eyebrow and repeated, "Are you sure you want to play this game? You know what they say about playing with fire." She winked as she pulled a knife from somewhere in her dress. "Still have the scars from last time?"

He clenched his jaw. Jennifer Vapros, like most descendants of the original families, had developed heightened abilities—a feat that he, Darius, still had yet to accomplish. Everyone else in his family had some form of extra ability: Michael, for example, could create small earthquakes, and their father could turn his skin into actual steel. Nobody knew for sure how to coax out the extra power, but Darius had a feeling it had to do with experiencing some kind of trauma. It would make sense, after all. He himself had never gone through anything that left him feeling like he couldn't go on, but he knew Michael had been in some tough situations. And Jennifer Vapros, if the rumors were to be believed, had experienced her fair share of trauma.

Jennifer lifted her hand, as if in a wave and revealed her palm to him. The skin was red, like a glowing ember, and Darius knew, from their last meeting that if it touched him, it would burn like fire and leave scorch marks on his skin.

He had once been on a raid of one of the Vapros' parties with Michael. All had gone well until he decided to go after the only Vapros actually attending the party—Jennifer. He had only just caught her when she grabbed his arm and, eyes blazing, burned into his skin. The burn had since healed over, but his pride had yet to recover.

He charged at her, hammer in hand. She disappeared before his eyes and rematerialized just behind him. With a smirk, she thrust her knife into a chink in his armor. It didn't pierce the skin.

If she was frustrated by her failure, she didn't show it; her face remained as calm and collected as ever. Darius increased his grip on the hammer. "You're quick," he growled, "but you'll tire."

He swung quickly. Jennifer dodged the blow and reappeared in the air behind him and quickly pulled the helmet from his head. She materialized across the room, cradling his precious piece of armor. "Yes," she agreed, "but not before ending you."

"Jen!" a girl's voice cried, and Darius turned in time to see Jennifer's twin sister hurtling down the hallway. Behind her was a boy dressed sloppily in commoner clothes with what appeared to be a borrowed noble's coat. Grunting, Darius threw his hammer at the boy. It only nicked his shoulder, but it was enough to send him sprawling to the ground with a cry of agony. The girl rushed to protect him.

Jennifer redoubled her grip on her knife. "No helmet and no hammer?" she asked, arching an eyebrow.

"All I need are my fists." Darius charged her.

She ran at him with equal vigor. Before Jennifer could rematerialize behind him again, Darius was able to make contact with her. The force of the blow sent her crashing to the floor. Breathing heavily, he grinned at her. "Tired yet?" he asked.

She struggled to sit up. A few feet away, the sister was sobbing over her groaning commoner. Darius bowed mockingly to the fallen assassin and began to walk away. With a little cry, Jennifer leapt to her feet and caught his hand in hers. He felt the familiar burning sensation and threw her off, sending her flying into the opposite wall. It snapped apart at the impact, impaling her with splinters of wood. She didn't try to stand again.

Victoria gasped and ran to kneel over her sister. Wood stuck out of her back like spikes, but they hadn't gone deep enough to pierce any vital organs. She rolled Jennifer over, clearly expecting the worst. "Jennifer?" she said timidly, shaking her sister's shoulder.

Her sister let out a groan of pain and brushed Victoria off. "I'm going to burn that bastard's face off."

Victoria sighed with relief and relaxed visibly. "I'm sure you will," she said soothingly, "he deserves it."

"I'm right here." Darius murmured, still standing to the side shaking his burning hand.

"You deserve it." Victoria repeated timidly. She was crying.

"Tell your boyfriend to visit a doctor," he said. "His shoulder's broken." A stream of guards rounded the corner and Darius decided it was time to make his exit. He picked up his helmet from where it lay on the ground and replaced it on his head.

He could hear Victoria yelling at the guards to take her twin and the commoner to a hospital. Darius listened bemusedly. She didn't exactly seem like the type to be good at giving orders, especially due to the fact that there were tears streaming down her face. He swaggered from the Opera House, cloak billowing behind him.

He had only made it a few paces down the street when he heard the telltale clamor of horses making their way after him. As he turned around, he came face to face with what seemed like an entire army of Imperial troops. The soldier at the front lifted a parchment. "Taurlum," he said solemnly, "you are wanted for vandalism crimes against this building and the murder of the Captain of the Guard."

Darius's jaw nearly hit the ground. "He *died?*"

"By order of the Emperor, you are under arrest."

"Wait," Darius said, holding his hands out in front of him, "the vandalism charge. It's on the Vapros Opera House. You all . . . you never interfere in battles between the families."

"Times are changing."

Darius let out a stream of curse words and turned to see if he could run. More Imperial troops were flooding the streets, swords trained on him. Too late—he regretted not retrieving his hammer. He raised his arms in an enraged surrender as the troops moved in around him.

Chapter Fourteen

CELERIUS ESTATE
LILLY CELERIUS

Lilly Celerius rolled over in bed for the hundredth time that night and verbally cursed her insomnia. She should have been used to it by now. She hadn't experienced a full night's sleep since her brother Edward had been murdered unexpectedly in his bed three years ago. But tonight, the condition seemed especially merciless. She had been up all night, worrying about Anthony. She'd run out of tears a few hours ago, and now all she could manage was a dry hiccup once in a while. *It must be nice*, she thought bitterly while squeezing her eyes shut, *to be able to escape into dreamland for a few hours.*

Footsteps outside her door made her open her eyes. Who else was awake at this hour? Maybe Jonathan was coming to check on her. She closed her eyes, listening for voices. The footsteps stopped outside her door. "Jonathan?" she dared to whisper. The word died on her lips as the person outside her room began to speak.

"I think they're in the west end of the house," the low, gravelly voice said, and Lilly sat straight up in bed. This wasn't the kind, familiar voice of her caring servant. This was an intruder.

Another unfamiliar voice chimed in, "We'll have a better chance if we spread out." With a pang of fear, Lilly realized there was an entire group of intruders, as many as five or six, gathered outside her bedroom. She slid out of bed as quietly as she could and groped around in the darkness for her sword.

"Look for offices," one of the voices said. "Anywhere they'd keep legal documents." The other intruders grumbled in agreement. She heard the footsteps disperse and dared to relax. Then the doorknob turned. Her heart leapt into her throat as she whirled behind the opening door, sword held at the ready.

A man poked his head in. An iron mask shaped like a snake concealed his face. Lilly bit her lip hard. She recognized that mask. It bore the emblem of the Brotherhood of the Slums, a cult of bandits that had appeared when the empire had taken an economic downturn. The cult member sauntered over to Lilly's desk and began to rifle through its drawers, scanning each piece of paper quickly before tossing it aside. Summoning all her courage, Lilly moved through the darkness to stand behind the man. Quietly, she drew her sword. "Find anything?" she asked in a low voice.

The bandit whirled around with a yelp and moved to pull a dagger from his belt. Lilly slashed her sword across his neck, her expression cold and hard, in spite of her pounding heart. The man gasped as he fell, clutching at the cut in his throat. He did not get up again. Lilly wiped her blade gently against the dying man's grime-coated shirt, cleaning the blood away as best she could. Something told her she would need that sword again tonight.

As she raced down the corridor to sound the alarm, Lilly collided with someone in the hallway. She hit the ground, bruising her elbow badly. She gritted her teeth and tried to ignore the injury. Luckily for her, nobody in the Celerius family felt pain for long. The figure she'd crashed into towered over her, leering from within his snake mask, and Lilly jabbed her sword upward, aiming for his throat. He dodged her blow and knocked the sword out of her hand. Lilly scrambled to retrieve it, but the bandit planted his foot on her wrist until he heard a telltale crack. The bones in her wrist began to repair themselves immediately, but Lilly screamed anyway.

"Come now," her attacker said soothingly, kicking her sword farther away from her groping hand. "Who are you? What are you doing out of bed so late?"

Lilly kept screaming. *Someone wake up!* she prayed. *Someone come help me!*

"Tell me who you are and I might let you live," the bandit offered.

"I'm a servant!" Lilly shouted.

"A servant with a sword?" The man cocked his head and gave her a small smile. "I think we both know that's not true."

"I took it from my master's room!" she yelled. Nobody could hear her. Nobody was coming.

The attacker leaned down and pressed his dagger to her neck. "I believe you," he told her, "but I can't let you raise the alarm." He pressed the dagger in hard and slit her throat. Lilly felt blood streaming down her neck and gasped for enough breath to let out a final scream, but all that came out was a weak moan. She closed her eyes. The murderer smiled, sheathed his bloody dagger, and walked away from the corpse.

As he neared the end of the hallway, he heard fast footfalls behind him. He whirled around just in time to see the girl he'd murdered inches behind him and wielding her sword. The cut in her throat had faded into a thin scar. "No," he said, eyes wide. "You're not a servant—you're—"

Lilly cut him down with one expert flick of her wrist. "I'm a Celerius," she told him as he died on the floor.

Lilly tore down the hallway and up the stairs into the guard tower. She heaved on the ropes to sound the bells. The bells rang so loudly she was sure everyone in Altryon could hear them. Someone would come now. She was safe. It was over.

One minute passed, then two. Nobody came. She pulled the bell ropes again. The house stayed quiet. Lilly's heart began to thud. She looked to the window of the guard tower and let out a gasp. The eastern tower of her family's estate was in flames. That's why no one was coming to help her. There were guards surrounding the flaming tower heaving buckets of water into the blaze. Down in the courtyard, two figures in iron helmets were sprinting for the exit. Jaw clenched, Lilly tightened her grip on her sword and flew down the stairs. She made it outside just before the bandits. "Stop!" she commanded, sword outstretched, barring the door.

The two men turned to each other, grinning. "What a brave little girl you are," one of them said, his voice raspy. "Coming after us in the middle of the night. You should be in bed," he snarled.

Lilly glared at them icily. "Find what you were looking for?" she asked angrily.

One of the men held up a few rolls of parchment and sneered gleefully. "We did, and now it's time for us to go. Step aside and we will let you live."

Lilly didn't budge. "Do you two know what lies beyond Altryon?" she asked stonily.

"Nobody's ever been outside these gates," the taller one scoffed.

"Move aside, girl."

"My brother has been outside!" Lilly shouted. "He goes outside every day to fight the savages and protect everyone within the city— even you two. And this is how you repay him? You rob his family? You burn his house?" She was breathing hard. The bandits looked nervous.

"Just move aside," the one holding the parchment said angrily. "Don't make me hurt you."

"You couldn't hurt me if you tried," Lilly spat. "Know this about my brother, the one who protects you. Before he became the leader of the military, he taught me how to fight." She flipped the sword expertly. "My name is Lilly Celerius; you will yield."

Without warning, the shorter man charged at her. She leaped aside and flicked her sword with lightning swiftness as he ran past. He landed on the ground with a cry. "Ready to join your friend?" Lilly asked the remaining intruder, cleaning her sword on his comrade's shirt.

The bandit reached for his pistol and fired a shot straight into her shoulder. She didn't even flinch. The wound bled for only a few seconds before the skin laced back together. The only evidence that the shot ever occurred was the smoking gun in the bandit's hand. He dropped his pistol and turned to run. He didn't make it far. Lilly's cold steel sliced into his back after only two steps. She could thank her Celerius speed for that. He fell to his knees and dropped the documents into the mud. Lilly walked around him and positioned her sword under his neck so she could look into his frightened eyes. She leaned in close. "Who sent you here? Why did you come?" she growled.

The bandit spat in her face. His saliva was mixed with blood. He gurgled, "I'll tell you nothing."

Lilly raised her sword in a high arc and brought it down hard on the man's neck. His head rolled into the mud after the parchment. Kneeling, Lilly wiped her sword clean and then began to gather the documents. It only took her a moment to realize what she was staring at: the architectural plans of the Celerius house, documents about banking and finances, figures she couldn't comprehend. The bandits had been after everything that made the Celerius estate run smoothly.

She looked back at the house and saw the fire was now under control. She pulled the snake-like helmet off the bandit and went inside, lost in thought. It was time to find her father.

⁂

"Lilly," Sir Celerius said, looking down at the papers spread across his desk, "I know you're worried, but this isn't anything for you to be concerned about."

"No?" Lilly sat in the high-backed chair in front of her father's desk and twisted her hands together. "I think it might be."

Sir Celerius set the papers aside. "We should just count ourselves lucky that the thieves didn't get away with any of our valuables. Or our lives," he added. Her father came around the desk to take the hand of his only daughter.

Lilly licked her lips. "That's what I don't understand," she said. "Why didn't they try to take our valuables?"

"I'm more concerned with this rumor about your brother." Sir Celerius lowered himself into the chair beside Lilly. "Tell me again what you heard?"

Lilly swallowed. It wasn't the first time she'd relayed the story, but that didn't make it any less painful. "They're going to execute Anthony. They want someone else in power, someone who isn't from our family, so they're going to kill him in order to send a message: the families aren't as powerful as the empire. And if he tries to resist, they'll come here and kill us instead."

Sir Celerius's eyes were blazing. He shouted, "They won't get away with this! I will make sure of it! It isn't right! It isn't honorable! How sure are you that this is legitimate?"

Lilly paused. "We've had scares like this before, what with the Vapros and their rumors. It could be a trick to get Anthony not to trust his men, or to distract us, or Anthony could be overly paranoid... but I'm not sure."

Sir Celerius said angrily. "Either way, I'll have some spies in the military get closer to this. I'm willing to go to war with the emperor over it."

Lilly focused very hard on the documents on her father's desk. "I'm scared, Father," she said quietly, even though Celerius never admitted they were scared. "I'm really, really scared."

"It'll be all right, Lilly." Sir Celerius leaned over to embrace his daughter. "It'll be all right."

VICTORY LIES WITHIN
THE ASHES

Chapter Fifteen

IMPERIAL PALACE
NEIL VAPROS

THE FOLLOWING MORNING NEIL PACED THE FLOOR OUTSIDE THE emperor's throne room, wishing desperately that he were somewhere else. Last night had been a whirlwind of confusion. A few minutes after he and Rhys made it home, Victoria burst into Sir Vapros's office in tears. Apparently there had been a scrape with Darius Taurlum at the Opera House, and Jennifer was in a hospital with minor stab wounds. Sir Vapros had pressed her for details, and Victoria let it slip that she'd been with her lover, and the rest of the night had been yelling and tantrums. When Sir Vapros calmed down enough to focus on the matter of the Imperial soldiers, he sent Rhys to spy in the markets and Neil to schedule an audience with the emperor himself. And so, Neil found himself here, pacing the halls of the palace.

He pivoted on his heels and faced the giant throne room doors. They nearly reached the ceiling and were made of what appeared to be ivory with gold embellishments. Neil remembered that this was the same palace where his ancestors had originally ruled, and if legend were to be believed, it was also where they were gifted with their powers. Neil focused on the empty space in the room and tried to picture a glowing deity floating in the air. He could almost see the Man with the Golden Light. Shining. Radiant.

The door to the throne room opened loudly and Neil's heart leapt to his throat. The emperor was unsettlingly cold, and he had a cruel sense of humor. Neil would give anything to be in the markets with Rhys. "Sir," he said, bowing hastily, but as he looked up, he realized with relief that he was looking at the empress and her personal guards. "Your highness," he amended, bowing again.

"Neil," she said, with a careful smile, hurrying toward him. The empress may have been a noble, but she was still a woman. Her hair bounced around her face in loose curls as she curtsied and flashed him a smile as she welcomed him. Suddenly, she halted as if she remembered not to get too close to him. She took a step back. "How are you? How is your father?"

He smiled hesitantly, noticing her sudden reservation. "We are well, thank you."

"I assume you are here to see my husband?"

"I am. We have matters to discuss regarding the city."

The empress looked at him, a newfound interest sparkling in her eyes. "The city? How ... interesting," she commented. She seemed to be choosing her words very carefully.

"It's just a passing rumor," he said trying to keep his voice free of suspicion. "Nothing too monumental."

She gave him a smile that didn't quite reach her eyes. "It's always something monumental with your family." She invited him inside the throne room. "Remember, Neil," she said thoughtfully running her hand over her husband's golden throne, "If you focus on the sparks, you might come to ignore the fire."

Neil nodded in agreement, but he wasn't quite sure what she meant about sparks, or fire. She was acting very strangely. Never before had a rumor concerned him like this. "If it were up to me," he said with a smile, testing the waters, "I'd be in the markets."

The empress looked up at him. "Chatting with the ladies?" she asked knowingly.

"Is there anything else to do?"

She threw back her head and laughed. "Not for a boy your age, I suppose." She turned and began to walk toward the door. She stopped and looked back at Neil for an uncomfortably long time, a strange expression on her face, before finally hurrying away. "I'll tell the emperor you've arrived," she said, pulling the door shut behind her.

Neil was sorely tempted to try sitting in the great golden chair before him. The empress would probably have let him do it if he'd asked, but she seemed so distant today that he hadn't bothered. Normally she was always jovial and excited, but today something clearly weighed on her mind.

The door opened again, and Neil whirled to bow. "Been waiting long?" asked the slow voice of the emperor. He strode toward his throne, followed by a trembling servant.

"No, your highness," Neil said. "I'm here to discuss some concerns."

The emperor reached his throne and sat without making a sound. The servant sat beside him in a small wooden chair. Neil glanced over a few times, but the servant wouldn't meet his eyes. His arms and face were covered in large purple bruises and he peered at the floor from behind his dark, matted hair. Neil felt a surge of sympathy for the poor man. It was a well-known fact that the emperor beat his servants.

The emperor leaned forward slightly and examined Neil. Neil tried not to stare back, but he couldn't help but scan the emperor's face a few times. It had no wrinkles, no discolorations, and no marks of any kind. It was as if he had been fashioned out of the purest marble. That face was both fascinating and terrifying.

"I wonder," the emperor said, running a long finger down the arm of his throne, "what it is about me that repulses you so?"

The question caught Neil off guard. "Excuse me?"

The emperor laughed once. "Look at you, Neil Vapros. You've been gawking at me since I walked in. I disgust you." He tapped his chin with a slender forefinger. "Is it my face?" he asked, eyes boring into Neil's. "Do I look ugly to you?"

"No, sir. I'm here about—"

"Is it my voice?" the emperor interrupted. "Do I sound like some sort of monster? You're looking at me as if I crawled out of one of your nightmares."

"I don't think you're a nightmare," Neil said uneasily.

"Come, now," the emperor chided. "You're afraid of me, I can see it in your face. You want nothing more than to run from my palace and never look back. Isn't that right?"

"No, sir," Neil said, but it was only partly true.

The emperor laced his fingers together. "You're lying to me, Neil Vapros. But I forgive you. I understand. There are certain times when it is wiser to lie."

"Yes, sir," Neil said. "Um, about the city—"

"For instance, if you were to tell me I looked ugly to you, or that I reminded you of a nightmare, I might be offended. I might become

. . . angry." He let his gaze drift to the servant at his side. "I can be unpredictable when I'm angry. Can't I, Saewulf?"

The servant trembled and nodded.

The emperor continued, "It's because I'm a man with power. And when a man with power becomes angry, you never know what he might do. He might throw you in a dungeon. He might have you exiled. He might use his power to destroy you—all because you made a mistake."

The servant inched away from the emperor's throne.

"But I'm a patient man, Neil Vapros," the emperor droned on. "I won't get angry because of one mistake. I won't even get angry about two mistakes. But when the mistakes begin to pile up, I'm afraid I lose control of myself." He looked pointedly at Saewulf, who was shuddering visibly. "So please, for everyone's sake, try not to make any more mistakes, Neil Vapros. Now, let's get down to business. Why are you here?"

Neil glanced at the servant once more before answering. "I came here to talk to you about some concerns I have about the city."

The emperor heaved a sigh and leaned back into his throne. "The city," he said uninterestedly. "The city your ancestors were sworn to protect until they threw it all away."

Neil forced himself to remain quiet. The emperor raised his eyebrows, silently egging him on. "They couldn't handle that kind of power, I suppose. Not strong enough. Not worthy. It's not their fault. Some men weren't born to be great."

Neil clenched his jaw. "I have some concerns, sir," he repeated.

The emperor grimaced. This was his game. Pushing Neil, testing him, seeing if he could get him to sweat. "It was this very room, if legend is to be believed."

"Yes, your highness."

"Savages broke through those very doors and stormed this hall, and then according to your little 'myth,' a deity came down and made you 'godlike' in your own way."

"I know the story, sir."

The emperor's face suddenly twisted into a violent sneer. "I'm sure you know it very well, Vapros," he hissed. "I'm sure you tell yourself that story every single night. I know it would make me feel less guilty if I believed there was some god justifying my actions. For how can you feel bad about stomping on the rest of us when it's 'his will.'"

Neil didn't quite know what to say. The emperor grinned when he noticed Neil's attempt to form a sentence. "Yes, sir. But I'm not here for that. I'm here because of our concerns about the city."

The emperor gave in and queried, "What sort of concerns?"

"I've been hearing strange rumors about the Captain of the Guard," Neil began, but the emperor cut him off.

"The Captain of the Guard," he said, "the one who died of a broken skull thanks to a *family member?*"

"Yes," Neil interjected. "Because of a *Taurlum* family member."

"But the Taurlum was only there because he was chasing a *Vapros*, isn't that right?" the emperor asked, raising one eyebrow.

Neil swallowed hard. "I'm not the one who threw your soldier into a wall."

"I didn't say you were."

"There are rumors," Neil pressed on, "that you are planning to retaliate for what happened. People are saying you're going to target the Lightborns. I just wanted to know, sir, if there's any truth to those rumors."

The emperor blinked slowly.

"I just—I don't think my family deserves to be punished for something a Taurlum—"

"Have you ever heard of the legacy phase?" the emperor asked.

"I, um, yes." Neil was trying hard to hide his frustration. "When a family's bloodline is threatened, the head of the family sort of . . . panics, I guess. He feels a responsibility to keep his family line from dying out. So he makes it a priority to produce more offspring, to pass on our powers to as many children as possible."

"And how many offspring inherit the powers, Neil?"

"All of them," Neil explained. "Our powers are always passed on. That's why we all still have powers."

The emperor smiled. Neil didn't like it. "So it is perfectly normal in your family to have one parent with powers," he said slowly, "and one parent without. That's what happened to you, in fact, is it not?"

Neil agreed, "That's how it is for everyone in my family."

"Who is more powerful, your mother or your father?"

"My mother is dead, so my father."

"Ah, that's right. Such a pity." The emperor looked off into the distance as if picturing something from the past. "I remember your mother: gorgeous woman. Your parents were treated like royalty. The people adored your mother. There was always a lot of nonsense about her clothes, what party they were attending. People actually referred to them as 'Altryon's first couple.'" He nearly spat the words. "The empress was quite upset when she heard that one. Really, people made such a fuss."

Neil swallowed. His father rarely talked about his mother. Neil hung on every word, not knowing if he wanted him to stop or continue. The emperor went on. "Your father adored her. He must have been completely devastated when she died." His eyes returned to Neil.

Neil felt his cheeks burn. He felt goose bumps up his arms, but didn't understand the conflicting emotions: outrage at the emperor's underlying scorn, pity for his father, a longing for the mother he never knew. Before he could sort through it all, the emperor interrupted his thoughts. "Anyway, back to the original question. Before your mother died then, who was more respected, more important in your family, your mother or your father?"

"I don't know. My father, I suppose."

"Why?"

This conversation didn't make sense. "He's a direct descendant of the Vapros line," Neil said finally.

"There it is." The emperor stood while declaring, "A direct descendant. You and your Lightborns, you think you're all so much better than the rest of us. We ordinary people, we're nothing to you. We are ugly to you." He ran a hand across his marble chin and continued. "You throw us into walls, break our bones, bend our laws, because once upon a time there was a leader who had powers and you are his direct descendant." The emperor wasn't shouting, but Neil still felt deafened by the words.

"Your majesty, I don't—"

"A Taurlum killed my father twenty years ago," the emperor said, trapping Neil in his gray glare. "He didn't agree with some of his new laws so he *murdered* him. This defiance of authority is not new to our city, and it will not be tolerated much longer. That I can assure you."

Neil shifted his weight from foot to foot for a tense moment of silence. "My family would never intentionally defy you, your highness."

"Of course not," the emperor replied, waving a hand dismissively. "It was the Taurlum, as you said before." He looked into Neil's eyes again. "You have nothing to worry about. Frankly, I'm surprised you bothered to come speak to me at all. It was so kind of you to converse with an ordinary person like me."

Neil opened his mouth to protest, but at the last second caught sight of the beaten servant, shaking his head very, very slightly. "It was a pleasure to meet with you, sir," he said as politely as he could. "I'm sorry for taking so much of your time."

"An apology," the emperor exclaimed as Neil walked away. "Did you hear that, Saewulf? How polite it is for him to apologize. You could learn a thing or two from Neil Vapros."

As Neil left the palace, he turned toward home and began to run. He had to see his father. Despite what the emperor had said about having nothing to worry about, Neil wasn't convinced in the slightest.

Upon returning home, Neil found his family convened in the Vapros war room. He took an empty chair next to Rhys and leaned over to ask what he'd missed, but stopped when Sir Vapros began to speak. "Now that we're all here," he said, looking pointedly at Neil, "we can begin."

Neil wanted to shout at him that he was only late because he'd been visiting with the emperor, something Sir Vapros had ordered him to do. While he was at it, he wanted to ask why he always had to do the worthless jobs and, more importantly, why he had to learn about his mother from the emperor?

He still had an uneasy feeling about that whole conversation, but kept his mouth shut. Throughout Neil's life, it was as if his father had always been wary of him. Uneasy around him, as if he wanted to be close, but there were barriers. Neil had always wanted to ask why. However, he couldn't do that. And he already knew why, anyway. He'd been born.

Sir Vapros pointed at Neil and he gave a quick summary of his conversation with the emperor, leaving out any mention of his mother.

Sir Vapros made eye contact with each of his children while noting, "Something is very wrong in our city. We have seen worrisome behavior among the Imperial Guards. Rhys had a troubling encounter with an arms dealer."

Neil scowled. His father hadn't mentioned his contribution, or Bianca's. Sir Vapros began to review the recent suspicious activity. "Today, two business partners have chosen to end their affiliations with our family. Meanwhile, Darius Taurlum has been arrested for attacking our Opera House, which means the emperor isn't turning a blind eye to our actions anymore. And last night, the Celerius house had a break-in and an attempted robbery. The culprits were members of the Brotherhood of the Slums." An uncomfortable murmur went up. "They tried to steal worthless documents," Sir Vapros continued a little more loudly, " and why they chose papers when they could have gone after jewels or money, we can't be sure."

"How is all of this related?" asked someone from the other side of the table.

"This is not just about our family," Sir Vapros said. "It concerns the three houses. For the first time in three hundred years, we may have a common enemy."

The room fell silent. Finally, Rhys spoke up. "The Celerius are moving a carriage today. I heard they are transporting something important away from their house, in case of another attack. I want to take Neil and Jennifer to raid it. See what they're so concerned about."

Neil was touched that his brother wanted him to accompany him on the mission, but Sir Vapros waved away the idea and said, "We can't risk any illegal activity, particularly when the Imperial Guards are arresting Lightborns."

Neil looked over at Jennifer. She seemed slightly relieved. She'd come away from the fight with Darius with nothing more than a few bandages wrapped around her torso, but Neil suspected she wasn't eager to jump back into action quite yet.

"We'll ambush them in the orchards," Rhys insisted. "It's neutral territory. We can hide in the trees until we see them. A sneak attack. We'll be in and out before they can do anything about it." He was getting excited. Rhys loved to plan battle strategies. "I can put them to sleep. They won't even see us."

Sir Vapros relented. "Fine. Proceed." Out of the corner of his eye, Neil saw Jennifer open her mouth, but then she closed it and arranged her face in her trademark smirk. "The rest of you should be on the lookout for more information. Spread no more rumors. Just listen." He stood. "This meeting is adjourned." Rhys jumped up and ran to prepare for the coming carriage raid. "Remember, Rhys, heart or head." Rhys nodded and darted out the door. The rest of the family funneled out of the room behind him. Sir Vapros was reminding his son of the fact that the only way to kill a Celerius was to damage their heart or their brain. This was another detail that Neil had known from the time he could walk.

Neil slumped in his chair and groaned. "How did things get so messed up?"

"Things always get messed up," a cold voice said from the other side of the table.

Neil looked up to realize he was alone with Jennifer. She slumped in her chair too, moodily examining her knife. He wanted to get up and leave, but Jennifer stopped him with a hard look. "Sure you feel comfortable going along with us?" she asked lightly, staring at him with icy eyes. Neil felt like prey caught in a hunter's trap. "After all, your powers haven't evolved at all."

A surge of anger coursed through him. How could Jennifer be so different from her twin sister? Victoria was kind to Neil. She encouraged him and helped him. Jennifer goaded him, mocked him, all the while knowing she was safe because she could kill him with one twist of her wrist. "Are you sure you feel comfortable going along with us?" he mimicked. "After all, dear sister, you did have half a wall pulled from your back last night."

Her eyes widened, and then narrowed. She materialized in front of Neil, her knife an inch from his eye. "Care to repeat that?" she snarled.

Neil materialized to his feet behind her. "You seem a little sensitive," he said, resting his hand on his own knife.

Jennifer's eyes began to burn. "People don't talk to me like that."

He saw her hands begin to heat up and knew it was time to go. "Maybe they ought to," he said with a mocking bow, and then he was out the door and materializing down the hallway as fast as he could. He reached the strategy room in record time. Rhys hardly took notice of his presence. He was pouring over a map and muttering to himself.

"We're not going to lose anyone on this one, right?" Neil asked, collapsing into one of the padded chairs positioned around the table.

"No. I've taken nearly every variable into consideration," Rhys replied without looking up. "The Celerius family is small. The only possible threat is Lilly, the daughter, but she doesn't have any advanced powers, so I've ruled her out as a danger. Her brother is the General of the Imperial Army, but he doesn't have time to sleep, let alone escort a convoy. Other than that, they're all either off on military business or powerless servants."

"Lilly doesn't have advanced powers?" Neil asked.

"No, not yet."

That struck Neil. He knew the Celerius girl was a year older, seventeen. If Rhys thought there was hope for her powers to develop, maybe there was hope for his.

"I'm a little concerned about the youngest brother," Rhys said and pointed at his right temple. "He reads minds. He might be able to see us coming. And he's decent with a sword. They all are. If he shows up, Jennifer and I will double-team him with our powers. So he'll either end up asleep or Jen will burn him until he surrenders." He finally looked up. "I think we should be on our way soon. We've only got about two hours to prepare."

Neil noticed that Rhys was squinting at his documents on the desk. "You need spectacles," he said.

Rhys looked up, his brow still knitted from concentrating. "Father won't allow it. He thinks it'll show weakness if we wear things that show our flaws."

Neil ran his fingers through his hair. "That's one of the dumbest things I've ever heard. You're practically an inch away from the paper and you're still squinting."

"Neil, I can't," Rhys sighed. "Will you tell Jennifer to get ready?"

"She's ready to slit my throat. You'd better tell her." He started toward the door, and then stopped. "Rhys," he said, a smile starting on his face, "would it help if I brought along a friend?"

"As long as you can meet up with us quickly. The Celerius carriage is probably already on the move."

VICTORY LIES WITHIN THE ASHES

Chapter Sixteen

THE ORCHARDS
NEIL VAPROS

"WHEN MOST BOYS INVITE ME OUT, THEY DON'T TAKE ME TO SIT AT the top of a tree and ask me to bring my knives," Bianca said.

Neil sharpened his knife and began testing it on a nearby branch. "What can I say? I'm not most boys."

She grinned and winked. "On that, we can agree."

Ambushes were usually boring, especially when remaining quiet was part of the criteria. Neil and Bianca had long ago given up on silence, and Neil was surprised at how quickly the last hour had passed. "You know you're going to stick out with your hair like that," he informed her.

She touched a strand of her ivory hair. "What do you mean 'with my hair like this?'"

"Well, we all have our black masks and hoods. We blend in. But you—"

"Have beautiful shining hair?" she supplied, tossing her head.

"Yes," he said rolling his eyes, "you have beautiful shining hair."

She smiled and checked her reflection in her knife and said, "Do you think your siblings are having an equally interesting conversation in the other tree?"

"No," Neil said immediately, "absolutely not. Rhys is probably enforcing the silence over there. And Jennifer doesn't like talking to us, anyway."

"Your family is so close," she said, a light, teasing sarcasm in her voice.

Neil scoffed. "We're a military unit. Not a family."

Bianca looked like she felt sorry for him. Neil wanted to defend his family's arrangement, to proclaim that it was fine how it was, but he said nothing. His family was far from perfect. Rhys and Victoria felt like family, but the others were allies, nothing more. His father didn't like him; Jennifer detested him. The older cousins didn't give him the time of day, and the younger ones were fidgety nuisances. His aunts and uncles were unapproachably aloof. His mother was dead. He made sure not to complain too loudly when he was with Bianca. He knew that she hated talking about her parents, or lack of parents. He found it astonishing and admirable that she had been able to survive by her wits alone since the ripe age of nine, but she refused to discuss any of the circumstances that had put her there.

Once Neil had met a girl in a bar that told him the Taurlum family ate and drank together every night, and for the first time in his life he'd been jealous of the brutes. He knew the Celerius family treated family customs with honor (but with them, everything was about honor. They got dressed with honor, ate with honor, went to the bathroom with honor and tied their boots with honor). He hadn't realized that even the barbarians had closer family ties than the Vapros. The closest thing they had to an event like that was the tattoo ceremony, and even that was a celebration of their progress in the feud. However, there was never any real progress. They took steps forward and then steps back.

As if reading his thoughts, Bianca said, "Do you remember when we were kids?"

"Of course."

"There was that one thing you wouldn't tell me." It wasn't a question, but he knew she wanted an answer.

"How my mother died?"

"You never talk about it." He looked at her silently, hoping she'd rescind the question, but she didn't. "You do owe me one…" she whispered quietly.

He took a deep breath. "Childbirth," he said finally, looking down.

Bianca blinked. "Oh. That's not what I thought it would be at all."

"No?"

"I was expecting some kind of . . . I don't know, horrible assassination or attack or something. Not just . . . an accident."

"Well, now you know."

Bianca put her hand on his shoulder. "I'm sorry," she said sincerely, "but at least you had a few years with her."

Neil shook his head. "She died giving birth to me."

Bianca's brow furrowed. "But Rhys—"

"Rhys is my half-brother. When she died, my father had this big revelation. He realized we're all mortal, you know? And he was afraid that if he died, he wouldn't have enough heirs to keep our family going. He wanted more kids, more security for our family line." Neil fiddled with the knife absently. "Rhys's mother was a waitress from one of the taverns my father owns."

Bianca's mouth fell open.

"It's called the legacy phase," Neil explained bitterly. "He thought he had some kind of responsibility to pass on our powers to as many children as he could have. Because, I guess, he didn't have enough faith in the kids he already had."

"Oh."

"Anyway, that's why my father doesn't exactly cherish me," he continued dully. "Because I took his wife away." He looked at Bianca with a small shrug.

Bianca grabbed his arm and said, "But you have to know that your mother . . . it wasn't your fault."

Neil laughed cynically. "Next time you come for family dinner, we can tell my father that. I'm sure it'll convince him."

She looked like she wanted to hug him but held back. "Where is Rhys's mother now?"

"She's dead. She came to a Vapros event when Rhys was five. The Taurlum raided it and killed her. He was there. I think that's why he wants to be a doctor so badly, because he didn't know what to do. One small consolation, he developed the ability to put people to sleep shortly after watching his mother's murder."

Before Bianca could respond, they both looked toward the road at the sound of hoof beats. "Here they are," Bianca murmured, poking his arm. The lavishly decorated carriage rolled down the road toward them, completely unsuspecting. The blue and gold carriage was a sitting duck.

"Ready to go?" Neil asked, unsheathing his knife.

"Born ready."

Neil prepared to materialize down the tree, but before he could move, Jennifer was already upon the driver. Neil watched, mildly disappointed that he hadn't made it there first, as she burned him to death and hurled his body to the ground. Neil materialized to the ground and Bianca landed next to him. Jennifer was smirking. "A little slow today?" she asked. A stream of smoke ascended from the driver's body.

Rhys appeared next to them and charged for the door, materializing every few steps. Neil never grew tired of seeing his family members appear and reappear. It looked as if a person had dissolved himself into ash, and then an entirely new person not too far away reformed himself out of the same ashes. The ability was gloriously beautiful. Rhys performed it effortlessly, barely taking notice of his change in location. Materializing was just like taking another step to him.

Rhys then threw open the carriage door, brandishing his knife calmly. He was wise to prepare for an attack. Lilly Celerius herself lunged from the cabin, swinging her rapier viciously. With a little surprised gasp, Rhys materialized out of range of her weapon. She lunged after him. He jumped back, luring her away from the carriage. "Lilly!" Neil called, trying to help.

Breathing heavily, she turned to Neil, weapon at the ready. "I'd address you by your name," she snarled, "but you're too much of a coward to show your face."

Neil pulled down his mask. "This ends better for you if you give up now," he said. "Hand over what you're transporting."

Lilly stared at him, eyes blazing, and hissed, "Neil, right?" He nodded, surprised that she knew his face. "I've heard of your stupidity and arrogance. Seems I was not misinformed. "

"I'm not arrogant," Neil argued, but he was grinning as he added, "I'm self-assured. I have every right to be. Look around you. I have three allies. You're alone. What's so stupid about that?" He kept inching backwards toward Jennifer and Bianca, hoping she'd follow. She didn't take the bait.

"What is stupid is not your numbers," she said, feet planted. "It's the fact that you attacked our carriage with no idea of what was inside. Is it worth risking lives to you, Vapros?"

Rhys cut in. "You seemed rather eager to move it. I calculated the risk. It's worth it, if the bounty is important enough."

Lilly kept her eyes on Neil. "I think you will return home disappointed."

Bianca moved forward. "Let's see what you're moving then, shall we?"

Quick as a whip, Lilly swung her arm around so her sword was pointed at Bianca. "Take another step and lose your head," she spat through her teeth. "I make that promise to you, street girl."

Neil was slightly surprised by the off-handed insult, but Bianca took it in stride. She palmed her knife and prepared to throw it. "Speak to me like that again and lose your eye," she said calmly. "I make that promise to you, rich girl."

A tense silence stretched over the entire forest as the two girls stared each other down. Jennifer smirked and folded her arms, but Neil was nervous. Suddenly, a small figure jumped down from the carriage and darted to Lilly's side. Neil couldn't help but chuckle as the tiny man waved around a tiny sword. "Jonathan," Lilly declared. "Are you prepared to fight for the honor of the Celerius family?"

Jonathan gulped. "Yes."

Bianca whipped her knife at Lilly; she sliced it out of the air with a flash of steel. Bianca looked surprised. "All right," she muttered, "you're fast. I'll give you that."

Bianca hurled a few more knives and was greeted with the same result. Neil tried to take Lilly by surprise, but she seemed to sense exactly where he planned to rematerialize and swiped at him, nearly slicing his throat. He staggered backwards, gasping, heart pounding from the close call. "Amateur," Jennifer said to him with a smile. She jumped into the fray and lunged at Jonathan, her glowing hands outstretched. The diminutive servant closed his eyes and swatted blindly with his blade. She ducked around his weapon and struck him across the face with the back end of her knife. He yelped and hit the ground. Lilly turned at his cry and Rhys, seizing the opportunity, materialized behind her, grabbed the back of her neck and closed his eyes. Lilly's eyes rolled back into her head and she collapsed into Rhys's arms.

"See?" he said, lowering her to the ground gently. "Not even a little risky."

Neil walked over to the fallen servant, who had his hands clamped over his cheek. He was groaning and rolling from side to side. "You'll pay!" he cried as he saw Neil coming. He struggled to sit up, but ultimately failed and fell onto his back. Neil planted his foot on the servant's chest. "Is Lilly ...." Jonathan asked fearfully.

"She's alive," Neil assured him, "but she's napping. However, you and I need to have a little chat."

From the back of the carriage, Neil could hear Rhys's voice: "Common documents? Architectural plans? Bills? Why was there so much fuss over this?"

Neil repeated the question to Jonathan, "Why so much fuss over these documents, servant? You were moving them quickly. Why are they important?" Jonathan tried to squirm away. Neil pushed down harder with his foot and called out, "Jennifer, come here. He doesn't want to talk." Jennifer would never take orders from her younger brother, Neil was well aware, but Jonathan didn't know that.

Jonathan let out a squeak. "Keep her over there," he cried. "I'll tell you! I'll tell you!"

"Good choice." Neil smiled a little. "I don't like to deal with her either," he said as if it were a big secret. The humor escaped Jonathan.

"Last night we were attacked," Jonathan said. "By the Brother-hood of the Slums. They were after our documents. Lilly managed to kill them but we found this on one of them."

He pulled a small paper from his coat pocket and tried to hand it to Neil. Neil looked at him skeptically for a moment, then met him halfway to retrieve the parchment. As he began to read it, his expression shifted from curiosity to confusion to fear. "Rhys!"

Rhys materialized next to them. "What is it?"

Neil handed the paper to him. "We have a problem."

Rhys squinted and brought the paper close to his face. Neil sighed. The kid needed spectacles. Rhys gasped. "Yes, we have a problem."

Chapter Seventeen

IMPERIAL MILITARY OUTPOST
CARLIN FILUS

"WE HAVE A PROBLEM," CARLIN SAID, SLAMMING HIS FIST AGAINST the table. The soldiers sitting closest to him jumped as the noise echoed through the war room of the Imperial Military Outpost. "The situation outside the wall has become dire, and ...." he trailed off. Nobody was listening. He coughed loudly to regain their attention, but everyone at the table was either staring at the general or at the floor. "We could be outnumbered in the West! One thousand men are too many to ignore!" Carlin said loudly. One of the soldiers glared at him; the rest remained motionless. A palpable tension hovered over the table like a thick fog, and Carlin eventually stopped trying to break through it and resorted to muttering under his breath every few seconds.

Finally, General Anthony Celerius cleared his throat. "Dismissed," he said shortly.

Nobody moved. One of the smaller men raised his hand slightly. "Sorry, sir?"

Anthony met the man's eyes and offered him a small, weary smile. "You are all dismissed. This meeting is adjourned."

The men rose and filed from the room, sneaking glances over their shoulders at their general. Carlin stayed in his seat. "I said you are dismissed, Carlin," Anthony said with all the conviction of a man who has given up hope.

"Forgive me, sir, but I think you and I have more business to discuss."

"Then discuss it."

"You and I have private business," Carlin amended, shooting a glare at the corner of the room where a single soldier remained.

Anthony met the eyes of the man in the corner and barked, "Virgil. I already dismissed you."

Virgil Servatus, third in command to Anthony and only one rank below Carlin, removed his golden helmet and shook out his shoulder-length brown hair. "I will not let this happen," he said.

Anthony looked at him for a long time with an expression Carlin couldn't quite read. "I don't know what you mean," he said finally.

"Don't lie!" Virgil cried, turning to Carlin in a rage. "Carlin, you're my oldest friend. Listen to me. This is wrong. There are other ways!"

Carlin scoffed, but this time there was a shiver of pain in his voice. "You don't know what you're talking about."

"Virgil," Anthony pleaded, "just go. It'll be okay. Trust me." He looked at the man with wide eyes.

Virgil dropped his helmet on the table and let the sound reso-nate through the room. "Are you really going to pretend that this isn't happening?" he shouted, taking a step toward Carlin. "This man gave us everything, Carlin. Could you really strike him down?" Virgil demanded. "Could any of us strike each other down? We've grown together, spilled blood together, changed this world together, for better or worse… Could you really murder your brother, Carlin?"

"Brother?" Carlin hissed, furious.

"Am I next?" Virgil continued. "Where does your ambition end?"

Carlin looked like he wanted to speak, but he couldn't. Anthony held up a hand for silence. "You know your orders," he said firmly, "and you know your place. Don't worry about me. This is not the end. I will say it one more time: you are dismissed, Lieutenant."

Virgil gave Anthony a long look. "Forgive me," he whispered, scooping up his helmet and heading towards the door. "Forgive him," he said softly as he left.

Anthony watched him go. "I do," he whispered.

Carlin stood and drew his sword. "Well, General," he said with a forced smile, "that was a touching little scene. The temporary loyalty that these men have shown you is inspiring. It's almost tragic."

Anthony sipped his wine and traced a river on the war map with his fingertip. "If I let you do this … my family will be safe?"

Carlin said, "You have my word. The emperor is just looking for a shift in power."

"I can see into your soul, Carlin," he said tiredly. "And it is lost."

Carlin leaped forward and pointed his sword between Anthony's eyes. The general didn't flinch. "Don't give me those Lightborn lies," he hissed, "I know you mighty Celerius think you're impressive with your advanced abilities, but all you can see is what's on the other side of a wall. You know nothing of my soul."

Anthony met the other man's eyes and addressed him quietly, "I don't need advanced abilities to know you're lost, Carlin. Your actions alone are enough to prove it."

Carlin narrowed his eyes. A moment later, the smug smile was back in place. "It's truly flattering that you're so concerned with my soul's well being, General," he said casually as he lowered his sword to the level of Anthony's heart. "But you don't need to worry. I don't have a soul. Neither do you. They don't exist, you know." *Argue with me. Tell me I'm wrong. Go on. Give me a reason.*

Anthony bowed his head slowly as he whispered, "I pity you."

Carlin's smile twisted into a maniacal sneer of rage as he plunged the sword forward. The blade slid easily between the general's ribs and came out on the other side, piercing the chair. With a gasp, Anthony snapped his head up and instinctually groped desperately for his own sword. It was as if he suddenly realized that giving up was a mistake, as if there was something else he could do. Skewered against his chair, he couldn't quite reach the hilt. Carlin pulled his sword out and began to wipe it clean of Celerius blood. "Long live the Emperor," he said quietly, walking away with a calm little smile as Anthony slumped forward over the table, knocking over his glass and spilling wine across the war map.

Chapter Eighteen

THE ORCHARDS
LILLY CELERIUS

LILLY CELERIUS'S FIRST THOUGHT UPON WAKING ON THE SIDE OF THE road was that she had never experienced such a deep, peaceful sleep in her life, and she probably never would again. Her second thought was that the Vapros brats had undoubtedly stolen her precious cargo. She jumped to her feet. "Jonathan!" she cried, peering inside the carriage. To her relief, all of the boxes appeared to be inside. "Jonathan?"

A loud cough came from the other side of the carriage. "I'm here," he said, flat on his back and desperately trying to dust off his oversized military jacket.

"What was the point of all this?" Lilly wondered aloud. "They didn't even take anything. And why would they bring that . . . that poor girl with them?"

Jonathan tried and failed to stand up, but managed to ask, "Do you know her?"

"She sneaks into parties a lot. I didn't know she could throw a knife."

Jonathan finally made it to his feet. "Just because she's poor doesn't mean she's useless," he said quietly. "I'm from the slums, too."

"You don't live in the slums," Lilly said with an eye roll. "You live in my guest house." She rifled through the papers. "I think everything is here."

"Not everything," Jonathan admitted. His face grew red. "I gave him the paper."

Lilly whirled around. "Who's him, Jonathan?"

Jonathan tried to fight his tears. "Neil Vapros."

Lilly pulled her rapier from the ground. "Well, now they know." She swung a few practice arcs through the air. "Stop crying, Jonathan. It's all right. It won't do them much good anyway. Unless we truly are at war."

Chapter Nineteen

THE MARKETS
MICHAEL TAURLUM

MICHAEL TAURLUM HAD NO TROUBLE WEAVING HIS WAY THROUGH the crowded marketplace; people saw him coming and dove out of the way. He swaggered down the street, dressed in a tight red and gold shirt that clung to his skin and showcased his muscles. He kept his eyes peeled for women to occupy his time.

A group of giggling girls caught his attention as they made their way into a shop. Grinning, he made his way across the street and fumbled with the doorknob for a moment before heaving his way into the store. His head swayed dangerously near the ceiling. "Hello, ladies," he said casually. The storekeeper winced as Michael nearly tore the door off its hinges.

The girls whispered to each other nervously. A girl with a red sash finally said, "I'll do it," and separated herself from the group. "Hello, Taurlum," she said. "How are you today?"

He ogled her. She was tiny, but everyone looked tiny to him. "I'm fine," he answered. "And better, now that I've had the pleasure of seeing such a beautiful woman."

The other girls giggled, but this one wasn't fazed. "I'm just surprised to see you here," she said, the beginning of a laugh on her lips. "Considering this is a woman's hat shop."

Michael froze. The other girls were laughing uproariously. "I know," he said, trying desperately to save face. "I just owe the owner some coin."

"Why?" the girl asked, biting back laughter. "Did you buy a hat from him earlier and forget to pay the bill?"

Michael slammed a few coins down on the counter. One of the girls let out a little scream, followed by an eruption from the others. "The hat was for my sister," he invented. Michael turned away from the girls and leaned toward the storekeeper. "Play along," he hissed, and the keeper nodded. "Anything these ladies want," Michael said more loudly, "is on me."

The other girls squealed and began running up and down the aisles of hats. The girl with the red sash didn't join them. "That was generous of you," she said, offering him a smile. He stared at her for a moment, scrutinizing her features. He peered over her head at the other girls who were running around the store. She blushed. It was evident that he was trying to decide whether or not she was the prettiest girl among the bunch. Taurlum weren't known for subtlety.

He turned his attention back to her and she seemed to be visibly relieved. "I'm a generous man," he replied, raising his arm in a stretch that showed off his bicep and his bracelets at the same time.

The girl's eyes widened as she saw his jewelry. "You have a lot of bracelets," she said. "You must be very wealthy."

"Oh, these?" he said haughtily. He pulled off a bracelet and threw it to her. She caught it. "I have thousands at home," he bragged. Then he looked at her thoughtfully and offered her a wink. "I can show you, if you'd like."

She slipped her wrist through the bracelet. It stood out radiantly against her shabby coat and worn shoes. "You want to take me home with you?" she asked.

Michael flexed again. "Why not?" he said lazily. "I can give you a tour. We can see the private bathhouse … my bedroom … you know, all the best parts of the Taurlum mansion."

She bit her lip and gazed up at him from beneath her eyelashes, all while asking, "Won't the other Taurlum mind?"

Michael scoffed. "I'm allowed to bring poor people inside," he said. "It's my house."

The girl looked hurt for a moment, but she covered it up quickly. "Of course," she said flirtatiously, touching the gold band on her wrist. "I bet no one in your family controls you, do they? You're too strong for that."

Michael grinned widely. She didn't know it but that was the perfect thing to say to get on Michael's good side. "Come on," he said, turning toward the exit. "Tell your friends you're leaving. I really want you to see my room."

The girl touched her new bracelet again and waved to her friends before hurrying out of the shop and following in the Taurlum's wake toward the mansion.

Chapter Twenty

IMPERIAL PRISON
DARIUS TAURLUM

Darius tried to move for the ten-thousandth time, but before they'd thrown him in the dungeon the Imperial Guards had fitted him with a wooden collar that bore down on his pressure points. With every shift in position, he could feel it dig into his skin and leech his strength. He had gone over every single member of his family, wondering which one was most likely to break him out. His father would be far too busy. His mother, only a Taurlum by marriage, was too frail. His sister Cassandra might show up, if she felt like it, but Darius eventually came to accept that his best chance was, unfortunately, Michael—the Nose, his idiotic, womanizing brother.

Sweat began to drip down his face as he tried not to struggle. Each movement was painful. They'd anchored his hands to the floor, and he could easily have broken the shackles if they hadn't been designed to hit him at the pressure points in his wrists. He was immobilized, powerless, and for a Taurlum, that meant he was nothing.

He heard footsteps coming down the hall, and he hoped it was his dinner. Last night, the guards had served him some sort of pig slop, spoon-feeding him because he could not move his arms, and he'd held eye contact with the guard for the whole meal, a vengeful fury brewing in his expression. The guard seemed terrified. Darius loved it.

The footsteps reached the door. Darius gurgled through his collar, "I think the chains are getting loose, buddy. Hopefully, I don't break free while you're feeding me." The person behind the door didn't answer. "Hello? I'm getting hungry," he prompted.

A tiny key shot through the crack at the bottom of the door and landed close to his hands. Darius grabbed at it clumsily and maneuvered it into the lock on his handcuffs. They sprung free. "Michael?" Darius asked. "Cassie? Is that you?" No answer. He felt at his collar, searching for the keyhole. To his surprise and relief, the same key unlocked the cuff around his neck. "Lazy bastards," Darius muttered with satisfaction. He wrenched off the collar and let it clatter to the floor. "Look out, Imperial Guards," he said a little louder, lumbering to the cell door and tearing it off its hinges. His strength was back. The abrasions on his neck and wrists were fading already. "The beast has escaped!"

His triumphant smile disappeared as he realized the person waiting on the other side of the door was not one of his siblings. It wasn't even his father. His savior was dressed in leather armor and camouflage green, jet-black hair pulled back out of her face, and a mouth set in fierce determination. She wielded a long chain with a single spike fixed to the end, and she had an unyielding expression on her face. "Who are you?" Darius asked.

The girl blinked her dark, slanted eyes, but didn't answer. He repeated his question more forcefully this time. She gave him a small smile and then hurled her spike straight into the vulnerable part of his stomach.

He stumbled back, impressed at the skill of the throw, but also furious that the foreign girl was not here to free him. He pulled the spike out of his navel and gave it a strong pull; she lost her balance and stumbled toward him. He prepared to club her to death with his arm, but she anticipated the blow and abandoned her weapon to barrel roll underneath it and into the cell. Darius felt his stomach begin to bleed. "Listen, sweetheart," he said, raising his giant fists into fighting position, "you're thin as a stick. Give this up before I snap you like one."

She smiled. "Poor baby," she cooed with a thin accent as she unsheathed a spare knife. "Scared and bleeding, so he has to make idle threats."

Darius replied, "Idle threats? We'll see."

She darted forward and carved a long cut into his arm. It began to bleed. Darius couldn't help but feel a little nervous. She was obviously well-trained. He knew better than to underestimate her based on appearance; he had learned that lesson from Jennifer Vapros. "You broke me out of prison to kill me?"

She grabbed her spike on a chain from the ground and answered, "Couldn't open the door. It was too thick and I couldn't find that key. So I needed some help."

"You're welcome."

She hurled the spike at his neck, but he saw it coming and jumped out of range. She narrowed her peculiar eyes. "You're quick. I was not told that you would be quick."

"What can I say, I'm full of surprises." He swung his arm out, sending her flying into a wall. With a cry, she dropped her knife and chain. He grabbed her by the throat and lifted her into the air with his remaining strength. "I ask again," he said, loosening his grip enough so that she could speak. "Who are you?"

She glared at him. "Anastasia," she spat.

"Anastasia." Darius lowered her to the ground, but kept his grip on her neck. "You clearly don't work for the Imperial Army."

"No," she said carefully. "I'm not a soldier. I'm an assassin."

"Oh, really?" Darius said sarcastically. "Is that so? I hadn't noticed." He examined her attire. "Where are you from?"

Anastasia tried to scoff. The effect was ruined by the fear in her eyes. "You wouldn't believe me if I told you."

"You look like a savage. I'd guess you have come from the outside."

"When did this become a casual conversation?" she growled.

"Fine. Let's get less casual." He lifted her off her feet again. "Why did you come to kill me?"

She laughed. "Because I was paid."

"Who paid you?" It came out as a snarl. He was getting impatient.

"A good assassin never reveals her employer."

"A good assassin wouldn't let me catch her." Darius threw her against the wall again. She fell to the ground, harder this time, and when he picked her up he saw she'd been knocked unconscious. He thought about killing her, but he was running out of time to escape. He left her limp body on the ground and hurtled out of the dungeon. He was alive, but someone wanted him dead badly enough to hire an assassin from some unknown place.

A pair of guards rounded the corner. One of them held a bowl of the slop they'd been feeding him for dinner. He dropped the bowl, stunned, when he saw the prisoner. Darius grinned and cracked his knuckles. "Who's first?"

Chapter Twenty-One

TAURLUM MANSION
MICHAEL TAURLUM

Michael Taurlum's eyes flickered open. He recognized the ceiling of his bedroom and instantly noticed he was violating his sacred code: he was cuddling. There was some girl latched onto his arm, sleeping peacefully. Without thinking, he quickly brushed her off, then winced as his Taurlum strength sent her over the edge of his bed and onto the floor. She squealed as she fell. Michael tried to resist doing the same. "What the hell was that, Michael?" she groaned, stumbling to her feet and wiping the sleep from her tired eyes.

Michael hopped out of bed and tied his red and gold pajama bottoms tighter with his ringed fingers. "You tell me," he breathed, heart pounding. "Why were you in my bed?" He grabbed a glass from a side table and filled it with wine.

The girl self-consciously adjusted her corset. "I fell asleep—so what?"

Michael drained the glass and poured himself another. "I prefer to sleep alone."

"Oh, really?" the girl remarked and moved to sit on the bed, but she backed off when he turned to glare at her. "Michael Taurlum, afraid to share his bed? I find that hard to believe, given your reputation."

"I'm not afraid," he insisted. "You're the one who should be afraid. It's dangerous to sleep near a Taurlum. If I rolled over, I could have crushed you."

"Like you care about what happens to me," she muttered. "Do you even remember my name?"

He turned away from her and began to pour another drink. The girl put a hand on his shoulder carefully. "Something tells me that isn't the only reason you're upset," she said soothingly. "Was it something I did?"

"It has nothing to do with you."

"Some other girl then?" she tried. "You can tell me. I'm a good listener."

"Leave it alone," Michael warned. He pulled away from her hand and dropped back onto his bed, throwing his empty glass carelessly across the room. It shattered. The girl winced.

"If you leave now, you can make it home by sundown. I think. I don't know where you live."

She stood over him. "Come on, Michael. You can tell me. You're strong on the outside, but I can tell there's something making you weak on the inside." She ran a hand down his bare shoulder. "Tell me. I'll help make you big and strong again."

She was trying to appeal to his ego. He saw right through her game, and part of him wanted to toss her out into the street, but instead he rolled up on his side to look at her. "The last woman who shared my bed was my fiancée," he said bluntly. The girl's eyes widened, and Michael quickly added, "She's gone now."

The girl didn't seem to understand and asked, "Where did she go?"

He laughed humorlessly. "Turns out, she was also sharing a bed with another man."

"Oh," the girl said. Her eyes had strayed from Michael to the extravagant tapestries on the wall behind him. "So you kicked her out." Her eyes fell to the intricately woven rug and the beautifully patterned blankets. Most commoners could only dream of seeing such luxuries.

"Not exactly," Michael replied, leaning back into the pillows and closing his eyes. "The other man was a Vapros."

The girl's eyes snapped back to the Taurlum. "Yeah," she said slowly, "those Vapros, so … immoral." They were nearing dangerous territory. The feud was a sensitive topic among the families. One wrong word could set him off like a bomb. "Is she with him now?"

Michael chuckled darkly, opened his eyes and answered, "You could say that."

The girl looked uncomfortable. "Maybe we should talk about something else?" she suggested, but Michael wasn't paying attention to her anymore.

Michael reminisced, "I confronted her, and she lied to my face. That was the first time I ever created an earthquake. It wasn't intentional. And it wasn't a very impressive one, compared to what I can do now. But it was enough." He heaved himself out of bed. The girl stood, too, and backed away a little. "I'm not even sorry," he said, "I was going to give up so much for her, and she couldn't even be faithful. Look around you. I was about to leave all of this for her. She deserved what she got."

"Of course she did," the girl soothed. "Of course she did …"

"I tracked down her lover and killed him, too," Michael continued. "It's my favorite death to date."

The girl was trembling. She attempted a smile. "You're a warrior," she whispered, more to herself than to him, as if she were trying to justify something.

Michael spoke with pointed sarcasm, "Thanks for bringing those memories to the surface. You've been very helpful." She attempted to sit back down on the bed, but he pointed to the door. "Now get out."

"Are you sure, Michael?" she asked. "I can help you. If you just opened up to me a little more, I could—"

Get *out!*" His volume shook the room.

She let out a little scream and ran, pausing only long enough to snatch her dress off the floor. Michael settled back into his giant bed. At last, he was alone—just the way he liked it. A tear drifted from his eye and he wiped it away in confusion. Taurlum don't cry, and neither did Michael. Weaklings cried. "Iron Flesh and Iron Will," he whispered to himself harshly.

He curled up in his blankets for another night alone. Michael Taurlum was many things, but he was no weakling.

Chapter Twenty-Two

CELERIUS ESTATE
LILLY CELERIUS

LILLY PACED AROUND THE CELERIUS TRAINING ROOM, SIZING UP HER adversary, and trying to shake the carriage fiasco from her mind. She lunged outwardly with her wooden sword and her brother blocked it easily. Thomas back-peddled a few paces and smiled. "You know you'll never be able to land a hit, Lilly." He teased, brown eyes twinkling. "I know what you're going to do before you do it."

She mentally focused and swung her sword again, and once more he blocked it expertly. "I'll hit you eventually," she said with another swing.

He parried and hit her hand. She winced and felt a cracked bone reset. "Sorry," he muttered.

She leapt forward and swung as quickly as she could, but he didn't try and block this time. The wooden sword collided with the side of his head, but he didn't even seem to register the blow. His eyes were closed in quiet concentration. "Thomas," Lilly said as she moved forward. "Are you trying to read my mind?"

He held up a hand. "People are screaming inside their heads. They're crying out in pain," he whispered.

"Knock it off," she said. It wasn't unlike her brother to pull stupid pranks with his powers.

He opened his eyes and tears leaked out. "Anthony," he whispered.

A blood-curdling scream pierced the stillness. Lilly stared at Thomas for a moment and then she dropped her sword. She dashed through the hallways and made it to the front door faster than she had ever run anywhere. Her father stood at the door holding a small wooden box. Her mother was on the ground sobbing. There was an Imperial messenger on the ground bleeding from his throat. "What …." She couldn't form any other words.

Her father turned to face her and she noticed his face was as red as it had ever been. She took a step forward and opened the box hesitantly. It was filled with ashes. She looked up at her father with disbelieving eyes, "Is it…."

He opened and closed his mouth, helplessly trying to choke out a few words. After a few seconds, he was able to manage, "It's Anthony."

VICTORY LIES WITHIN
THE ASHES

Chapter Twenty-Three

VAPROS BUNKER
NEIL VAPROS

"WHO THE HELL IS CARLIN FILUS?" SIR VAPROS SHOUTED. THEY were all crammed in his office, describing the events that transpired with Lilly Celerius and the carriage. Sir Vapros stood behind his massive desk drumming his fingers, his piercing green eyes staring pointedly at his children. His sleeves were rolled up, and it was possible to see more of his tattoos. Neil couldn't help but think about how many lives they represented. There was one in the shape of a broken sword on his forearm and Neil was willing to bet it had come from a Celerius.

Neil shifted uncomfortably in his seat and finally said, "He's the second in command in the Imperial Army. Or, he was, until the general was murdered. Now he's number one." The Vapros network of informants worked swiftly and efficiently.

"He has power," Jennifer said. "He can get around certain laws."

Sir Vapros sat down in his black leather chair, rubbing his hand thoughtfully over his black and grey stubbled chin. "So what does this mean?"

Neil seized his opportunity. "The Celerius servant gave me this," he said, pulling the crumpled piece of paper from his pocket and passing it across the table. "It's a document Carlin wrote up. It authorizes all crimes committed by the Brotherhood of the Slums."

"Only crimes against the families," Rhys corrected.

"So their attack on the Celerius house that night was legal," Neil finished hurriedly.

Sir Vapros was quiet. He held the document in both hands and scanned the lines several times. "Crimes against the families," he repeated slowly. "*All* the families?"

Rhys nodded. Sir Vapros let out a snarl of fury and turned his hands to smoke, consuming the paper and turning it to ash.

"We're going to be next," Jennifer drawled, looking at her fingernails. "The Celerius were robbed and there's a Taurlum in the dungeons. We're the only ones who haven't been touched yet."

"We have been touched," Sir Vapros said. "Our records keeper was murdered. They found his body this morning."

"Records," Neil said thoughtfully. "That was what was in the Celerius carriage: boxes of their records. That's what the Brotherhood tried to take."

Sir Vapros looked at Neil for the first time. He really looked at him and seemed to truly appreciate his son's contribution to the conversation. "It's a legitimate connection," he said. "What would this Carlin want with family records?"

Rhys frowned slightly and joined in. "I have a theory. What if Carlin wants to study us? Track our habits, find out about our businesses and discover how we go about our daily lives. But he hasn't actually attacked us. What if he isn't the main threat? What if he's a spy for someone more important?" He turned to Neil. "You said the emperor was acting strangely."

Jennifer interrupted. "There's no motive," she said flatly. "The emperor is already the most powerful man in Altryon. What can he gain by starting a war with us?"

Rhys said. "Maybe he's afraid we'll try to take over again, like the old days."

Sir Vapros turned to Neil. "You talked to him. Did anything seem out of the ordinary?"

Neil ran his hand through his hair. "I don't know, he was incredibly creepy," he admitted. "He acted cold, but that's not unusual for him. He played games and clearly had been beating that poor servant. He tried to make me uncomfortable." Suddenly, a memory tugged at his brain. "But his wife acted distant, too, and that's unusual for her. He did say he was going to retaliate against the Taurlum; it's not unreasonable to assume we could be next."

"Rhys," Sir Vapros said suddenly, "I want you to look into the Taurlum records. See if anything's happened to them."

Now that missions were being assigned, Jennifer, who was much more interested in the discussion, asked, "Why don't we have someone gather information on the Brotherhood? I can find out how Carlin got them in his pocket."

"He probably offered them food," Neil said. "Things are so bad in the slums now—"

"Neil," Sir Vapros snapped. "Enough." Neil closed his mouth. "I care about my family, not the poor. If the emperor decides to make an enemy out of the Vapros family, then we will strike him down and leave his throne in ashes. I hope he's not that stupid." Sir Vapros left the room. Jennifer followed.

Neil leaned over and whispered to Rhys, "Do you actually think we have a chance of defeating the emperor?"

Rhys thought for a moment, and then said. "Not alone."

Chapter Twenty-Four

IMPERIAL PALACE
CARLIN FILUS

CARLIN WATCHED THE EMPEROR AND HIS SERVANT NONCHALANTLY playing chess. He was sweating. They'd done a very bold thing today in sending Anthony Celerius's ashes to his family home. The Emperor, however, seemed unfazed by the possible danger they could face at the hands of the Celerius family.

Anthony had told Carlin a lot about his father over their years as friends and rivals. According to Anthony, Sir Celerius had always been one for following procedure. He tried his utmost to do everything as correctly and politely as possible, without breaking rules or endangering his honor. Reputation was, for a Celerius, the most important thing for a man to protect. Bodies died, but reputations lived forever.

Today, all formalities were abandoned. No one had ever barged in on the emperor before; Sir Celerius made himself the first.

"You bastard!" he screamed, charging into the throne room without even so much as a knock.

The emperor didn't even look up from his chessboard. "Check, Saewulf."

Carlin stood and drew his sword but the Emperor waved him away. Carlin stepped back but kept his sword at the ready. "You had my son murdered!" Sir Celerius shouted. The emperor raised a hand for silence, but his enraged visitor ignored it and continued ranting. "You invaded my home and put my daughter's life in danger. Are you trying to destroy my family? After we have been nothing but loyal to you for all these years? I heard the rumors, but I never thought you could be this ruthless."

The man called Saewulf moved his queen diagonally a few spaces. The emperor pondered a moment, hovering his hand over a few different pieces as he tried to decide on a move. "Have you met Saewulf?" he asked calmly.

Celerius knocked the chessboard across the room. "You killed my son!" he roared. "You had his ashes sent to my house in a box!"

Sighing, the emperor finally looked up at the furious man. "Saewulf is my humble servant," he explained. "He looks different, doesn't he? We've realized how special he is. We've gotten him all cleaned up, and I'm starting to look at him in a new light. I used to play chess with myself, you know."

Celerius, breathing hard, looked at Saewulf. His body was unmarked by the bruises that usually covered servants around here. He had orange hair that had been pulled back away from his face. His skin looked rough and tan as if from constant work in the sun. Celerius snarled, "I don't care about your servant." He drew his sword. "I'll kill you all! I'll kill you myself! You're unarmed and this poor excuse for a general, couldn't stop me if he tried!" he yelled gesturing dismissively at Carlin. "It will be easy. It will be a pleasure."

The emperor gazed at him with an expression that almost looked like boredom. Carlin approached Sir Celerius from behind but he lashed out in a wide arc and Carlin backtracked a few steps. "Is this a genuine threat?" the Emperor asked.

Sir Celerius made a sound halfway between a laugh and a sob and lunged with his sword.

Suddenly, he was in the air, suspended as if from unnoticeable wires. He struggled to break free, but the most he could do was swing his sword harmlessly three feet from the emperor's head. "What's happening?" he screamed.

"What the…" Carlin trailed off. This was something he'd never seen before.

The emperor nodded toward Saewulf. The servant had his arms raised, palms facing Celerius, holding him immobile with some invisible force. "What's happening?" the emperor echoed vaguely as Saewulf silently held Celerius in place. "What's happening indeed, my dear Celerius? I've been wondering exactly that. What's happening behind the closed doors of the families? Are they planning to overthrow me and climb back to the top? Are they plotting ways to kill my Captain of the Guard? Who will they hurt next with their ambition? Me?" He looked pointedly at the sword still dangling from his prisoner's hand. "That would be a shame."

Sir Celerius dropped his sword with a clatter. There were tears in his eyes.

"A shame, indeed," the emperor said. Saewulf's eyes had turned frighteningly black. "I'll take care of your family once you're gone," the emperor promised. "Don't you worry."

Saewulf punched straight through Sir Celerius's chest, destroying his heart so thoroughly that even his ability to heal was not quick enough to save him.

The emperor rose and walked over to the body, which Saewulf had let fall to the floor. "What a pity," he said softly, nudging the corpse with his toe. "Saewulf, gather the chess pieces."

His servant obeyed. "I was about to beat you, too," Saewulf complained in a raspy voice as he set up the pawns with bloodied hands.

Carlin stared at the servant in awe. "How long… how long has he been able to do that?"

The emperor ignored Carlin as he smiled and gestured to Saewulf to make the first move. "We should try to get through this game before the siege," he said methodically. "There won't be much time afterwards."

The servant moved a pawn forward two spaces. "We'll have to finish quickly," he said. "It all begins tonight, after all."

VICTORY LIES WITHIN
THE ASHES

Chapter Twenty-Five

VAPROS BUNKER
NEIL VAPROS

NEIL LAY ON HIS BACK IN THE BUNK BED HE SHARED WITH HIS BROTHER, staring up at the mattress over his head. He'd been lying here for hours, unable to fall asleep. "You still awake?" he whispered to the darkness.

"Yeah." The mattress shifted, and Rhys's head appeared over the side of the top bunk. "Do you really think the emperor is coming after us?"

"I hope not."

"But do you think it's likely?" Rhys's eyes were wide with something close to fear. It was an expression Neil hadn't seen since he was five years old, when Rhys had still been afraid of the dark. Neil had always let him crawl into bed with him, acting like a tough older brother, but secretly a little scared himself.

"I think it's likely," Neil said, wishing he had a different answer.

"Do you think he'd kill us?"

Neil wanted so badly to say no, but chose, "I don't know. He never seemed all that evil before, but people wear masks." The man made of marble wasn't ruthless or tough the way the Taurlum were, but he had a cold, inhuman kind of mercilessness according to his enemies. If his plans were to destroy the families, he would not hesitate to murder everyone in his path. "If he attacks us, will you stay and fight?"

Rhys didn't answer.

"I think I would run," Neil said to break the silence. "I don't stand a chance against the emperor's forces."

"What you're describing is desertion," Rhys said quietly.

"Is it, though?" Neil sat up and whispered, "We were born into this. We never took an oath. We never made any promises. Everything we've done so far was out of loyalty, hatred, or revenge."

"I'd leave, too," Rhys whispered. "Going up against the emperor is suicide. I'd go with you." He gave a little, disbelieving laugh. "We're talking about abandoning our family, Neil."

Neil's thoughts flashed to Darius Taurlum, who got to drink with his family every night, and then to Bianca, who didn't have any family left to abandon. "To be honest, we aren't exactly the closest knit family around," Neil said.

Rhys looked at him. "You think?"

"I've gathered a few clues over the years." Neil fiddled with the edge of his comforter. "So it's decided? If this turns into a war, we run?"

"We run," Rhys confirmed. "And then we'd live in the slums, I guess."

Neil closed his eyes for a moment, and then opened them as wide as he could to stave off sleepiness. "What about . . . beyond the wall?"

Rhys scrunched up his eyebrows and recited:

"There is no story sadder than that of little Billy.

He thought he'd have adventures if he could leave the city.

He made it through the wall and quickly lost his head-

For the savages were waiting and they cut him up instead."

"Don't quote the emperor's nursery rhymes at me," Neil said.

"You know what's beyond the wall … desert, desert, and savages. Why do you think people who are exiled are forced to leave the wall? Because it's certain death, Neil, certain death."

"But where did the savages come from?" Neil pressed. "They have to be from villages. They have to have families. Otherwise, they would've died out. We can't be the only city out there."

"Even if there are other cities, we'd die of hunger—or stab wounds—before we made it anywhere. Altryon is in the middle of a wasteland. It's a fact. I've read about it. It's essentially suicide."

"Staying here is just as much of a suicide, if this turns to war. At least out there, we'd have a chance—"

"No, Neil, there is no chance."

"But if there was, just think about it for a second. What if there are other civilizations? And what if there are civilizations where they've never heard of the Man with the Golden Light, or the families, or the feud, or any of it?"

Rhys said, "It's a nice thought. I'd love to leave behind the feud. I get the feeling Dad sort of likes keeping it alive. He adds fuel to the fire sometimes. Like when he sent you out to kill a Taurlum. It wasn't necessary. It was just to rile them up." He yawned. "It's all part of his hatred. I'd like that to go away, I think. No more assassinations. No more strategizing. No more plotting."

"I thought you loved to plot, Rhys."

"I do. But sometimes, I wish I didn't have to." There was a long pause, before Rhys spoke again. "We should bring Victoria."

"Yeah, of course," Neil said as he buried his face in his pillow. "She'd love a world like that."

Rhys let out a yawn. "So it's decided. If a war starts, we get the hell out of here."

"We get the hell out of here," Neil confirmed quietly.

Chapter Twenty-Six

CELERIUS ESTATE
LILLY CELERIUS

Lilly felt like this horrible day would never end. Those meddling Vapros had attacked her carriage, and then she had returned home to the horror of seeing her brother's ashes hand-delivered in a box. Her father had raced out to heaven knows where in a blind rage.

Lilly made a habit of refusing to drink. She hated alcohol, hated its taste and its side effects and the headache it caused the next day, but tonight was an exception to the rule. Her brother was dead. Anthony, who had long ago promised to protect her no matter what, was gone, just like the rumors had said he would be.

It didn't even feel real yet, maybe because they only saw each other on special occasions. If she tried, she could almost convince herself that he was still alive and well at the military base. But the truth always settled back in like dust over her skin, and never again would she see that big, toothy grin he reserved just for her, or hear his belly laugh, or feel his strong embrace. She was already forgetting the color of his eyes.

She poured herself another glass of wine. She was being silly. Death was just a part of life. She'd lost people before. Before today, the one that had hit her the hardest was her brother, Edward, victim of an assassination a few years ago. He had been found dead in his bed; they never did find out who was behind the murder. His death had crushed her. But time had eased that pain; this loss was fresh, new, agonizing. And this time, she knew exactly who had taken the victim away from her.

"Miss," Jonathan said quietly. "I think you've had enough."

She looked right at him and drained the glass, daring him to speak again. "They sent my brother's ashes in a box," she said hoarsely, refilling the goblet and wishing her house had something stronger than wine. "Killing him wasn't good enough. They had to burn him and scoop him into a box and send him home." She was out of tears. She gripped her glass and whispered, "I can't believe I have lost another brother."

"No more wine," Jonathan said quietly as he reached for the bottle.

She said something under her breath.

"Pardon?"

She made eye contact and said with steely resolve, "He dies."

Jonathan touched the buttons on his coat nervously and asked, "Who?"

Lilly threw her full glass against the fireplace. It shattered. "Carlin, and I'm going to cut out his black heart and burn it to ash, same as he did to Anthony."

Jonathan was quiet for a moment. "Good," he finally replied.

If Lilly had been able to feel anything but fury and numbness, she would have been surprised. Jonathan was not the vengeful type. "He will regret the day he betrayed my family."

Jonathan went to fetch another glass from the cabinet. He filled it halfway with water and offered it to her. "I'd love to be there when it happens," he said.

She ignored the water and took a gulp of wine, straight from the bottle. She glanced at Jonathan. It was improper to create a bond with a servant and she'd always been told to avoid treating Jonathan like a part of the family. However, the constant dedication and support that he showed her made that a difficult task. "I want everyone there," she said finally.

A fire of rage ignited in her chest, working with the alcohol to dull her pain. She promised herself she wouldn't extinguish the flame. She would let it burn.

VICTORY LIES WITHIN
THE ASHES

Chapter Twenty-Seven

VAPROS BUNKER
NEIL VAPROS

NEIL DODGED THROUGH THE MARKET STREETS, MATERIALIZING AROUND corners and tearing down alleyways to get away from the stampede of people following him. He finally ducked behind a fruit stand, hugging his knees to his chest and listening to the thudding footsteps of his adversaries as they raced past.

"Neil! Wake up!"

Neil blinked a few times. "What?" he mumbled groggily.

Rhys was standing over him. "Do you hear that?"

"Hear what?"

"Listen!"

Neil sat up. Overhead, on the floor above them, he could hear footsteps running in all directions. "People," he said stupidly.

"A lot of people," Rhys said urgently. "How many people live in this house?"

"I don't know. Thirty?"

"I hear a lot more footsteps than that."

Neil listened again and then everything clicked: the raid they had feared was happening—tonight, right now. He jumped out of bed and threw on his assassin cloak. "We have to go now," he said, suddenly wide-awake. Rhys ran to get his things. As they barreled out into the hallway, they nearly crashed into Jennifer and Victoria. "You heard?" Neil asked, pointing up at the ceiling.

"We were just coming to get you." She and Victoria were both wearing their battle cloaks. The latter looked extremely uncomfortable. "Never been so glad to be sleeping on the bottom floor," Jennifer said.

"We don't have time to talk," Rhys said. The four of them started for the stairs. "We should find Father first," Rhys decided. "He's the strongest. He's the best equipped to deal with this."

"Taurlum?" Victoria asked, pulling her hood over her head.

"I don't think so," Rhys said. "The footsteps aren't loud enough to be Taurlum. And our hallways are too small for them to fit."

"Celerius, then?"

"Doubtful. It's not like them to make the first move. And they wouldn't cut us up in our beds. It's not honorable."

"Then who?" Victoria and Jennifer asked together.

Rhys and Neil shared a look. Neil said, "It's the—"

"Look out," Jennifer hissed, throwing out an arm to stop her siblings from proceeding. "We have guests."

At the end of the hallway, unaware that they'd been spotted, were three soldiers clad in Imperial armor and some sort of mask. "I'll take the one in the middle," Jennifer said from the side of her mouth. "Rhys, you get the guy on the left. Neil, you can have the one on the right."

As soon as she finished giving orders, they were sprinting down the hall toward their adversaries. Jennifer reached her soldier first, burning straight through his mask with her palms and sliding a knife across his throat. Neil hit his target next, materializing behind him and stabbing his heart through his back. Rhys brought up the rear, calmly putting his man to sleep before throwing his limp body to the ground.

Victoria finally caught up with her siblings. "Why are they wearing masks?" she asked, looking a little pale. She had never admitted it, but killing made her sick to her stomach.

Rhys bent down and removed the mask in fascination. "I could be wrong, but it looks remarkably like an apparatus for protecting against asphyxiation via smoke inhalation."

The other three stared at him blankly. "Talk like a person," Jennifer grumbled.

Rhys slid the mask over his own face experimentally. "It's a gas mask," he said, voice slightly muffled. "If there's a fire or something, this can help you breathe through the smoke."

Jennifer ran her hand across the man she'd just killed and cremated him. "How do you know all this stuff?" she asked, picking up the gas mask from the pile of ash.

Rhys pulled off his gas mask, looked at it and spoke thoughtfully. "I think I invented it." The other three stared at him. "I mean," he clarified, "I think I talked to the guy who wanted to invent them. I helped him work out some flaws in the design. It was supposed to help save people. He told me he was part of the doctor's guild and was a philanthropist."

Jennifer narrowed her eyes. "And now the army has them. " She tightened her ponytail and grumbled. "The same army that wants to go to war with us. Good going, Rhys. You practically handed them their victory."

Rhys stared at the floor. "You're right. I'm sorry. I didn't know."

Neil glared at Jennifer. "Leave him alone."

In a flash, Jennifer had her knife in her hand. "Don't tell me what to do."

Victoria stepped between her sister and brother. "So the soldiers have gas masks," she said, trying to guide the conversation back to the matter at hand. "So they were going to set fire to our house?"

Rhys shook his head. "They wouldn't have come all the way down here just to start a fire." He began fishing through the fallen soldiers' pockets. "Ah," he said quietly, pulling out a small canister filled with a pin on the top. "Of course. I've seen these before. It all makes sense now."

Jennifer exhaled heavily. "Are you going to enlighten us?" she asked with exaggerated patience, "or just talk to yourself?"

"These canisters have gasses inside that make people fall unconscious or suffocate," Rhys explained. "It doesn't usually kill them, just puts them to sleep for awhile. It would be a good way to capture us because we need air to materialize."

Neil waited, but Rhys didn't continue. "So?" he prompted gently.

"So they don't want us dead," Rhys elaborated. "They want to take us prisoner. They were going to find our bedrooms, release the gas—they'd be safe because of the gas masks—and bring us to … well, wherever they want."

Victoria tried to look calm. "So here's the new plan," she said as forcefully as she could. "We get out of here. We'll warn people on the way when it isn't too risky, but above all else, we have to escape."

"Taking charge," Jennifer said, patting her sister on the back. "I like it. You heard her," she said to Rhys and Neil. "Let's go. Run."

"Wait." Neil knelt to pick up the masks from the fallen soldiers. One of them had a giant hole burned through it from Jennifer's hands, but the other two were still whole. "Put these on," he said, offering them to Victoria and Jennifer. "Just in case."

Victoria took hers and slid it over her face, but Jennifer waved hers away. "You wear it, Neil," she said with a foreign kindness. He was about to thank her when she added, grinning, "After all, you need all the help you can get."

Scowling, Neil handed the mask to Rhys, who pulled it on without hesitation. The four Vapros started down the hallway, pounding on doors and yelling about the invasion as they went. Jennifer kept her knife in her hand at all times.

They rounded a corner and found themselves face to face with a large group of masked soldiers. Jennifer lunged at one of them, sinking her knife into his arm and yanking his mask off his head and onto her own. Victoria hung back, holding a knife in her hand just in case, but Neil knew she had no idea how to use it. He jumped into the fray, stabbing and dodging and materializing out of the way as the Imperial soldiers swung at him. He wondered desperately where the rest of his relatives were. Maybe the soldiers had already gassed them. Maybe he, Rhys, and the twins were the only ones left.

"Look out!" screamed Victoria. Neil turned just in time to see one of the soldiers pull the pin on a canister full of the foggy vapor. He groaned. He was the only one without a mask. Holding his breath, Neil materialized behind one of the soldiers and tried to pull off his mask. But fighting without breathing was hard work, and the man was struggling hard. Any second now Neil knew he'd have to take a breath.

Just as his lungs began to burn, something heavy was shoved against his face. Neil gasped against his will. Instead of breathing in the toxin, however, he found himself inhaling clean air. He pawed at the object against his face. He pulled it the rest of the way over his head, quickly finished off the soldier, and looked around for his savior. The only one in his vicinity was Jennifer. "You?" he called to her over the noises of combat.

"Thank me later," she yelled back, burning through the masks of two soldiers at once. The holes she made rendered their masks useless, and after three seconds of breathing in the gas, both soldiers were lying motionless on the ground. He looked around for more men to fight, but there was nobody left standing other than his siblings.

"I think we beat them," he started to say, but stopped himself. Waiting on the stairs in a stiff formation stood more soldiers. The room was silent except for the heavy breathing of Jennifer, Rhys, and Neil. One of the new soldiers stepped forward and approached them. "Vapros children," he said in a cold voice, "surrender now. We will not harm you unless you resist."

"Go to hell," Jennifer said through her mask, throwing her knife directly into his stomach. The soldier hit the ground screaming. The group on the stairs began to file down, swords outstretched, and Neil prepared to charge them. Suddenly, a scream went up near the top of the stairs. The soldiers paused. More screams joined the first one, and then the soldiers were gone and Sir Vapros appeared on the bottom step. The stairs behind him were littered with small heaps of ash.

Victoria paled. "How many did…?" She couldn't finish her sentence.

"I consumed about ten," he answered. "We're leaving. Now! It is no longer safe here."

Victoria pulled a mask from a body on the floor and offered it to her father, but he shook his head. "There's a gas," she started to explain.

"The gas cannot harm me," he assured her. "I am smoke." He let his body transform back into a giant cloud and glided up the stairs. His family followed, watching in horror and awe as he enveloped every soldier they met and turned them into little piles of dust.

When they reached the second highest floor, Sir Vapros took human shape again. "We met much less resistance than I expected," he mused. "The emperor sent a rather weak—"

Before he could finish, he was lifted off the ground by an invisible force. A figure emerged from the shadows, eyes an otherworldly black, hands outstretched. He had a familiar face, but Neil couldn't quite place it. Victoria let out a scream.

Sir Vapros dematerialized out of the man's hold, but before he could revert back into smoke the invisible force had taken hold of him again. The man clenched his outstretched hands into fists; Sir Vapros went flying into a wall headfirst. He landed on the ground with a thud and didn't get up.

Neil ran to his father's side. Sir Vapros's chest rose and fell slightly, but his head was bleeding badly. "Who are you?" Neil demanded, standing to face the intruder.

The man looked at Neil, an odd smile playing at his lips. "You don't remember me?" he said in a raspy voice. "I'm insulted. We've met before. I suppose I looked a little different."

Neil squinted, trying to remember. It came back to him in a sudden burst. "You're the emperor's servant," he said. "The one he beats. You were there when I went to see him."

The servant bowed. "Saewulf."

Saewulf looked strikingly different. Apparently when clean, his hair was actually a burnt orange color. It was pulled away from his face and lapped down near his shoulders. His ragged servant-wear had been exchanged for well-made, tight-fitting, black clothing.

Victoria couldn't take her eyes off her father's unconscious form. "What are you?" she asked, with her voice catching.

He turned his gaze to her. "Not a student of history, I see."

Jennifer stepped forward. *"Answer her."*

Saewulf laughed. The sound sent chills down Neil's spine. "You know the legends that surround your family. You tell me."

Before any of them could respond, Saewulf whirled around and stretched his arms out toward Rhys. Neil's brother was lifted into the air. He flailed and began to scream. Before Saewulf could do anything further, Neil and Jennifer were upon him. Saewulf dodged Neil's blade, but Jennifer was able to nick him with her red-hot hands, and his concentration was broken. He dropped Rhys, who rematerialized on the other side of the room and sprinted up the stairs. His siblings followed. As they materialized through the small door and pulled off their gas masks, Neil could hear Saewulf charging after them. "Split up," he said, panting. "Meet at the Opera House later."

"But Dad," Victoria began.

"He's alive," Neil assured her. "He was breathing. Split up!"

For once, nobody argued with him. They headed out into the night, dematerializing to avoid being seen. Neil had made it onto the rooftop when he heard the iron door being ripped off its hinges. Saewulf swung his arm and it clattered into the darkness. Neil turned to flee, but he heard his sister scream. He looked down to see Victoria, who had almost escaped, being lifted into the air. Saewulf dragged her back to the entrance of the house using his invisible force. "Surrender or she dies!" he screamed into the night.

Neil whipped his head around to look at Jennifer. For the first time in his memory, he saw real fear in her eyes. She took a half step back toward their house. "Don't do it, Jen," Neil cautioned. She looked at him, trembling, and he could see the conflict in her face.

"It's your last chance!" Saewulf yelled. "I'll kill her in front of your eyes!"

Victoria wasn't screaming, but she looked out of her mind with terror. Jennifer made eye contact with Neil. "I'm sorry," she mouthed and then materialized to the ground. "Don't touch her!" she shrieked, running toward her sister. "I surrender! Let her go!" After a moment of internal struggle, Neil materialized to the ground and followed Jennifer up the street. He didn't see Rhys. His brother had probably made it far away before Victoria's capture. "Jen!" Victoria cried. Her voice echoed oddly, as if she were trapped in a giant bubble, "Don't do it! Run!"

Jennifer stopped a few yards out of Saewulf's reach. She was crying. "I'm not leaving you." She turned to Saewulf, her knife drawn. "I'm here," she said. "You have me. Let her go."

Saewulf didn't drop Victoria. She struggled to dematerialize away the way her father had, but she didn't have enough energy. "Jennifer," she begged, "you have to get away. Find Robert. Tell him . . . tell him I can't meet up with him."

Jennifer's face was bathed in tears. "You're going to get out of this. We all are. I'm here, Saewulf. Put her down."

Saewulf smiled. He pulled Victoria in closer, keeping her suspended. "Something you should know about me since we only have just met," he said lazily. "I'm a liar."

He pulled Victoria in so close that he could reach out and grab her. He caught her neck in his glowing hand. Jennifer and Victoria screamed together. With a quick flick of Saewulf's wrist, Victoria fell to the ground, neck twisted at an unnatural angle, eyes wide and blank.

Jennifer let out a snarl of rage and pain as she materialized in front of Saewulf faster than Neil had ever seen a human being move.

She wrapped her hands tightly around his throat, and Neil swore her entire body glowed red as she burned him. With a yell, he threw her off; she landed in the street next to Victoria's body. With a shuddery gasp, she gazed into her twin's eyes and then began to sob uncontrollably. Neil ran to help her to her feet. "We can't win this," he gasped. Saewulf had his hands clasped around the raw skin on his neck, howling in pain.

Jennifer let Neil hold her. "He dies right now," she vowed through sobs.

"He'll die," Neil promised, "but not now. We have to regroup first and then get stronger."

Jennifer groped for her knife. "Now," she snarled. Her hair was coming down from its ponytail, but she didn't reach up to fix it. Neil let go of her. This was not a Jennifer he'd seen before. Gone was the poised assassin; this Jennifer was wild, like a savage, like an animal.

"Please, Jen," he begged. "Not tonight. We have to get out of here before he calls in reinforcements. We'll die."

"I don't care if I die!" Jennifer screamed.

"Victoria would care," he insisted.

At the name of her sister, something in Jennifer collapsed. New sobs filled with anger and pain racked her body as she sheathed her knife. "He will die," she whispered to Victoria as she placed her hand on the back of her sister's neck. They spent a few precious seconds watching the ash float away into the distance as Victoria dissolved. Then with one final look back, they ran into the darkness.

The empty Opera House felt ominous, Neil noticed, but his siblings didn't seem to care. Jennifer had run out of tears hours ago. She turned her knife over and over in her hands, sniffling and hiccupping. Rhys wept silently in the corner, head buried in his cloak. Neil was still in shock. No tears fell from his eyes because none of this felt real. It was all a dream, just a continuation of the nightmare he'd been having a few short hours ago. Any second now he'd wake up in his room and Victoria would be fine.

"So we're on our own now?" Jennifer asked bitterly.

"I think we're the only ones who escaped," he answered.

"Do you think they'll kill the others?" Rhys asked.

"No," Neil said. "Why bother using gas to knock us out if the plan was to kill us? They want us alive."

"We have to save them, " Jennifer said. "We have to overthrow that bastard."

Rhys laughed humorlessly and muttered, "You really think the three of us can topple the strongest man in Altryon?"

Jennifer looked at both or her brothers, a hint of steel returning to her voice. "We're going to build an army. We'll start with Robert."

"Robert?" Neil asked.

"That boy from the slums—the one who followed Victoria everywhere." Jennifer closed her eyes and took a deep breath. "She was in love with him. She never told me but I could tell. They were going to run away together. She never told me that either. But I know they were planning it. I saw how they looked at each other." Jennifer wrapped her arms around her chest, as if she were physically coming apart. "If anyone will fight to avenge her, Robert will."

"Who else can we find?" Rhys asked.

"I don't care who we team up with," Jennifer said stonily. "I don't care who we have to convince or what we have to do. Tomorrow I'm starting a revolution. Saewulf and the emperor are going to die."

Neil and Rhys exchanged a glance. "I know we talked about leaving, but..." Rhys trailed off and gestured at their sister.

Neil pushed a hand through his hair and said. "I know, we can't." He stood up and walked backstage, searching for bottles of alcohol. He grabbed a large one and threw it to Jennifer. "To Victoria Vapros," he said as she popped open the top and took a long drink. She passed it back and he followed suit. "It's in her name that we start this revolution."

Rhys had already begun strategizing. "They had those canisters specially filled with hazardous gas," he said thoughtfully. "They could only have gotten that kind of weapon from an arms dealer. There aren't too many dealers around here. I could track him down. We know it wasn't the Celerius."

"And you already know the man who sold them the gas masks," Neil reminded him. "You said you helped him out."

Jennifer traced the rim of the bottle with her finger. "I say we start from the bottom and work our way up until the empire is in ashes." She reached up to tighten her ponytail, the familiar determined gleam back in her eye. "We ravage until the emperor is entirely alone."

Chapter Twenty-Eight

CELERIUS ESTATE
CARLIN FILUS

CARLIN STOOD AT THE TOP OF THE HILL OVERLOOKING THE CELERIUS estate. Across the city, he knew Saewulf had already begun the siege on the Vapros bunker. "Virgil, get the men in formation," he commanded. "And then I'd like to talk to you." He examined the estate, taking note of all of the exits. Not a single Celerius would escape him tonight.

"We are prepared, sir," Virgil said a few minutes later. "Rifles loaded, men in position."

Carlin grinned. "Just think, tonight every single Celerius in Altryon will be dead or a prisoner. It's a beautiful thing."

Virgil didn't budge. "You wanted to talk to me, sir?"

Carlin turned from the house. "Will you look at me, please?" Virgil made eye contact with the new general. "Look," Carlin said, putting a hand on Virgil's shoulder, "I know you were close to

Anthony. I'm sorry I had to kill him. I had my orders. There was nothing I could do."

Virgil didn't say anything.

"I'm in charge now," he continued, as he straightened his red cloak proudly. "And as my second in command, I hope you will put aside your emotions and act with professionalism."

Virgil finally spoke up. "My allegiance lies with this army and whoever leads it. That was the oath I took when I enlisted. I tried to save Anthony because it was my duty. Now my duty is to protect you. I don't blame you for being the soldier that the emperor instructed you to be. Emotions have nothing to do with it, sir. If you'll allow me, I'll cut down the Celerius myself."

Carlin smiled and patted Virgil's shoulder. "Good, excellent," he said gruffly as he turned his sights back to the house and raised his sword. "Time to interrupt a funeral!" he cried and led his army down the hill with Virgil at his heels.

Chapter Twenty-Nine

CELERIUS ESTATE
LILLY CELERIUS

LILLY WAS ON HER FOURTH GLASS OF WINE AND SHOWED NO SIGN OF stopping. Jonathan, who was on glass number three, was having trouble staying awake. "I'm too small to drink as much as you, Miss," he slurred. He'd taken off his military coat and attempted to drape it across the back of his chair, but it had fallen onto his lap an hour ago and he'd accidentally kicked it onto the floor. It lay in a heap at his feet.

Lilly tilted her glass and sent a river of wine down her throat. "I don't care how much you drink," she muttered. She wished she could feel as intoxicated as he looked, but grief kept finding her through the alcohol. "I should stop. It's not even helping."

Jonathan tried to sit up. "It would be rude to keep drinking alone," he said as formally as he could manage. "I should stop, too." He let out a small burp and then turned bright red. "Forgive me. I . . . excuse me."

Lilly cracked a smile. "You look terrible," she said, polishing off her glass.

Jonathan rubbed his eyes. "I feel terrible."

"Don't we all."

They heard footsteps coming down the hall in their direction. Jonathan jumped out of the chair and then toppled over, his feet tangling in the jacket he'd left on the ground. "Allow me to hide your glass," he panted, trying to stand.

Lilly waved her hand. "Don't bother. This is the least of my worries."

"It's just . . . drinking with one's servants—it's not—"

"Proper?" Lilly interjected with a humorless laugh. "Anthony is dead. Being proper is not important any more."

The door swung open. Jonathan began to bow and then let out a cry of surprise. An Imperial soldier burst into the room and struck the servant across the face with the butt of his rifle. With a cry, Jonathan hit the floor. Lilly jumped up, reaching for her sword. She grabbed the hilt clumsily, finally feeling the effects of the wine and rolled behind one of the cabinets for cover. She held her sword up from behind it as steadily as she could. "Lilly Celerius," the soldier boomed, "we have orders to capture you. If you come quietly, you will not be harmed."

More soldiers gathered in the doorway. Lilly redoubled her grip on the sword and tried not to sway into range. Why was the alcohol kicking in now? "Who gave you your orders?" she asked, fixing her eyes on the leader. "The same person who told you to stand by and let Carlin murder my brother?" Tears stung her eyes but she willed them away.

"Put down your sword," the soldier ordered, but Lilly didn't move. Jonathan lay unconscious at her feet. For a terrifying second she thought he was dead, but then she heard him snoring faintly.

"I will die before I go anywhere with you," she spat.

The soldier reached down to draw his weapon, and Lilly noted with dismay that they were all equipped with powerful rifles. Her heart sank. She couldn't outrun a gun or dodge a bullet.

"I'm hard to kill," she said quickly. "People have tried before. I can heal from any wound. Think about that before you waste your ammunition."

The soldier smiled ruthlessly. "I know how to kill you. All I have to do is hit your heart or your head. You can't recover from that. And I'm more than capable."

Lilly took a deep breath. "Shall we test that theory?" she asked and before any of them could respond, she rolled out of her cover and was upon them. She swung her sword wildly at the leader, slicing cleanly through his neck. His body hit the ground almost a full second after his head. None of the soldiers were prepared to face someone so fast. One of the soldiers behind him panicked and shot his rifle. The shot went wide, and the bullet buried itself in her shoulder, but a bullet was nothing compared to losing Anthony, and by the time she'd killed the shooter, her arm had already expelled the bullet and healed over into a scab. The other guards had clearly not expected this much resistance. As they began to fumble to load their guns, Lilly cut them down like weeds.

Gasping, Lilly sank to the ground and began to sob. "Anthony," she whispered, sword slipping from her hand, "help me …."

A low chuckle came from the doorway. One of the soldiers, in spite of a large gash across his chest, had failed to die. "You'll be with him soon," the man gurgled, lifting his rifle as best he could from his position on the floor, and Lilly was almost glad that it was about to be over.

As the soldier put his finger against the trigger, a large vase sailed through the air and connected with the side of his head. His body went limp. Lilly looked around in confusion and saw Jonathan, grim-faced, struggling back into his military coat. "Are you all right?" he asked, helping her to her feet.

Lilly wanted desperately to hug him, to sob into his shoulder and let him tell her she would be okay, but she refrained and declared, "I'm fine. Thank you."

"It's just my duty, Miss," he said humbly, bowing and stumbling a little.

A group of Celerius guards entered. "We heard a shot," one of them said. "Are you all right?"

Lilly nodded. "Are there any more of them in the house?" she asked.

"We've been fighting them off in the courtyard," a guard answered. "It's nearly the entire Imperial army. We can't keep up with their guns. I'm sorry, Miss Celerius, they've captured your mother. She's unharmed, but I'm afraid your brother Thomas is dead."

Lilly's heart stopped beating. "Thomas?" she whispered. "How?"

The guard bowed his head. "Your brother fought hard," he said, "but swords are no match for rifles."

Lilly couldn't breathe. "Who killed him?"

"I didn't see. None of us did. We just found the body in the main hallway."

"Maybe he wasn't dead," she insisted. "Maybe he was still recovering."

The guard said quietly, "His heart was gone."

She blinked. "His heart was...."

"Someone cut it out of him. It looked like a wide blade, maybe a broadsword."

She was going to be sick. "They cut out his heart?"

"Probably to make sure he was really dead," a guard supplied.

Lilly closed her eyes. "Carlin," she growled. "He's behind it; I know he is. With Anthony gone, he's the leader of this army." She opened her eyes. They were blazing. "He will bleed for what he's done."

"Do you think he's here?" Jonathan asked.

She hadn't thought of that. "I'm going after him," she said, retrieving her sword. "He won't be on the front lines. He's probably inside somewhere … looking for the real challenges. I'll destroy anyone who stands in my way of killing that bastard." Her brain no longer felt fuzzy. Anger destroyed the dull calm she'd tried to weave earlier. "You prepare the horses," she commanded, addressing the guards. They began to file away. "Wait!" They paused. "Half of you get to the treasury. Empty it. We will not be returning." The guards obeyed.

"Me, Miss?" Jonathan asked.

She barely looked at him. "Go with them."

He looked disappointed, but he ran to catch up with the guards, nearly tripping on his coat.

Lilly strode down the hallway as fast as she could without running, throwing open every door she passed. The first room was empty. The second had an overturned dresser partially blocking the door but nobody inside. The third room: Lilly clamped both hands over her mouth to hold in a scream upon seeing the bodies of two servants stabbed through their hearts. She nearly retched when she recognized them—Jonathan's parents. *Don't think about it,* she told herself. *Not now. Not yet.* She closed the door and moved on to the next one, her father's bedroom. Inside was a troop of four men, headed by Carlin himself. They were rooting through drawers and overturning furniture, laughing cruelly. Lilly kicked in the door. "Carlin," she roared, swinging her sword.

He jumped at her voice and turned to her. His face cracked into a dangerous smile. "Oh my," he laughed, "you came right to me."

She let out a wordless snarl. "I am going to kill you for what you did to my family."

Carlin unsheathed his broadsword. Against her will, her eyes strayed to the blade. It was caked with the dried blood that she knew belonged to her brother. "You sound so upset," he said delightedly. "It's adorable."

"There is nothing adorable about this," she said coldly. "No more politics. No more deception. This is pure unadulterated revenge."

His men looked uneasy and shifted uncomfortably. Carlin chuckled. "I bested your brothers," he reminded her. She bit down hard on her tongue to keep from screaming at him. "They weren't quite ... fast enough. So what is it that makes you think you can escape my blade?"

Lilly's face stretched into a savage grin. "Trust me," she said viciously. "I'm fast enough." With a blur of movement, she lunged at one of his men and sliced through him. Carlin jumped forward and tried to cut her legs out from under her, but she whirled out of the way and stabbed his remaining companions before he could suck in a breath to gasp.

"So you're fast enough to defeat these pathetic fools," Carlin spat as he kicked a half-alive body to the floor at her feet. "Have a go at me."

She laughed without humor. There were tears in her eyes. "My pleasure."

She swung, ready to cut his arrogant throat, but her sword collided with steel, and with a shock she realized he'd blocked her blow. That had never happened to her before. He lashed out at her, and it took everything she had to twist out of the way in time. He swung his sword like a maniac, and she let out a cry as she realized she wasn't strong enough to block him every time. His weapon nicked her side, making her bleed, and she stared up at him in fear. "You're…"

"Faster?" he supplied. He knocked the sword from her hand. "Stronger?" He missed her neck by a fraction of an inch. "Better?"

She dropped to the ground and dove for her sword. He kicked her hard and trapped her neck beneath his boot. Flipping her onto her back, he positioned his broadsword against her heart which pounded so fast she could barely breathe. "Yes," he said. "I am."

An arrow came flying out of nowhere and embedded itself in Carlin's hand. He howled in shock and let the sword fall; it left a shallow scratch just over Lilly's heart, which healed over before she even felt the pain. Carlin hit the floor as an arrow whizzed past, embedding itself in the wall. Gasping hard, Lilly jumped to her feet and fled.

As she raced down the hallway, thankfully deserted, she allowed herself to glance over her shoulder to see if Carlin had begun to pursue her. The corridor behind was empty, but Lilly put on a burst of speed just in case, threw herself around the corner and ran directly into a tall Imperial foot-soldier holding a bow and arrow. She gasped in surprise as she collided with his armor and started to fall backwards, but he caught her and held her arm firmly until she regained balance. She couldn't see his face through his helmet, but she felt his eyes on her. With a grunt, she twisted out of his grip and reached for her sword before realizing she'd left it back in her father's room.

Lilly backed away down the hall, eyes on the bow in the guard's hand, waiting for him to fit an arrow into it and shoot her. He remained motionless. When she was halfway down the corridor, she turned and bolted. The soldier didn't chase her.

Lilly was puzzled. Other than Carlin, that soldier was the only one on this floor and he was definitely the only person she'd seen all night carrying a bow and arrow. He must have been the one to shoot the arrow into the room. No doubt he was aiming for her and had only hit his leader by mistake. But that was quite a mistake. She'd been on the ground at Carlin's mercy. There was no need to shoot an arrow at her if she was already about to die. And why hadn't he finished her off just now, when she was clearly weaponless and vulnerable?

She reached the back door of the house and stumbled out into the night. The Celerius guards had loaded the horses with bags of the family treasure. Lilly mounted one of the steeds hastily and urged it to turn around so she could face the men. "Carlin is still alive," she admitted. "He's strong. I need to get stronger before I can face him again." She took a deep breath. "Too many people have died. It cannot be ignored. I am fighting for the memory of my brothers and for the guards and servants who fell tonight." She fought back tears, exhausted. This was too much. She needed sleep, or at the very least more wine. "I, Lilly Celerius, will lead this rebellion against Carlin and the emperor and every one of the Imperial bastards who attacked my family. Who will ride with me?"

Jonathan urged his horse to the front of the group. His cheek bore a large black bruise, but if he was in pain he hid it well. "I will, Miss," he promised.

The Celerius guards echoed his vow, and Lilly nodded gratefully. "Follow me," she cried, turning her horse and nudging him into a gallop. "The Emperor of Altryon will fall."

Chapter Thirty

THE TAURLUM MANSION
MICHAEL TAURLUM

MICHAEL SAT IN HIS BED, GROANING AND RUBBING HIS TEMPLES. *WAS it possible to be hung-over during the middle of the night? Apparently, it was. Waking up had been a mistake.* He crawled out of bed and walked over to his side table with a groan that was almost a roar. He heard a few family members singing a drinking song downstairs, but he didn't care to join them. He grabbed a bottle of gin and poured a glass. "Are you my best friend or worst enemy?" he asked the bottle with a small grin. "Bit of both," he decided with a sip.

He drained the glass and had it refilled within a minute. It was funny how alcohol was the only thing that ever made him feel any sort of pain. At the same time it was the only thing that granted him a bit of peace. It was as if every time he held the cup he was holding a loved one's hand. In recent months, his drinking schedule had changed. Formerly, he would drink in the Taurlum dining room with his father. Things were different since the night he barged into his father's office and told him he was leaving to marry his fiancée. He'd known picking his own wife, and a poor one at that, would never be tolerated. Michael had stupidly thought the girl had been worth it. Despite the fact it all blew up when he discovered her cheating, his father refused to forgive him. Michael no longer felt welcome. The glass exploded in Michael's hand and he realized that he had been clutching it a little too tightly. That wasn't a problem. He had others.

He heard the drinking song cease suddenly. That was odd. It wasn't like the Taurlum family to leave a song unfinished, no matter how drunk they were. The silence was quickly followed by loud crashes and Michael's ear perked up in interest. *Did they all pass out drunk at the same time?* He closed his eyes and waded through his sheets into the center of his bed. Suddenly the smashing grew louder and echoed down his hallway. "What the hell was that?" Michael muttered to himself.

Then he heard the racket closer to his bedroom and a rifle being fired. He threw his sheets off and leapt to his feet. These noises were not an after-effect of his family's antics. Someone was in the house. He threw open his door and was instantly greeted by a volley of fire from a small squad of Imperial soldiers.

He stumbled backwards and toppled to the ground. One of the soldiers pulled a pin on a canister and threw it at his fallen body. As he staggered to his feet, Michael noticed that the canister expelled smoke at an alarming rate. He knew not to inhale, even in his intoxicated state. While holding his breath, he grabbed a bottle from his side table and chucked it at one of the Imperial guards. The bottle flew so straight and swiftly that it knocked the guard off his feet. Michael grabbed the table by one of its legs and charged at the soldiers. One managed to reload his gun and fire in time, but the bullet ricocheted off Michael's chest and found its way into the soldier's vulnerable neck. Michael followed up that maneuver with a swing of the table. The two remaining soldiers were knocked clean off their feet in an explosion of splinters, glass, and alcohol. Michael took a deep gulp of air as he teetered back and forth in the doorway, furious and confused. *Why were they here?*

He stepped out fully into the hallway, holding one leg of the table that had broken off. He heard a soldier on the floor groaning so he stepped on him. Michael turned to his right and realized he was staring at nearly ten Imperial soldiers who were trying to quickly reload their rifles. "Oh," Michael said quietly as he dropped the leg and turned to face them head on. They were about thirty feet away and standing in front of a giant glass window.

The silence was nearly unbearable as they tried to load their guns with care. Michael picked up one of the unmoving soldiers by the foot and with a mighty roar, he hurled the body at the throng. One or two soldiers fell, but that was only the distraction. Michael began his charge. He barreled at full speed down the hallway before the soldiers even had a chance to regain their formation. He was going too fast to slow down, but that was okay. Michael didn't want to slow down. One second he was running and the next he and three soldiers were falling from the third story window. He hit the pavement on all fours, crushing a soldier in between his iron skin and the street.

He stood up and looked back to see a few soldiers gathering by the broken window staring down at him. He vaguely remembered somehow being involved in a similar situation earlier that week. He turned to see the three soldiers in a broken mess on the street behind him. He scoffed and thought to himself: *Good. That's what they get.*

He took a moment to readjust to the change in scenery. Glancing around the side of the house, he could see what looked like half the Imperial army leading members of his family into a wagon. They had some kind of strange collar around their necks. Michael wanted to race to their aid, but he was grossly outnumbered and still hadn't escaped the rifle fire. A few bullets bounced off his back and he began to run in a panicked fashion. He glanced back at the mansion one last time, then bolted off into the markets for shelter.

Chapter Thirty-One

THE MARKETS
DARIUS TAURLUM

DARIUS KEPT HIS HEAD DOWN AS HE PUSHED THROUGH THE CROWDED streets. He'd only been out of prison for a few hours and he wasn't looking to go back. The markets were usually deserted after sundown, but tonight the alleys were packed with civilians. Maybe there was a riot. He readjusted the cloak he had stolen to cover his golden hair. If anyone here recognized him, he'd be thrown back in the dungeon for sure.

The Taurlum mansion was barely visible in the distance. Darius took a long look at it and sighed. There was no way he'd be able to live there anymore. He was a fugitive now. He'd have to hide out in the slums, or worse, the sewers. Never again could he enjoy the bath-house with Michael, or have a drink with his father, or even feel the adrenaline rush of holding a hammer above his head.

"Hey!" someone shouted, and Darius turned to see someone running toward him holding a weapon. For a split second, he was sure he'd been discovered, but then realized the person charging at him was none other than Michael Taurlum.

"What the hell's wrong with you?" Darius exclaimed, putting up his hands to stop his brother.

Michael stopped in his tracks. "Darius?" He looked confused. "Is that you?"

"Of course it's me!" Darius pulled off his cloak and revealed his hair. "Who did you think it was?"

"I don't know," Michael offered, looking weary. "You shouldn't walk around here with your face hidden like that. People will be suspicious. There's been an attack." He was still looking at his brother skeptically; as if he wasn't completely sure Darius wasn't a threat. "I thought you were in prison."

"I made it out," Darius quickly explained. "There was an attack?"

"Yeah." Michael looked up at the mansion as he spoke. "The emperor. He brought an army. I think he got everyone except me. And you, apparently."

"Everyone?" Darius gasped.

"They're not dead," Michael reassured him. "I saw them being taken away, probably to the dungeon."

Darius slammed his fist into a building. The bricks shattered loose with a crunch. "Why would someone do this?" he yelled, attracting the attention of everyone around him. An Imperial soldier at the other end of the street turned his head toward them and began shoving through the crowd.

"Darius," Michael hissed, yanking his brother's cloak back up over his hair. "Run!"

He didn't need to be told twice. The brothers took off down the street, shouting and waving to startle people out of the way, diving around corners and zigzagging through alleys, trying more to lose the soldier than to actually get anywhere. Their noise attracted more attention, which in turn attracted more soldiers. Arrows began to fly; one of them bounced off the back of Darius's head, missing a pressure point in his neck by inches. "We have to hide!" he screamed, putting on a burst of speed. Michael roared and slammed his ringed fingers into a building, effectively blocking the alley with a good amount of debris.

Michael was falling behind though. "Where?" he yelled back.

"Orchards!" Darius replied and pointed to the grove of trees a quarter mile down the road.

"Why there?" Michael panted.

"Trees!" Then Darius was out of breath. He couldn't manage more than the one word, but Michael understood. Trees were easy to climb, easy to hide behind, easy to use as shields. They raced for the orchards, Imperial soldiers hot on their heels. A volley of arrows slammed into Darius's back. He reached around, still running, to feel for blood, but his impossible luck held out and the arrows missed his vulnerable points.

They reached the edge of the orchard. "I want to try something," Michael said, slowing to a stop.

Darius dove into the forest gasping and pulled himself up into a tree. "What are you doing?" he hissed. Michael had knelt to the ground and pressed his palms against the dirt.

"I just want to try."

Darius realized what was going to happen only a second before it occurred. "Have you been practicing?" he shouted. "Michael! Can you control it?"

Michael grinned. "Nope."

The earth began to shake. Fissures erupted in the ground, beginning where Michael's hands touched the soil. Darius's tree shuddered.

The soldiers came closer, almost there. They were going to catch them—

And then a cavern opened in the ground and swallowed the guards. Michael's earthquake ripped through the ground, sending trees toppling into the chasm, crushing the Imperial soldiers. Darius held on tightly to the branches of his tree, praying it wouldn't fall.

Then it was over. The earth closed up, and Michael, sweating profusely, dusted off his hands on his cloak. "There," he said casually, as if he hadn't just killed a handful of men.

"Damn, Michael," Darius said, sliding down from his tree. "That was insane."

"I don't think I could do it again," Michael admitted. "It took a lot out of me."

Darius pulled off his cloak and said. "We can't stay here."

"I know."

"Where can we go?"

Michael suggested, "The sewers, maybe? Like Uncle Nicolai did?"

Darius snorted. Nicolai Taurlum, according to legend, had attempted to murder the previous emperor. He'd been successful, and when the soldiers pursued him, he'd escaped into the sewers where he had supposedly been living ever since. "You know that's just a story, right?"

"What do you think happened to him?"

"They probably caught him and killed him. He's not living in the sewer. That's ridiculous."

Michael said, "They never caught him. He's still at the top of the most wanted list."

"Then he died some other way. You can't survive in a sewer for twenty years. It's not possible. We're not hiding there," Darius said sitting on the trunk of one of the fallen trees. "We have to save everyone else. That assassin girl, she broke me out in less than a day."

Michael stared at him, "What are you talking about?"

"Someone sent a girl to assassinate me. She broke into my cell so I was able to escape after I kicked her ass."

Michael leaned against the trunk and closed his eyes. "So go find the assassin girl," he suggested wearily. "I'll wait here." The night's events, coupled with the energy to create an earthquake had exhausted the warrior.

Darius snorted. "I don't need her. If she can do it, I can do it. I'll have them out by the end of the week and then we'll leave. We'll go outside the wall. Start a new life far away from here. Live in the savage's tribe or something."

There was no answer from Michael other than a faint snore. Darius pulled his cloak up over his head. "Fine," he muttered. "Sleep for now. But tomorrow we have a family to rescue."

Chapter Thirty-Two

IMPERIAL PALACE
CARLIN FILUS

Saewulf pushed open the large door with his mind and stepped back to allow the emperor to enter first. "I swear you do that just to show off," Carlin muttered, bringing up the rear.

Saewulf smiled serenely. "If you could do what I do, you'd show off, too."

Carlin put his feet up on the large war room table. "Yeah," he admitted. "Probably."

The emperor stood at the head of the table and contorted his face into a grin. It made Carlin wince. "Tonight was a success," he announced to his panel of soldiers. "There were a few holdouts, a few—mishaps—but on the whole, I am very pleased."

Every eye in the room flickered to Carlin's bandaged hand. He scowled and hid it under the table. Saewulf nudged him. "Did you ever find out who shot you?" he asked.

Carlin repressed a growl. "No, and I don't intend to search. It was just an accident."

Saewulf smiled slowly. "Of course. An accident."

Carlin clenched his teeth. "Are you suggesting it was not an accident?"

The servant said. "I don't presume to know anything about your army."

"What if it wasn't an accident?" someone asked. Carlin whipped his head around. His eyes widened as they found the man who had spoken.

"Virgil? I ... what do you mean?"

Virgil stood. "Every man in this army took an oath to protect the emperor," he said. "But none of them took an oath against the families. The Celerius did good things for Altryon. One of them formerly led this army." He paused. "Some of the soldiers have loyalties to the families. Maybe one of them wanted to protect the girl you were trying to kill."

Carlin looked down at his bandaged hand. "You think we have a traitor?"

"I do. And I hope you will let me uncover him."

Carlin looked thoughtful. "Find this traitor," he told Virgil. "Interrogate every man who was there that night. And if none of them seem suspicious," he added, glancing at Saewulf, "we will know it was only an accident."

Virgil took his seat, and the emperor regained control of the room. "Only a few people escaped us last night," he said. "They are all children. Three of the Vapros, two Taurlum, and the Celerius girl."

How do you like that, Saewulf? Carlin thought bitterly. *You let three of them get away. I only lost one.*

"We have the houses in our possession," the emperor continued. "We are seizing control of their assets. The plan is working. The families are no longer a threat to my rule." A light applause went up from the table. "And as for the ones we failed to capture, they will be hunted. They will be caught. They will kneel before me, and they will be killed."

The emperor addressed the men at his right. "Saewulf and General Carlin, you will track down the rest of the children. When the final one is executed, we will have not only eliminated the families, but their legacy as well. They will be scrubbed from the history books. No one shall ever speak their names again." The gruesome smile stretched across his face again. Chills flew down Carlin's spine. "Their time playing God is over."

PART TWO

TWO MONTHS LATER

The Fugitives

VICTORY LIES WITHIN
THE ASHES

Chapter Thirty-Three

HOME OF QUINTUS
NEIL VAPROS

NEIL WAS ABOUT TO PUSH HIS HAND THROUGH HIS HAIR AND GROAN in frustration when he saw it—an open window. He smiled and nudged his brother. "Look who decided to enjoy the night air?" he whispered, nodding at the opening in the wall. The window was small and a little too high to climb through, but it was enough.

"Thank God something's open," Rhys said. "I've never tried to materialize through a solid wall before."

Neil poked his head around the corner and waved to catch his sister's attention. "We found a window!" he mouthed, and she abandoned her post and materialized next to her brothers. Smiling, Neil looked up at the window. "Two months since the raid on our house," he said fondly, "and see how much our army has grown!"

He turned to face his army, which still consisted of only Rhys and Jennifer. "You're hilarious," she said with an eye roll. "Has anyone ever told you you're hilarious? Because you are."

Neil bowed. "Well it's not just us," Rhys said. "There's Robert too."

Over the last two months Robert Tanner, Victoria's old boyfriend, had begun recruiting anyone he could find to grow the revolution. Unfortunately, he made himself hard to find, which was a detriment to his allies when they needed his help. He was most likely spending his evening preaching to starving people and tearing down the Emperor's new propaganda posters. It was getting easier to get citizens to join the revolution every day, mostly because the emperor's attempts at seizing the Lightborns' businesses had resulted in economic collapse. While the empire struggled to reestablish the businesses, many were out of work, and thus more willing to share their disdain for the Emperor in public.

"Okay," Neil said seriously. "Recap time. When we get inside, we take out the guards. Once they're taken care of, Jen and I will provide Quintus with a necessary show of force." Jennifer reached up to tighten her ponytail. "Rhys, you get to the front doors as fast as you can and let our friends inside. Don't let them out of your sight. They'll ransack the treasury and split the money with us." He looked at Rhys and repeated, "Make sure they split the money with us." Rhys nodded. "I'll find Quintus and have a conversation with him." Two months of spying, bribery, and trading rumors had revealed that the emperor's advisor had played a major role in the attack on the Vapros bunker. "Rhys, when you're finished in the treasury, meet back up with us by this open window. We won't leave until we're all together." He pulled up his hood. "Got it?"

Jennifer and Rhys both whispered, "Yes."

"Then let's go. Good luck, everyone." Neil materialized up to the roof and then, with a deep breath, jumped off. He kept his eyes fixed on the tiny open window. Just before he fell past it, he materialized through the opening and appeared inside with a light thud. Jennifer followed a second later. She hit the floor soundlessly, landing in a crouch like a cat. Rhys was not quite so graceful. His landing made the loudest noise of all, echoing down the hallway and startling a sleeping sentry to his feet.

"Who's there?" the watchman slurred groggily. Neil slid a knife into the nape of his neck and neatly severed the spinal cord. The sentry died without another sound. Jennifer reached out and gently closed the guard's eyes before turning his body into dust. She'd become less ruthless since the night her sister died. All her life, she'd been trained to look at her targets as just that—targets. *But now*, Neil thought, *now she couldn't help seeing them as human beings who could breathe and laugh and hurt, just like Victoria.* Gone was the merciless assassin whose eyes blazed when she killed. The only thing filling Jennifer's eyes nowadays was grief and revenge.

"Are there any more?" Rhys asked, looking up and down the hallway. It appeared to be deserted, and Neil told him so. "I'll go open the doors, then," he whispered and started down the hallway, materializing every few steps. Neil watched him go.

"Quintus's door," Jennifer reminded him. He turned. She pointed at an extravagant double door made of marble. He reached for the handle. Jennifer opened her mouth and then quickly closed it.

"What's wrong?" Neil asked.

"Nothing," she said. "I'm just wondering how many guards are on the other side."

"Probably none," Neil said. "He had a sentry. He has no reason to expect an attack, except for the obvious reason."

"Right." Jennifer still looked troubled, but she pushed past Neil to throw open the doors.

As Neil predicted, there were no guards in Quintus's bedchamber. The emperor's advisor sat up when the doors opened, then stumbled out of bed in his nightgown and tried to flee. "Quintus!" Neil cried jubilantly, "It's been too long!"

"Guards!" he shrieked as he frantically searched for an exit. He apparently had no trouble recognizing them, even though they'd abandoned their typical Vapros clothing.

Jennifer was across the room in an instant. Quintus desperately flailed out at her, but she dodged his attack and clasped her hand around his throat. He started to struggle but instantly stopped when he felt the intense heat coming. "Your guards can't hear you," she cooed as he fell to his knees. Her grip remained strong. A shadow of the old bloodthirstiness crept into her eyes.

"What do you want?" Quintus sputtered as he tried to avoid being burned alive.

Neil walked to Quintus's bedside table and selected a bottle of wine from his vast array of bottles. "You know," Neil said, "the night right before my family was imprisoned, we were spreading rumors about you, Quintus. We told everyone you were an alcoholic. I thought it was just a rumor, but look at this. You have an entire cellar right next to your bed." Neil's ease was all an act, but it was necessary. Interrogation relied on a show of power.

Quintus stared at Neil in confusion. Neil lowered the hood of his cloak and waited as recognition finally dawned. "You're the Vapros kids that escaped."

"And people say you're slow witted," Neil said in mock disbelief.

Quintus growled and attempted to shift his position, but Jennifer held him in an iron grip. Letting your brother make all the speeches?" he spat.

She smiled and her hands grew a little hotter. "I don't mind. I like my current job well enough."

Quintus glared at Neil and spoke as slowly as he could. "Why are you here Vapros? To kill me? For what? All I am is an employee of the emperor. I had nothing to do with the capture of your family."

Neil dropped the wine bottle. It shattered as it hit the floor. Wine splashed onto one of Quintus's extravagant rugs. Quintus winced. "You don't give yourself enough credit, my friend," Neil said as he took a step closer to him. "In recent months, I've learned a lot about you. Mostly because a lot of fingers seemed to be pointing clearly at you when we asked who planned the attacks."

"Why don't you get your sister off me so we can converse like gentlemen?" Quintus groaned as a portion of his neck became visibly discolored.

Jennifer glanced at Neil who nodded. She dropped Quintus, who fell to the ground, panting. "Fine, let's talk," Neil said, his theatrical voice fading away and turning to one of anger. "I want answers, and you're going to give them to me. Otherwise, Jennifer will melt your throat and you'll choke on the flesh."

Quintus patted his ginger curls into his usual hairstyle. "What do you want to know?" he asked, clearly attempting to maintain a bit of dignity.

"I know one thing for sure: the emperor didn't imprison us because we're a threat to the people. He did it for some sort of personal gain. That's why he took over our businesses and our money."

"Well …." Quintus's eyes narrowed as he spoke and a bead of sweat dripped down his face. "As you probably know, based on our pasts, I'm not exactly pro-family. Neither is the emperor. He's wanted you out from the moment he took the throne. But who is he to change two centuries of tradition? He had to let you live. He had no choice.

"But then he found that new servant, Saewulf, and the two of them started speaking about the issue behind closed doors. It was like he started to actually consider wiping out the families. He made plans, discussed tactics... I, of course, was against all of it."

"The truth, Quintus," Neil snarled as he pulled his knife from its sheath.

Quintus sighed. "I wasn't against it, but I knew it would be difficult. You all owned so many businesses, and Anthony Celerius was leading the military. You had too much power. People actually *liked* you, despite your childish fighting. We needed a way around all that. The general was easy to dispose of, but the business part was a trickier challenge. We couldn't just overtake businesses without knowledge of how they worked. It would cause an economic disaster."

Jennifer's eyes were narrowed. "So you decided to study up on us."

Quintus gulped. "We made plans to steal documents, study how your assets operated. That was my contribution. It was supposed to be a gradual takeover. Then the Captain of the Guard was killed and the emperor snapped. He felt the manslaughter was an act of defiance. He wanted to speed things up."

"So you put your little plan into action?" Neil asked.

"We had already planned to get rid of the general. Now we had a reason to go after the families. We had a reason that the people could understand, anyway. So Carlin killed the general and I collected the documents. Then Sir Celerius tried to kill the emperor, which was when we decided to act that night."

Neil stared at Quintus. "That was a lengthy explanation," he said warily, "but I'm not sure I believe all this. What did we ever do to the emperor? Where did all this hatred come from?"

Quintus started to snicker, but stopped when nobody else joined in. "It's obvious, isn't it? He lost his father to a Taurlum. That's not something you ever forget. If you saw your father shot with a gun, every gun you saw would bring up an unpleasant memory, right? His father was murdered by a super-human show of force. It's not exactly a mystery as to why he wants your kind gone, is it?"

For once, Neil allowed his icy expression to melt as he glanced at Jennifer. Having an enemy who wanted something from you was one thing, but having an enemy who despised your entire being was something completely different.

The doors burst open, and for a split second Neil thought another guard had discovered them. Then he recognized his brother. He ushered in about a dozen men from the hallway. Each man was armed to the teeth and bore helmets designed to look like snakeheads.

Neil smiled. Good old Rhys. "You're familiar with the Brotherhood of the Slums, aren't you, Quintus? I believe you hired them to raid the Celerius Estate, right?" he asked cheerfully. Quintus didn't move, but Neil continued anyway. "Yes, these men are crooks and mercenaries, but tonight we have hired them to help us carry off your valuables." He swept a bow. "Thank you for your donation to the cause."

Quintus opened and closed his mouth rapidly. "Please," he said finally. "Please don't kill me. I'm sorry. I'm sorry!"

Neil laughed. "Kill you? No. We aren't barbarians. We've spread rumors about you, robbed you, dealt with your guard out in the hallway, and told everyone you're unfaithful to your wife, but we would never kill you. By the way, I've noticed you're sleeping alone. I hope we can take credit for that. From experience, we know there are fates worse than death." He saw a shadow pass over Jennifer's face. "We just want your money to finance our revolution and to feed the people starving in the streets because of your laws. But don't feel too bad for the poor people, Quintus. Soon you'll be one of them."

Quintus stared at him in shock throughout the entire speech. "You're not going to kill me?" he stammered.

"No. Just leave you penniless."

"Don't, don't do this to me," Quintus said, but he looked relieved.

"You did this to yourself," Neil said carelessly. "Goodnight, Quintus." Jennifer let go of his arms and planted her foot in his back. She kicked, sending him sprawling across his bed. He didn't get up. The Vapros children, flanked by the Brotherhood, left Quintus's room and shut the door behind them.

"Did you get the treasure?" Neil asked Rhys as they marched back to their open window.

Rhys nodded. "It fills three carts."

"Did you run into any trouble?"

"Ten guards who are all asleep downstairs."

Neil smiled. "Good work."

"What now?" Jennifer had caught up to her brothers.

"We have to pay the Brotherhood, of course," Neil said. One of the Brothers grunted. "We promised them half. And then we have to take the rest of the money to the safe house."

"Anything else?" she asked.

"No." He looked at her. "Why? Did you have something in mind?"

The old glint was back in her eye. "I want to give this house a proper send-off."

"A send-off?"

She held up her hands. They were glowing red.

"We can't," Neil told her, sighing. "Quintus is still inside. We need him to take news of our raid back to the emperor. It's our only hope that our family will hear the gossip and know we are trying to save them."

"We'll get him out," she said. "He's unconscious anyway. I kicked him pretty hard." She looked at her brother. "Let me do this, Neil, for our sister."

Neil pushed his hand through his hair. "Fine." He looked around and picked the smallest Brother. "Take Quintus outside," he instructed, "and leave him across the street." The man grunted and turned back toward the marble doors. "The rest of you, get out of here." When the hallway was deserted, he signaled to Jennifer. "Go."

Grinning, she seized a curtain in both hands. It ignited immediately. She materialized down the hall a few feet and grabbed a tapestry, and then ran her hand along a long velvet couch. She stooped to touch a carpet. The entire hallway was in flames. Neil materialized out through the window, expecting Jennifer to follow, but it was several minutes before she finally appeared. "Where were you?" he asked. Smoke billowed through the open window.

She grinned and pulled him a few yards down the street, away from the heat of the building. "I had to hit every floor." She tightened her ponytail. "Why, were you worried about me, little brother?" she teased.

Rhys came around to meet them before he had time to answer. Two Brothers trailed behind him, dragging carts full of rubies and gold. "Got the money," he said. "We divided it all up already. I can't believe you burned down his house."

Neil reached into one of the carts and pulled out two gold rings. He handed one to each of the Brothers. "For your trouble."

The Brothers exchanged glances and grinned within their helmets. "Pleasure doing business with you," one of them said, pocketing the ring.

Neil bowed. "The pleasure was all ours." The mercenaries disappeared into the night.

"Now what?" Rhys asked, eyes locked on the carts.

"For one thing we should get out of the street," Neil said.

His siblings agreed. Being out in the open was incredibly dangerous at any time of day, especially with the entire Imperial army searching for them. Even in disguise, they'd had several close calls and they were jumpy whenever they had to leave their hideout. Living in constant fear had taken a toll on all of them, even more than the weight loss from never having enough to eat. At least with Quintus' gold, the constant hunger would be over.

"You two go home," Neil answered. "I'm going out."

"Out?" Jennifer had already started dragging a cart down the road. "Out where?"

"Socializing," Neil said as he grabbed a sack of coins and walked away. "I'm going to make us some new friends."

VICTORY LIES WITHIN
THE ASHES

Chapter Thirty-Four

THE POWDER BARREL PUB
NEIL VAPROS

NEIL WALKED INTO THE BAR FEELING NERVOUS. HE HAD NEVER BEEN IN A bar outside the nightlife district, much less a bar in the middle of the markets. The markets weren't Taurlum territory anymore—the emperor had taken over everything in the aftermath of the attacks—but it still made him uneasy to walk through these streets. He always had a faint suspicion that Darius Taurlum was waiting around the corner, hammer raised, ready to pummel him. But Darius was long gone. All the Taurlum were.

Neil poked his head inside the bar and looked around for Imperial soldiers. In the old days, finding a soldier in a bar was lucky, but now it was a death sentence. He relaxed slightly but he didn't lower his guard completely. Even in disguise, he feared he might be recognized. When he didn't find any guards, Neil sauntered up to the bartender. Reaching into his pocket, he pulled out a few gold coins he'd snagged from the carts at Quintus's house. "I'd like to buy a round," he said, dropping the money on the table.

The bartender raised his eyebrows. "For whom?" he inquired.

Neil smiled wistfully. He missed the days when bartenders knew exactly what he meant when he put money on their counters. "For everyone."

The bartender slid the money off the table and into a pocket of his apron. "Everyone!" he called out. "Next round is on this guy!"

Total silence, and then a disbelieving cheer from the patrons greet-ed his announcement. This clearly wasn't the norm around here. Neil ducked away from the counter as the customers rushed toward it and went to sit in the back and eavesdrop. He didn't take a drink himself. He needed a clear head tonight.

A large bearded man was having a heated discussion with his table. Neil caught the word "emperor" and shifted a little closer.

"… Never been worse!" the bearded man was saying. "I haven't had a job in months. My children go to bed hungry. This nation used to be great! The emperor ruined us." He took a long swig of brandy and raged on. "If it weren't for that stranger, I wouldn't even have been able to afford a drink tonight."

A smaller man said. "This kind of thing used to be common," he reminisced. "Remember the old days? Go to the nightlife district, wait around for one of the you-know-who to come buy a round of beer and then head off to the opera?"

Another man gestured knowingly. "I was there the night Darius Taurlum stormed the Opera House. I wish I'd known it was the be-ginning of the end. I might've stayed a little longer." His companions laughed.

"The families were generous," the bearded man said. "They made sure we had jobs. They were generous to people. Not so much to each other, but to us, they were kind."

Neil decided this was the best opportunity for him to join the conversation. "The families were kind," he said, pulling up a chair. "I remember those times well. They cared. Not like the emperor. He's supposed to be a leader. He's supposed to protect us, but he doesn't give a damn. We should do something about it."

The bearded man looked skeptical and glanced around the bar for soldiers. "Since you bought me a drink, I'll humor you. What do you suggest we do?"

Neil smiled. This was his favorite part. "The emperor decimated the families and told you all it was for the good of the people. Do any of you feel better off? People are starving in the streets. The emperor has failed us, and a man who fails his people doesn't deserve to keep his position." People at other tables were listening now, leaning in as inconspicuously as they could. But it wasn't enough. Neil stood on his chair and began to speak loudly. "The emperor doesn't deserve to reign!" he cried. "He deserves to lose his head. I suggest revolution!"

The bar fell silent. "You can't say things like that," the smallest man whispered from the back of the bar.

"I do not fear him," Neil lied with a cocky smile. Nobody scared him like the emperor.

"Those are big words," the bearded man said finally. "Who's going to start this revolution? You?"

Neil rubbed his hand through his hair. "You still don't know who I am, do you?"

"Enlighten us," the bartender spoke up.

"Look at my hair," Neil said patiently, dropping the cloak to reveal his dark hair, which had grown long and unkempt, but still was the dangerous telltale Vapros color. "Look at my eyes." He felt everyone in the bar studying him. People began to gasp. "Need another hint? I bought you a round. Who does that sound like, I wonder? This cannot be this hard for you."

The bearded man's eyes grew wide. "My God," he breathed. "We could be beheaded for talking with you, Raven."

He whispered the Vapros nickname as quietly as he could. Neil smiled and extended his arms. "Yet, here you are."

"Which one are you?" asked the small man from the back.

"Neil."

The bartender pointed to a sign tacked to his wall. "According to my wall, you're one of six remaining Lightborns."

"There are only three Vapros left," Neil confirmed. "We can't win this war alone. We need help."

A woman at a nearby table asked, "How did you escape?"

"We heard them coming and ran," Neil said. "We left behind our family. Some of them died that night. Some of them are in the emperor's dungeon. We will do anything to get the remaining ones back."

"So you don't care about us," the bearded man declared. "You just want your family back."

Neil took a breath. He'd been prepared for this. "I've spent the last two months on the streets. I have been hungry and scared and homeless. I have gone to sleep wondering if I will survive to see the sunrise. Nobody should live like that. I love my family," he emphasized, "and I want them to be free, but I want all of you to be able to eat first."

"Why shouldn't we just turn you in and get the reward?" the bearded man asked.

"Two reasons," Neil said holding up two fingers. " First, I'm a Vapros. Good luck with that." Several people chuckled and Neil continued, "Second, that might help you, but what about your neighbors? Don't you care about the future of Altryon? Putting me in jail isn't going to change the emperor's oppressive policies. In fact, you will be worse off. If you are going to fight the emperor, you need every Lightborn you can get."

That seemed to do the trick. Neil could see the fire of inspiration in every pair of eyes in the pub. "I'm not saying I'm interested," said the bearded man, "but if I were willing to join you, how would I begin?"

"For now, it's all about waiting for the right time. Stockpile weapons. Spread the word. Disrupt the empire when you can. Small isolated attacks keep the empire off balance and stretches their resources." He couldn't keep the grin off his face. He had them. "Just remember: we were beaten, but we have not been defeated. When you see us revolting in the streets, I hope you will join us. Goodnight gentlemen." He stepped down off his chair and the bar began to buzz with conversation. He was almost out the door when a voice stopped him.

"So, I've been searching for you for months and all I had to do was give up and go to a bar? You have truly impeccable timing, Neil."

Neil closed his eyes. Even after two long months of absence, that silvery voice was just as familiar as it had always been. And tonight, it sounded furious. He pivoted on his heel and faced Bianca. "It's been awhile," he said lamely. Her ivory hair was unchanged, but her eyes had an intensity he'd never seen before.

"We need to have a conversation," she said. Her eyes didn't leave his.

Neil took a deep breath. "Yeah, I know."

He reached for a chair to pull up to her table, but she shook her head and stood. "Not here." She wouldn't stop looking at him. He knew he must look terrible. His clothes were ragged and he was thin and unshaven. But all she said was, "Follow me."

He followed her out of the bar, pausing to throw several coins on the counter before he left. "Make sure everyone gets some food and another round." The bartender nodded and Neil followed Bianca out into the dark night. They walked in tense silence. "Are you going to kill me?" he asked, trying to sound like he was joking but genuinely afraid to hear the answer.

She stopped and looked at him for a few seconds. "I haven't decided yet," she admitted, but she didn't look quite so dangerous anymore and resumed her quick strides down the street. Exhaling with relief, Neil followed her through the dark streets.

Chapter Thirty-Five

BIANCA'S APARTMENT
NEIL VAPROS

"THIS IS WHERE YOU LIVE?" NEIL ASKED AS HE FOLLOWED BIANCA INTO the small but nice-looking apartment. They were on the third floor of a building in the working district. He had no idea how she was able to afford something in this part of the city.

"We are not going to discuss my living arrangements," Bianca said shortly as she took a seat on her couch. Neil sat beside her. "We are here to talk about why I shouldn't kill you."

Neil shifted in his seat. "I'm sorry about everything that happened over these past months. I don't know what else to say."

Bianca nearly growled. "You don't know what to say?"

"That's not what I meant," he backtracked. "Listen, you have to have some sort of idea of why I—"

"Abandoned me?" she offered. "Left me an emotional wreck as I wondered whether or not you were alive?"

"I was just going to say left, but that works too," he said sheepishly and brushed the hair out of his eyes. It had gotten longer since they had been on the run. "The situation's been complicated."

"Complicated? The situation's been complicated? I have been worried sick, not knowing if you were dead or alive, and you say it was complicated? No note, no nothing? You just vanish without a trace and that's your answer?" Her voice was hard, but tears burned her eyes. She took a breath and stared down at her hands as she said softly, "You were my best friend, Neil. How could you just disappear like that?"

Neil swallowed and bit back emotion as he took a finger and used it to lift her chin. She looked at him with those sad, grey eyes. "Bianca, I watched my sister die and practically my entire family was arrested and thrown into a dungeon. You've been my best friend since I was six. I don't know what I would do if I lost you, too. Look, I only have three people left in this world that I care about: Rhys, Jennifer, and you. I can't lose you too. I didn't want to put you in danger. Anyone who knows or cares about me is in jeopardy. I couldn't risk leading them to you. I thought when all of this was over I could come find you then."

"You couldn't have sent a note?"

"I couldn't risk it. You had to have seen the 'most wanted' signs and at least known I was alive and that they were hunting for me."

She nodded reluctantly. "I hoped and I heard rumors." She looked at Neil for a long moment and then squeezed his hand. "What about Victoria? You saw it happen?"

Neil winced. He still felt the pang of Victoria's death like a knife through his heart, but he tried to maintain his composure and said slowly, "The emperor's servant, Saewulf, killed her in cold blood."

Bianca's expression softened. "I'm sorry."

He said, "Don't be. Sorry doesn't bring people back."

"Saewulf." Bianca turned the name over on her tongue. "He's the psychic everyone's talking about. The one who can torture you without touching you, the emperor's new favorite."

"Sounds like him. He's the most terrifying human being I have ever met."

"How's Jennifer?" Bianca asked with trepidation.

Neil felt a sharp pain in his heart. "She doesn't think we notice, but we do. She's broken. She tries to hide it though." That was a very subtle way of saying it. Jennifer wasn't just broken. She spent nearly every night alone and sobbing.

Bianca closed her eyes. "What have you been doing for all this time?"

"As much as we can without going against the empire directly. We raid the homes of city council members who approved laws against the families. We stockpile weapons. We've been working with the Brotherhood of the Slums, but now we're starting our own group down in the poor district. We take out Imperial Guards. We go to bars at night and try to get people fired up. In the beginning, we eliminated arms dealers but the emperor has the Celerius's assets; he doesn't need them."

"What about the other families?"

Neil said, "I don't know much about them, actually. I guess Lilly Celerius is living with some guards and a servant. She took out a military outpost, but that's all I've heard. The two Taurlum are still alive. Darius tried to free his family, but he failed. He's a complete drunkard. I don't know how he's been avoiding capture if he's spending all his time in a stupor."

Bianca opened her eyes widely and stared at him. "You're all idiots," she said bluntly. "You have the same goal as the other families, and you haven't thought to ask them to team up with you yet?"

"Of course we've thought of it," he said, mildly offended. "We've spent endless hours arguing the pros and cons. But we always come to the same conclusion. There's no way it would work. The scars of this feud are too deep. We'd kill each other before we ever got to the emperor."

Bianca pressed on. "You can't disregard them. You're the only ones who have any advantage over the emperor and his guards—your powers. You have to reach out to them, or the whole thing is hopeless."

"Part of me knows that," he said reluctantly, "but the other part of me is having trouble accepting that my enemies since birth could help me save my family."

Bianca countered, "The old legend says your families have to protect Altryon—together. This could be what the prophecy was talking about! You have a duty."

"Maybe," he mused quietly. Neil leaned forward, placing his hands on his knees. "I'm going to have to go. Rhys and Jennifer will be worried. Life as a fugitive keeps everyone a bit on edge." He took her hand and squeezed it. "Are we good?"

She smiled a little and stood up. "Do I get a hug?" she asked. "I've missed your stupid face, Vapros."

He leaned in and hugged her tightly; he felt a sudden rush of emotion as they embraced. It had been far too long since he had experienced a sincere moment. He almost felt a sense of peace with his arms wrapped around Bianca's signature black leather armor. It, too, had changed slightly since he saw her last. It was trimmed with some kind of fur. "What's with the fur?" he asked.

As they separated, she glanced down as if she had forgotten. Her eyes lit up. "I've been planning a trip," she said excitedly.

Neil raised a questioning eyebrow. "What kind of trip?"

"The kind no one in all of Altryon believes is possible."

"Oh great, you're being cryptic," he said with an eye roll. "I see. I'll play along." He cleared his throat. "What kind of impossible trip, Bianca?"

She laughed, but still didn't give him a straight answer. "I met someone in the slums who said he was from somewhere very interesting."

"And where did he say he was from, exactly?"

"Oh, nowhere." She was drawing this out on purpose. "Just . . . beyond the wall."

Neil leaned in slightly and dropped the act. "Tell me more." In spite of the revolution he was trying to start, he'd never quite forgotten the plans he and Rhys had made to escape it all on that fateful night.

"Well," she said, shaking out her ivory hair, "he told me what's on the other side of the wall."

Neil could hardly contain himself. "Well? Desert and dead earth or?"

She smiled. "Cities—villages—civilization."

Neil exhaled. "Impossible."

She said, "Neil, we have been so sheltered. Everything we think we know is a lie. Altryon is just one city. There are villages outside the barrier. Some of them are at war with us—most of them, actually. The emperor isn't just defending us from savages; he's fighting a war with several villages full of other civilized people that are being enslaved by the empire. The emperor has been lying about what really goes on out there so that the people in Altryon won't join the so-called savages in their revolution. So that they won't feel bad about the oppression that's happening out there, and so that they'll keep obeying his orders. We think it's a wasteland of savages but it's actually not."

Neil's world began to spin. He let himself sink into the couch. "Who was this guy? How do you know he's telling the truth?"

She remained standing and began to pace excitedly. "He found a way to sneak through the wall. He has proof. He showed me documents that represented five different villages. Five! And all of them are outside the wall."

Neil raked his hand through his hair. "How the hell did you get this guy to tell you all of this?"

She paused. "Well," she admitted carefully, "I might have done some interrogating."

"Why am I not surprised?"

"I really wanted to know!" she said defensively. "He let something slip about life outside the wall and I couldn't let him stop there."

"Do you realize how incredible this is?" Neil said. "I've been trying to start this revolution for months, but there's already a war against Altryon! And there are several villages involved! If we could join them, if we could make it past the barrier somehow, we sure as hell can't stay inside the wall much longer without getting caught...." he trailed off, lost in thought.

Bianca was getting excited. "We could bring the other families," she suggested, and Neil groaned. "I know you don't want to, but it's our best bet. You need them. They're strong. We already know at least one of them is stronger than you," she finished with a wink, and Neil knew she was remembering the time she'd saved him in the markets.

"I'll admit I've been thinking about it for awhile now. I just don't know if they'll go for it." Bianca batted her eyes and waited. She always knew exactly how to wear him down.

"They might not want to end the feud," he said stubbornly.

"Is that any excuse not to try?" she persisted. "Getting through the wall would really help if we had a Taurlum's strength. They're probably tired of being hunted too."

Neil rubbed his eyes and tried to focus. "Okay, you could be right. And speaking of Darius Taurlum, I guess I'll try and track him down first. He's the one who needs the most help."

"When will you go?"

"There's no time like the present. I have some underground sources that may be able to help.. How much time do we have before you plan to leave?"

"Not a lot. I was planning to leave in five days. It's the day before the Emperor's ridiculous new curfew goes into effect. It will be too difficult to travel at night after that."

He stared at her for a moment. "What if you had left and I didn't know where you had gone." His stomach dropped at the thought.

"Unlike you, I had planned to leave a few clues that only you would have understood."

Neil's eyes widened in surprise. "Really? Ok, you can tell me about that later," he said as he ran his fingers through his hair. "For now, give me details. Everything I need to know."

She quickly explained and he listened intently. When she finished he smiled. "I think we can make this work. But I've got to leave now. We don't exactly have a ton of time. Any idea how I can contact you? I can't risk coming back here. It's too dangerous for you."

Bianca's eyebrows furrowed. "Leave a letter with Bill the Bartender at the Poor Chap's Tavern."

"We can trust Bill?" Neil asked.

"He's always looked out for me," she replied.

"Okay, perfect. It'll take me some time to find the other fugitives. I'll leave you a message that afternoon if I can get the others to help us escape," Neil said. He turned to leave in a hurry but stopped. He turned back to Bianca and wrapped her in a tight hug. "Thanks."

She smiled. "You're welcome. Now go try and end your stupid feud."

Chapter Thirty-Six

THE FALLEN GOD'S PUB
DARIUS TAURLUM

Darius staggered into the bar and hobbled over to the bartender. "Hello," he slurred. "A glass of ale, please, Mr…" He trailed off as he tried to remember the bartender's name.

The bartender continued to wipe off the counter. "You've got about seven tabs you need to pay first."

Darius smiled sheepishly. "Why don't we try for a record?"

The bartender pulled a glass from the sink and wiped it down before placing it on a shelf behind him.. "You set the record two tabs ago. You can't drink here. Either you pay or you get out."

Darius grumbled a string of creative curses under his breath and hobbled into the street. He looked around, remembering simpler times when he was allowed to show off his impeccable strength to all the civilians. It had been a long time since he had been able to cause unbelievable amounts of property damage. He hummed a few off-key bars of his favorite Taurlum drinking song. He wasn't worried about being recognized. He hadn't showered in about a month and his usual blonde locks had become matted and dark with filth. He wore a brown, filthy cloak that he kept pulled down over his forehead. His usual upright posture had been abandoned for a heavy slouch and his body had thinned from months of eating sparsely.

A small commotion was happening at a nearby stand. Unwilling to be left out, Darius half-ran, half-stumbled across the street to join the crowd. A vendor was attacking someone who had tried to steal from him. Darius raised his fist in the air. "Let me take care of this!" he shouted.

The shopkeeper glared at Darius. "Go home, drunk," he said. "Let me handle my own problems."

Completely undeterred, Darius plucked the crook out of the vendor's grasp with one hand and hurled him into the wall. He beamed at the crowd, ready to be praised. He was greeted instead by uneasy silence as the people in the crowd started to back away from him. Through his intoxicated haze, Darius realized that using his power had probably not been his wisest option. *No,* he thought moodily as he turned to sulk off into an alley, *the wisest option would have been to sit quietly in the bar and drink another ale. Why didn't I do that? Because you can't pay for it.* He sank to the ground and rested his cheek against the pavement. Oh, how his head ached.

"Well, you've certainly handled your change in circumstance well," the voice came from the entrance to the alley.

Darius didn't lift his head. "If you're here to kill me, do it before I sober up."

"I knew it was bad," the voice said, coming closer, "but I had no idea you were this bad."

Darius rolled over until his face was pressed completely against the ground. "Do I know you?" he growled, voice muffled by the street.

"Is that comfortable?" the voice asked sympathetically.

"No," Darius replied.

"Well, I'm not surprised that you don't remember me." Darius wondered idly if he were already dead and this voice his conscience. "After all, the last time I saw you, you were kicking me through your window."

Darius picked his head up and finally met the eyes of the young man standing over him. It slowly dawned on him that he was looking at another fugitive. A Vapros, he knew, but he couldn't think of the name. "What do you want, boy?"

The Vapros gave him a smile that was barely more than a grimace. "Neil," he said. "I'm Neil. And I need your help."

Darius moaned. "I don't help people, and especially not a Vapros."

"There's a revolution coming, Darius, and I want to know if you'll be a part of it. Someone has got to save your family."

Darius sat up angrily. "Listen," he growled, swaying a little, "my family can't be saved. I can't do it. I tried already. I'm the only hope for the Taurlum name now. I have to have as many children as I can. All the girls will be my wives!" He began to laugh. "And then I can have my own, new family. And drink until my steel heart stops beating!"

Neil sat on the ground next to him. "You're legacy phasing?"

"Call it what you want."

"That's unfortunate," he said. "My father went through a legacy phase once. He just wanted to protect his family line. He needed more kids, and it didn't matter where they came from. Your family and mine, they aren't so different."

Darius pulled a flask from the inner pocket of his cloak and took a large gulp. "You're talking to a wall, Vapros. I'm done. So is Michael."

Neil was unfazed. "We could always use your help, and so could your family."

Darius growled, "Don't try to guilt me into this, you little bastard!"

Neil pressed on. "I'm not. But you have to make a decision soon. You can drink yourself to death, or you can help save your family and right the wrongs that have been done. The feud ends here, Darius. We can end it."

"My God," Darius said as he took another sip. "What the hell are you talking about? You sound like a preacher."

"I am preaching," Neil said confidently.

"Listen, kid," Darius mumbled, fumbling with his flask. It slipped between his clumsy fingers and hit the ground, but didn't break. "One day, you're gonna give up hope just like I have. And when you do, I invite you to grab a drink with me. Maybe I'll let you buy me a round." He looked excited by the prospect. "But until then, get out of my face with your damn hope. It's making me feel sorry for you. I don't give a damn about the feud. I was born hating your kind, but now I don't care."

Neil stood up and looked down at Darius's pitiful, hunched form. "In three nights," he said, "we will be at the First Church of Enlightenment deciding on a plan of action." He had decided on the meeting place based on their encounter with the preacher so many months ago. The Man with the Golden Light was the one who gave them the powers that started the feud; it was fitting that his shrine was the place for the feud to end. "I think we are going to find a way beyond the wall. You can either be a part of that or not. But we'd love to have you. At least think about it. We don't need to interact ever again after we get through. We could go our separate ways forever."

Darius scoffed and stowed his flask in his pocket. "Night, kid," he said and rolled over.

"Think it over. Goodbye, Darius."

Darius waited for Neil to exit the alley before pulling out his flask again. He knew that it was inscribed with his family crest's motto, "Iron Flesh and Iron Will." He stared at it wistfully, remembering when it had been the source of his greatest pride instead of his greatest failure. He remembered what it felt like to be so sure that he would be with his family again. He felt sorry for Neil. The Vapros boy had been right about one thing: the two of them, in spite of being from different families, weren't so different at all. Nobody stayed hopeful forever. Darius was sure Neil would soon give up and find a place in the gutter next to him.

Chapter Thirty-Seven

CELERIUS HIDEOUT
LILLY CELERIUS

JONATHAN STUMBLED UP THE STAIRS WITH A BOX TWICE AS LARGE AS HE was. "Did we have to settle on the top floor of a building, Miss?" he asked from behind the box.

Lilly stood at the top of the staircase, examining the cargo her small army had accumulated. "This is discreet and out of the way. Don't complain. Just be happy we have a place at all."

"Yes, Miss," he said, finally reaching the top step and dropping the crate with a sigh of relief. "It's just . . . I fear each one of these steps is half as tall as I am. I just wish we didn't have to buy everything and move it in when it's the middle of the night."

She smiled for the first time in days. "You'll get used to it."

He sat on the crate and arched his back, trying to stretch out his aching muscles. "Are we still rich?" he asked hopefully.

Lilly gave him a distracted nod. She was inspecting cargo. "We're armed, too," she murmured a minute later. "We've been lucky." She turned to face her tiny army of Celerius guards. There were five of them left; they proudly wore their armor even though they were caked with mud to hide their original blue and gold colors. They all looked as exhausted as Lilly felt. Sleep had been scarce over the last two months. But things were finally turning around for the fugitives. With a heavy amount of bribery, Lilly had procured the attic above a bakery. It wasn't very big, but it had enough room for all of them to sleep comfortably on the floor. The owners of the place turned a blind eye to the fugitives' comings and goings.

"So," Lilly said to her guards, "here we are. We have a place to live, and we still have enough money from the treasury to afford weapons. I think the next step is obvious: recruiting. We have to make our army bigger, and I say we start in the slums."

The guards looked uneasy. "With all due respect, Miss," one of them said, "the slums and the Celerius aren't on good terms."

"They're poor," Lilly said. "We're rich. We can offer them money to help us. I don't see the problem."

The guard answered, "That is the problem. They won't be sympathetic to our cause. Your family turned a blind eye to their suffering. They'll be glad to return the favor."

"Anyone can be bribed," Lilly insisted, but the guards still looked troubled, so Lilly refined her plan. "The military, then. We'll see if anyone abandoned the army when the emperor attacked us. There could be allies there, right?"

The men nodded and Lilly smiled. "Fine," she said. "Tomorrow, we will start our recruitment. And in no time, the emperor will be dethroned!"

The men cheered half-heartedly and wandered toward the beds on the floor. Lilly went back to inspecting cargo. Weary as she was, she couldn't afford to sleep yet. There was planning to be done.

Chapter Thirty-Eight

VAPROS HIDEOUT
NEIL VAPROS

NEIL AWOKE WITH AN IDEA. HE GROANED AS HE SAT UP AND LOOKED around for his brother. His new room consisted of a mat on the floor with a dusty pillow. Rhys was across the room, sleeping soundly on another mat. Their "house" consisted of an empty abandoned building they found in the working district. So far, it had sufficed as a suitable base. Neil walked over and lightly nudged Rhys with his foot. "Hey," he said. "Get up. I think I have a way to find Lilly Celerius."

Rhys didn't open his eyes or react to the nudge, but replied immediately, his voice clear of any hoarseness that usually accompanied waking up. "How do you know she'll come with us?"

Neil stared at his brother's motionless form. "Were you even sleeping?" he asked incredulously.

"Yes, until you kicked me." Rhys finally rolled over and looked up at his brother. "How do you know Lilly will come with us? Darius

212

didn't want to. And I'm not even sure we should be looking at them for allies."

Neil turned to the closet and fished out his cloak. "Darius will come around if he sees other people joining us. After Lilly, we can look for his brother, Michael."

Rhys closed his eyes. "Michael's still in the markets," he said. "Someone told me he's all over the girls there. More than usual, he's trying to breed more Taurlum."

Neil raised an eyebrow. "How is he running around the markets and not being captured? That doesn't make any sense. Who told you that?"

"I don't remember," he said. "My brain needs a few moments to operate correctly. I was sleeping a few seconds ago, remember?"

Neil smirked. "Keep that brain operating; it might be the only thing keeping us alive."

Rhys smiled and opened his eyes again. "So, Lilly Celerius …." He got up and stretched. His hair stood out at funny angles, and Neil bit back a grin. "You think you can find her?"

Neil began fastening his cloak. "Rumor has it Lilly escaped with some guards."

"And?"

"Lately, someone has been buying weapons and armor from our arms dealer friend in the working district. Do you remember what was sold out the last time we went to buy knives?"

"Rapiers?" Rhys said with a smile.

"Rapiers."

Rhys grabbed his cloak from the closet. "I'll get Jennifer up," he said. "It's a good theory, Neil, a really good theory." He reached beneath his pillow and pulled out a knife. "Last time we saw her, Miss

Celerius wasn't a big Vapros fan," he said, stowing the knife in his pocket. "I hope she won't hold a grudge."

Neil mused, "Tragedy has a way of erasing past relationships."

Rhys gave him a half-smile. "I think that's a truth we can all appreciate."

Chapter Thirty-Nine

CELERIUS HIDEOUT
LILLY CELERIUS

"Jonathan," Lilly said for the third time. "Do not touch the grenades."

Jonathan pulled his hand away from the weapon. "But Miss," he said dreamily, eyeing the grenade with fascination, "if I could learn to use one, I could help your army."

Lilly gave him a glare, and he snapped out of his trance. "I'm not a soldier, of course, Miss," he said sadly, "so I'll stop touching the grenades." He gazed at the crate longingly, but stopped when Lilly cleared her throat at him.

"Was it just me," she asked. "Or was the arms dealer who sold us these unbelievably creepy."

"Well, Miss, I don't wish to be vulgar, but that man is referred to as the Pig."

Lilly laughed. Jonathan looked confused and slightly hurt. "Jonathan, I don't think referring to a man as a pig is considered vulgar by any standard."

Jonathan loosened his collar. "But don't you want to know how he got that name?"

Lilly laughed again. "I think I can infer, Jonathan. Thank you very much."

"Just be careful of him," he said. "I don't want you getting hurt."

"Jonathan, that is truly adorable. I'm a Celerius. I have nothing to fear from a perverted merchant."

Jonathan slumped. "I've just heard stories, Lilly." Her eyebrows shot up. He had never used her first name before. "Miss Celerius," he amended quickly, reddening as he realized his mistake.

"I'll be careful," she promised. His gaze strayed to the grenades again. "You know," she said hurriedly, and he looked at her again, "you've gotten quite protective of me lately."

He gave her a sad smile. "You tend to become protective of someone when you realize that they're the only thing you have left, Miss."

"Lilly," she said clearing her throat. "You can call me Lilly if you want to, Jonathan."

Chapter Forty

THE MARKETS
NEIL VAPROS

THE PIG SMILED, REVEALING A MOUTHFUL OF ROTTING, YELLOW TEETH. "Gee," he said smugly, "I'm not sure if I've sold anything to Light-borns. That would be illegal."

Neil rolled his eyes. "Now, we both know that's a lie. Don't play games with me. Have you seen Lilly Celerius or not?"

The Pig said, "I mean, maybe I saw her. I just can't seem to re-member. Maybe some coin would get me thinking."

Neil dropped a pouch on the counter. The Pig snatched it up, squealing greedily. "Have you seen her?" Neil repeated through grit-ted teeth.

"She picked up twenty boxes of weapons just last night. She had a few guards and a comically small servant come pick them up. They were on foot. Had to make a couple trips. The little one could barely carry one crate." The Pig chortled. Neil waited for him to finish. "And between you and me, Mr. Vapros…." The Pig looked around dramatically and leaned in to share his secret, "she was quite enticing. You Vapros are gonna kill her, aren't you?"

Neil wrinkled his nose as the Pig's breath hit him. "What?"

"You're going to hunt her down and kill her, yeah?"

"No," Neil said thoughtfully. "Something else is going on. Hopefully she won't kill us. Thanks for your help."

"So if you're not gonna kill her then why are you looking for her?" the Pig asked while obviously pretending to be nonchalant.

"Why do you care?" Neil asked.

The Pig overdramatically winced in emotional pain. "Why are you being so rude Raven?" He was almost spewing fake tears. "That's the problem nowadays. People don't understand that sometimes I'm just trying to be courteous or that I'm just a friendly chap."

"I hear from the women in town that you're a bit too friendly," Neil said.

The Pig gasped in horror. "Stop it!" he wailed. "I'm as delicate as they come!"

Neil raised his eyebrows. "We're going to get a group together and leave the city," he said, finally giving in. It wasn't like the Pig had any reason to share that information with anyone.

The Pig's eyes sharpened. "So you won't be buying any more weapons?"

"I'm afraid not," Neil said.

The Pig patted Neil on the shoulder from across the counter. "Well, at least let me leave you with a parting gift!" the Pig said as he lumbered out from behind the counter and over to a small cabinet by the backdoor of the shop. "You Lightborns were great customers."

He pulled a small pistol from the cabinet and shoved it in Neil's face. Neil backtracked a step and the Pig followed. "But now that I can't count on your business I think the reward will do well enough."

Neil groaned, "You are a spectacularly terrible human being."

The Pig shook his head vigorously. "I'm just a good businessman, kiddo!"

"Same thing," Neil murmured under his breath.

"Keep your social commentary out of my kidnapping, brat," the Pig demanded. "And no using your special little powers."

"Okay," Neil said. "Any other demands?"

"You bring your sister with you today?" the Pig asked.

Neil didn't answer. As the Pig squealed in delight, he absently lowered his gun a fraction of an inch. Neil used the minor distraction to materialize behind the Pig. Before the Pig could turn around Neil had his knife pressed against his neck. "I want to renegotiate," Neil said.

The Pig growled, "You're making a big mistake, brat."

"No, I think you'll have to get by without that reward," Neil said.

Before the Pig could respond, Neil felt a cold bar of steel come in contact with the back of his head. He fell to the ground with blurry vision and ears ringing. The Pig laughed loudly and sneered at Neil's nearly unconscious body. "Stupid kid!" he taunted. "I'm the richest guy in town! You don't think I've got guys watching my store?"

Neil rolled over and realized his assailant was one of the Pig's employees wielding a metal club. Neil wanted to fight the vertigo but his attempts to roll over only made it worse. "Boys! Get out here!" the Pig yelled.

A crew of out of shape men assembled in the main shop room. None of them paid Neil any mind. One of them belched. The Pig didn't bother to look disgusted. "The Vapros kid's siblings are nearby," he said, with a belch of his own. "Check all the nearby alleys and bring me whoever you find. Try to keep the girl from getting dinged up. I want her in mint condition."

Neil rolled over and tried to stand up. The Pig placed his fat foot on Neil's chest. "After we get them, then we should search the surrounding buildings for Lilly Celerius. The Vapros thinks she's nearby. Let's find her."

The men looked confused. One spoke, "You want us to kidnap a Celerius girl?"

The Pig nodded. "She's tiny. She won't be so hard. Knock her out while she's sleeping." He ran a hand over his bald scalp. "Just think," he said gleefully, "by the end of the night, I'll have a Celerius girl and a Vapros girl tied up in the back of my shop!"

The bell over the front door rang, signaling that a customer had arrived. The Pig glared at his men. "Go!" he mouthed, and they disappeared out the back door. He rushed around to the counter and put on a cheery grin. "Welcome!" he said.

The customer was a tall man in a mask. The customer didn't seem to care that Neil was nearly passed out on the floor. As he approached the counter, the Pig craned his neck back to meet his eyes. "Nice mask, guy," the Pig said. "What's that made of, steel?"

The man behind the mask just stared at the Pig. It even made Neil feel uneasy. He had a bow over his shoulder. "What's that bow made of?" the Pig asked. "Could you be convinced to sell it?"

"I heard the conversation with your men," the man in the mask said softly.

The Pig raised his eyebrows and looked at the door. "No way you could have heard that through the wall," he said stupidly. "You were outside the shop when we were talking."

The man pulled the bow off his shoulder. "Nevertheless," he said quietly, fitting an arrow against the string.

The Pig looked around anxiously. "What the hell are you doing, guy? Vapros! Help me!"

"Pig," the man said. "You have posed a danger to the one I am sworn to protect. For that, I am afraid you must die. I hope you find peace in the end."

Before the Pig could react, an arrow fired straight through his eye and he fell to the ground like a mason's sack of bricks. Neil wanted to stand and face the attacker but he couldn't. The masked man slung the bow back over his shoulder and exited the shop, leaving the arms dealer to rot behind the counter. After a couple of minutes Neil stumbled out of the shop after him. He stopped and put up the closed sign on the door. No reason to alert people to the Pig's demise while they were still in the area. He trotted across the street to the alley where his siblings had been waiting. Jennifer was standing near the entrance. When Neil got closer he realized there was a pile of bodies lying behind her. She didn't look phased in the slightest. Rhys looked slightly frightened. "So I assume the Pig wanted to make some coin?" Jennifer asked, gesturing toward the bodies.

Neil said breathlessly, "Yes, but he's taken care of. Some guy shot him."

"Someone we know?" Rhys asked.

Neil started to shake his head, but the pain stopped him. "I don't think it had anything to do with us."

"So what about Lilly Celerius?" Jennifer asked as she methodically turned the bodies to small piles of ash.

"It was her," he informed them as he rubbed his head where a knot was already swelling. "She sent her guards to get the weapons. And they came on foot. They're close."

Rhys peered at Neil, "Are you ok?"

"Took a metal rod to the head. I'll be fine and I'll tell you later. Right now, we need to find Lilly."

Rhys furrowed his brow, thinking. "There was a room for rent above one of the bakeries around the corner," he said. "Remember? We checked it out before we found our house."

A thrill coursed through Neil's veins, clearing his foggy head. "So we'll go ask the owners if it's still for rent," Neil said, his excitement building. "And if they say no, then we've got her!"

Jennifer rubbed her hands together, clearing the dust. "Or we've got some other poor sap who's renting the space and has nothing to do with the families."

"It's worth a try," he insisted turning toward the bakery.

Rhys grabbed his arm to stop him. "Aren't you forgetting something?"

"What?"

Rhys gestured toward the Pig's store. "There's a whole lot of weapons that suddenly just became available at a price that we can actually afford."

"Too bad he didn't sell groceries," Jennifer said. "I'm starving."

Neil patted Rhys on the back. "Good thinking. I was so obsessed with finding Lilly, I didn't even think about the weapons. Let's check out the bakery and then I'll head out to find Robert. He can gather up some men to come add this to our arsenal. He'll be thrilled."

Chapter Forty-One

CELERIUS HIDEOUT
LILLY CELERIUS

LILLY HEARD A NOISE ON THE STAIRS AND IMMEDIATELY SPRANG INTO action. She grabbed a rapier from the nearest crate and pointed it at the door, ready to slice the intruder in half. The door creaked open and she came face to face with three Vapros. It wasn't exactly what she'd expected, but she swung her sword viciously at Neil's neck for good measure. "What are you doing here?" she growled as she repositioned it right beneath his chin.

Neil raised his hands to show that he was unarmed. Behind him, his sister and brother mimicked his surrender pose. "Listen," he said, "we heard you're starting a revolution. We'd like to invite you to the one already in progress."

"You've started one?" she asked, not lowering her sword.

"Yeah," Rhys piped up. "And we are gathering up all the others who want the emperor to die."

Lilly didn't take her eyes off Neil. "I'm in it to kill Carlin, mostly."

Neil smiled the best he could with a sword at his neck. "That can be arranged, too."

Lilly lowered her sword and ushered Neil and his family into her makeshift house. She closed the door tightly behind them. "How did you find me?" she asked. "I was hoping to stay hidden."

"The Pig told us you bought weapons from his store," Jennifer said, examining her fingernails coolly. "We narrowed it down from there."

Lilly shuddered at the mention of the Pig. "How large is your rebellion?"

Neil said. "We have no way of knowing actually. We are doing what we can to disrupt military operations within the city and to arm the people. We have new intelligence that says there are five villages outside the barrier that have been at war with the empire for years. We think that with their help we can win this thing. But we need to get outside the wall to coordinate an attack on the empire. We could use your help."

She tried to keep her confusion concealed. "You know about the villages outside Altryon?"

Neil stared at her. "You already knew?"

"The Celerius have been in the military for about a century. Even though soldiers are given orders to be silent about what's out there... I've heard bits and pieces," she said. "I don't know if you're really going to find what you're looking for out there. From what I hear, even though the empire is forcing the idea of savages down our throats, things are still pretty rough out there. I can't believe that there might be a perfect revolution brewing."

"I know this is a lot to wrap your head around," Rhys said gently, "but if you're really considering the offer, come to the First

Church of Enlightenment in two days. Once the sun sets, we will be there. Hopefully so will the Taurlum."

"You're trying to unite the families?" Lilly said dismissively. "It won't work."

"We think it could. Let's be honest, we can't stay in the city. We've experienced close call after close call. I'm sure you have too," Neil argued.

A small man in a blue coat came rushing out from around the corner. "Intruders!" he exclaimed, raising his arm. His hand clenched a small round object. "Shall I throw, Miss?"

Lilly looked down and gasped. "Jonathan. Put the grenade down." The servant, looking sheepish, gently replaced the weapon in a crate by the door. "They aren't intruders," she said. "I can't believe I'm saying this, but . . . they could be allies—maybe."

"Allies?" Rhys said hopefully. "Does that mean you're in?"

Lilly hesitated. "I don't know yet. I . . . we have to discuss it first. I'm not sure you can be trusted. You Vapros are known for tricking people in such a fashion."

Neil looked at his siblings. "We hope to see you at the church. I know we've fought before, but I think it's time to bury the hatchet. We don't really have another option. We need each other, if we're going to make it past the wall. Once we get outside this city, you can go wherever you want. We can all go our separate ways. But before any of that, we need to make it past the barrier."

She turned her sword over in her hands. "I'll keep that in mind," she said finally.

Jennifer reached around to open the door, and the Vapros materialized down the stairs and away. Lilly closed the door. "Get the guards in here," she said to Jonathan. "We need to talk."

Chapter Forty-Two

THE OXBLOOD INN
DARIUS TAURLUM

DARIUS AWOKE IN HIS RICKETY MOTEL ROOM BED FEELING LIKE HE'D ingested acid. He stumbled to the window and groped for the latch before he realized it was already open. He pushed his head outside and took a gulp of air. The night wind against his skin was cool and refreshing. In only a few seconds, he felt alert enough to realize two things: first, that the window had been shut when he'd collapsed into bed, and secondly, there was someone else in the room with him. He whirled around just in time to see a long spike soar toward him. He ducked and the weapon embedded itself in the window frame.

Heart pounding, Darius stood up and yanked the spike out of the wall. It was attached to a long chain. He hadn't seen a weapon like this in months. The memories came rushing back instantly, and he closed his fist around the chain and turned away from the window. "It's been awhile," he said to the darkness.

A figure stepped out from the shadows and moved to stand in a pool of moonlight pouring in from the window. "It's been awhile since anyone wanted you dead," Anastasia said. She held out her hand. "I'd like my rope dart back, please."

He set her weapon down on the windowsill and stood in front of it. "Plenty of people want me dead."

She smiled confidently, her slanted eyes narrowing ever so slightly. "You won't trick me into revealing my employer," she said.

He took a step toward her. She held her ground. "I don't have to," he said. "I already know who it is. It's obvious."

She raised her eyebrows. "Is it?"

"You work for the emperor," he said, taking another step toward her. Anastasia smiled slightly, as if she knew the punch line to a joke he hadn't heard before.

"Not quite," she said, and before he could stop her, she dodged around him and lunged for the windowsill, catching the spike in her hands. He tried to grab her, but she slipped through his fingers. He lost his footing and staggered into the wall. She laughed. "You aren't so quick anymore, are you?" He swung his massive fist at her, but she dodged it effortlessly. He was breathing heavily. "What have you been doing?" she asked. Her tone almost sounded worried. "You're clumsier than last time—much clumsier."

"I'm a little out of practice," he panted.

She looked at him patronizingly. "Need a minute to catch your breath?"

He grabbed the bed and hurled it at her. She jumped back with a cry, but the bedpost struck her feet and sent her spiraling to the ground. Darius grinned. "No, thank you."

He approached and bent over to grab her, but she kicked him in the side of the neck. Her foot connected with a pressure point; Darius gasped and reeled backward.

"You're not as slow as I thought," Anastasia murmured, working her way to her feet.

Darius stood by the window, hand pressed against his neck. He prayed he wasn't bleeding. "I guess I'm not so out of practice after all," he said, hesitantly removing his hand and examining it in the moonlight. It was mercifully clean of blood.

Anastasia hurled her spike at him with a grunt, but this time he was ready. He caught it in midair and pulled hard. She went skidding across the floor, still gripping the chain. "I'm not going to die today, Taurlum," she hissed, jumping to her feet and throwing herself out the window. He saw her land on her feet like a cat on the street below.

In a rage, he threw the spike down after her. It landed almost two yards to the left of the target. Anastasia grinned up at him. "Until we meet again," she yelled, bending down to retrieve the rope spike and dashing down the street.

Darius stared at the retreating form in disbelief and then turned to push his bed back into place. When it had been reset, he sat and buried his head in his hands. "I need to find Michael," he groaned, collapsing back into sleeping position and cursing himself for letting the assassin escape.

Chapter Forty-Three

IMPERIAL PALACE
CARLIN FILUS

CARLIN BRUSHED PAST THE GUARDS AND PUSHED THROUGH THE DOORS into the throne room. The emperor didn't acknowledge his presence. He was lounging in his throne, gazing off into the distance. Saewulf sat by his side. Carlin cleared his throat. The emperor didn't move. "You wanted to see me?" Carlin said finally.

The emperor slowly turned his head toward the general. "I'm disappointed, Carlin," he said as he intertwined his fingers. Carlin couldn't help but notice Saewulf's stony face break into a tiny smile. "I am so very disappointed."

"About what?" Carlin demanded. "I've kept the savages under our boot. Our army is doing just as well as ever." Saewulf let out a small chuckle. Carlin glared at the servant and let his hand drift to the hilt of his sword. "Do you have something to say to me?" Saewulf didn't flinch.

The emperor stood and held up a hand for silence. "Two months ago," he said softly as he took a step down onto Carlin's level, "I sent you to murder the Celerius family. One of them escaped. Is she still at large?"

Carlin's jaw tightened. "Yes."

"And these Vapros, are they still at large?"

Carlin pointed desperately at Saewulf. "They were his responsibility!"

"And the Taurlum?" the emperor asked calmly, but there was a storm in his eyes.

Out of the corner of his eye, Carlin saw Saewulf smirking. "Still at large," he admitted, bowing his head.

"Still at large," the emperor repeated. "As the general of my army, I expected you to be able to handle this in a matter of days. Not months."

Carlin gritted his teeth. "I've more important responsibilities than worrying about a few missing teens. We are fighting a revolution outside the wall. What do you care about a few kids that don't pose any danger to the empire?"

"Oh, so now you get to pick and choose which of my orders are convenient for you to follow? Is that what you are saying?"

Carlin backtracked quickly. "Of course not. But we have bigger problems than a few kids. And this is a city of over a million people. We've had several close calls but the people are helping them. They're hard to find."

The emperor narrowed his eyes. "Oh, they're *hard to find?* My apologies, General; your total incompetence is forgiven in that case. I didn't realize they'd be *hard to find.*" Saewulf chuckled. Carlin wanted to plunge his sword into the servant's eye.

"Since they're so *hard to find*," the emperor was saying, "I'll give you a little hint. Darius Taurlum is hiding in plain sight, drinking his pathetic life away. You just can't seem to find the right gutter to pick him out of. And Michael Taurlum, he's in the markets, seducing every young woman he can find. Not exactly subtle, and not exactly *hard to find*."

A bead of sweat traveled down Carlin's forehead.

"Lilly Celerius is prancing around the city flanked by an entire squad of armed men. And the Vapros spend their time either burning down the houses of my associates or recruiting prospective combatants in public places. And you can't catch a single one of them? Did you never think to send someone to a bar and wait for the Vapros to just drop in?" The emperor began to pace in front of his throne. "Did I put the wrong man in charge? Virgil could have done this by now. Saewulf could have done this by now. Anthony Celerius could have done this in one night, if his own flesh and blood weren't involved."

Carlin couldn't look the emperor in the eye. "Father, I—"

The emperor whirled to face him. "Don't you *dare* address me that way." The smile was gone from Saewulf's face and an eerie silence filled the room. The guards in the room nervously shifted back and forth, unsure of where to go or how close to get to Carlin.

Carlin tightened his grip on the hilt of his sword. "Why not?" he asked. "Afraid your servants will find out you have a bastard for a child?"

The emperor stood completely still for a few seconds. The guards posted at the door sensed it was time to intervene and they approached Carlin. "Settle down, sir," one of them muttered in his ear. Carlin brushed him off.

"Never say anything like that again, boy," the emperor hissed, "or I will have your subordinates cut you down. I don't care who your father is."

A guard put his hand on Carlin's shoulder (whether to comfort or restrain him, Carlin didn't know), and whispered, "General, maybe you should leave."

Carlin punched the guard so hard it sent him unconscious to the floor. The other guard attempted to subdue him, but Carlin's sword was through his chest before he even drew a weapon. Saewulf started to stand, but the emperor raised a hand, and he sat back down. "Calm down, Carlin," he boomed. Carlin froze, panting. "You have another chance. But I want to see progress. Start with the Taurlum."

Carlin sheathed his sword and glared at Saewulf, who returned the look with a lazy, little smile. "Yes, sir," he said, straightening his coat. The guard he had punched stirred and tried to stand; Carlin brought his foot down hard against the man's face. A sickening crack filled the throne room. "Keep your psychic on hand," Carlin said coldly as he walked toward the door. "I might need him later."

The room was silent as the giant double doors closed behind the general. "Your son is a bloodthirsty maniac," Saewulf observed casually. The emperor nodded as he retook his seat. "I know," he said with the ghost of a smile forming across his lips. "That's what will make him so effective in our war."

VICTORY LIES WITHIN
THE ASHES

Chapter Forty-Four

VAPROS HIDEOUT
NEIL VAPROS

"WE'RE NEARLY OUT OF FOOD ALREADY," NEIL SAID TO JENNIFER AS he rummaged through their cabinets. He had successfully tracked down Robert, and his men were looting the armory at this very moment. The events of the day had left Neil excited, but famished. "I wish Lilly would have offered us some food. But then again, she wasn't exactly a gracious host." Neil smiled at Jennifer, but the joke was lost on her. Neil gulped down a stale piece of bread and continued his search.

Jennifer said, "Maybe Rhys will bring some back?"

Neil handed Jennifer the last piece of bread.. "Now that we might have the Celerius on board, Rhys is out trying to verify the legitimacy of Bianca's claims. He isn't looting tonight."

"Oh." Jennifer stared vacantly into space as she chewed. "Maybe Rhys will bring some back."

Neil stopped rummaging. "You already said that."

"I did? Oh, forget it then."

"It's fine," he said nervously, moving to sit next to her. She had pressed herself into a corner of their tiny kitchen and hunched over to rest her chin on her knees. She didn't acknowledge her brother. "Are you okay?"

"Yes."

"Are you sure?"

She closed her eyes. "Yes."

"Are you lying to me?"

She finally looked at him. "Of course I'm not okay. I don't understand why you're okay."

Neil pushed his fingers through his hair. "I take it one day at a time."

"She was your sister, too," Jennifer said bluntly. "And you and Rhys just keep acting like we didn't lose her." There were tears in her eyes. "Didn't you care about her?"

"Of course!" Neil felt his eyes widen as Jennifer's tears spilled over onto her cheeks. "Of course we did. But if we're ever going to avenge her, we can't waste time missing her."

It was the wrong thing to say. Jennifer let out a sob. "Waste time missing her?"

He looked alarmed. "No, that's not what I meant. It came out wrong."

He expected her to pull out a knife and stab him then and there, but all she said was, "I've lost a lot of people, Neil."

He waited, but she didn't say anything else. "I've lost a lot of people, too, Jen." He wasn't used to comforting his sister. "I lost Victoria with you. And we both lost Mom."

She wiped her cheeks, trying to erase the stream of tears cascading down her face. "You didn't know Mom. You don't have memories of her tucking you into bed and reading stories to you, and teaching you how to walk." She stopped, interrupted by a hiccup, then continued, "And you didn't lose Victoria the same way I did. When you have a twin, you're born together, you spend your lives together and you have a connection. You can tell each other anything. Even all your deep dark secrets." Her nose was running and she scrubbed at it furiously with her sleeve. "But I did. And now I'm going through everything alone."

Neil didn't know what to say. "You have me," he tried lamely. "You can tell me your darkest secrets, if you want to." He pulled her into an awkward, one-armed hug. "I know I can't replace either one of them for you. But I can try, if you'll let me."

Jennifer sniffled. "Have you ever betrayed anyone?" she asked quietly.

Neil hadn't, and he told her so.

"When I was young, maybe Rhys's age, I had this friend," she said, wiping her eyes and sitting up. "Edward. I met him at the Opera House. He came out of his box, and Victoria and I went to talk to him. This was back when Victoria was too shy to go get gossip on her own." She remembered this with a giggle. It had been so long since Neil had heard her giggle. "He was sweet," she continued. "And he always said exactly what I was thinking. Nobody's ever thought like me before. Not even Victoria, really." She gave a shuddery sigh. A fresh wave of tears started down her face. "So we talked to him for awhile, I don't remember about what, and then the opera ended and we had to leave. Edward said he'd walk us out. Victoria went ahead of me, so I could hang back and have time with him alone. She could tell we had a connection." Jennifer unwrapped her arms from around her legs. "He walked me all the way home. I don't think he meant to.

We just couldn't stop laughing, you know? And when I was about to go inside, he kissed me."

Neil tried not to look surprised. Jennifer had never seemed to be the romantic type.

"We made plans to meet again. We found each other at the Opera House, in the markets, in restaurants. We used to write letters in secret code and leave them at an abandoned stand in the market." She smiled faintly. "I think I loved him."

Neil couldn't help it. "What happened to him?"

Her smile faded. "I started my assassin training. I was busy all the time. And he was busy, too. He was going to join the military. He didn't want to, but it was his duty. It was a great honor to be a Celerius and go into the military."

Neil nearly jumped to his feet. "Your boyfriend was Edward Celerius?"

Jennifer swallowed. "I never told anyone but Victoria. I knew people wouldn't understand."

"Jennifer!" Neil shoved his hand through his hair. "You can't just date a Celerius! Don't you see how wrong it is?"

Jennifer's eyes were shining with tears again, and Neil almost regretted his words. "The families aren't even technically related anymore. It's been nearly three hundred years," she said defensively.

"That's not why it's wrong. We were at war."

"Don't you see I didn't have a choice?"

"You could have chosen not to see him again."

She shook her head. "I couldn't have. He was so perfect for me, Neil." She took a deep, shuddery breath. "Dad sent me out on a few assignments, and I passed them all easily. He told me I was the best assassin candidate he'd seen in years. And then he gave me my first actual assassination. It was a more difficult test than the others, but

Dad said he knew I could do it." She ran her hand over her ponytail. "It was Edward. I refused, of course. I told him I didn't want to be an assassin anymore. I couldn't tell him the real reason. He was enraged. He said he had information that, at that very moment, the Celerius family was plotting to kill me. My talents had not gone unnoticed. He told me they would be clever in choosing an assassin or a situation that I wouldn't suspect."

Neil's heart sank.

"I went to see Edward that night. I brought my knife. It was the first time I'd been to the Celerius estate. He let me in. He knew something was wrong. He saw me shaking." Jennifer was about to cry again. "He brought me up to his room and told me everything would be fine and that he loved me ... but he reached for something in his pocket too quickly and I thought it was a weapon. I—"

"Stop!" Neil felt like he was being strangled. "You don't have to say the rest."

She closed her eyes and took deep breaths. "It was one of those secret letters we communicated with. I thought it was a weapon. I couldn't cremate him," she whispered. "I couldn't."

The room was uncomfortably silent as the gravity of Jennifer's story began to settle on Neil's shoulders.

"That's why I warned you. About Bianca, I mean. When she helped you in the markets, a long time ago. Assassins shouldn't have friends. It's too hard that way. I don't want ... I won't let you put yourself through everything I went through. It's not fair. None of it is fair."

"Jen ..." He didn't know what to say.

"And I know you want to be an assassin," Jennifer went on. "I know you want it more than anything. You think it will bring you glory and make you a Vapros hero and help you find your advanced abilities. None of it's worth it, Neil. *Not one second* is worth it because you have to live with yourself afterwards. And now I have to remember it forever. Now I have this." She pulled her shirt to the side to reveal a tattoo slightly above her heart. It was a skeletal hand clutching a heart. "I told Father I seduced Edward, so this was the tattoo he gave me."

They sat in silence for a few minutes. "I'm sorry," Neil said. "About everything you've gone through. But you can't blame yourself for Edward. You didn't know. You thought he would kill you first. You have to forgive yourself."

"I don't know how much longer I can keep this up," she said. "Any of it. The planning, the recruiting. This is all hopeless."

"This can't be hopeless. If we give up, they win. Saewulf wins."

"I know. But it's hard." She sat in silence for a few moments. "What are you going to do when all this is over? Could you really just put all this behind you?"

"I'd try. I'd keep the family going. But not like it was before. I'm going to have a real family. A family that doesn't fight all the time."

"Every family fights, Neil. It's part of loving each other. Look at the two of us."

He couldn't quite believe his ears. "You love me?"

"Of course I do!" She punched his shoulder gently. "You're my baby brother."

"I know, it's just . . . you've never acted like it." He let out a breath. "What do you think you'll do when it's over?"

"I'm going to do something for Victoria," she decided. "It will be something big—maybe a memorial."

"I'll help you," Neil promised. "We'll build a statue of her and put it right in the nightlife district."

"You really think we'll make it out of this?"

"We will," he said. "I promise."

Jennifer laughed a little through her nose. "Don't make promises you can't keep, Neil."

"I can keep this one. I can try."

She stood up and dusted herself off. "I'm going to bed," she said. "It's been an emotional day. When Rhys gets home, tell him good-night for me."

"I will." Neil stood up, too. "Jen?"

She was on her way to her bedroom, but paused. "Yeah?"

"I, um … I love you, too."

She nodded appreciatively and disappeared into her room. Neil cocked his head, listening carefully, but for the first time in months, he didn't hear quiet sobs coming from Jennifer's bedroom. He tried to process everything she had just told him. Neil ran his fingers through his hair. He stared in the direction of Jennifer's door and smiled faintly. At last, all he heard was silence. Maybe there was hope for her, yet.

Chapter Forty-Five

THE MARKETS
DARIUS TAURLUM

MICHAEL WANDERED THROUGH THE MARKETS LOOKING FOR A woman to occupy his time. He wasn't drunk yet, but planned to be by the time he hobbled home. He noticed a pretty young woman at one of the stands and he grinned. Target acquired. Before he could reach her, he was grabbed by the shoulder and yanked around.

"Darius?" Michael said, confused. "What are you doing here?"

"Someone just tried to kill me," he said bluntly.

Michael still looked confused. "But you're alive."

Darius seemed exasperated. "I'd realized that by myself, actually. I fended her off."

Michael wrinkled his giant nose. "That's curious. Who was it?"

"Remember that assassin who tried to kill me in the Imperial dungeon?"

"No."

"Oh, I see your mind's as sharp as ever. Look, I'm in trouble. I need a new place to stay. Where have you been sleeping?"

"Calm down, kiddo." Michael said, "Let's take this one step at a time. Who would want you dead?"

"The emperor does, but I don't think it was him."

"Maybe it was the other families," Michael suggested, sneaking a look over his shoulder. The woman was gone. A little dejected, he turned back to his brother. "They might want to take you out."

Darius said dismissively, "No, I talked to Neil Vapros the other day. He wanted to help me. He's trying to get the families together. Think Michael! Who wants me dead?"

Michael's ears perked up. "He wants to get the families together?"

"Yeah, they're meeting tomorrow night at the First Church of Enlightenment. They're trying to find a way over the wall using some back gate of some sort. Focus, Michael! There's an assassin after me!"

There was panic in his voice, but Michael barely noticed. He rubbed his chin. "We should go," he said finally. "To the church, I mean."

Darius looked at him incredulously. "Are you serious? I thought we gave up on the revolution thing."

"We did," Michael answered. "But if people are going over the wall, you and I should be among them. Once we're outside Altryon, we're free men. No more being hunted." He leaned closer. "No more assassins."

"No more assassins." It sounded nice. "Fine, I'll be there. You too?"

"Absolutely, brother. I'll see you tomorrow night."

Darius turned on his heel and walked back the way he had come, leaving Michael to scan the streets, looking for another girl to occupy his time.

Chapter Forty-Six

IMPERIAL DUNGEON
CARLIN FILUS

CARLIN STARED THROUGH THE BARS AT HIS CAPTIVE WITH A WISTFUL smile on his face. Ever since he had achieved a position with the empire, he had loved spending time in the dungeons. A new wing had been added and nothing supplied him with more joy than wandering around the dark halls. A raspy voice called from the top of the stairs. "Oh, Carlin," Saewulf hissed. "You've picked such an odd place to pout."

Carlin scowled in Saewulf's general direction. "Leave me alone, servant."

Saewulf effortlessly used his powers to glide down the staircase to Carlin's side. "Such an interesting revelation that was," Saewulf mused with a dark smile. "I can't believe the emperor never thought to tell me about his connection with you."

Carlin glared forward, not bothering to face the psychic who was practically dancing around him. "I don't understand why he would. He's not particularly proud."

Saewulf thoughtfully pulled his long, orange hair away from his eyes and tied it into a ponytail. "If you would, I'd love a little clarification. How did you come to be?"

"Well," Carlin said bitterly, "when a man and woman like each other very much...."

Saewulf chuckled, his voice trickling out like cold water. "Was that a joke? From you?"

Carlin continued to stare through the bars. "The emperor once had a mistress before he was actually the emperor. I was born. I shouldn't have been."

"Interesting," Saewulf said. "It seems even he had a legacy phase. It's not just Lightborns."

"You don't need to be trying to spread your legacy to have children," Carlin responded. "He wasn't, anyway."

Saewulf peered into the cell at a prisoner for a moment. "Well, this explains your latest promotion."

Carlin finally turned to face Saewulf and his hand moved to the handle of his sword. "Pardon me, Saewulf. Care to repeat that?"

Saewulf wasn't intimidated; instead, he looked rather amused. "Carlin, are you honestly trying to tell me you were promoted purely because of your skills as a tactician or a strategist? Grow up."

Carlin looked ready to pull his sword. "I was given no advantage," he replied. "Ever! I grew up poor and joined the empire the second I could. And then I worked for it. I worked every blasted day until my fingers bled and I couldn't continue."

Saewulf said, "It's just odd. I heard that you blew through the ranks to your current position. It takes most generals nearly their entire lives to reach such a status. Well, all generals except Anthony Celerius. But with his strategic mind and swordsmanship, how could he not reach general quickly? How old are you Carlin? Forty? Forty-five? Celerius was only thirty when he became general."

"And look where he is now," Carlin spat as he drew his sword. "I put my blade through his chest and then I had his body burned. And he deserved it."

Saewulf sneered. "Because he was better than you? Because he was in your way of becoming a man your father would notice?"

Carlin clenched his sword and hissed, desperately trying to avoid playing Saewulf's game. "No," he managed, "he deserved it. I trained with him and rose through the ranks with him, but he was always praised because of skills he was born with."

Saewulf back-pedaled a few steps as Carlin advanced. "Oh, I see," he cooed. "It wasn't fair?"

"You're damn right it wasn't fair!" Carlin roared. "I spend every second training and bettering myself and some kid speeds through the ranks because he was born with certain skills? People who take advantage of their birthright and hold it over the rest of us are not to be admired as gods. They're to be exterminated as abominations."

Saewulf bobbed his head thoughtfully and his smile began to fade. "That's a popular theory," he said. "But not everyone who's born into privilege is an abomination, Carlin."

"The Lightborns are," Carlin said. "Them especially—the Vapros, the Taurlum and the Celerius. They don't belong out there with the innocent people. That's why I come down here. To remind myself where they really belong." Saewulf pivoted on his foot to look into the cell where Carlin had been staring. Inside was a body with arms outstretched, straining against chains that suspended him from either wall like a demented scarecrow. An iron mask had been fitted over his face and small air holes were visible. "They belong in one of two places: here in these cells or in the ground."

"That's Sir Vapros, eh?" Saewulf asked. "What's with the mask?"

"It limits his air," Carlin said. "He needs air to materialize. They all do. With the limited supply, he's left helpless."

Saewulf paused for a moment and then turned to leave. "It's been good to speak with you, Carlin. It's always interesting to see what makes psychopaths like you tick."

"Go to hell," Carlin murmured as he was left to examine the helpless prisoners.

Chapter Forty-Seven

FIRST CHURCH OF ENLIGHTENMENT
NEIL VAPROS

"No one is going to show up," Jennifer said glumly. She was lying flat on her back behind the alter, throwing her knife into the air and catching it by the handle before it hit her face. The trick made Neil nervous, but Jennifer never missed.

The First Church of Enlightenment wasn't a place Neil had ever spent a lot of time. He didn't believe in The Man with the Golden Light as deeply as his father did. He'd never really stopped to consider religion at all. He didn't know why the "Man" had chosen his family to gift or why he'd picked them to protect the city or why he'd never intervened when the feuding became heated.

Maybe he thought the feud couldn't be fixed.

"I say we head home now and pretend we never had this terrible idea to rely on our greatest enemies," Neil said.

"Yeah," a booming voice said from the door. "Enemies can be a bunch of flaky bastards, can't they?"

Neil jumped up from his sitting position on the stage and materialized down into the pews to get a better look. "Darius?" he said, squinting. The Taurlum swaggered down the aisle. "You look sober. And bathed."

Darius rolled his eyes. "That's because I am. You're a deductive genius." He leaned against the pulpit. "I'm not used to being in the same room as a Vapros without trying to kill it," he admitted, looking down at Jennifer.

"Welcome to desperation," she said, tossing her knife up again. Darius plucked it out of the air, catching it by the blade, unaffected by its sharpness. She glared at him, but didn't get up. "Did you bring your brother?"

"Michael's supposed to meet me."

Rhys poked his head out from the back room where he'd been combing the cabinets for bottles of wine. "There's nothing back here," he reported. "Which is a shame because I doubt Darius Taurlum will be able to see straight without a little—" He cut himself off quickly when he saw Darius standing on the stage wielding a knife. "Hello," he said nervously. "I don't believe we've met. I'm Rhys."

Darius handed the knife back to Jennifer and lumbered over to Rhys. "Darius," he said, catching Rhys's palm in a crushing handshake. Rhys winced.

"Don't hurt him, Darius," Neil said. "We need him in top shape. He's the brains behind this operation."

"Oh, you're a brain?" the Taurlum asked, dropping Rhys's hand. "What good is a brain in a fight?"

"I do battle strategy," Rhys said calmly.

"Battle strategy?" Darius looked thoughtful. "Okay. Let's say I'm going up against four Imperial Guards armed with bows and arrows and I'm not wearing any armor. What weapon do I use?"

Rhys's calm expression didn't falter. "Easy. You're a Taurlum, you would use a hammer." Darius opened his mouth, but Rhys wasn't finished. "But if you want to know which weapon you should choose, I would suggest a shield. You could use it to block arrows since you don't have armor and then, when they're out of ammunition, you could swing it like a club. Most people don't carry them because they're large and impractical, but that wouldn't matter to you."

Darius almost looked impressed. "That's not too bad, little raven."

Rhys said, "I just know a lot about battle strategy."

"Don't be modest," Jennifer called from her place on the floor. "Rhys knows a lot about everything."

"Everything?" Darius repeated.

"Almost everything," Rhys amended quietly.

"So, you know what the most sold item was in the market last year?"

"Apples," Rhys said without missing a beat. "Followed by salt, bread, and rice."

Darius wracked his brain for a harder trivia question. "Richest merchant in the market?"

"Well, it was Sir Taurlum, until the attack," Rhys said, brow furrowed. "But once he was gone, the man who runs food distribution was the richest. But then the Pig started branching out and selling more products. He used to sell exclusively weapons, but then he added masks and armor to his inventory and profits shot up. So the richest man in the markets is the Pig."

"He was the richest man in the markets," said a feminine voice from the very back of the church, "until two days ago, when he was murdered along with all his employees." Lilly Celerius glided down the aisle, head held high. Jonathan followed close behind.

Darius looked slightly let down. "Don't let it get to your head, kid," he told Rhys. "Celerius, I reckon?" he said, turning to the newcomer.

She barely nodded at him before ascending the steps onto the stage and turning to Neil. "When you told me you talked to the Pig, you neglected to mention that you killed him."

"I didn't kill him," Neil said defensively.

"Oh, please. They found arrows in his body. The Vapros are well known for using crossbows."

"That's true, but not anymore," Rhys said. "Until recently, we couldn't afford them or their ammunition. The Pig tried to kill Neil, and he sent his men after Jennifer and me. They were coming for you next."

"I'd believe him," Darius muttered to Lilly sarcastically. "This kid knows everything."

"So yes, we killed his men in self defense, but someone else walked into the store while I was subdued and shot him." Neil said.

"You didn't think to mention this earlier?" Lilly asked.

"I wanted to get you to the church," Neil said. "Honestly, it wasn't the first thing on my mind."

"Well, I would be lying if I said I was distraught. Given the state of the city, it comes as no surprise. Poverty drives people to extremes."

Neil considered bringing up the fact that the Pig's murder seemed deeply personal, but he refrained. Why should Lilly care why the sleaziest merchant in town was killed? He probably had hundreds of enemies. Lilly walked by the group and planted her feet next to Jennifer. "Are we all here? Can the planning begin?"

"The Nose isn't here yet," Neil pointed out, glancing at Darius. The Taurlum didn't look offended by the use of his brother's nickname.

"We'll catch him up," Darius said. "Let's get down to it. I say we start by finalizing the plan to make it past the wall."

Jennifer scoffed. "Subtlety be damned, I suppose."

Darius eyed her indignantly. "We Taurlum aren't known for subtlety."

Jennifer raised her eyebrows. "So I've gathered."

"I have a friend who knows a way out," Neil said hurriedly before a fight could break out. "I didn't bring her to this meeting because I was under the impression it was a Lightborn only sort of gathering." He glanced pointedly at Jonathan.

The small servant reddened. Lilly looked mildly annoyed. "He goes where I go."

"Just like a Celerius to make a power play on our first peaceful meeting," Darius grumbled.

"Actually that seems more like a Vapros kind of move," Rhys whispered.

"Anyway," Neil pushed on, "there is only one main door in the wall. It's used by soldiers and is heavily protected. I don't like our chances of sneaking through that way. But there is also a lesser-known back door."

"Explain," Lilly said.

Neil wanted to snap at her. He smothered the instinct and continued. "There is a special gate protected by a small guard house. It's near the Taurlum mansion and the Imperial Outpost. Guards use it to bring supplies out to the army, without attracting enemy attention. Sometimes they bring things in from the outside, too, like prisoners of war or negotiators. It opens once a month during the full moon."

"I think I've seen that building," Darius muttered.

"The next opening is tomorrow night," Neil said.

Lilly looked skeptical. "So soon?"

Darius looked at Rhys and grinned. "I'm sure there's a battle plan, right, buddy?"

Rhys didn't return the smile, but he explained calmly. "We go as fast as we can. We bring everything we have. We attack with our powers and we don't give them any time to regroup or call for reinforcements. Once we make it out, we scatter into the wilderness."

It wasn't exactly what Darius expected. "Sounds a little risky."

"I know," Rhys said, "but it's the best we can do."

"Why can't I just punch my way through the wall?" Darius asked. "Then we could go whenever we want."

"The wall is near thirty feet thick, two hundred feet high, and made completely of solid rock. It was built by dozens of Lightborns. It is truly the greatest architectural marvel to date," Rhys said. "The wall is also constantly manned and guarded. Tunneling would be loud and by the time we were halfway through we would have the entire army on our backs."

"One question," Darius said. "Will there be booze outside the barrier?"

Rhys said, "Maybe. If not I could teach you how to make it before we all split up."

Darius gasped. "You can do that?"

"Yes. It's simple fermentation."

Darius threw his hands into the air happily. Lilly rolled her eyes and cut off his cry of jubilation. "My group is five soldiers and four dozen crates of weapons. How do you propose we transport that?"

Rhys thought for a moment. "You might have to leave it behind."

Lilly looked offended. "I don't have impenetrable skin or materializing powers! I need armor. I need weapons!"

"You can bring some of it," Rhys said, "just not all. Darius could help you carry a crate or two."

"Anything for you," Darius said mockingly.

"You'll have to leave the guards, too. We can't sneak that many people through the wall. They need to stockpile weapons and prepare for the revolution," Rhys said.

Lilly looked like she wanted to argue more, but Neil cut in. "Listen, Miss Celerius. I understand you have different needs than we do. And you're used to being in control. Not now though. Everyone needs to check their ego at the door. That includes you, Darius and us."

She opened her mouth to respond but suddenly tensed up and raised one hand in the air. Her eyes closed. "Miss?" Jonathan said urgently, speaking up for the first time all night. "Is it happening again?"

Lilly snapped out of her trance and gasped. "Don't panic," she said, "but there are twenty men gathering outside."

Jennifer jumped to her feet. "What makes you say that?"

Lilly trembled. "Over the last month, I developed advanced abilities," she whispered. "I can feel sound waves and vibrations in the ground. I sense a large gathering of people walking outside. They're making a formation around the front doors. They know we're here. They're coming for us." She closed her eyes and stretched her arms out, reaching through the empty space in front of her. "There's a back door, yes? I can feel it."

"There's a door, yes," Neil said, a pang of jealousy coursing through him. Was he the only one without a heightened ability? "What brought upon your new powers?" he asked.

"I heard my father had been murdered," she said, and it wasn't in her usual icy tone. It sounded sad, and Neil remembered that he wasn't the only person who had lost someone in this war.

"We should split up," Darius suggested. "Meet in the orchards before sunrise. It's easy to hide in there. I've done it before."

"Okay," Neil said. "Lilly, you and Jonathan take the back door." They sprinted away, Jonathan falling behind almost immediately. She paused for a moment to let him catch up. "Darius, you—"

Darius grinned like a madman and charged straight through the wall and into the street, effectively forming his own way out. "Damn Taurlum fool," Jennifer grumbled.

"A fool who's on our side," Neil reminded her. "We can take the rooftop exit." He materialized to the uppermost balcony and then over to a ceiling beam. He grinned as he rematerialized, remembering the days when using his powers like this winded him for days. Now it was as natural as breathing. Jennifer and Rhys joined him on the beam and together they materialized toward the small door that opened up onto the roof.

Rhys led the way onto the rooftop and was immediately greeted by a volley of arrows. He gasped and materialized across the street on a new rooftop; the arrows continued toward his siblings. Neil felt a sharp pain across his arm and let out a cry. Jennifer sliced an arrow out of the air with her knife. "Neil, go!" she screamed as she began to panic. She had taken care of the first arrow, but seemed too disoriented to dematerialize. Neil grabbed her hand, gathered his concentration, and used his energy to materialize both of them across the street next to Rhys.

Rhys was putting archers to sleep right and left. Neil ducked behind a chimney and pressed hard against the wound on his arm. It wasn't much more than a cut but it was bleeding a fair bit.

Jennifer looked more disoriented than Neil had ever seen her. Neil grabbed her wrist. "Come on!" He summoned the extra energy to materialize with her to the street. The arrows followed them, shooting in perfect arcs over the roof of the building. They took off running but Jennifer lagged behind, gasping sharply with every step. Neil slowed and pulled Jennifer around a corner, out of range of the archers, and slid to the ground. When Jennifer collapsed next to him, he wrapped her in a hug. "We almost lost you."

A few tears fell down her face. "I …." She took a few shallow breaths. "I can't … do this."

"You can do this," he assured her. "Remember what I said? We can't give up. Or they'll win."

"I can't, Neil," she said softly.

Rhys knelt beside them solemnly. "Neil," he said, "her back." He looked like he was going to be sick. Neil ran his hand down his sister's back. His stomach turned as his palm slid over a jagged fragment of an arrow. The end had broken off, making it harder to see, but the tip wedged tightly into what could only be her lung. "Jennifer?" he said cautiously. "Do you feel okay?"

She smirked. Her ponytail had come undone, but she didn't care, or maybe just didn't notice. "Don't patronize me," she said faintly, "I'll be fine."

Neil rolled her onto her side and examined the wound. He and Rhys exchanged a glance. Rhys shook his head. "Neil," he whispered. "I don't know."

"It's bad, isn't it," Jennifer said. "You don't have to pretend."

Neil let her lie down. "It'll be okay, Jen," he said. "I promise."

"Don't make promises you can't keep, Neil."

Neil felt his eyes welling up. "No, Jen, I can keep this one. We just need to find someone who can heal you—a doctor."

Jennifer put her hand on Neil's arm. "Don't. I'd honestly rather just let it end now."

Neil pounded his fist into the ground. "Don't say that!"

"It's okay," she breathed. "You know better than anyone that I can't keep going through this without Victoria—"

Neil cut her off. "This wound is not that bad," he told her fiercely.

"I couldn't do it without her," she managed. Her eyes fluttered closed. "Couldn't do it alone."

Rhys lost his composure and began to sob.

Neil grabbed Jennifer's hands to comfort her and realized with a sinking heart that for the first time in her life they were cold. She sputtered for a moment and managed to keep speaking. "Don't be an assassin," she begged Neil. "It's not how you think it is. I spend so much time being angry … and alone."

"I won't," he promised, gripping her hands tightly. "I won't."

A smile ghosted across her face. She whispered something hoarsely and then with one last sigh of relief went limp in his arms. Neil buried his face in her body and wept as he felt the crushing weight of another loss.

It could have been hours later, or maybe only seconds, but the next thing Neil knew was Rhys's hand on his shoulder. "I don't think we can take her to the other side of the barrier," he said, voice cracking with tears. "We have to … you know."

Neil looked up at Rhys with red-rimmed eyes. "I don't think I can do that."

Rhys said, "I know. But she deserves to be … she doesn't deserve to be left here all alone." He put his hand against her neck. "I'll do it, if you don't want to."

Neil wiped his eyes and put a hand on her neck next to Rhys's. "I can do it," he said. Together, they watched Jennifer's body slowly dissolve into ash and float away, carried up over the rooftops by the wind.

Chapter Forty-Eight

THE ORCHARDS
DARIUS TAURLUM

DARIUS MADE IT TO THE ORCHARDS BEFORE ANYONE ELSE. **H**E HAD BEEN sitting in a tree for over an hour, holding as still as he could in case any soldiers had followed him. In spite of the danger he'd narrowly escaped, a thrill built in his stomach. He'd forgotten how much he loved going into battle.

Dawn was just breaking when he heard voices coming from below his perch. He swung himself down, grinning as he prepared to pummel the enemies. He stopped his fist just in time as he recognized his new unlikely allies. "You made it!" he said to the Vapros boys, smiling at Rhys. He didn't smile back. "What's wrong?" Darius asked casually. "And where's the girl?"

Neil looked at the ground. Rhys shook his head silently.

"Oh," Darius said. He tried starting a sentence but the words wouldn't form correctly. He tried again. "Well, if it means anything, I fought her a few times. She was brave and strong as hell. "

Neil looked up. "Yes," he said. "She was." Darius pretended not to notice the tears in his eyes.

A rustling in the trees made Darius's ears perk up. "Careful," he whispered, crouching over like a predator about to pounce. "There's someone here."

Neil and Rhys materialized into the branches of the tree, but Darius stayed on the ground. The thrill in his stomach was back. The rustling came closer, and he knew he should hide. He couldn't take on an ambush without his hammer, but he couldn't help it: he wanted to fight again.

A figure burst through the bushes and before Darius could make out a face, four hands came down from the tree and grabbed the unwanted guest. In a flash, Neil and Rhys materialized to the ground, holding a struggling girl between them.

"What the hell was that?" the girl gasped.

Neil threw her to the ground. "You just materialized," he said, panting a little. Materializing with another person was a lot harder than going alone. "Why did you follow us?"

The girl struggled to her feet and pushed her hair out of her face. Darius finally recognized her. "Anastasia," he growled. He planted his foot against her shoulder and kicked her hard. She toppled over. "You might be the most persistent person I've ever met. That doesn't seem to have worked out for you too well." He leaned over her. "Who sent you?" His voice came out in a roar that was so loud the Vapros boys flinched.

She didn't flinch, just turned her head and spat on his boot. "Go to hell."

Two sets of footsteps rustled into earshot. Darius groaned. "Who is it now?"

The footsteps stopped. "What happened here?" Lilly's voice asked.

Darius glanced up. "This girl has tried to kill me three times. It's time to find out why."

Lilly cocked her head and looked at Anastasia. "She won't talk?"

"No," Darius said. "And I think I'm going to pull off her fingers."

Anastasia gasped.

Lilly stepped forward quickly. "No, allow me," she said. "I'll make her talk."

Jonathan (*of course Jonathan was here*, Darius thought) spoke up. "Miss, I don't know if you should do this."

"Jonathan," she said calmly, "I can handle it." She bent down to place her hand on Anastasia's forehead. "You see, this power I've developed started out as a weapon of sorts."

Anastasia began to shake spastically.

"What's happening to her?" Rhys asked curiously.

Lilly kept her eyes closed. "I can send energy through things. When I do it to the ground and the air, nothing really happens. But when I do it to people they react poorly."

Anastasia screamed.

"Just tell us why you're trying to kill the Taurlum," Lilly said soothingly, "and I'll make it all go away."

"The Nose!" the assassin screamed. "Michael Taurlum hired me!"

Lilly took her hand away. "There's your answer."

"She's lying," Darius growled. "Michael is my brother."

Lilly moved to put her hands back on Anastasia's forehead, but the hostage shrieked, "I swear it was him! He wouldn't tell me why! Please, don't touch me!"

"If Michael hired you, then you must know where he is," Darius said. "If you don't tell me now, I will crush you in my hand like a stick."

Anastasia trembled. "He's in the old Taurlum mansion. The Imperial Guards know he's there, but they haven't captured him. I don't know why."

Darius looked confused. "He's living in my house?"

Anastasia nodded, but he wasn't paying attention to her anymore. "I have to find Michael," he said to his group of allies. "I have to get to the bottom of this."

Neil reached for his knife, his face red with fury. "This was you!"

"What?" Darius asked turning his attention away from Anastasia. Neil was upon him in a second, swinging his knife rabidly. It bounced off Darius's stomach and he stumbled backwards. "Whoa kid! What the hell do you think you're doing?"

"Someone ratted us out. Someone told the empire where we were going to be and now Jennifer is dead. This is because of you and your damn family!" Neil advanced slowly. For a moment Darius was sure that there was steam coming off of Neil's body. Rhys stepped in front of Neil and raised his hands calmly. Neil said, "Don't defend him."

"I'm not." Rhys had tears in his eyes too. "But think, Neil, settle down and think. Darius was there, too. So was Lilly. If Michael knew we were going to be at the church, then it must have been him. If this was anyone's fault, it's purely Michael's. And Darius is just as confused as we are. He was betrayed."

Neil glared at Darius over Rhys's shoulder. "This was such a mistake—trying to get the families back together. This feud is in our blood. Trusting you is just going to get us all killed."

"Listen kid," Darius said slowly, "I'm just trying to figure this out. I had nothing to gain from your sister getting killed. All I want is to know what's happening. I'm going to find Michael right away."

Neil sheathed his knife and stumbled backwards. He ran his fingers through his hair and tried to think. "I'm sorry, but you can't," he said. "Every day we stay here is another day we risk our lives. The gate won't be open for another month. We're leaving tonight, with or without you."

Anastasia took this opportunity to jump to her feet and sprint away through the brush. Lilly started to chase after her, but Darius grabbed her arm to stop her. "Don't bother," he growled. "We have to find Michael."

"What if she goes to the emperor?" Lilly said.

"She's not working for the emperor," Darius growled. "She's working for someone else."

"And that someone else appears to be Michael," Rhys said.

"Look," Darius said growing annoyed, "I'm confused about all of this. I don't know why Michael would do this, but I've got to go see him. I've got to know what's going on."

"If you go after your brother, you'll have to go alone," Neil said. "The rest of us are getting out of here."

"I'll meet up with you before we leave, then."

Rhys's brow was furrowed. "Michael never showed up to the church ..."

"He's the one who told me I should go," Darius said. "He said he'd meet me."

"But he never did," Rhys confirmed. "And instead, we were ambushed by the Imperial Army. The same Imperial Army that's letting Michael live in your old house."

"What are you implying?" Darius said as he noticeably clenched his fists.

"Michael could be feeding the emperor information in exchange for his own freedom," Rhys said.

Darius punched a tree trunk so hard it toppled over. "My brother is not a traitor. This is something we just need to clear up."

"Maybe not, but it all adds up, don't you think?"

Darius started walking. "I'm getting to the bottom of this," he said.

Rhys scrambled after him. "I'll go with you," he said. Darius felt a rush of gratitude at not having to face his brother alone. Darius felt confused about his feelings. Why would he want a Vapros to accompany him anywhere? For a moment Darius felt hope, maybe they could actually learn to overcome the feud. But those feelings were quickly replaced with skepticism when he heard Neil rush to catch his brother.

"Oh no, you won't!" Neil grabbed Rhys and pulled him back. "There is no way in hell you are getting in the middle of this." Darius glanced at Neil who was glaring at his brother protectively. It was clear that Neil definitely didn't want Rhys to be alone with two Taurlum, especially if one was working for the emperor. "Rhys—" Neil started, but his brother interrupted.

"If Michael ordered this attack, then it's his fault Jennifer is gone. I want revenge too, Neil." Rhys lowered his voice and pulled Neil to the side but Darius overheard him say, "We need to know who we can trust and who we can't, Neil. Michael might be able to fool Darius, but I will know the truth. It has to be me. You have to get word to Bianca. Let me do this."

Neil didn't look convinced. Darius's head was swimming and he was sure that the Vapros boy felt the same. "Fine," Neil said as he rubbed his temples. He raised his voice to include Darius. "You can go kill Michael, but not yet. None of us has slept all night. You need a few hours rest before you kill anyone."

"We aren't going to kill him," Darius protested, but he did feel exhausted. "We're going to get an explanation. My brother would never betray our family."

Neil looked like he wanted to argue but he simply nodded. "Just rest first. Rhys and I have had a hard day."

"Well then follow me," Lilly said. "My home can accommodate us all."

VICTORY LIES WITHIN
THE ASHES

Chapter Forty-Nine

LILLY'S HIDEOUT
NEIL VAPROS

LILLY LED THEM TO HER SAFE HOUSE, AND THE GROUP FOLLOWED
her up to her rented attic. "This is definitely nicer than where I live,"
Darius said as he took a seat at Lilly's kitchen table.

"We took a lot of money from my home before it burned," Lilly
explained. "We can afford the rent here. And we paid off the owners
to keep their mouths shut about us living here."

Jonathan went to the cabinet, pulled out a loaf of bread and a
bottle of wine, and placed it in the center of the table. No one took
a drink and Darius noticed. "Nothing to drink, tiny shadow man?"
he taunted.

Jonathan seemed more confused than offended by the insult. "It
is improper for servants to drink with their superiors," he said. "And
… tiny shadow man?"

Darius tore off a piece of the bread. "You're never far behind … Lilly." It was a struggle to use her given name. "Kind of like a shadow."

"I am like her shadow," Jonathan said emotionlessly. "I won't let harm come to Miss Celerius."

No one else reached out for the bottle. Not even Darius. "You don't drink?" Darius asked the table.

Lilly said, "Not anymore. Not after it almost cost me my life."

The Vapros boys murmured in agreement. Darius sighed and handed the bottle back to Jonathan. "I guess there's no time like the present," he grumbled.

Jonathan replaced the bottle in the cabinet, exchanged it for a pitcher of water, and returned to the silent table awkwardly.

"So, we already know you're always at her heels," Darius said to the tiny servant. "Say a horde of troops came after 'Miss Celerius.' What would you do?"

Jonathan looked determined. "I would not have to do anything," he said confidently. "Miss Celerius is fully capable of handling attackers herself. But if I needed to step in, I would kill them."

Darius chuckled. "You?"

"Yes," his eyes narrowed fiercely. "All of them."

Darius grinned. "Well, I'm glad to have you on our side, tiny savage," he said, patting Jonathan on the back. He pitched forward, unprepared for the Taurlum's strong hand against his shoulder. Darius pulled back immediately, muttering an apology.

"What do you guys think you're going to do when you get outside the wall?" Rhys asked, chewing thoughtfully on a piece of bread.

Lilly drummed her fingers on the table a few times. "Well, I had an uncle who was banished," she said finally. "I'll try to find him."

"What about joining the war against Altryon?" Neil asked.

"I'll get to that eventually. I want to find my uncle first." She ripped off a chunk of bread as properly as she could. "I've lost a lot of people in this war. I'm not so eager to jump right into another one."

"I understand. I'm not sure if I'd join the war, either," Neil admitted quietly.

Rhys nearly dropped his bread. "What?"

Neil covered his face with his hands. "Do you ever think about how things could actually be better if we didn't have to be a part of the Vapros family?"

"We have to save our family," Rhys said.

"I know that," Neil muttered. "But do you really miss it? Do you miss the pressure? Do you miss being beaten? Do you really miss everything Father did to us?"

"Stop." Rhys said. "I know you got the worst of it, but Father was good to Jen and me."

"Really? Because to me, it looked like he wouldn't let you be a human being. Do you ever wonder what it would be like to be able to be a normal person or even wear spectacles for that matter?"

"Okay, so he wouldn't let me wear spectacles, but that doesn't mean I want to abandon him. And he never did anything to Jen. She was fine—"

"You're a smart kid, Rhys," Neil interrupted. "You're smarter than I am. So don't sit there and pretend that at the end of the day Jennifer was okay. Don't pretend that you didn't notice anything."

Rhys was silent, but his jade eyes teared up. Neil's eyes flicked over to Lilly. "Look, we can talk about all of this later but I think we both know that there were a lot of things we didn't know about Jennifer. Let's not insult her by saying she was 'fine' when we both know she wasn't."

Neil stared at him for a moment and then ran his hands through his hair. "I love our Father," he continued, "and I want to see him and the rest of the family free, but I've lost a lot of people, too. I only have two really important people left. I would rather take them and run far away. Just keep them safe with me."

"Two important people?" Darius echoed. "Who's the second?"

"She's a girl from the streets. You wouldn't know her." Neil thought for a second. "Actually, you would. Do you remember the girl who knocked you out in the markets once? The day before you attacked the Opera House?"

Darius laughed a little. "How could I forget?"

"Well, that's Bianca, my best friend. She's the one who told me about the back gate in the barrier."

Darius said, "I can't believe I'm relying on a street girl who made me a laughingstock."

"She's not part of your family, though," Lilly mused. "This isn't her war. Would she still want to leave with you?"

"Would Jonathan want to leave with you?" Neil countered.

All eyes turned to the servant. "Miss Celerius is my duty," he said formally. "I have no choice but to leave with her."

"Right," Neil said. "But do you want to? Are you happy about going?"

He didn't miss a beat. "Of course I am."

"And what about the fighting?" Darius jumped in. "This isn't your war, Shadow Man."

Jonathan reddened. "My family has served the Celerius for generations. I may be a servant, but I still wear a Celerius military coat." To prove it, he carefully adjusted one of the buttons on his oversized jacket.

Darius wasn't satisfied. "If Lilly died, would you continue on?"

Jonathan looked at his hands. "I serve the Celerius family, in life and in death." He didn't sound completely sure. He wouldn't meet anyone's eyes.

Darius, sensing it was time to let the subject drop before Jonathan cried, moved on. "What about you, Lilly?"

"What about me?"

"You have a military coat. Why? Most Celerius girls don't choose to look poised for battle at all times."

She smiled. "I am not most girls."

Darius opened his mouth to continue his interrogation, but Neil jumped in before he could offend anyone else. "Why are you asking so many questions, Darius?"

Darius said, "I've spent my life hearing stories about how horrible your families are, and now I'm about to go into battle with you. It's probably about time I learn some truths, don't you think?" He looked at Rhys. "I already know you're a brain. But what about your brother?" His eyes settled on Neil. "What about you, kid? Got any stories to tell? You seemed like a more enthusiastic guy when we first met. I miss the preaching."

"I don't feel like preaching anymore," Neil replied. "I've lost both of my sisters, I'm not sure how I feel."

"I'm used to losing people," Darius said, trying to be comforting. "It's been happening since I was born. Taurlum would go on raids, and a few wouldn't come back. You learn to live with it."

This didn't make Neil feel better. "Well, I'm running out of people to lose." A silence settled over the table as each person remembered the loved ones lost.

"I have a question for you," Jonathan said boldly to Darius. The Taurlum looked mildly surprised. "Sir Anthony used to talk about his adventures in the Taurlum Coliseum. Is that a real place?"

Darius said, "Of course it's real!" The Coliseum was in the basement of the Taurlum mansion. It was a giant battle arena where prisoners were pitted against animals, soldiers, and sometimes members of the Taurlum family. He'd grown up watching fights to the death.

"And is it as horrible as they say?" Jonathan asked.

"I used to play in it with Michael when there were no battles going on. It was like a playground as a kid. I even fought in it for real once. I won—clearly."

"Did you fight my brother?" Lilly asked.

"I don't remember Anthony Celerius, but if he lived to tell the tale, then whoever he was fighting is long gone. Coliseum battles are to the death."

Lilly shuddered. "That is absolutely gruesome."

"What about Nicolai Taurlum?" Rhys asked. Neil felt a thrill course through his veins. Nicolai Taurlum, the Sewer Man, was one of his favorite myths. "Is he real?"

"Yeah, Uncle Nicolai was real. People talk about him, but I don't really remember him too well. People say he was the biggest Taurlum."

Neil's jaw dropped. "He's real?" he said incredulously. "Did he really escape the Imperial Guards and live in the sewers?"

Darius said, "I have no idea. He probably ditched the sewers years ago, if he did survive."

"Oh." Neil was disappointed.

Rhys yawned. "I'm going to sleep," he announced, rising from the table. Darius followed suit. "We have a big day ahead of us."

Neil agreed. "A gate to get through, a Taurlum to kill—"

"We aren't going to kill him," Darius interrupted. "He's innocent."

"A Taurlum to talk to," Neil amended. "Either way, we should all get to bed."

They began to strip off their armor. "So, the Vapros eating children: true or false?" he heard Darius ask Rhys as they settled into their positions on the floor. Neil closed his eyes. The last thought that entered his mind, before he drifted off to sleep, was one of confusion. For once in his life, he had shared an amicable moment with his lifelong enemies. But where did the feud end? Was it something that could be overcome or was it something destined to continue forever? Could he ever really trust Darius and Lilly or were they just using him to escape? Would they then try and kill him and his brother?

Neil awoke to the sounds of Jonathan sweeping the room. He sat up and rubbed a hand through his hair. "You do this every morning?" he asked, eyes squinted against the light pouring in through the window. It had to be about midday.

Jonathan didn't look up. "Anything Lilly needs," he said, not pausing in his diligent cleaning.

Neil whistled. "Why didn't we ever have servants as loyal as you? When we were attacked, all our servants ran for the hills."

Jonathan said, still staring at the floor, "I don't have anyone else. Carlin's men killed my parents that night. Lilly is the only family I have left. I took a vow to care for her a long time ago."

Neil groaned as he stood up. "Have you seen my armor?"

"It's being cleaned by one of the guards," Jonathan replied, sweeping his small dust pile into a dustpan. "I'll have it to you soon."

"Wow. Thanks." Neil flopped back down onto the floor. "Any ideas about what you're going to do once we're outside the wall?"

"Lilly's going to join the rebellion, eventually, of course," Jonathan said, tucking the broom away in the corner. "But I'm not cut out for that life. I'll wait until she joins up and then I'd like to settle down. Find a nice girl, start a family. Lilly pulled me aside last night to talk to me and told me that once we're outside the wall she wants to free me. Let me live some other kind of life."

"Any wife of yours would be lucky," Neil said.

"Well, one thing is for certain. She'd never have to lift a finger."

"It's funny," Neil said, folding his hands behind his head and looking up at the slanted roof, "I've spent all this time wanting to start a revolution, but now that it's happening I think I want the same thing you want."

"A family?"

"Yeah." He rolled over to look at Jonathan. "Do you think that's weak?"

Jonathan shook his head. "I think it's admirable. War is fueled by hatred. A family is something to love."

Neil smiled slightly. "How many hours until sunset?"

"About six. You all slept very late. But I suppose you deserved it."

"Well, now I'm up," he declared. "Time to train."

"So, tonight's the night," Darius said, dropping into push-up position in the middle of the room. "How do you Vapros prepare for a battle?"

Rhys watched Darius do a few push-ups. "We practice our balance. It helps with materialization." He looked toward the door as Neil entered. "You're awake," he noted. "Finally. Where's Lilly?"

"No idea," Neil said.

"Miss Celerius is preparing for the day," Jonathan supplied.

Darius paused mid-push-up. "So she's training?"

"She's doing her hair."

"What?" Darius almost dropped himself. "That's how she prepares? She combs her hair?"

Jonathan seemed confused by the question. "Um . . . yes?"

Darius rolled his eyes and muttered something that sounded distinctly like, "Women."

Neil materialized up to the rafters of the attic and let himself fall. A few inches before he hit the ground, he materialized back up to the ceiling and caught a rafter in his hand. Meanwhile, Darius dusted himself off and moved to sit on a dusty couch. "That's all you do to warm up?" Neil asked between materializations. "A handful of push-ups?"

Darius followed the bouncing Vapros with his eyes. "I weigh four hundred pounds," he said casually. "It's a good amount of lifting. And anyway, I'm already stronger than the Imperial Guards. I was just working out because Rhys says it's 'necessary' if I'm going to go into battle."

"You weigh four hundred pounds?" Rhys asked with interest. "I never would have guessed that. Your footsteps aren't as loud as I would have expected."

Darius flexed his bicep. "Skin of steel comes with the weight of steel."

The door to another room opened and Lilly stepped in. Her hair and makeup were done to perfection. Neil let himself land on the ground and pushed a hand through his hair a little self-consciously. He'd hardly even looked in a mirror the better part of two months. "Good morning, gentlemen," Lilly said, taking a seat beside Darius on the couch. "Training for this evening?"

Darius nodded and fell back into push-up position, this time using only one arm. Rhys looked impressed. "Four hundred pounds," he said under his breath. "Unbelievable."

"Does anyone want to spar with me?" Lilly asked. "You know, to practice for tonight?"

Darius laughed. "You don't want me," he assured her. "I'm nowhere near as fast as you."

"I'll do it," Neil said.

Lilly pulled two wooden swords out of the crate on the floor and tossed one to him. "Be careful, Vapros," she warned as she whipped her sword around in a circle. "I've been training." Neil brandished his sword confidently and lunged at her. She was expecting it, blocked him effortlessly, and parried. Before she could finish him off, he materialized behind her. She ducked beneath his weapon and blocked his sword. But just barely. "You've been training too," she exclaimed, preparing to strike again.

"Living as a fugitive gave me a little practice," Neil said, swinging his sword toward her neck.

She dodged the blow and quickly swiped her sword against his back. "Gotcha!" Neil stumbled forward, wincing a little at the pain. Lilly smiled triumphantly and patted daintily at her hair. Inexplicably, it had all stayed perfectly in place. "Best two out of three, Vapros?"

"Apologies Miss Celerius," Neil said with a sarcastically elegant bow. "I've got a little errand to run."

VICTORY LIES WITHIN
THE ASHES

Chapter Fifty

THE POOR CHAP'S TAVERN
NEIL VAPROS

Neil did his best to make it through the city quickly, but his fugitive status made it especially difficult. Wanted posters were plastered around every square and on every major road. To make matters worse those roads were also the most popular, which meant he'd have a greater chance of being recognized despite his disguise and turned in for the reward. These factors, working in tandem with the fact that it was the middle of the day, made it nearly impossible to get anywhere quickly, even if he wasn't travelling very far. Neil darted from alley to alley and never lingered anywhere so that no one would be treated to anything more than a passing glance. The streets were unusually crowded today and Neil had to revise his route several times. Since their escape that terrible night, Neil and his siblings had picked up new clothing around the city and burned anything that was remotely purple. He now wore a tight brown coat that covered his midsection just enough to hide his armor. Rhys had also sewn on a brown hood to match and Neil kept it pulled far over his forehead to hide any stray, raven-colored hairs.

He eventually reached his destination, The Poor Chap's Tavern, and slipped inside. He'd decided to come in the middle of the day because usually bars and taverns were vacant before the factories closed, especially in the working district, but to Neil's surprise he noticed that the bar had over a dozen patrons. It was probably because of the Emperor's new economic policies. Despite his attempts to study up on the families before seizing their businesses, the economy was falling apart. Factories closed left and right and some products stopped appearing in the markets all together.

Neil noticed Bill the Bartender and approached him casually. Bill placed a drink on the bar and then turned toward Neil. Bill did a double take as recognition dawned. "Bianca says you're bringing me some sort of letter?"

"Yes sir," Neil said as he pulled the letter from his inside pocket. "I appreciate you doing this," he told Bill quietly. Neil had known Bill the Bartender since he was a child when he'd worked in one of the Vapros bars.

Bill the Bartender didn't reply. He just nodded. Neil looked at him curiously and noticed that his hands were shaking. Neil turned and surveyed the room again. "Lot of customers today, Bill," Neil said carefully.

Bill shrugged. "They don't have much else to do now that the Emperor closed their factory."

Neil's hand was now wrapped around the hilt of his knife. "Why aren't they drinking, Bill?"

Bill the Bartender stared Neil down. "They're not thirsty," Bill said frantically.

Neil turned to face the patrons again and realized that they'd blocked the door and that they were now armed. "Seriously?" Neil growled.

Bill came out from behind the bar. "I've got nothing but love for you and Bianca, but this bar is all I have. And five thousand gold pieces would really go a long way to helping me keep it, Vapros."

Neil realized quickly that he was surrounded and that his enemies were armed with knives, shanks and metal bars. A few men even had pistols trained on him. Neil had a sinking feeling as he realized that he couldn't fend them off. "If he looks like he's gonna teleport, shoot him," Bill said.

"You can't do this, Bill."

"I really don't want to," he said as he pulled out a knife of his own and joined the circle surrounding Neil. "But I've got to eat. I've got to put food on the table for my family."

Suddenly the door burst open and sunlight streamed in. A drunken teenager hobbled in and fell to his knees seemingly disoriented. "We're in the middle of something," Bill yelled.

The teenager swayed dizzily and hugged his bottle of liquor closer to his chest. Neil stared at the teenager and tried to stifle his excitement. "Any time, Robert," Neil said.

Robert dropped his façade and hurled his bottle at the closest attacker. Before anyone could react, Neil materialized behind the bar. Robert pulled a small pistol from his coat and fired off a shot as he leapt over the bar and behind its sweet cover. As Robert reloaded his gun Neil desperately searched the cupboards, still in shock that Robert Tanner, Victoria's old boyfriend, was coming to his rescue. "You're a very convincing drunk," Neil said as Robert fired off a shot at the attackers who were now shooting at the bar.

"I appreciate that," Robert replied. "Do you have a plan to get us out of here?"

Neil began hurling bottles over the bar. "I do."

After Neil was sure that his attackers were ankle deep in alcohol, he risked the chance to grab a candle off of the bar. He heard Bill the Bartender yell at the men to get down but it was too late. Neil threw the candle into the puddles of alcohol and the bar sprung into flames. "You're gonna burn it down?" Robert asked incredulously.

Neil just grinned. "Ready?"

Robert nodded. They popped out from behind the bar and Robert shot the first man who tried to shoot them. Neil materialized to the other side of the bar and cut down the only man who wasn't on fire or fleeing in fear. In the confusion Robert hopped over the bar and the two young men escaped into the street. "Follow me," Robert said as they sprinted away from the blazing bar. "I've got a place where we can talk and lay low."

The neighborhoods got worse and worse as Robert led Neil towards his hideout in the slums. He'd brushed away a tear when Neil told him about Jennifer. Neil figured it was probably because she looked just like Victoria, his lost love, and therefore he'd lost her again in a way. Obviously Robert was trustworthy so Neil filled him in on the events since their last meeting. Neil trusted Robert because of his history with Victoria. This trust was further reinforced by the fact that he'd protected Neil with his life, even though five thousand gold pieces would put him out of the slums forever.

"You're sure you can get us to your hideout without being seen?" Neil asked.

"You're a nervous guy, aren't you?"

Neil laughed mirthlessly. "That's what being a fugitive does for you. You saw what just happened. Life on the run isn't all it's cracked up to be." Neil paused. "How'd you know to show up, anyway?"

"Bill the Bartender was hiring guys out of the slums to be his muscle. I heard in some of the underground markets that you were going to deliver him some letter for Bianca and he was going to jump you. I heard too late to bring some muscle of my own so I had to improvise."

Neil looked at Robert gratefully. He'd shown an enormous amount of courage coming alone to an ambush. It was very clear why he had to leave the city now. When everyone in town had five thousand golden reasons to stab him in the back, every second of life was a luxury. "I appreciate it," Neil said.

Robert waved away the gratitude. "I can get your letter to Bianca. I already sent word for her to meet me after I heard about Bill's plan. She should be here before sunset."

Neil ran his hand through his hair. "I can't thank you enough, Rob."

Robert just waved him off again. Neil wondered if he'd always been so serious or if that was an aftereffect of losing Victoria. "Why do you keep your hands so deep in your pockets when you walk?" Neil asked.

Robert looked down at his hands, which were deeply shoved into his coat pockets. "It's so none of the coins in my pocket hit each other or jingle at all."

"Why's that?" Neil asked.

"Because if someone hears that I have coins in my pocket, they'll kill me for them."

"Oh," Neil said. It dawned on Neil how tough life had become for everyone since the toppling of the families.

"So you're really leaving, huh?" Robert asked.

"If we stay in this city we're gonna die, Rob. There's no scenario in which we're able to start the revolution before we get caught and killed. We have to leave."

"You think you're gonna find your revolution out there?" Robert asked.

"Honestly, I don't know," Neil said. They'd stopped walking and were standing in an alley. "I just know I can't make it any longer inside the wall. I can't start a revolution if my head's on a pike."

Robert stared at him. After a while he scratched his head. "Yeah, I suppose that makes sense."

He turned around again and led Neil to an unassuming shack. "This is...?" Neil asked.

"My home," Robert replied as he opened the door and gestured for Neil to enter.

Neil entered the hovel and tried not to wince. It was even more dilapidated than the hideout that he and his siblings had been living in. Neil tried to ignore the family of cockroaches in the corner and the spider webs that were hanging from the ceiling. "You live here?"

Robert said. "For the time being, yeah. I used to live in the working district but things are getting worse. This revolution is all I have, Neil. I mean, what would you do if you were me?"

"If I were you I'd shoot me in the face and take that reward," Neil said.

Robert laughed. "Don't tempt me."

"Is that why I'm here?" Neil asked.

"Nope." Robert said as he walked over to the center of his "living room," if it could even be called that. He rolled up his tattered rug and showed Neil a small hatch in the ground. With a grunt and a heave, Robert pulled it open and stood next to it.

"Is that your murder hole?" Neil asked.

"Just look," Robert said.

Neil walked over and peered into the dark hatch. His jaw dropped. "How many?" he asked.

"I'm not sure. I think I'm nearing two-hundred," Robert said.

In Robert's hatch there were hundreds of rifles and pistols lying side by side. He actually had enough firepower to arm a small militia. Now it was evident why Robert didn't just burn the place down and live in an inn. "This is more than I expected," Neil said.

Robert grinned. "I thought it might be. A small group of men and I stormed an old Celerius workshop and found dozens of guns in the basement. That combined with all the weapons we got from the Pig's place has left us with a pretty substantial armory.

"I'm still leaving, Rob," Neil said. "I've got to. Despite how many guns we have, we're still going to need a lot more people and firepower to make this a reality. It's only a matter of time before we're captured or killed, if I stay."

Robert said, "I understand that. I'm just showing you those because I want you to remember that you still have very capable friends in this city. I've heard the rumors, same as everyone else, that there's something outside the wall other than desert."

"Villages, I'm told. An army," Neil replied.

"Villages isn't exactly a term that inspires a whole lot of confidence, Neil," Robert said. "I'm just asking you to keep this fire power in mind. I'm just getting started, Neil. If you don't find your giant revolutionary army out there, I still want you to consider coming back."

Neil stared at the floor. He didn't respond. "The revolution isn't dead inside this wall," Robert continued. "I'll keep fighting it. But

I'm not confident that I won't end up facedown in the river. I need help."

Neil finally met Robert's eyes. "I'll consider it," he said.

Robert gave him a half smile. "That's all I ask."

Neil finally looked at Robert's coat. Jennifer had told him about it a few times, but Neil had forgotten to ask. "Is that it?" Neil asked gesturing to his green faded coat.

Robert looked down at himself. "Yeah," he said quietly. "Victoria bought it for me about a year ago. I'd wear it so that I could go to parties and not be thrown out."

A few of the buttons had broken off and it was stained by what looked to be mud and blood. "Doesn't wearing it make you a prime candidate for mugging?"

Robert said absently, "Yeah, I suppose it does." He ran one hand across the sleeve. "But I don't care."

Neil pulled a pouch of gold from his pocket, a leftover from Quintus's house, and tossed it to Robert. Robert caught it. "It might not be of use to me outside the wall," Neil told him. "Might as well give it to someone who'll make the best of it."

Robert didn't say anything. He just pocketed the coins and smiled awkwardly. He probably didn't know how to thank anyone for giving him money. It had been a long time since Neil had seen someone do something honorable and he wanted to do it for Victoria. He now understood why she risked their father's wrath for this brave, young man. "I hope to see you soon, Rob," Neil said as he waved goodbye and walked toward the door.

Robert chuckled. "Yeah. I hope you do too."

And with that Neil exited Robert's shack and proceeded down the road in the direction of Lilly's hideout. He was worried about Robert. Sure, he was charismatic and dedicated, but those were the kind of people that the empire put the most energy into crushing. Hopefully he'd still be fighting if Neil ever came back. And hopefully he'd still be wearing Victoria's coat.

Chapter Fifty-One

CELERIUS HIDEOUT
DARIUS TAURLUM

FOR THE FIRST TIME IN TWO MONTHS, DARIUS SLIPPED ON HIS strategically placed armor, covering his pressure points. It took a few minutes to get used to the weight, but he felt powerful with it on his shoulders. "Everyone ready?" he asked, turning to his fellow warriors. Everyone had bathed and looked considerably better. The Vapros boys were still strapping on their leather armor, but Lilly looked prepared for battle in her blue and gold military coat. "Tonight's the night we leave Altryon behind," Darius said as he flexed his muscles experimentally in his armor.

"It's weird," Neil said, flipping up his hood. "This is where I was born, took my first steps, said my first words."

Lilly weighed different swords in her hands. "Hopefully we'll take our last breaths here, too," she murmured. "Once this war is won, we'll be back."

Rhys said, "We leave as fugitives, but we will return someday as free men. And women," he added quickly at a glance from Lilly.

"The sun is setting, Miss," Jonathan said nervously. "It's time!"

Lilly sheathed her sword. "My guards have elected to remain in the city so that we can move more inconspicuously. It means fewer weapons, but it's also a greater chance of survival."

"Is Bianca coming with us?" Rhys asked Neil.

"I don't know. She was planning on leaving anyway, with or without us. She might already be there. I sent a letter with Robert, so hopefully that'll reach her."

"No more stalling," Darius ordered. "Let's go!" He led the way down the steep staircase and out the back door, heaving a large cloak over his shoulders to hide his shining armor. He needn't have bothered; the city was nearly empty tonight.

The group walked together down the quiet streets to the market, sticking to the shadows in case a stray civilian happened to walk by. The Taurlum mansion loomed in the distance. Darius kept his eyes fixed on his old home. *Michael was in there. Could Michael have told the emperor about the meeting in the church? Was it Michael who had hired an assassin to kill him? No,* Darius thought furiously. *Michael would never do that. Michael would have an explanation.*

They reached a road that split in two directions. One was paved with marble. It led to the front hall of the Taurlum mansion. The other was a small dirt road that curved around behind the mansion, ultimately to the secret barrier gate. "Well," Darius said. "I guess this is it." He took a step onto the marble path. Rhys followed.

"Be careful," Neil said softly. After a second of hesitation, he pulled Rhys into a hug. "Don't trust either of them," Darius heard him whisper. "I don't feel good about this whole thing."

"See you on the other side, Shadow Man."

Rhys and Darius walked side by side down the road. "Darius," Rhys said. "You do know there's a chance we'll have to fight him."

Darius stopped in his tracks. "Michael and I are brothers. He would never try to hurt me."

"Right." Rhys let silence fall over them for a few minutes as they resumed walking. "Darius?"

"Yeah?"

"You trust me, right?"

Darius snorted. "You're a Vapros. I trust you as much as I would trust a Vapros, I suppose."

"Ok, do you at least agree that my knowledge about things is usually pretty accurate?"

Darius didn't like where this was going. "I suppose."

"I'm just saying that there are a lot of things that just aren't adding up. You have to prepare yourself for that."

Darius said reluctantly, "I will. But he's not behind this. Trust me. I know my brother."

"I hope you're right," Rhys said softly. "I truly hope you're right."

Chapter Fifty-Two

THE ALTRYON GATE
NEIL VAPROS

Neil saw Bianca before she saw him. His pulse quickened. She was leaning against the nearest building, still wearing her armor trimmed with fur. He quickly materialized next to her. "Hello," he whispered in her ear. "What's up?"

"Neil!" She wrapped her arms around him almost sympathetically. His letter had detailed the situation with Jennifer.

He returned the hug. "What's the situation?"

"Five guards," she replied. "I could have taken them out on my own, but I'd like someone to get rid of the bodies. Also, it doesn't seem fair that I get to have all the fun."

He grinned. "What about outside the wall?"

"No idea." Lilly and Jonathan approached. "Ah," Bianca said, "it's the rich girl. How've you been, rich girl?"

Lilly offered a little smile. "I've been working hard," she said. "You still couldn't beat me, street girl."

"I remember you being pretty quick," Bianca said. "Ready to take out some guards?"

Lilly whipped out her sword. "Born ready."

Bianca led them around the corner and pointed up. Two soldiers patrolled the top of the wall. "Watch this," she mouthed. She pulled out two knives, one in each hand, and threw them at the same time. Both met their marks; the guards fell off the wall, shouting. Neil materialized right below and caught them by the necks, cremating them before they even hit the ground.

One of the guards on the ground heard the commotion and came running toward the Vapros boy, but Lilly jumped out of the shadows and sank her sword through his heart. Neil sprinted over to disintegrate him while Lilly and Bianca each took out another guard.

It was over in less than ten seconds. Neil kicked through piles of ash. "That's the most people I've ever dematerialized in a row," he panted.

"My God," Jonathan breathed. "That was incredible. They just dissolved!"

Neil nodded, trying desperately to catch his breath. "It takes a lot out of you."

Jonathan didn't seem to notice Neil's exhaustion. "Those first two didn't even land!" he said, awestruck.

Neil laughed a little at Jonathan's incredulity. "It's a handy little talent."

"How do you do it?"

"It takes concentration. We take the same energy we use to teleport, but we channel it into another person instead of ourselves. They aren't capable of reforming, like we are, so they just turn into ash." Jonathan's jaw was hanging open. Neil smiled. "It's a lot easier to do it to people who are already dead. When you try to cremate living people, their bodies fight back. They have their own energy that keeps them glued together. My father can manage it, but I'm nowhere near strong enough yet."

Lilly and Bianca caught up to them. "Ready?" Lilly asked, "We have a city to escape."

Neil walked up to the giant gate and pulled it open. Instead of spitting them out into freedom, it opened into a long corridor with another gate at the end. It was so close he could have materialized right up to it.

Unfortunately, there were several soldiers standing in his way.

"Well, well, well," said a voice from behind the guards. "That was almost too easy."

The soldiers parted and General Carlin walked between them, brandishing a broadsword. Lilly snarled and raised her own weapon.

"Oh, please." Carlin said, rolling his eyes at Lilly. "Did you really think we wouldn't find out about your escape attempt? The Vapros brats have been advertising it all over town."

Neil reddened. Carlin noticed.

"We have our spies," he said, smiling. "Michael Taurlum was very helpful."

Lilly gasped. "I knew it," she muttered. "Stand down, Carlin," she commanded. "In the name of my brother, Anthony Celerius, I order you to call off your soldiers!"

Carlin laughed. "In the name of Anthony Celerius? Anthony is dead. I killed him myself. Sent you the ashes in a box, remember?"

Lilly narrowed her eyes. "Stand down or I will—"

Before she could finish the threat, she and the rest of her group were thrown against the wall and suspended in midair by an invisible force. "I'll take it from here, General," a cold voice said. Neil's heart sank as he recognized Saewulf. "Ah, one of you is a Vapros," he said delightedly, making his way through the ranks of soldiers. "Do you remember me? It's been too long!" His hands began to glow. "Let's see if you die as easily as your family members."

Chapter Fifty-Three

TAURLUM MANSION
DARIUS TAURLUM

THE TAURLUM MANSION DIDN'T HAVE A LOCK. THE FRONT DOOR WAS designed to be so heavy that only a Taurlum could heave it open. With a grunt, Darius forced through the door and beckoned Rhys inside behind him.

Their footsteps echoed against the marble floor. Rhys let out a low whistle. "Nice place," he said, admiring the high ceilings. "Much different from our house."

Darius didn't say anything. He couldn't quite believe he was home. He had long ago accepted that he would never set foot in this entryway again, yet here it was, looking as splendid and regal as the last time he saw it. He pressed his palm against one of the columns and closed his eyes. It was like he'd never left. If he concentrated hard, he could almost hear his family's voices echoing down the hallways.

"Where's Michael's room?" Rhys asked.

Darius opened his eyes and exhaled. "Upstairs," he said quietly. "I'll show you." He led the way through a maze of staircases and hallways, pausing at each one to touch a portrait or gently straighten a tapestry. It didn't feel like his house was deserted. Any second now, someone would come around the corner and ask him if he wanted to go out and get a drink. It would be like nothing had ever happened; the past two months were just a dream.

"This is his room," Darius said, rapping his knuckles against the door. It fell open. Michael's room was empty. His bed was stripped of its sheets, his dresser overturned, his clothes spilled out over the floor. A fine layer of dust covered it all.

"It doesn't look like anyone's been here for a long time," Rhys whispered.

"Why are you whispering?" Darius asked, lumbering into his brother's bedroom and pulling the dresser into its upright position. "You're acting like somebody died in here."

"Somebody did die here. A lot of people died here." Rhys still wouldn't set foot in the room. "Did you not realize that?"

"Taurlum don't die," Darius insisted. "They're all imprisoned."

Rhys persisted, "Taurlum have weaknesses, same as everybody else. You and your family aren't gods. You're mortal men. And some of you died in the attack that night."

"You may know a lot," Darius said, steadying himself against Michael's dresser, "but you're wrong about this."

"I'm sorry," Rhys whispered, "but I don't think I am."

Darius held perfectly still for a moment, then stormed past Rhys and down the hallway. "Michael's not here," he said. "We're leaving."

"Wait!" Rhys had to materialize every few steps to keep up. "Is there anywhere else he could be? Any places he used to spend a lot of time?"

"The roof," Darius said, not slowing down. "That way." He gestured vaguely. "Find it yourself."

"Darius!" Rhys grabbed his arm and held on tightly. The Taurlum didn't even slow down. "We need to find your brother!"

"Maybe my brother is dead," Darius growled. "Just like the rest of my family apparently is! I don't need to listen to your condescending Vapros attitude."

"He's not dead," Rhys said calmly. "You saw him two days ago. He has the answers you need. Remember why we came here?"

Darius finally stopped. "Right." He put his face in his hands and took a few deep breaths. "The roof—this way." He started up a long staircase and threw himself against the door at the top. It burst open with a noise so loud that, for a moment, Darius thought he'd ripped it completely off its hinges. "Michael?"

Michael turned around and gazed with droopy eyes at his intruders. "Darius," he said lazily as he raised his jeweled arms. "Glad to see you made it home."

"What do you . . . you never showed up at the church. You said you'd meet me and then you didn't come."

Michael gave him a slow smile. "No, I didn't. I had more important things to do."

"That assassin came back," Darius said. "She tried to kill me again."

"Did she?" Michael took a step toward them. The jewelry on his wrists clinked softly, like cruel, quiet laughter. "But she failed, I see."

"I'm still alive, aren't I?" Darius didn't like the look in Michael's eyes.

"Indeed." Michael stopped. "What a pity," he said harshly.

Darius stared. "What a ... a pity? Michael, what are you talking about?"

"Anastasia," he said loudly, and the assassin stepped out of the shadows. "He's still alive."

Anastasia looked furious. "Not for long," she growled, reaching for her spike. Michael held out a hand to stop her.

"You have tried to kill him three times," he said softly, and Darius felt his jaw drop. "Give up. You clearly aren't capable. I'll do it myself."

"Michael?" Darius's throat was dry. "What are you talking about?"

Michael turned and gazed over the city. "A couple of months ago, when that Vapros boy attacked our house, I realized how easy it would have been for him to kill one of us," he said. "We were stronger, of course, but he had the element of surprise. We barely saw him coming. And I started to wonder. What would have happened if he'd reached his target? What if he had killed our grandfather? Or even our father?"

"Neil's not so bad," Darius said quickly. "The Vapros aren't so different. I actually think the feud can end. Stop what you're doing Michael."

Michael didn't appear to hear him. "So I took a look at Father's will, just to see how things could have ended up. You can imagine my surprise when I discovered that he left everything to you."

"So what? I'm his son!"

Michael turned back and glared at Darius. "His *youngest* son," Michael hissed. "He didn't leave anything to me. The elder. The rightful heir. You would be the new 'Sir Taurlum.' He preferred you. He's always preferred you."

Darius could barely breathe. "So you tried to have me killed over some money? I would have shared it with you. You know that."

"It's not about money!" Michael was starting to lose his composure. "It's about the fact that our father loved you more than he loved me! Our entire family did! And for what? I decided to leave for a girl and despite our 'break-up,' I am still considered a deserter. A failure. As long as you're alive, Darius, I will always be second best. And it's not in a Taurlum's nature to settle for second." Michael gestured toward Rhys. "I see you brought a friend. Now you're fraternizing with a Vapros. This is exactly why you have always been completely incapable of leading this family. You are consorting with our greatest enemies."

Out of the corner of his eye, Darius saw Rhys start to reach for his knife. "So you hired an assassin to kill me once I was in prison?" he asked.

Michael laughed hollowly. "I'm the one who put you there."

"I don't understand."

"How do you think the Imperial Guards found you so quickly? Who do you think alerted them that someone would be attacking the Opera House that night?"

Against his will, Darius whispered, "It was you?"

A few raindrops fell from the sky. Michael shrugged his shoulders. "Of course it was me. I was hoping you'd die resisting but there was no such luck. So I took other precautions. I didn't plan on the army ousting us, though. I was forced to hide for a while. One night, Carlin caught me in the markets. He was going to kill me, until I offered him something better: every other family member. I told him I could find all of you, and he told me he'd give me my weight in gold for each one. I sent my assassin again, but then you found me and gave me everything—five fugitives under one roof. I'm a free man, thanks to you. I can walk down the streets with my head held high. Now I'm free to build my legacy: a legacy where I can be free of the things that haunt me. Free of my mistakes." He straightened a few of his bracelets and continued to stare into the distance. "And tonight, I'm going to kill you."

"Are you that stupid? You really think the emperor is going to live up to his end of that bargain? Once he captures us, you will be at the top of the most wanted list."

Michael said, "You're wrong. The emperor needs me. He attacked our family without knowing enough about our businesses. He can't run them without my help. He realizes my value in restoring economic order," Michael continued, his voice dangerously calm. "So tonight it ends, brother. Part of me always knew I'd have to be the one to do the deed. Part of me knew I couldn't have someone else do it for me. It'll be over quick. You've lost a lot of weight."

"This is crazy," Darius said. "You're crazy."

"Shut up!" Michael roared deafeningly loud. "I will not have my motives questioned by the likes of you. What were you doing with your life, anyway? Drinking it away? Your death won't even matter." Anastasia began to spin her spike-chain. "This is where it ends, Darius."

Darius clenched his jaw. He trembled. "Then let's end it—bare hands, man to man."

Michael curled his hands into fists and leaped at Darius, who met him halfway with a force just as mighty. They collided with a sound as loud as thunder. Michael recovered first. He swung his full might into Darius's jaw; the blow sent a shockwave through the air. Anastasia tried to hurl her spike at Darius, but Rhys materialized in front of it and deflected the blow with his knife. Anastasia growled and slammed her foot across his face in a roundhouse kick. He tried to materialize behind her to put her to sleep, but she anticipated it and whipped the spike at him, forcing him to dodge and duck.

Across the roof, Michael was quickly getting the better of Darius. He swung faster and harder than his brother and Darius was having trouble getting his arms up to block. "You never understood!" Michael roared as he swung with all his might. "I have the strength of a god! Why should I be treated like a mortal man?"

Darius delivered a punch to Michael's stomach that would have killed a normal man. "You're not a god," he yelled back angrily. "Taurlum have weaknesses, same as everybody else. You are treated like a mortal man because you can die like a mortal man!"

The rain fell hard now. Michael lashed out with a strike Darius wasn't strong enough to block. He hit the ground so hard it left a Taurlum-sized crater. "All evidence to the contrary," Michael retorted, grabbing Darius by the front of his armor and slamming him back into the floor. Darius struggled to get up, but Michael pinned him down with one hand and began to beat him with the other. "Am I not a god?" he shouted. "I don't bleed. Mortals bleed!'

Darius's breastplate crumpled. Michael ripped it away and delivered more blows to his now-unguarded upper body. "I have never felt tired. Mortals tire!"

He punched Darius's face. "I've never been hungry. I've never felt weakness. I have never been in pain. Am I not a god?" he roared.

Darius kicked his feet up into Michael's chest, sending him staggering backwards. He rose, panting, and raised his fists.

Rhys materialized behind Anastasia and grabbed her neck, but before he could put her to sleep she pulled her elbow back into his gut. He stumbled and materialized out of range of her spike. He was growing tired. The energy it took to teleport was taking its toll.

Darius leapt at Michael like a feral animal. He ripped off his brother's breastplate and delivered a crushing blow to his chest. Michael staggered but didn't fall. He charged his brother with enough force to crush a boulder. Darius yelled and began to fire punches at Michael, who grabbed Darius around the waist and hurled him across the roof. With his brother out of the way, Michael dropped to his knees and planted his palms on top of the mansion. A dark grin crossed his face.

Darius realized what was going to happen a mere second before it occurred. "Rhys!" he screamed. "He's going to…."

Large cracks in the marble radiated from around Michael's ringed fingers and spread across the roof. Darius ran to Michael and kicked him hard enough to break his concentration, but the damage was done. The roof began to crumble under the weight of the Taurlum boys. Michael didn't seem to notice, or maybe he just didn't care. He leapt with reckless abandon at Darius. He landed on his brother's back. The rain made the marble slippery. Darius dug his heels in to avoid going over the edge. "As I recall," Michael hissed as he caught Darius around the neck, "creating earthquakes is quite godly."

"You sound tired," Darius said, bucking Michael off his back. "That's strange. Do gods tire, Michael?"

Michael fell into a crouch, smiling evilly. "You fought well, brother," he said. "But those words will be your last." And he pounced with all his might at Darius.

VICTORY LIES WITHIN
THE ASHES

Chapter Fifty-Four

THE ALTRYON GATE
NEIL VAPROS

CARLIN PACED THE GROUND IN FRONT OF THE IMMOBILIZED AND suspended intruders. "Your little servant is still trailing after you?" he said to Lilly with a slow smile. "I killed your parents, you know," he added, looking at Jonathan with cold eyes. "They were tiny, stupid looking slaves, too."

Jonathan tried to reply, but Saewulf's powers made it impossible to open his mouth. Carlin laughed. "So," he said conversationally, "who shall we dismember first, Saewulf?"

Saewulf shrugged.

"I say we start with the weakest and work our way up," Carlin continued without waiting for a response. "We can start with the girl with the knife."

Saewulf squinted, and Bianca began to shudder.

"Stop!" Neil breathed even though no one could hear him. "Don't hurt her!"

Bianca screamed. Neil desperately tried to focus his energy to dematerialize out of Saewulf's hold, but he couldn't muster enough energy. Bianca's cries distracted him. He struggled, concentrating harder than he ever had before, and felt the energy run through him in an unfamiliar way. It coursed through his fingers instead of settling in his stomach. Something was happening, something different, something he'd never felt before.

Suddenly, a bolt of smoky fire exploded from his fingertips and landed straight in Saewulf's eyes. He howled and clapped his hands over his face, dropping his prey. The soldiers stared at him in shock. A few of them clumsily assembled their weapons, but Neil threw another bolt of smoke and fire that tore through their formation. He looked down at his hands incredulously. This must have been his advanced power, finally coming into play!

Neil ran past Saewulf's screaming form and knelt down next to Bianca. Carlin started to swing his sword down on the Vapros, but he was blocked by Lilly. "Carlin," she said calmly. "You and I have unfinished business."

"Get out of my way," he snarled.

Lilly lashed out so quickly her blade was invisible and nicked his shoulder. He howled and jumped backwards, then narrowed his eyes. "All right," he said, "you first, then your fire-throwing friend."

Lilly raised her rapier. "You're going to die here, Carlin. For everything you've done to my family, death is a mercy."

He grinned. "Then allow me to be merciful," he said with a mock bow, and he lunged at her.

Neil pulled Bianca out of range of the sword fight and helped her sit up. "Are you okay? What hurts?"

She groaned and stood up. "I'm fine. Take care of the psychic. Jonathan and I will take care of the guards."

Jonathan, who had been trying his best to stay out of the way of any fighting, looked up at her with wide eyes. "Really?"

She reached into a pocket in her armor and handed him a flint-lock pistol. "Really."

He closed his fingers around the gun and smiled. "Let's do this!"

"Be safe," Neil pleaded, and then he turned to face Saewulf. The psychic had regained standing position. A red scorch mark covered his neck and crept onto the right side of his face. A few strands of his orange hair were singed. Neil's thoughts flashed instantly to Jennifer.

"That was a nice trick, Vapros," Saewulf spat. "But you're still going to die. I will rip your bones out of your flesh."

Neil smiled sweetly. "Are you sure you're okay to fight, Saewulf? You've looked better." He let his energy flow down to his fingertips. His hands glowed white with heat, and just as Saewulf raised his arm to immobilize Neil, he let fire explode from his body. Saewulf dodged around the ball of fire, but his concentration was broken.

"It seems we're evenly matched," Neil said, heating up his hands again.

"Don't insult me," Saewulf growled. "I am superior."

"Prove it." Neil felt his hands getting hot.

Saewulf scowled as he raised his arm. "I'm about to."

Chapter Fifty-Five

TAURLUM MANSION
DARIUS TAURLUM

"**How many more times can you vanish, kid?**" **Anastasia taunted** as she whirled her chain. "You look sleepy."

Rhys panted heavily. "I could do this forever," he gasped, "but I don't think I'll have to."

She laughed. "You're right." She wasn't even out of breath. "You'll die before you get the chance to do it again." She whipped the chain at him fiercely. He dodged it without dematerializing. The roof beneath him was crumbling thanks to Michael's earthquake. He could barely keep his footing.

Behind Rhys, Michael pounded on Darius, who had retreated to the edge of the roof and was trying desperately to protect the pressure points in his neck. "I thought you were a warrior," Michael grunted. "Sorry—my mistake." He shoved Darius hard. "I wonder if a fall from this height would kill you?"

Anastasia threw her chain at Rhys one more time. The Vapros let himself collapse, and the spike sailed harmlessly over his head and instead nicked Michael Taurlum's neck. Anastasia gasped. Rhys grabbed the weapon before she could get it back and threw it expertly into her stomach. She fell to her knees.

Michael pressed his palm against his neck, eyes wide. "No," he whispered, pulling his hand back and holding it at eye level. It was covered in blood. "No!"

Darius lunged and wrapped both hands around his brother's vulnerable throat. "You made a horrible mistake, Michael. It didn't have to end like this."

Michael cried out and frantically tried to pry Darius's hands off his neck, but when he spoke, his voice was almost calm. "Are you going to do it, Darius? Are you going to kill me?" he asked, while tears of anger raced down his cheeks. "You're my brother. Do you think you can do it? Can you send me to the place where I've sent so many: countless men, warriors or not? Not to mention the woman I loved." Darius's eyes softened. "Let me go, brother. Think about the future of the Taurlum family."

Darius loosened his grip, and Michael wrenched himself free. He pulled a small knife from the back of his armor and tried to jab it into Darius's stomach. Snarling, Darius yanked the blade away from him and caught him by the throat again. "I have thought about the future of the family," Darius growled. "And you don't deserve to be part of it."

Michael screamed wordlessly as Darius kicked out and sent his brother over the edge of the roof. They heard him hit the ground, his armor clanging against the marble road. Darius peered over the edge. His brother's limbs were twisted into a broken mess. He was covered in blood. There was no chance he'd survived, not when he was already vulnerable. Darius closed his eyes and sank to the ground. He'd done it. Michael was dead. He'd killed his own brother. He didn't feel accomplished. He didn't feel relief. He felt like a monster.

"Is he dead?" a small voice asked. Darius opened his eyes to see Rhys, his hair plastered to his head by rain.

"Yeah," Darius croaked.

Rhys patted Darius's shoulder. "You did the right thing."

"Doesn't feel like it." They shared a moment of silence as they reflected on the conflict that had just occurred, "What about her?" Darius asked.

Rhys looked over his shoulder at Anastasia, who was lying on the ground with her eyes closed. "I just put her to sleep," he said. "She'll be okay, if she finds a doctor when she wakes up."

Darius sighed. "We should go. I don't want to ever come back here."

Rhys said sympathetically, "Okay. Let's go. We have to meet the others outside the wall." He and the Taurlum walked side-by-side back into the house. "And be careful," Rhys added as they started down the stairs. "This house could collapse at any second."

VICTORY LIES WITHIN
THE ASHES

Chapter Fifty-Six

THE ALTRYON GATE
NEIL VAPROS

"Shut the damn gate!" Carlin roared as he swung at (and was blocked by) Lilly. "Don't let them slip past you!"

The guards made for the exit, but Bianca and Jonathan got there first. Bianca began to cut down any guard who came her way while Jonathan held out his pistol threateningly. Carlin scowled. "This won't last," he said as he brought his sword around hard enough to disarm a normal man.

Lilly's blade flashed like lightening. "I'm faster than I used to be."

She twirled and whipped the sword past his knees. He jumped backward silently, then lunged so quickly she didn't see it coming. His blade only grazed her thumb, and it healed over quickly. Lilly couldn't help but cry out in surprise. Carlin gave a maniacal laugh and swung the sword within an inch of her neck. "Still faster," he hissed, eyes shining.

A few feet away, Neil threw a fireball right at Saewulf's chest; Saewulf caught it with his psychic powers and hurled it back at him. Neil materialized out of the way just in time.

"Come on, cousin!" Saewulf snarled. "Can't you do any better than that?"

Neil sent another fireball at his adversary. "Cousin?"

Saewulf grinned and raised his arm, catching the fire with his powers again and this time letting it burn out in midair. "Don't tell me you actually haven't figured it out yet," he said idly. "Look at me. I have otherworldly powers. Sound like anyone else you know?"

"You're from the fourth family," Neil said. "I think I've known for a while. There used to be four brothers, but one of them was killed in the first great battle."

Saewulf laughed. "And they all said he was killed by savages, didn't they? They forgot to mention that they're the ones who killed him." He cackled at Neil's confused expression. "Oh, yes, Vapros. My ancestor was the strongest of the brothers. Of course he survived that battle! He should have gone on to rule Altryon. He wanted to lead the Imperial Army, eradicate the savages, and make Altryon safe forever. Perhaps even eliminate the need for a wall. His brothers weren't quite so ambitious. So they killed him."

"I have a feeling there's more to the story, Saewolf. If they killed him, he was probably a power hungry, maniacal bastard like you."

Saewulf wrinkled his nose in disgust and continued. "No! They were threatened by his power. Fortunately, they didn't know he had already sired a child. The legacy phase is a beautiful thing, don't you agree? My ancestors escaped the city and began their life out there." He raised his arm and trapped Neil with his powers. "I spent my entire life enduring hell you couldn't even imagine. But now my family has returned for one reason—to end your miserable little lives." Neil made two fireballs in his hands and blasted Saewulf's force field apart. Neil landed on his knees, panting. "You're getting weaker," Saewulf said confidently. "You just gained your new abilities. You can't hope to control them so early."

Neil struggled to his feet. "I wasn't planning on controlling it," Neil said as another blast of fire sent Saewulf stumbling backwards.

Saewulf raised his hands just in time to ward off the flame. Neil could see him buckling under the pressure, but his own vision became blurry, too. He took deep breaths and forced himself to keep going. "That's a lot of fire," Saewulf called from behind his defenses. "Must take a lot of energy."

Neil felt the heat in his hands begin to fade. His lungs weren't working anymore. Saewulf laughed and cleared away the smoke with his powers, then lifted Neil and slammed him against a wall. "It's over," he hissed, and in that moment, Neil realized what scared him so much about Saewulf. He had darkness in his eyes, with the desperation of a survivor; someone who was starving for something. Neil could do nothing but close his eyes and wait for the end.

Chapter Fifty-Seven

THE ALTRYON GATE
LILLY CELERIUS

Lilly knew she'd been getting stronger, but apparently Carlin had been training hard, too. "Give up?" he asked, repeatedly swinging his broadsword against her rapier.

She slashed so close to his head that she sliced off a few strands of his hair. "Never."

He swung down so hard that he let out a grunt. It was enough. She dropped her sword. Grinning, he swung again and gave her a shallow cut on her shoulder. It healed over before she had time to bleed. She dove for her sword, and he sliced into her side. This cut took longer to heal. "You're afraid," Carlin said, an evil grin splitting his face. "I can feel you losing hope."

Out of the corner of her eye, Lilly saw Saewulf lift a struggling Neil against a wall. She looked into Carlin's cold eyes. "Give me a second," she said as she made eye contact with the suffocating Neil. Moving as fast as she could, Lilly grabbed her fallen sword and ducked under Carlin's next swing. He swung again but she weaved out of range. Before he could regroup a throwing knife imbedded itself in his shoulder, courtesy of Bianca, across the room. Lilly bolted over to the psychic and tore into his back with her sword. Saewolf screamed and dropped Neil. Staggering to his feet Neil sent a jet of fire just over Lilly's shoulder to where Carlin was standing with his sword above her head poised to strike. The general was knocked off his feet and to the floor with a loud thud. "Thank you," Lilly said. Neil leaned heavily against the wall, gasping, and gave her a nod.

Suddenly, a loud clang echoed through the entire room. Lilly turned to see that the gate that led to everything beyond Altryon was sliding closed. "We're almost out of time!" Lilly yelled. "Come on, Neil!"

Evidently, a guard had managed to cut its supports before he was killed. Bianca and Jonathan came running toward them. "The gate!" Bianca screamed. "We have to go now!"

Neil was shaking his head. "Rhys," he breathed. "Darius."

"We might not get another chance!" Bianca begged. "They'll find their own way out!"

The gate had fewer than forty feet left. Suddenly, the room began to shake as loud footsteps came running down the hallway. "Reinforcements have arrived!" bellowed Darius, tearing through the hallway. Rhys followed at his heels.

Darius leapt in front of the closing gate and shoved against it. It shuddered, but he was strong enough to keep it from closing any farther. "Go!" he yelled. Rhys ducked through first, followed closely by Bianca and Lilly. Neil, still drained of energy, threw himself through next and collapsed to the ground. Jonathan brought up the rear. Just before he made it to the gate, he tripped over the blue military coat that had always been too big for him. Before he could scramble to his feet, he froze and began to rise into the air. Behind him, Saewulf had his arm raised, fury in his eyes. "Lilly," he taunted angrily. "Come back inside and lay down your weapon. Or watch your little friend die an agonizing death."

Lilly gasped and started back through the gate. Darius, who was starting to lose his grip, wouldn't let her through. "Don't do it," he groaned in pain. "He'll kill you."

"I don't care!" She tried to push past him, but at that moment, for the first time in his life, Darius's strength failed. He let go of the gate and collapsed to the ground outside the wall.

Lilly threw herself against the bars, screaming, "Jonathan!" She reached through the gate, trying to grab him, but he was out of reach.

Saewulf said, "No matter. Your friend will die, and then we will make it through the gate after you. I'll have you in my grasp by morning."

"He's not a Celerius!" Lilly screamed. "He's not in a family! You have no reason to kill him!"

"There is always a reason!" Saewulf roared as his eyes began to blacken again. A dark grin crossed his face and he lowered his arm. Jonathan dropped to the ground. "Lilly!" he cried, rushing to the gate.

Tears streamed down Lilly's face. "Your coat," she lamented quietly. The jacket had a huge tear ripped in the side where he'd fallen.

"It's okay," he assured her. "It's fine. The thing never fit me anyway."

"Any last words, Celerius slave?" Saewulf asked lightly.

Jonathan didn't take his eyes off Lilly. "Miss," he said. "I only disobeyed one order you ever gave me."

"It's okay, it's okay, I forgive you."

Saewulf clucked his tongue. "Those are terrible last words," he said, reaching out to crush Jonathan's neck. Lilly screamed.

"And for that disobeyed order," Jonathan choked, as he reached into his pocket and pulled out the grenade, "I am sorry."

Lilly knew what was going to happen and had time to throw herself out of the way. Saewulf saw it a second too late, and all he could do was raise his arms to protect himself. "Goodbye, Miss," Jonathan said, closing his eyes.

Lilly screamed as the grenade went off, consuming Saewulf and Jonathan and all the guards behind the gate. The deafening sound rang through the air and, in an instant, silence fell. The only audible noise was the crackling of the remaining embers and Neil's wheezing. "Jonathan!" Lilly staggered to her feet and tried to run back. Darius got up and dragged her away from the gate. When he set her down next to Neil, she collapsed into a heap and sobbed.

Neil looked helplessly at the sobbing girl. He met Bianca's eyes but she just shook her head, obviously also at a loss for how to comfort Lilly. Instead he turned his head away from her and looked out over the horizon for the first time.

The vast rolling hills of green grass were illuminated by the full moon. This was the same full moon the teens had seen a thousand times inside the city, but somehow out here it seemed brighter. Its light was strong enough to reflect off the lush blades of grass, so the whole landscape glittered as if the ground was adorned with the finest jewels. Layer upon layer of sparkling hills laid out at their feet, each one a little taller than the one before. And yet, the most unsettling, wonderful thing of all was that no wall interrupted nature's flow. It was breath taking.

Neil sat staring at the hills with his mouth gaping. He was obviously lost in the beauty of the landscape. Lilly's voice broke him out of his trance. "His ridiculous coat," she said hoarsely as Neil remembered Jonathan. "He would never take it off."

"We have to keep going," Rhys said as gently as he could. "It's only a matter of time before they open the gate and come after us. We need to be far away by then."

Lilly wiped tears out of her eyes. "Yes," she said. "We have to press on. I believe that was what he would have wanted."

Bianca started to put a hand on Lilly's shoulder, but thought better of it. She turned to Neil instead. "Where do we go from here?" she asked. The landscape was vaster than anything they had ever known.

Neil pulled his hood over his head and pointed out into the distance. "We move forward," he decided. "Wherever that may be."

"Time to run," Darius said, flexing a bicep experimentally.

"Yes," Lilly said, rubbing more tears out of her eyes. "Hopefully for the last time."

Chapter Fifty-Eight

THE MARKETS
CARLIN FILUS

CARLIN SPAT SOME BLOOD INTO THE STREET AND STOMPED AWAY IN FURY. He'd avoided the blast from the grenade, but it had caused damage to his army. Not to mention his gate. The heat had fused the door into the wall. There was no way to open it now. The brats were lucky this time, he fumed, but he'd get them in the end. As he walked, he thought about what was to come—telling his father of his failure. He would be scolded and possibly even demoted. His hatred and anger grew until he couldn't stand it any more. He reached the nearest stone building, removed his glove and began to strike his fist against the wall. He felt his face grow hot as blood dripped down his hands and he screamed in fury. After a minute or two, he began to tire and slipped his glove over the bloodied hand.

He continued down the street, calmer this time. Just when he was exiting the markets and nearing the nightlife district, an arrow flew and embedded itself into his shoulder. It had been perfectly aimed so that it went straight through the chink in his armor. Carlin howled and ripped the arrow out of his skin. He whirled around, looking for the source, but the streets were deserted. "Who's there?" he yelled, drawing his broadsword and whirling it threateningly.

A calm voice came out of an alley. "Seek out the families," it said, "and the next arrow will be in your neck."

Carlin stepped closer to the alley. "I'll kill you for this."

A man in an iron mask and a blue coat emerged from the shadows. He pulled out a thin sword of his own and leapt through the air. Carlin raised his sword to block but his hurt shoulder and damaged hand slowed him enough for the masked figure to gain an advantage. Carlin's sword fell to the ground with a clang. He gasped and backtracked hurriedly, examining his surroundings for another useable weapon. "Who are you?"

The masked man lowered his sword. "You have been a danger to the one I am sworn to protect," he said in a hard voice. "I advise you not to remain a threat any longer." Carlin leapt for his sword but the masked figure was too fast. He brought his foot across Carlin's head so hard that he saw stars. He tried to stand but the figure stomped his head against the cobblestone street. Carlin felt his nose crack. He remembered that he had a pistol in the back of his armor. He pulled it out and fired blindly at his assailant.

He lifted his head and, with relief, realized that his attacker had vanished. He was able to pull his damaged body off the ground and spat a mouthful of blood into the street. He exited the alley, limping and bleeding heavily from his nose. As he walked down the street in the opposite direction of the gate, he fumed to himself about how badly things had gone. If the Vapros boy hadn't suddenly developed his advanced powers, the Empire would be sleeping soundly. He heard footsteps running down the street after him and drew his sword viciously. A small soldier raised his arms in fear. "What do you want?" Carlin roared furiously.

"We ... we're still digging through the wreckage, sir," the soldier said quietly. "The emperor needs to be alerted of our progress. What should we tell him?"

Carlin sheathed his sword and exhaled deeply as he began to remove the armor covering his shoulder wound. "First, get me a doctor and prepare my convoy. Tell him we lost his psychic but we're on our way outside the wall. The fugitives will die. I'll make sure of it."

VICTORY LIES WITHIN
THE ASHES

Chapter Fifty-Nine

OUTSIDE THE WALL
NEIL VAPROS

"How's Lilly?" Bianca asked, staring at the rising sun in the distance. She was fascinated with this new world; Neil could see it in her eyes. After traveling for hours, they'd made camp on top of a distant mountain. They had taken turns staying awake to watch for any soldiers who might be following them.

"She'll survive," he said, sitting down next to her. "Darius and Rhys were both with her all night." Neil thought about Lilly sobbing beside him when they escaped through the gate. He'd wanted to comfort her but couldn't. They all should have been used to this by now. He had wanted to say something, to tell Lilly her servant was a hero, or assure her that the pain of her loss would fade with time, but he couldn't quite form the words.

Neil glanced covertly at his comrades. Darius was telling some loud, ridiculous story about his drunken, teenage grandfather unknowingly taking home some cross-dressed man. Rhys was smiling and writing in a small notebook, only half-listening. It was obvious that Darius was trying to cheer up Lilly and, surprisingly, it actually seemed to be working. *That's brave of him*, Neil thought. Darius was covering it well, but Neil knew killing his brother had seriously traumatized him. Darius put on a courageous smile and told a story about his grandfather's drunken exploits.

"It's easier to hate people you don't know," Neil muttered to Bianca.

"What?" she asked.

"Nothing," he said. "It's just an odd feeling. Being here with them…"

Bianca nodded in understanding. Darius appeared to be nearing the end of the story because he was getting louder and Lilly and Rhys laughed out loud. Neil was curious about the ending, but something weighed on his mind: a Taurlum had killed Rhys's mother, Jennifer had killed Lilly's brother, and Neil, if he had completed that first mission, would have killed Darius' grandfather, the very same grandfather who had mistakenly brought home a rather questionable date. That nameless, faceless target that Neil had been coldly assigned to assassinate was someone's grandfather. Neil thought about the countless others who had been murdered: the centuries of hatred and senseless violence, with each family convinced their side possessed righteousness and justice. And yet, there they were, sitting and laughing in each other's company. It wasn't the end of the feud, and such hatred and meaningless death could never be erased in a day. Neil knew that. But it was a step in the right direction.

"And how do you feel?" she asked quietly. "About being out of Altryon, I mean."

He thought about it for a minute. "Free." He raised a hand to shield his eyes from the brightness of the rising sun. "And I'm glad you're here with me."

She smiled, eyes still trained on the sunrise. "I'm glad to be here. I'll be with you until the very end."

He looked down at her, and she finally lifted her eyes to meet his. "I'm very glad you're with me," he repeated quietly, and before he could think, before he could talk himself out of it, he leaned down to press his lips against hers.

"You're up early," Rhys said from behind them.

"Just watching the sun come up," Bianca said briskly, but she was grinning. "Excuse me." She walked away toward the others and began to gather her gear.

The ground shook as Darius rolled up into push-up position and began to pump his arms vigorously. He let out an exhilarated yell. "First day outside the city!" he grinned. "Let's go!"

"So are we splitting up now, or are we going to keep this partnership going?" asked Rhys.

Neil looked at the group and noticed that they appeared to be silently asking the same question. "Why don't we stick together until we find someplace to settle—some civilization."

Lilly cracked her knuckles and sighed loudly as she prepared to stand. Her eyes had a fading redness that had been caused by all her crying. She picked up her sword and stroked the blade thoughtfully. "So, Captain Vapros," she said, looking at Neil as she stood up, "what are we looking for?"

"A new place to call home," Neil said, giving her a half-smile. She returned it.

"Then let the search begin," Darius said. He trotted down the mountain and into the unfamiliar expanses.

For the first time in his life, Neil felt truly free—free from the city that expelled him and his family, free from the emperor that wanted him dead, and free from the feud that had consumed his life. An unfamiliar feeling settled in his heart as he led the group down the mountain. For the first time in so many months, he felt hope.

ABOUT THE AUTHOR

Kyle Prue is an award winning author, actor and comedian. Kyle wrote *The Sparks: Book One of the Feud Trilogy* when he was just 16 years old. The next two books in the series are *The Flames* and *The Ashes*. The Flames will be published in April, 2017 and *The Ashes* will be available Fall, 2017. Kyle has spent the past year on a national book tour visiting over 80 middle and high schools and meeting over 60,000 students. Kyle is now a freshman at the University of Michigan, studying acting and creative writing. He is a popular keynote speaker at conferences and his assemblies are a huge hit with teens. To book an event, email Kyle at kyleprue@kyleprue.com.

The Sparks has won numerous national and international awards including Best Book and Best Fiction for Young Adults 2015. *The Sparks* was runner up for Best Young Adult Fiction at the Florida Book Festival and won Honorable Mentions at the New England Book Festival, Midwest Book Festival, Southern California Book Festival, and the International London Book Festival. Kyle also won an International Moonbeam Award and a prestigious Indie Fab award for Best Young Author.

Kyle is the founder of Sparking Literacy, a non-profit dedicated to lowering the high school dropout rate by inspiring teens to read, write and follow their dreams. You can learn more at sparkingliteracy.org.

CONNECT WITH KYLE

Follow Kyle on social media:
Facebook: facebook.com/kyleprue
Twitter: @kyleprue
Instagram: www.instagram.com/KylePrueOfficial

If you've enjoyed this book, sign up to receive our newsletter and you'll be entered to win a $50 Amazon gift card and a Sparks t-shirt. Members receive free gifts and updates about new releases. Join at kyleprue.com
If you would like to connect with other fans of the Feud series, join our Facebook group at www.facebook.com/FeudTrilogy

One more thing, If you liked this book, please leave a review. As a new author, I really appreciate your help to spread the word about my books. Thank you so much!

OTHER BOOKS BY KYLE

Book II: The Flames
Release: Aprial 25, 2017

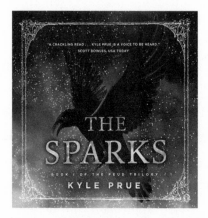

Audiobook
Release: Feburary 28, 2017

ACKNOWLEDGEMENTS

I would like to acknowledge and thank the following people for their special contribution to *The Sparks*.

First and foremost, I want to thank my parents, Kelly and Steve Prue, for their incredible support and endless man-hours as early readers and editors.

Secondly, I wouldn't have been able to accomplish this without the help of the editors who pushed me into endless revisions over the past year. Elizabeth Feins, who was spectacular at trimming the fat and bouncing ideas back and forth; Kelly McNees, for 14 pages of single spaced feedback that forced me to dig deep and mold the book into something I could be proud of; Julie Mosow, who helped as a fresh pair of eyes and was able to give instrumental plot advice; and Jim Basile, whose eagle eyes caught those punctuation and plot holes that touched up and finalized the book.

I would also like to thank those who we were willing to give me advice and guidance in my initial venture into publishing. That includes Michael Neff and everyone at the New York Writers Pitch Conference who initially taught me about what it meant to be original and assured me that I was on the right track with this novel; my acting manager, Cinda Snow, who has always stood by me and who I hope to repay when I'm a big movie star; and Howard Schott for teaching me to put in every last bit of work and for inspiring me to love reading and writing.

Thanks to Ashley Ruggirello at Cardboard Monet for the awesome cover design for the series. Thank you to Sari Cicurel, my PR agent, for her excellent work in making sure the book could get into the hands of as many readers as possible.

A big thank you to my fabulous agent, Veronica Park at Corvisiero Agency, for believing in me from the very start.

David and Courtney are, of course, to be included for being the original inspiration for the book and my writing. I couldn't have asked for better siblings. Also, to the rest of my wonderful extended family for being incredibly supportive of everything I do.

Above all, Seacrest Country Day School in Naples, Florida for their endless support, love and time. Erin Duffy and their entire faculty have been absolutely fantastic in encouraging me to follow my dreams and making Seacrest my second home. Not to mention my wonderful classmates who have inspired me daily to pursue what I love.

Last, but certainly not least, Drew Harrison. He was my first best friend and I've yet to meet another person with his unique intelligence and creativity. Without him, I never would have had the courage to disregard the naysayers and follow my dreams.

MISSION TO MONTE CARLO

Before Craig sat down he looked at her, thinking how lovely she was and how, with her hair falling over her shoulders, she looked very young, little more than a girl.

"I love you," he said. "I was aware of it just now when I saw what was happening in the Casino."

Aloya made an inarticulate little sound and her eyes filled with tears. Slowly Craig bent his head and very gently his lips found hers. Only when he felt that they were one with the stars and the moon, and at the same time enveloped by a glory that was not of this world, did he raise his head and she said in a whisper:

"I love... you... and I ought not bring you into this... ghastly situation which is... very dangerous... but there is no one... else I can turn to."

"You must tell me about it," Craig said, "but first I must kiss you again...."

Bantam Books by Barbara Cartland
Ask you bookseller for the books you have missed

Barbara Cartland's Library of Love Series

Mission to Monte Carlo

Barbara Cartland

BANTAM BOOKS
TORONTO · NEW YORK · LONDON · SYDNEY

MISSION TO MONTE CARLO
A Bantam Book / August 1982

ISBN 0-553-22876-5

Published simultaneously in the United States and Canada

Bantam Books are published by Bantam Books, Inc. Its trade-
mark, consisting of the words "Bantam Books" and the por-
trayal of a rooster, is Registered in U.S. Patent and Trademark
Office and in other countries. Marca Registrada. Bantam
Books, Inc., 666 Fifth Avenue, New York, New York 10103.

PRINTED IN THE UNITED STATES OF AMERICA

O   0 9 8 7 6 5 4 3 2 1

Author's Note

Monte Carlo in the last years of the last century was the smartest place in Europe. The guest-list to the small Principality reads like a mixture of the *Almanach de Gotha* and *Debrett*.

Yet, the division between the social classes was unbridgeable. During her honeymoon in Monte Carlo after her marriage to the ninth Duke of Marlborough, the Duchess, formerly Consuelo Vanderbilt, pointed out to him the elegance and beauty of some of the women to be seen in the Casino.

To her surprise, he forbáde her to mention them or to recognise the men who accompanied them, even if she had dined with them in the same party the previous night.

Only gradually did she understand that the lovely women were the leading Courtesans of Europe.

Other guests were the fascinating and extravagant Grand Duke Serge of Russia, the Grand Duke Nicolas, the Aga Khan, the beautiful, alluring Lily Langtry, the Duke of Montrose, the Prince of Denmark, and inevitably the Prince of Wales.

Countless novels, plays, and thrillers have been written about Monte Carlo, but there is no other place in the whole world which is synonymous with Kings and Princes, Grand Dukes, tricksters, cocottes, cocaine, systems, and suicides.

Mission to Monte Carlo

Chapter One
1900

The carriage drew up outside the Foreign Office and a tall man got out and walked in through the massive pillared door.

As soon as he appeared, and before his servant could speak, a young man in a frock-coat came hurrying forward.

"Mr. Vandervelt?"

The newcomer nodded.

"The Secretary of State for Foreign Affairs is waiting for you, Sir."

"Thank you," Craig Vandervelt replied.

He was escorted along the high-ceilinged, rather gloomy corridors until his escort opened a door into a large, impressive office.

Seated at a desk in front of a window which overlooked a small garden at the rear of the building was the Marquis of Lansdowne.

A very good-looking man, already going grey, he rose to his feet and held out his hand as Craig Vandervelt was announced.

"I heard only yesterday, Craig," he said, "that you were in London. I am delighted to see you."

"How are you, My Lord? I am on my way to Monte Carlo," Craig Vandervelt replied.

There was something almost defensive in his tone, as though he was warning the Marquis that he was only passing through England.

As if he understood, the Secretary of State said:

"Sit down. I have a lot to tell you."

Craig Vandervelt laughed.

"That is what I was afraid of!"

However, he seated himself in a comfortable chair, crossed his legs, and seemed very much at his ease.

The Marquis sat down opposite him, thinking, as a great many women had thought before him, that it would be hard to find a better-looking, more attractive young man anywhere in the world.

It was not surprising. Craig Vandervelt's father came from Texas, and it was his astute and brilliant brain which had turned what had been the Vandervelt misfortune into one of the greatest fortunes in America.

His mother, a daughter of the Duke of Newcastle, had been one of the great beauties of her generation. It was therefore not surprising that their only son would be not only extremely good-looking and irresistibly attractive, but also, although many people were unaware of it, had a brain which matched his father's.

Because he had no inclination to add to the enormous wealth his family had already accumulated, Craig had, from the world's point of view, become a "playboy."

He travelled extensively, and enjoyed himself not only in the great Capitals which catered for rich young men but also in more obscure, unknown parts of the earth, where a man had to prove his manhood rather than rely entirely on his pocket-book.

"I was thinking about you only a few days ago," the Marquis said, "and then, almost as if my prayers were answered, I was told you were actually here, and I was wondering how I could get in touch with you."

"I am staying with my cousin in Park Lane."

"I realise that now," the Marquis said, "but I had some anxious hours trying other places before I ran you to ground."

"You are making me feel rather like a fox," Craig protested, "and I have already told you, My Lord, I am on my way to Monte Carlo."

"That is what I might have expected," the Marquis said with a smile. "I am told that the Season there is gayer than it has ever been, and the beauties of the *Monde* and the *demi-Monde* glittering with jewels and covered in ospreys are dazzling!"

Craig threw back his head and laughed.

"I sense a note of envy in your voice, My Lord. You should accompany me to Monte Carlo."

"There is nothing I would enjoy more," the Marquis replied. "Unfortunately, I have to be here at the moment, although doubtless you will find the Prince of Wales amongst other Royal visitors at the green tables."

Craig smiled as if it was only to be expected, and the Marquis said:

"As it happens, if you had not been going to Monte Carlo, that is where I was going to ask you to go, and to cancel any other plans you had made."

There was a little silence. Then Craig said with a different look in his dark eyes:

"You speak as if there is something urgent."

"It is very urgent," the Marquis replied quietly, "and I believe that only you can help me."

Craig did not answer.

He knew that the Marquis would not speak in such a way unless what he required of him was something of international importance.

In fact, the Marquis of Lansdowne, before he became Secretary of State for Foreign Affairs, had enlisted Craig Vandervelt's help in ways which, if they had known about it, would have confounded those who looked on the American millionaire as an incessant seeker of pleasure.

It was the Marquis who had sensed that Craig was becoming bored with the role that had been thrust upon him and was growing cynical about his success with the women who flocked round him like bees round a honey-pot.

The Marquis had therefore enlisted his help in a small but important mission which concerned the German ambition for supremacy in Europe.

Craig had played his part so brilliantly that he had been thanked for what he did not only by the Prime Minister but also by the Queen.

The Marquis had continued to enlist the young American's assistance in one way or another again and again.

Because it was so secret and so very different in every way from his other pursuits, Craig had found himself intrigued and amused by what became at times a very dangerous pastime.

Twice he had missed by a hair's breadth being shot, and once an assailant's knife had been diverted by a split second of good timing.

The thrill of it, and the excitement of what he thought of as "dicing with death," was something which had become a part of his life, and he knew now that whatever the Marquis asked of him, he would agree to do it.

However, the Marquis seemed to have a little difficulty in choosing the words in which to explain the task that lay ahead.

As if he knew that Craig was waiting almost impatiently, he said:

"Forgive me if I seem hesitant. It is not because I am keeping secrets from you, but I am finding it difficult to explain how very little I know of the brief that I should have prepared before you arrived."

"The first thing to do," Craig said with an amused smile, "is to tell me what is the name of the enemy this time."

As he spoke, he thought that this was extremely

important because on one occasion when he was helping the Marquis he had been misinformed, or rather not told specifically, who was against him.

Only his intuition and his sixth sense had saved him from walking into a skilfully prepared trap from which it would have been impossible to extricate himself.

"The difficulty is," the Marquis said in reply to his question, "that as yet I have only suspicions rather than facts to justify my conviction that you are desperately needed in Monte Carlo at this particular moment."

"Then let me hear your suspicions," Craig suggested. "I am quite certain, My Lord, that when the time comes, I shall find them fully justified by something more lethal than a bow and arrow."

The Marquis laughed, but there was not much amusement in the sound.

"The trouble is, Craig," he said, "I am very apprehensive about what I am letting you in for. Our own Agents so far have come up with very little, and quite frankly, the men we have in Monte Carlo at the moment are unable to move in the right circles, where I believe they are needed."

"That, at any rate, should present no difficulty!" Craig remarked drily.

No-one knew better than he did that because he was so rich he was welcome wherever he went.

Yet, at twenty-nine years of age, it was a pity that when crowned Kings linked their arms with his, and Queens held out their soft hands in welcome, he inevitably wondered whether their enthusiasm for him was a response to his charm or to his unlimited Bank-balance.

As if the Marquis knew what he was thinking, he said:

"You are popular everywhere you go, Craig, and that is your great advantage from my professional point of view."

He lowered his voice instinctively as he said:

"I believe and hope that nobody has the slightest

idea outside these walls that your connection with me is anything other than that, through your mother, we are related. And they assume that it is only your search for amusement which takes you to strange places."

"I hope you are right, My Lord," Craig replied. "If it were not so, in some of the situations in which I have been involved I would not have been likely to last long."

The Marquis frowned.

"Perhaps I am wrong, Craig, in asking so much of you," he said, "but I hardly need tell you how useful you have been and how grateful we are."

His voice deepened as he continued:

"No-one else, and I mean *no-one* else, could have obtained the information which you have given us and saved us from being involved in disastrous circumstances which might have had far-reaching consequences for the peace of the world."

"Thank you," Craig said quietly. "And now suppose you tell me exactly what you want this time."

"I wish I knew," the Marquis replied, "but let me give you an outline."

Craig listened attentively as he began:

"As you understand, because you have helped us before, our position in India appears to be threatened by Russian advances in Central Asia."

Craig nodded, and the Marquis continued:

"Because Russia extends her Sovereignty towards Afghanistan, we have pushed the Frontiers of India farther to the west and the northwest."

This was so well known to Craig that he did not even trouble to murmur agreement, and the Marquis continued:

"Tibet, once dominated by China, is still independent and very hostile to outsiders, but we are worried."

Now Craig bent forward.

"Why?"

The Marquis dropped his voice even lower, almost as if he suspected that the walls had ears.

"A coded message from the Viceroy," he said, "has told us that he believes a secret Treaty exists between Russia and China, giving the former special rights in Tibet."

"It seems almost impossible."

"I agree with you," the Marquis answered, "but Lord Curzon is sure that Russia has sent arms to Tibet, and he suspects that there will soon be trouble induced by Russia on India's Tibetan border."

The Marquis fell silent, and after a moment Craig said:

"I thought you wanted me to go to Monte Carlo."

"I do," the Marquis agreed, "because I have learnt that Randall Sare arrived there three weeks ago without our being aware of it."

Craig looked up in surprise.

"Randall Sare? I do not believe it! I never thought he would come home. When I last saw him in India, he said he intended to live the rest of his life in Tibet."

"So you told me at the time," the Marquis said, "but obviously he has changed his mind, and since he arrived in Monte Carlo without getting in touch with us in any way, I can only think the explanation is that he is in hiding because of the information he carries in his mind."

"But why Monte Carlo?" Craig asked. "Why did he not come straight back to England?"

"That is something I do not know," the Marquis answered. "I agree with you that it seems a strange place to stop, and I never thought that Sare was a likely person to be addicted to gambling."

"No, that would be impossible," Craig agreed.

He sat back again in his chair, and there was a frown between his eyes as he concentrated.

"I can only think," he said after a moment, "that he had some particular reason for disembarking at

Villefranche, where whatever ship he was travelling in would have stopped. But if he got as far as that, did he then go on to Monte Carlo?"

"It is too difficult for me to answer," the Marquis said, "and that is why I am asking you—no, I am begging you, Craig—to go to Monte Carlo as quickly as you can and find Randall Sare."

"You mean your people have not been in touch with him?"

"No. They saw him, I think in a street, then lost sight of him before they could make contact."

"It seems incredible," Craig murmured, "and very inefficient."

"You must not blame our men too harshly," the Marquis said. "As the one I interviewed explained, he was told never to intrude on anybody of Randall Sare's importance without being quite sure that he would not be detected doing so, or that Sare would welcome the contact."

"That I can understand," Craig said. "But if, as you suspect, he is bringing back information of such importance, he may have gone into hiding until he can shake off his pursuers."

"That thought did cross my mind," the Marquis replied. "It might also account for the fact that he left the ship he was on."

He paused before he added:

"The sea is a very convenient way of getting rid of anybody who is unwanted."

"I agree," Craig said, "but I cannot believe that if Randall Sare was spotted three weeks ago, he is still sitting in Monte Carlo."

"I said he *arrived* three weeks ago," the Marquis corrected, "and he was seen a week later. It was after that that one of our men came back to tell me he was there, leaving two others to continue the chase, so to speak. They may of course have found him by this time, but if they have not, then I am praying that you will succeed where they have failed."

Craig's voice was rather cynical as he said:

"I fear you are being optimistic. Knowing Sare, the sort of places in which he might be hiding are not those I am expected to frequent when I am in Monte Carlo."

"I am aware of that," the Marquis said, "and that brings me to the second part of my mission."

"What is that?"

"My informant who returned to tell me about Sare also told me that he is somewhat anxious about Lord Neasdon."

"Do I know him?" Craig asked.

"I do not think you have ever met him, because since he is a comparative newcomer to the Foreign Office, I thought it would be a great mistake for him to know that you and I have any connection with each other except that we are somewhat distantly related."

"Of course," Craig murmured.

"He is quite an attractive man, about ten years older than yourself, and he has worked hard in the Diplomatic Service to get the position in which he is now. Because my predecessor had known him for years and was very fond of him, he was put in line for being accepted here on the permanent staff while he was still serving his time in the Embassies of Europe."

"I understand."

"Neasdon is unmarried, although I do not need to tell you that he has had a great number of *affaires de coeur* with the Beauties that are to be found at Marlborough House."

The Marquis paused for a moment, then as Craig did not interrupt, he went on:

"Now I understand that there is a new woman in his life, and from all I have heard she may be dangerous."

"Who is she?" Craig enquired.

"Her name," the Marquis replied, "is the Countess Aloya Zladamir."

"Russian, I presume?"

"I think so, although apparently nobody is quite certain. The Russians here to whom I have mentioned her name casually have never heard of her."

"There are, I believe," Craig said, "over two million Counts in Russia, so it would be impossible for anybody to be acquainted with all of them!"

The Marquis frowned.

"It only makes your task more difficult."

"Then I am going to search not only for Sare but also for Aloya Zladamir?"

"Exactly!" the Marquis agreed. "I am well aware that there may be nothing in Neasdon's interest in her. At the same time, the Russians are very clever with their spies and are determined to ferret out a great deal that we have no wish for them to know. That is especially true of Tibet."

"Do you think there is any link between Sare and the Countess?"

"None that I know of, but that is for you to find out," the Marquis replied, "and I think it would be a mistake for me to give you an introduction to Neasdon. It might be too obvious."

"I am sure there will be no difficulty in my getting to know him," Craig said.

"He has a great many friends in Monte Carlo who I am sure will be yours too. All I can beg you, Craig, if you think that Neasdon looks like being indiscreet in any way, is to step in and prevent it."

Craig raised his eye-brows, and now there was a definite twinkle in his eyes and a twist to his lips as he asked:

"Are you really suggesting. . . ?"

"I am merely pointing out," the Marquis said, "that if any woman had a choice, I am certain she would prefer a young American millionaire to a rather dull, none-too-wealthy English Peer!"

Craig laughed.

"This time, My Lord, you really have thought out a

melodramatic situation which is more suitable to Drury Lane than to the Casino in Monte Carlo!"

"I would not be too sure of that," the Marquis said, "and, quite frankly, Craig, I am perturbed."

"Why?"

"It was only in the last two days that I discovered that in mistaken zeal, one of my subordinates informed Neasdon of our concern over Tibet and that we have undercover Agents who attempt to keep us informed of the Russian attitude in that far-away, little-known country."

He paused before he went on:

"It seems almost too far-fetched to be anything but sheer melodrama, but if Randall Sare is being shadowed by Russians, and if Neasdon inadvertently reveals to the delectable Countess what information we already have, the two combined would be explosive to the point where the work of years could be undone and a great many lives put in jeopardy."

"I understand," Craig said, his eyes twinkling, "and of course it would be a pleasure to make the acquaintance of the Countess."

"They tell me she is very beautiful," the Marquis said with a slight smile.

"Then that at least should make my task more pleasant. Is that all you have to tell me?"

The Marquis rose from his desk.

"I have here the names of our men in Monte Carlo, but as you know, it would be very unwise to contact them unless it is absolutely necessary. They should not know that you have any connection with us. In fact, I hope no-one in Monte Carlo will be aware of it."

"That is how I prefer it," Craig said. "If there is one thing I dislike, it is working with other people."

"I know that, and perhaps that is why you are so successful. At the same time, be careful!"

Craig raised his eye-brows as he took the piece of paper from the Marquis's hand.

"I do not remember you ever saying that to me before."

"I am saying it this time. I take the Russian menace very, very seriously. I also believe they will stop at nothing to gain their objectives."

"You mean India!"

"Yes. They have already shown us how ruthless they can be in Afghanistan, and there is no doubt at all that the money, the weapons, and the inciting of the tribesmen on the Northwest Frontier all originate from St. Petersburg."

"You have certainly given me an unusual and intriguing assignment this time," Craig said. "I only hope I will not fail you."

"You have never done so yet," the Marquis replied, "and because of your unique position in the Social World, there is nobody else who could help me as you can at this particular moment. If you have anything to communicate to me, do it in the usual way. I am certain the code we have used before has not yet been broken."

"I hope not!"

Craig put the piece of paper in his pocket and held out his hand.

"Thank you," he said, "and I mean it! This is just what I needed at a moment when life in New York had become monotonous, and for the same reason I do not wish to stay in London."

"What you really mean," the Marquis said, "is that your heart is unoccupied, and that is exactly what I hoped it would be!"

Craig laughed.

"I am not even certain if I have a heart, but shall I say my eyes find the landscape too familiar, and 'pastures new' would be a welcome change."

The Marquis knew without his saying any more that Craig was really insinuating that he had finished with one love-affair and the lady's place in his life had not yet been filled.

Too, he had heard many women complaining that Craig Vandervelt was cruel, ruthless, and heartless, and that he was always the one who was bored first, while the woman who had once engaged his attention was left weeping and bewailing her dismissal.

Because Craig's affairs were always with sophisticated beauties who were safely married, there was no question of his being forced to the altar by an irate father, although occasionally a jealous husband would threaten to "call him out."

But in some skilful manner of his own he had managed over the years to avoid any open scandal, although it was impossible to prevent his attractions from being whispered about from *Boudoir* to *Boudoir*.

The Marquis, having shaken his visitor by the hand, walked to the door and thought as he did so that he not only wished he was young again but also regretted that when he was the same age as Craig he had let far too many opportunities pass him by.

Then he told himself that as a respectable married man, those were not the sort of thoughts he should be having!

Yet, he was quite sure that all over the world there were men like himself who were envious and jealous of Craig not only as a millionaire but also as a man.

The door of the office opened, and as if Craig understood the importance of the object of the interview being kept a secret, he said in a voice that could be heard down the corridor:

"Well, good-bye, My Lord. Give my love to all our relatives and say how sorry I am not to see them this trip. Perhaps I will be able to drop in again before I return to New York."

"Yes, do that," the Marquis said affably. "Enjoy yourself in Monte Carlo, and I hope you win at the tables."

"I doubt it," Craig said with a laugh as he walked away. "But there are other things to entertain one there besides cards."

There was an obvious innuendo in his voice, and the gaiety with which he spoke brought a knowing smile to those who were near enough to hear what had been said.

Then Craig walked jauntily down the corridor to where his carriage was waiting for him in the street outside.

* * *

The next day Craig Vandervelt left on the boat-train to Dover.

He travelled with a Courier, two Valets, and a secretary, and an entire coach was engaged for him and his staff.

At Dover, two cabins on the boat were reserved for him and his *entourage*, and again there was a private coach reserved for him on the Calais–Mediterranean Express.

As was usual, his secretary provided him with every newspaper and magazine that was published, and there was also a hamper consisting of his favourite drinks and several dishes prepared by his cousin's Chef at Newcastle House.

Craig sat alone, thinking out what he had learnt from the Marquis and finding the prospect in front of him intriguing and stimulating.

It was nearly a year since he had last undertaken a mission at the request of the Marquis. Although he had known it would be a great mistake to become involved again too soon in Foreign Affairs, and that it was wise that people should forget his existence in that sphere before he appeared again in a world that was very different from his own, he had begun to find that time lay heavily on his hand.

He was growing more cynical than ever about the society which welcomed him in London, Paris, and New York.

He knew he owed his entree into every Capital to his father's wealth. At the same time, because he had had such a cosmopolitan education, the Social World opened its arms to him and considered him as part of it wherever he went.

Even the most disdainful French aristocrats offered him their hospitality, and although it might originate from the fact that the French respected the fact that his grandfather was a Duke, they soon found that his charm, his almost perfect knowledge of their language, and the fact that he was extremely proficient at their sports all combined to make him a real friend.

He was invited not only to Balls and Receptions in Paris, which were normally exclusively French, but also to go boar-hunting, to shoot, and to sail with the young French aristocrats who usually preferred to bar outsiders from their pastimes.

Where women were concerned, the French were no different from the English or the Americans. They had only to see Craig to behave as if he were the Pied Piper, who must willy-nilly be followed.

Sometimes he told himself it was the golden coins which attracted them, but he would have been very obtuse if he had not realised that they also found him fascinating as a man and unique as an ardent lover.

"Je t'adore!" the French women murmured against his lips, and it was a refrain which was repeated in almost every language from the North to the South Pole.

And yet it was something which Craig himself had never said to a woman.

He could not remember when he had first told himself that he would never say those three words that every woman craved, until they could be spoken not only with his lips but also with his heart and perhaps, although he was not sure if he had one, his soul.

It was his mother who, because she was so beautiful and he loved her so overwhelmingly, had ingrained in him when he was a child the ideals of chivalry, and that love between a man and a woman at its best and its highest was sacred.

Lady Elizabeth, eldest daughter of the Duke of Newcastle, had fallen in love with Cornelius Vandervelt when he came to England as a young man, ambitious, positive, rather aggressively American, and determined to be a millionaire.

He was already rich by European standards, but as far as he himself was concerned, this was only the beginning of the ladder he intended to climb, and no-one should stop him from doing so.

He had met Lady Elizabeth in London at a party, and had fallen madly, head-over-heels in love with her.

Like everything else he coveted, he had swept her off her feet and by sheer drive and determination persuaded her to marry him.

It had not been easy, for her father, the Duke, had been violently opposed to the marriage, but Elizabeth had loved Cornelius in the manner of Romeo and Juliet, Dante and Beatrice, and the Troubadours in the Courts of Love.

Theirs had been a blissfully happy marriage until she died when her son was only sixteen.

By that time she had implanted in him her own ideals, her own desire for perfection, and he knew that until he could find a woman as beautiful, as sweet, and with the same nobility of character as his mother, he would never be in love.

It was this reserve within him which, because they could not reach the heights he demanded of them, drove women wild.

They had only to meet Craig to fall in love, and almost before he was aware of them they would throw themselves and their hearts at his feet.

He would not have been human if he had not accepted the favours that were offered him ever since he had grown up.

At the same time, over the years he became more

and more fastidious, and had grown used to hearing even those he accepted asking:

"What is wrong, Craig? Where have I failed you? What do you want that I have not given you already?"

It was impossible to explain, impossible to put into words where they did fail him.

Sometimes he would think, when some exquisitely beautiful creature held out her arms to him and her eyes lit up at his approach, that he had found what he was seeking.

But always in a short while he was disappointed, disillusioned, and was back seeking again for what he sensed was just over the horizon and yet could never reach.

Of course he had not put all this into words, not even to himself, but sometimes he thought his life was a pilgrimage and he would never reach the end except in death.

Journeying to Monte Carlo, he was thinking not so much about the Countess Aloya Zladamir as of Randall Sare.

Nobody knew better than he did the importance of his research in Tibet for the British Government.

The son of an explorer who was also an Asiatic Scholar, Sare had grown up partly in India and Nepal, and then had been sent to School in England, and to Oxford University.

He had done brilliantly in both, then returned to the land where he had been born and which he loved, to become of inestimable value to the British in what was known as *The Great Game*.

All over India there was a secret espionage organisation which recruited men who were trained and initiated in working, and at the same time taking their lives in their hands, for the protection of India and the peace of the Eastern world.

The Great Game had a network which extended into

Afghanistan and involved not only Europeans but a great
many Indians as well.

In a locked book in the Indian Survey Department
was a list of numbers which represented a variety of
secret Agents by whom the Russians and enemies of the
country were often rendered powerless or exposed
when they least expected it.

Randall Sare became an anonymous number in *The
Great Game,* in which his brilliance brought him to the
top of the list for those who understood the spider's-
web which hid such vital secrets.

To Craig it seemed incredible that Sare should first of
all have returned from Tibet without anyone in the
Foreign Office knowing of it, and secondly that he
should have stopped at Monte Carlo, and again not
communicated with the English Agents there, who
should have been known to him.

He began to suspect, as the Marquis had, that he had
a good reason for keeping out of sight, which suggested
that he was being followed and his life was in danger.

Because he not only admired Randall Sare but also
liked him as a man, he could only pray that he would
be successful where the others had failed and find him
as quickly as possible.

He did not underestimate how difficult it would be
and the risk that if he blundered into something which
did not concern him, he might endanger both Randall
Sare's life and his own.

It was only when he had thought for a long time
about a man who knew Tibet perhaps better than any
other white man, and whose secrets would be a prize
beyond price if they fell into the hands of the Russians,
that he allowed himself to consider the second mission
he had been given—the Countess Aloya Zladamir.

Here again he suspected, as the Marquis did, that if
she was pursuing Lord Neasdon there was a good
reason for it. At the same time, he could not believe
that Neasdon would be so stupid as not to realise in his

position how careful he should be in choosing those
with whom he associated.

'Russians! Always Russians!' Craig thought to himself.

At the same time, he remembered with satisfaction
that there were a number in Monte Carlo with whom
he was friendly.

The Arch Dukes, who were enormously wealthy, and
most of them extremely attractive, had made Monte
Carlo a special haven when they became bored with the
pomp of their own country and the troubles that seemed
to increase in the reign of every Tsar.

Once a year they would gravitate like migrating birds
towards Monte Carlo, where they built themselves
magnificently ornate Villas, pursued the most beautiful
women, whom they hung with emeralds and pearls,
and gambled with astronomical sums in the Casinos, to
the immense satisfaction of the authorities.

There was no race of men who could be more extravagant, more flamboyant, and at the same time more
attractive.

Craig looked forward to renewing his acquaintance
with the Grand Duke Boris and the Grand Duke Michael,
besides being certain that in their circle would be the
most alluring and exotic women to be found anywhere
in Europe.

He wondered if the Countess Aloya would be amongst
them, then some instinct, he was not certain why, told
him that it was unlikely.

* * *

As the train puffed early in the morning into Nice,
Craig wondered for a moment if he should leave it
there and seek his yacht, which he had ordered to come
from Marseilles to Monte Carlo.

He was certain that it would only just have had time
to reach Villefranche, and it might be more enjoyable to
go by sea to the harbour at Monte Carlo, rather than to
do the rest of the journey by train.

Then he told himself that that would take time, and as it was he could be in Monte Carlo in another hour.

He therefore stayed on the train, and although his secretary came to his compartment to ask if there was anything he wanted, he merely told him to buy the French morning newspapers and perused them until the line came to an end at the station in Monte Carlo.

From there he walked outside to where an open carriage was waiting for him, leaving his servants to cope with the luggage and follow in another carriage.

He drove off alone, taking off his hat as he did so to feel the sea breeze and the warmth of the sun on his forehead after the heat and stuffiness of the train.

As the horses went down a small incline towards the harbour, he saw a large number of yachts at anchor, some large, some small, all flying the flags of their own countries.

Craig's eyes went from a large number of French flags of red, white, and blue, to the White Ensign of the British ships. Then he was aware that there were two Russian yachts, side by side, both of them carrying the Imperial Eagle on their flags.

He thought the first thing he would do would be to find out to whom they belonged.

As the horses started to climb the steep hill towards the gold-domed Casino ahead, he looked back almost as if the Russian ships drew him like a magnet and they held the secrets that he was seeking to solve.

When Craig Vandervelt stayed in Monte Carlo, being a bachelor, he did not rent a Villa, which would have been quite easy for him to do, but preferred to stay at the Hôtel de Paris and also to have his own yacht in the harbour.

This meant that he was not restricted in any way from leaving at a moment's notice, or, if he wished to be alone or with some very attractive Siren, he could steam along the coast of Italy for a day or two and return when it suited him.

At the Hôtel de Paris he was greeted with great respect, and the Manager personally took him up to his Suite.

It was very palatial. Not only was it the best in the whole building, but because he liked quiet and privacy, Craig usually engaged several rooms on each side of it.

His Sitting-Room was filled with flowers, which might seem unusual for a man, but he not only liked their fragrance but disliked the unlived-in look of Hotel rooms.

There were flowers also in his bedroom, and as he looked out the window he saw his yacht arrive in the harbour below him.

Its lines not only looked beautiful, but the inside of the vessel incorporated every comfort known to those who sailed the seas.

Craig Vandervelt's mind was never still, and he had invented a number of gadgets, some of which had already been adopted by other yacht-owners, while some were so new that no-one else had as yet become aware of them.

He thought with satisfaction that he would be able to test some of his most recent innovations in the next few days, but at the moment the most important thing was to find his bearings and take the first step in his plan to find Randall Sare.

Half-an-hour later, however, nobody seeing him saunter out into the sunshine would have suspected that Craig was thinking of anything except his own enjoyment of the frivolities of the small Principality of Monaco.

Already, although it was still early, many of the more important guests were taking the air, walking along the terraced garden behind the Casino or across the Square towards the tables outside the Café de la Paix, where the gossips sat drinking *aperitifs* and criticizing one another.

Almost before he had gone a few steps Craig was greeted by friends and acquaintances.

"Craig! I was sure you would be here!" exclaimed one lovely woman wrapped in sables and wearing a King's ransom in jewels.

And Gaby Delys, the most talked-of and acclaimed actress in Paris, wearing a hat covered in ospreys, kissed him on both cheeks.

"*Mon cher* Craig! I am enchanted to see you!"

Craig bowed, kissed the soft hands, and, as the morning progressed, moved from one table to another, from one group to the next.

He was always sure of his welcome, always certain that there would be an invitation in the sparkling eyes of the women who saw him and a provocative pout to their red lips.

When finally he had ordered himself a very small *aperitif* and was seated beside Zsi-Zsi de la Tour, who was a notorious gossip, he asked:

"Tell me, Zsi-Zsi, who is in Monte Carlo?"

"As far as I am concerned, *mon brave*, there is only you!"

Craig twisted his lips.

"What would the Grand Duke say to that?"

She shrugged her shoulders in a typically French manner.

"He will be jealous, which is good for him!"

Craig laughed.

"I have no desire to disrupt His Imperial Highness's happy time with you."

"Which is a polite way of saying in English that you have other fish to fry,'" Zsi-Zsi answered.

Craig laughed.

Zsi-Zsi was always unpredictable, and although the fiery love-affair they had had together was over five years ago, they had remained friends and he would never have thought of going to Paris without visiting her.

Craig looked round.

"I see very few new faces and quite a lot of them have grown older."

"That is definitely unkind of you, Craig, and not like the pretty speeches you used to make."

"I am not referring to you," Craig protested. "You know as well as I do that you are eternally young and more beautiful with every year that passes."

"That is better!" Zsi-Zsi approved. "I only wish it were true. However, at least Boris still finds me irresistible."

"I am glad about that. I like him, and I see he has given you some very pretty baubles."

As he spoke Craig looked mockingly at the huge emeralds that encircled Zsi-Zsi's neck, and the one that was almost the size of a louis on her finger.

She gave him a provocative little glance from under her mascaraed eye-lashes before she said:

"Do you know which one I treasure most of all the jewels I have been given?"

"I have no idea."

"The little St. Christopher you gave me, and you may believe me when I tell you that I always carry it in my bag. It is my luck, my talisman, and inevitably a *bon chance* in the Casino."

"I am glad," Craig said with a smile. "And now I return to my original question. Who is here with whom I can amuse myself, since you are definitely *engagée?*"

"Now let me think..." Zsi-Zsi pondered. "I understand you would not wish, as the English say, to 'boil your vegetables in the same water twice.'"

"Certainly not."

Zsi-Zsi pursed her lips together.

"Now that I think about it, there are very few new faces!" She paused, then she added: "There is one, but I have no idea from where she comes."

"Who is that?" Craig asked in a voice of indifference,

his eyes moving over the crowd drinking and talking round them.

"She calls herself," Zsi-Zsi replied, "the Countess Aloya Zladamir, but Boris says he has never heard of her."

Chapter Two

When Craig returned to the Hôtel de Paris he went first to the Reception Desk to ask if there were any letters for him.

While the man was looking, he glanced quickly at the Hotel Register which stood open on the counter.

He had long ago taught himself to read upside-down, and amongst a long list of celebrities he saw the name for which he was looking.

It was a great satisfaction to know that the Countess was under the same roof, and when the man returned to hand him several letters bearing American stamps, Craig said casually:

"I am pleased with my rooms, but I hope you have not placed a lot of noisy people on my floor, as you did two years ago."

"I am sure, *Monsieur* Vandervelt, you will find it very quiet," the Receptionist answered quickly.

"I hope you are right," Craig said with a doubtful note in his voice.

The Receptionist looked at the keys behind him.

"One of the guests near you, *Monsieur,* is the Duke of Norfolk, who always retires to bed early, and another is the Grand Duke of Lichtenstein."

Craig nodded as if he was more or less satisfied; then,

as if he was eager to please him, the Receptionist added:

"Another is the Countess Aloya Zladamir, a newcomer to the Hôtel de Paris."

"I do not think I have heard of her," Craig said casually, and walked away with an air of indifference.

However, he had discovered what he wanted to know, and asking more or less the same question of the waiter who brought him some Evian water, he learnt that the Countess's room adjoined the last one which was a part of his own Suite.

This meant that the balcony of her Sitting-Room looked out in the same direction as his, at the magnificent view of the sea, the harbour, and the Palace perched high on the promontory.

Craig already had an invitation to luncheon, and as he went downstairs he found his friends drinking in the ante-room of the Restaurant and wondered if he would see the Countess and if he would be able to recognise her.

He had known a number of Russian women who were exceedingly beautiful, and he thought they usually had a flamboyance about them which appealed, as their male counterparts did, to the romantic notions which the rest of the world had about the Russians.

It might be true of the aristocrats, but no-one knew better than Craig how completely ruthless and often brutal the Russian soldiers were in Afghanistan and in other countries under their control.

In the crowded Restaurant, with its painted walls, crystal chandeliers, and gold ornamentation, were a great number of people he knew and who greeted him with varying degrees of delight, but he thought there was no-one who was likely to be the Countess.

He also saw Lord Neasdon lunching with two gentlemen of about the same age as himself, but without any female companion.

When luncheon was over, Craig with some difficulty

disentangled himself from his friends, and saying he needed the exercise walked from the Hôtel de Paris down the hill in the direction of the harbour.

He knew that his yacht had arrived, but he had another mission on the way, which took him, surprisingly enough, to the small Church under the railway-arch where few of the gambling visitors to Monte Carlo were ever seen.

The Chapel of St. Dévoté had been built at the foot of a deep ravine so that little light penetrated through the stained-glass windows, and inside it was dark, save for the candles flickering in front of a statue.

There were only two old women with shawls over their heads kneeling in prayer as Craig entered, and he moved softly up the side aisle to where there was a Confessional Box.

He entered it, and was aware that there was a Priest on the other side of an open grating.

They could not see each other, but the Priest obviously sensed his presence, and after a moment he said in Latin:

"*In nomine Patris et Filii, et Spiritus Sancti, Amen.*"*

Craig knelt so that his face was near to the grating, and he said in a low voice that it would have been impossible for anybody outside to hear:

"Is that you, Father Augustin? This is Craig."

There was a silence of surprise before the Priest said:

"I had not heard, *mon fils*, that you had arrived."

"I only got into Monte Carlo a few hours ago."

"It is agreeable to know that you are back with us again."

"I am glad to be here, but, Father, I need your help."

There was a faint note of amusement in the Priest's voice as he answered:

"I might have guessed that would be the reason for such an immediate visit."

*"In the name of the Father and of the Son and of the Holy Ghost, Amen."

"I am searching for somebody," Craig said, "who is, I believe, in great danger."

"And you think I may know of him?"

"I have no other way of contacting him, and you, Father, have helped me in the past to prevent a man from losing his life, which is a gift from God."

"Tell me the name of the man you seek."

"Randall Sare."

"Should I have heard of him?"

"You may have done. His father, Conrad Sare, was a great Oriental Scholar whose books are read all over the world by those who would learn from the East. I am sure most Monastery Libraries contain his work on Buddhism."

The Priest gave a low exclamation.

"Now I know of whom you speak. It is his son you are looking for?"

"I know he was in Monte Carlo a few weeks ago, but I think he is now hiding from men who are pursuing him."

"Where did he come from?"

Just for a moment Craig hesitated. Then, knowing that he could trust the man to whom he was speaking, he said quietly:

"From Tibet."

He knew there was no need to say any more. Father Augustin was extremely intelligent and, as Craig had found in the past, well informed.

There was a pause before he said:

"I will do what I can."

"That is all I ask," Craig said, "and thank you, Father. I am quite certain you have a large number of poor who need the solace of a few American dollars."

"Do not thank me until I have been able to help you," the Priest answered, "and come, if you can, again tomorrow."

"I will do that, and thank you, *mon père*. I would like you to know that the last man you helped is living comfortably outside New York and is very content to be an American citizen."

"I will thank God for His help in enabling me to rescue him," the Priest said quietly.

Craig rose from his knees.

"Good-bye, Father, and I cannot tell you how grateful I am for your help."

In a voice that carried beyond the thin walls of the Confessional, the Priest said:

"*Misereatur vestri omnipoteus Deus, et dimissis peccatis vestris perducat vos ad vitam aeternam.*"*

As Craig parted the curtain and went back into the Church, he saw that there was only one elderly woman waiting to take his place at the Confessional Box, and she did not even raise her eyes as he passed.

At the same time, he knew that he could not be too careful, and as he reached the statue of Joan of Arc he lit a candle and dropped a few coins noisily into the box in front of it.

Then he walked out into the sunshine, feeling as if he had transferred some of his problem onto shoulders that were broader than his own.

Nobody who knew Craig would have expected him to be friends with a Catholic Priest, and as he walked quickly to the road leading directly to the harbour, he hoped he would not be noticed.

However, there was little likelihood of that, since at this time of day the visitors to Monte Carlo were either sleeping off the very large luncheon they had eaten, or already were finding their fingers itching for the cards in the exclusive *Salle Touzet*.

The main Casino, to which the *Salle Touzet* was a recent addition, would be filled with the ordinary people of the town and the unimportant visitors, hypnotised by the rolling balls of the Roulette-tables, and Craig was glad that he had no reason to join them.

*"May Almighty God have mercy upon you, forgive you your sins and bring you to life everlasting."

He reached the harbour and found as he expected that his yacht was already moored and the gang-plank was down on the Quay.

He walked aboard to be greeted by his Captain and First Officer, who were obviously genuinely delighted that they had been ordered to put to sea after spending the winter in harbour at Marseilles.

"Where do you plan to go, Mr. Vandervelt?" the Captain asked eagerly, and Craig knew he was hoping they would not linger too long in any harbour.

"I do not know for the moment," he replied, "but I would like you to be ready to leave at a moment's notice. You know how restless I become when I am confined to one place."

"That is what I was hoping you would say, Sir," the Captain replied. "The Greek Islands are very attractive at this time of year."

"I had not forgotten that," Craig agreed, then added in a more practical tone: "Are all the new gadgets I ordered installed?"

"Aye, aye, Sir, and I hope you will come see them."

Craig started with the bridge and saw some of his inventions in action, then walked round the yacht, noting that the paintings he had ordered had been hung, a new idea for keeping the tables steady in a storm had been installed, and the very much larger bed he had bought for his State-Room because he found the last one too cramped was in place.

It was only when he went back on deck again that he said:

"I see there are two Russian yachts in the harbour. Will you find out to whom they belong?"

"I have already asked that, Sir," the Captain answered, "but when I enquired I could not obtain an answer. However, the Duke of Westminster's yacht is magnificent, and Mr. Pierpont Morgan is aboard his, which I was told arrived here last week."

Craig was listening and he was also noting that there

was a mooring between the Duke of Westminster's and the first of the Russian yachts.

After a moment he said:

"As I am rather interested to see if the Russians are as advanced as we are ourselves, I think it might be a good idea if we go out to sea for the next hour, and when we return, move into the mooring next to the first yacht carrying the Imperial Flag."

"I am sure that can be arranged, Sir," the Captain replied. "I will just go and have a word with the Harbour Master."

The Captain went ashore, and Craig spent the time on a further inspection of his yacht.

She was named *The Mermaid* and he has supervised every inch of her while she was being built. In fact, he thought he would be very piqued if any of the other expensive and magnificent-looking yachts in the harbour had more advanced technology than his or were in any way more comfortable.

He did not have to wait long before the Captain returned, and he knew before the man spoke that his request had been refused.

"I am sorry, Mr. Vandervelt," he said, "but the Harbour Master tells me that the Russians are not at the moment using that particular mooring but have reserved and paid for it."

Craig raised his eye-brows but did not say anything, and the Captain went on:

"It seems extraordinary and rather high-handed, but the Harbour Master told me that all the best places, which are those straight onto the Quay, are fully booked, and he has already had three requests this morning which he has had to turn down and offer the applicants a mooring out in the harbour."

Because this meant being rowed ashore every time one left the yacht, Craig knew that most owners found it extremely irritating.

Now with a smile he said:

"Well, we should be thankful you were clever enough to get this place. Now show me what speed *The Mermaid* can do with her new engine."

Two hours later, when Craig left the yacht, he again walked up the hill towards the Casino.

He had his own car in Monte Carlo, although he had not yet asked for it, and he was aware that his chauffeur would not only be wanting to see him but would also be eager to enquire if he would enter in the *Concours d'Élégance*, which had been inaugurated two years ago and proved a tremendous success.

This thought gave Craig an idea, as he remembered that those who owned their own cars would be looking for beautiful ladies to show off.

He had taken part in the *Concours* the previous year and remembered that the motor-cars were exhibited on the terrace below the Casino, where they were examined by a Jury.

At 3:00 P.M. they went in procession round the gardens, then pulled up in front of a grandstand where the prizes were awarded. After this they circled the gardens again and a further prize was given to the most elegantly dressed woman in a car.

Last year, Craig had taken the *Grand Prix d'Honneur* as the chief award. Although the policy was never to give second or third prizes, the announcements gave not only the names of those who were first in the *Prix d'Honneur*, the *Grand Prix d'Honneur*, and the *Premier Prix*, but also the names of the ladies, their dressmakers, and their milliners.

This ensured frantic competition amongst both the ladies themselves and those who dressed them.

Craig remembered with amusement that the very alluring beauty who had won the prize with him had told him that this ensured that she would be dressed by her Parisian dressmaker for the rest of the year in gowns which would either be free or half-price.

Because he was looking for somebody spectacular

whom he was certain he would recognise on sight, he walked into the Casino, through the ordinary Gaming-Rooms, and into the *Salle Touzet*.

There were lovely, elegantly dressed, beautiful women at almost every table, their eyes glued to the cards or the Roulette-wheel, and therefore paying little attention either to the men who sat beside them or to those who wandered about, looking for somebody to entertain them.

Craig found the Grand Duke Boris smoking a large cigar while Zsi-Zsi was for the moment intent only on staking the gold louis he had given her on what she considered her "lucky numbers."

Craig was well aware how superstitious Zsi-Zsi was, but that was nothing new, for most gamblers had what they believed were lucky charms which would ensure their winning at the tables.

He had known women who carried with them the skin of a venomous snake, an eagle's claw, a rabbit's foot, and even a piece of a hangman's rope.

He had also known men who put spoonfuls of salt in the pockets of their evening-coats to induce the cards to bring them luck.

He had always thought them ridiculous, since all a man really needed was an intuition which warned him of danger and a perception which told him there was trouble ahead.

However, this was something he would not have said to the Grand Duke Boris, who, like most of his countrymen, believed that luck was a lady and could therefore be wooed.

"How are you, Craig?" the Grand Duke asked genially.

"All the better for seeing you, Sir," Craig replied. "Are you enjoying yourself?"

"Things seem to be pretty dull at the moment," the Grand Duke replied. "But I must certainly give a party now that you have arrived. What about tomorrow night?"

"I shall be very honoured," Craig replied.

"I will tell Zsi-Zsi to ask all your particular friends, but none of your enemies, if you have any."

"I am always hoping they are few and far between."

"There you are right," the Grand Duke said. "You are a very popular man, Craig, and as I understand you are alone, we must find somebody who is beautiful to keep you anchored here for at least a little while."

He paused before he added:

"I see that your yacht is in the harbour so that you will be able to steal away without our being able to prevent you."

Craig laughed.

"I have every intention of staying for a while. I find New York boring, and I have no wish to be in London at this time of the year."

"I expect it is raining."

"I am sure it is," Craig said, laughing.

As they were talking they had moved across the room to where there was an open window and sat down at a table in the centre of it.

A waiter came hurrying to the Grand Duke's side.

He ordered a bottle of champagne, then said to Craig, as if it was on his mind:

"There is one damned pretty woman I have not seen before, but she seems to be caught up with one of your countrymen. I expect you know him—Lord Neasdon?"

"Actually, I have never met him," Craig replied. "What is he like?"

"Pompous, and I find it strange that anything so attractive as the Countess Aloya Zladamir should find him interesting."

Craig did not answer for a moment. Then he said:

"With a name like that, I suppose she is one of your countrywomen?"

"I suppose so," the Grand Duke said. "I have never met any Zladamirs, but that is not to say that they do not exist."

Craig laughed.

"You could hardly be expected to know everybody in a country the size of yours!"

"She is also very young," the Grand Duke continued, as if he was following the train of his own thoughts, "and I cannot make up my mind whether she belongs to the *Monde* or the *demi-Monde*."

"Surely that is not a very difficult decision, at least for somebody as discriminating as Your Imperial Highness."

"I have an idea that you are 'pulling my leg,'" the Grand Duke said, "but I admit this woman has me baffled. I got myself introduced to her, and believe it or not, she made it very clear that she was not interested in me!"

The Grand Duke spoke in an ingenuous way which made Craig want to laugh.

He was well aware that to know the Grand Duke Boris, handsome, rich, exceedingly generous, and with a flamboyant personality which dominated the social scene of Monte Carlo, was the ambition of every woman whether she belonged to the *Beau Monde* or the *demi-Monde*.

In fact, Craig was certain that if what the Grand Duke had said was true, it was the first time he had ever shown an interest in a woman of any social class and not been responded to with enthusiasm.

What had happened had obviously piqued him, for he continued:

"I should have thought that being here alone in Monte Carlo for the first time, she would have jumped at the opportunity of extending her acquaintances. But no! She is seen either with Neasdon or alone."

"A possible explanation is that she is in love with him."

"I do not believe it!" the Grand Duke replied. "He may be a very good Diplomat, but I am quite certain he is as much of a bore in bed as he is at the dinner-table!"

Craig laughed again.

"That is certainly condemning, especially when it is the opinion of an expert like yourself, Sir."

The Grand Duke had the grace to laugh as well.

"I am probably making a fuss about nothing, Craig," he said. "At the same time, it really annoyed me. But do not say anything to Zsi-Zsi. Of course she has no idea that I approached this woman."

"You know that anything you say to me is in confidence."

"Well, I shall try asking her to the party tomorrow night, and you can have a look at her," the Grand Duke said a little heavily, as he sipped the champagne which had just been poured out for him. "But I doubt if she will come."

"Why not try asking Neasdon and suggest that he bring her with him?"

The Grand Duke chuckled.

"I might have known you would have a solution to the knotty problem! But of course! That is the ticket! And Neasdon, I should imagine, will be quite pleased to be invited to one of my parties. I have never sent him an invitation before."

"I am sure he would be delighted, Sir. And do make quite sure that the invitation is a dual one."

"I will!" the Grand Duke agreed firmly.

They talked of the *Concours d'Élégance*, and the Grand Duke had invited himself aboard *The Mermaid* before Craig left him.

As he walked back to the Hôtel de Paris, he felt he had done a good day's work, although he had not actually made contact with the two people with whom he was most concerned.

Then as he walked along the corridor to his own Suite, he saw in front of him a very elegant figure.

His first impression was of a woman moving with a grace that was unusual, and she was also exceedingly slim.

Then as he stopped at his own door and she turned in

at a door at the far end of the corridor, he realised he
had seen the back of the Countess Aloya Zladamir.

As he entered his own Suite he thought again what a
lucky coincidence it was that she should have rooms
connecting with his, and that actually the room next to
hers was empty.

"My luck has not failed me," Craig told himself. "I
have no need of snakes, hangmen's ropes, or black
cats!"

He read the newspapers until it was time to dress for
dinner, and when he had changed into the smart,
close-fitting tail-coat which, like all his other clothes,
was made in London's Saville Row, he went downstairs
to find the party with whom he was dining.

They were old friends he had encountered on the
terrace in front of the Casino this morning, and they
had insisted on his joining them, and he was only too
willing to do so.

He was already making a list in his mind of the
people with whom he wished to renew his acquaintance
and those he wished to avoid.

The Prince and Princess of Braganza, who were his
hosts this evening, were charming, and she was very
attractive.

They were only a party of ten and were seated at one
of the best tables at the side of the room where the
windows overlooked the garden in front of the Casino,
which was brilliant with fairy-lights.

There were also fairy-lights in the trees, and with the
stars coming out and a pale moon shining its light on
the dome of the Casino, the whole place looked
enchanted.

The guests in the Dining-Room of the Hôtel de Paris
looked enchanted too, and Craig wondered if anywhere
else in the world one could find in one place more
beautiful women or more handsome, aristocratic men,
all the finest representatives of their different nations.

From the moment they sat down at the table the

conversation was sparkling, and Craig found himself
talking in first one language, then another, and contriv-
ing in his own inimitable way to be witty in them all.

Everybody was laughing, and it seemed as if a cre-
scendo of voices was rising from all the other tables,
when suddenly by the door there seemed to be a
sudden hush, which spread gradually over the room.

Craig looked round, saw the reason, and was not
surprised.

Moving into the Dining-Room was the most beautiful
and unusual woman he had ever seen, and as he looked
at her and saw who walked behind her, he knew who
she was.

One man at the table murmured:

"By Jove! That is something to look at!"

Craig thought he could have echoed his words.

She was, as he had noticed when he had seen her
walking down the passage, very slim. She was also
taller than many other women in the room, and if she
had dressed in order to cause a sensation, she had
certainly succeeded.

Every other woman was clothed in the colours of the
spring fashions: green, blue, pink, yellow, and a great
deal of soft white chiffon or tulle.

The Countess Aloya was wearing black. It was quite a
severe black, and the bodice was plain and very tight,
accentuating the soft curves of her breasts and her very
small waist.

Her skirts, billowing out, were not ornamented, and
what at first glance seemed so extraordinary was that,
unlike every other woman in the room, she was not
glittering with jewels.

Craig, as a connoisseur of women, knew there was no
need for them, for the whiteness of her skin was a jewel
in itself, and her hair, so fair that it seemed almost
silver in the light from the chandeliers, appeared to
glitter without the aid of diamonds.

Only when she had drawn nearer to a table not far

from Craig was he able to see that on one side of her bodice was pinned a brooch with one enormous stone the same colour as her hair, and he knew it was a yellow diamond.

She was spectacular, but, far more important, she was really beautiful. Her eyes were enormous, slanting up a little at the corners, and her eye-lashes were very dark.

Although he could not see the colour of her eyes, he suspected that because she was Russian, they would be green.

Without that colour hair she could easily have belonged to another nationality, although for the moment he could not think what it might be.

Almost as if he were a Producer of a Play, the *Maître d'Hôtel* ushered the Countess to a table for two which was next to the one occupied by Craig's party.

The Countess sat down facing him, and now he could see the exquisite symmetry of her small straight nose, and strangely he thought that her lips, which were softly curved, gave the impression, although of course it was ridiculous, that she was a little unsure and apprehensive.

Then he told himself that he was imagining things, and yet he knew he was looking at a face that was so different, and so unusual, that it was hard to find words to describe it even to himself.

For the moment all the conversation at the table at which he was sitting had ceased. Then his hostess, the Princess, said:

"I must admit, she is surprising! Last night she wore dead white that was almost like a Grecian gown, and her only jewel was a pearl ring the size of a pigeon's egg."

"Have you met her?" Craig enquired.

The Princess smiled and shook her head.

"My husband has not yet made up his mind whether it is *comme il faut* for me to do so."

Craig laughed.

"The Grand Duke Boris is just as undecided as you are," he said. "But surely this is a very unusual enigma in Monte Carlo of all places?"

"Very, very unusual," the Princess agreed, "but I assure you, every man in the place is trying to discover the secret of the Sphinx, and every woman, including myself, is hoping they will not do so too quickly."

Craig laughed again.

As the conversation returned to normal, however, he found it hard to take his eyes from the woman sitting almost opposite him.

Although he could not hear what she said, he knew that Lord Neasdon was droning on with a monologue which he was quite sure was very boring.

His companion appeared to be listening attentively and, Craig supposed, encouragingly.

At the same time, she was certainly not being in the least flirtatious, nor did she appear to be enticing him with glances or provocative pouts of her lips as almost every other woman in the room was doing.

He looked round and saw La Belle Otero, one of the most famous Courtesans in the whole of Paris, making the men with whom she dined sit spellbound as she talked to them.

They raised their glasses again and again to drink her health, and undoubtedly they promised that sooner or later they would add to her famous and priceless collection of jewels.

When he had first seen her, Craig had thought it was impossible for any woman to be more alluring, and he had not been surprised when he had learnt that the cupolas on the corners of the new Carlton Hotel at Cannes were shaped to resemble La Belle's breasts.

At another table was La Juniory, who had had a bed made in the shape of an enormous conch-shell, and Gaby Delys, the toast of Paris, whom he had seen earlier in the day and who was as usual festooned in pearls, each string longer and more valuable than the last.

But all these women paled beside the beauty of the Countess Aloya, and Craig found himself wondering what there was about her that made her unique.

He told himself after studying her for some time that it was not only her features, her unusual eyes, or her hair, which she swept back in the elegant but simple style made famous by Dana Gibson.

There was, he thought perceptively, something deeper, something that emanated from her almost as if she were surrounded by an aura of her own personality.

Anyway, as far as he was concerned, she was as brilliant as if she were enveloped in light.

It might be, he told himself scornfully, that he was intrigued because of what the Marquis of Lansdowne had said, yet all through the long meal that followed, he found it difficult to take his eyes from the woman at the next table.

He was determined to meet her, and he thought it was far too long to wait until the next evening to find out if Neasdon had taken the bait offered to him by the Grand Duke and would bring her to the party at his Villa.

But try as he might, when they all went on to the Casino he found it impossible to find anyone who could introduce him to the unknown Countess.

He thought of walking up to Neasdon and introducing himself and saying that the Marquis of Lansdowne had told him they would meet in Monte Carlo. But that was something he had no wish to do.

But he could not think of any other way of talking either to Lord Neasdon or to his companion.

They were in the *Salle Touzet* at the Casino, but Neasdon did not gamble, nor did she.

Instead they sat at one of the tables, talking to each other and drinking champagne, but, although Lord

Neasdon had obviously a great deal to say and took a long time in doing so, neither of them seemed particularly animated.

As Craig moved round the room, talking to friends, pretending to watch what numbers came up on the Roulette-tables, or standing behind those who were playing Baccarat, he thought he had never been so frustrated or so helpless.

In the past, every social problem had seemed far easier. In fact, he could never remember wanting to get to know somebody, especially a woman, without it happening almost before he thought of it.

Although he went very near to the Countess at times, he was aware that she never once raised her eyes to look up at him or at any other of the people in the room.

She merely appeared to be listening attentively to Lord Neasdon, occasionally speaking to him, sometimes making a gesture with her left hand.

"What can I do?" Craig asked himself, and felt like swearing when half-an-hour after midnight he saw the Countess rise to her feet.

Lord Neasdon obviously expostulated with her, doubtless begging her not to retire so early, but she moved insistently towards the door, and Craig unobtrusively followed.

She obtained a black velvet cape from the Cloak-Room woman, placed it round her shoulders, and walked ahead towards the door.

Again, because he could not help himself, Craig followed, and as she went down the steps and out into the moonlight, he saw her raise her face up towards the sky.

He saw the long line of her white neck, and he thought, although he could not be sure, that she wished upon a star, as women have done since the beginning of time.

Then, with Lord Neasdon still muttering, she walked

quickly towards the lights of the Hôtel de Paris and disappeared up the steps and through the door into the Reception-Lounge.

Craig, without even thinking that he should have said good-night to his host and hostess, walked after her at a discreet distance.

By the time he had reached his own floor, he was not surprised, although he thought he should have been, to see the Countess walking alone ahead of him as she had done earlier in the day.

Even as he went into his own Suite he heard her door close decisively.

It was then that he told himself that whatever her association with Lord Neasdon might be, he was not her lover, and, what was more, it was unlikely that he would join her later.

Craig felt sure of this because he had sent his Valet downstairs to find out if Lord Neasdon was staying in the Hotel.

The Valet had returned with the information that His Lordship was in fact at L'Hermitage, which was a little higher up the town, and the next most important Hotel in Monte Carlo.

In his own Suite, Craig stood for a moment, thinking.

Then, as if his instinct told him what to do, he walked through the communicating door of his Sitting-Room into his bedroom and opened another, almost identical door, which led into the empty room which communicated with that of the Countess.

He was well aware that the door, both on his side and hers, had been locked by the staff, and would only be opened if they asked for the key.

Again following his instinct, he opened first the window, then the shutters, and went out onto the balcony.

The spring air was cool as he moved out, and the vista below, with the lights in the yachts in the harbour and on the promontory above, was very beautiful.

The stars were reflecting in the sea, and the white

light of the moon turned everything to silver, which made him think of the Countess's hair.

Then as he thought of her he heard her come out onto the next balcony, and as she did so she sighed.

She obviously had no idea that he was there. She had taken off her cloak, and the moonlight was on the whiteness of her neck and arms and the silver of her hair.

She stood at the front of the balcony with her hands on the stone balustrade, and once again as she looked up at the stars Craig had the strange feeling that she was praying.

She stood there for some minutes. Then he said very quietly and softly:

"I have always thought that this is one of the most beautiful views in the world."

She started as he spoke, and turned her face to look at him, then looked quickly away again.

He did not say any more, but almost as if he compelled her to answer him, she said after a moment in a voice that he thought trembled:

"I . . . I did not know that . . . you were . . . there!"

"I only arrived today."

There was silence. Then he said:

"I always feel as if those yachts below us are straining at their moorings, longing to leave in search of adventure which lies somewhere beyond the horizon."

He spoke in the voice he might have used to a child when telling a fairy-story, and almost as if she entered into the fantasy she replied:

"That is what I would love to do . . . to sail away and . . . never come back!"

"Do you mean to this world, or to Monte Carlo in particular?"

"To Monte . . . Carlo."

Because her voice was different from the way she had spoken before, he had a feeling that her answer was personal and impulsive.

Then, as if she regretted what she had said, she added:

"I must go in. I am told the nights here can be very . .. treacherous."

"That is true," Craig replied, "but actually the temperature today has been very mild, and unless you feel cold, I do not think you will come to any harm."

"I hope not!"

As she spoke, once again Craig's perception told him that she was not thinking of herself.

Almost as if the words were put into his mind, he said:

"Of course, with the elderly it is always wise to take precautions in this climate, which can be very changeable. They should be well wrapped up at night and should remember that the wind that comes from the Alps can definitely be treacherous."

There was then no doubt that she drew in her breath sharply, and she said as if she spoke to herself:

"If that is true, then one should be very, very careful if one has come from a hot climate."

"Of course," Craig agreed. "I remember once when I returned from India and stopped at Monte Carlo that I was laid up for several days, entirely through my own fault."

"You have been to India?"

"Several times," he answered. "It is a country with which I have a deep affinity."

There was silence. Then the Countess said:

"I am sure if you have . . . once been there you could never . . . forget it."

"Of course not," Craig agreed, "and when I am in India I think how foolish we are not to listen to what it has to say."

She turned her face towards him, and he knew that for a second she looked at him in surprise. Then she looked away again and said:

"In the West . . . everything is very . . . different."

"Yes, but that is not to say that we know more or are any better as human beings."

Again there was silence, before she asked almost as if she could not help herself:

"Where have you . . . been in India?"

Craig gave a little laugh.

"It would be almost easier to tell you where I have not been. It is a country of such beauty that it captivates the eye, and also, as I expect you know, holds the mind spellbound. From the moment one steps onto Indian soil, one starts to learn, and goes on learning."

"How do you know, and how can you . . . think like . . . that?"

"I might ask you the same question," Craig replied. "And shall I say that as India has introduced us to each other, there is so much I would like to talk to you about."

The Countess made a little gesture which he felt was one of eagerness. Then suddenly she looked down into the harbour before she said in a voice which he thought trembled:

"I . . . I must go to bed . . . good-night, Sir."

Without waiting for his reply, she turned and left the balcony, closing the window behind her.

Then as he stood without moving, wondering at her haste at leaving him, wondering at the strange tremor in her voice, he heard somebody else speak in her room.

For a moment he thought it was a man.

Then as he listened, not sure, the window was opened and somebody pulled the shutters to and bolted them.

It was a maid, and he knew that it was her voice he had heard, and she had been speaking in Russian.

Chapter Three

The next day Craig was determined to find out more about the Russian yachts in the harbour.

He thought he had not done too badly so far in making contact with the Countess, but, although that was fairly satisfactory, what he was really concerned about was Randall Sare.

Ever since he had met him in India when he was only twenty-one, in his eyes Randall Sare had been a hero, somebody he admired more than any other man he had ever met.

It was the Viceroy who had first spoken of him in a way which told Craig that there was something special about the man, for he awoke a look of admiration in the Viceroy's tired eyes and brought to his voice a note which Craig had recognised as one of respect.

The Viceroy of India had an importance that was incomparable with that of almost any other Ruler in the world.

There was no King or Emperor who had more power or who, in a huge country where white men reigned supreme, lived with more pomp and circumstance.

Needless to say, the British took their games with them wherever they went, and sport being their chief spiritual export, the young soldiers, full of dash and energy, spent every moment enjoying their national games when they were not on duty.

It was inevitable that as soon as Craig Vandervelt arrived in India, with his aura of wealth glowing round him, he should be taken to Calcutta for the races.

From Calcutta with its race-dances, public breakfasts, and curious alternations of sweep-stakes and country dances, he went on to Simla, where the race-course on a high plateau of Annandale was surrounded by tall pines and deodars and was deliciously secluded.

Because Craig not only owned with his father the best race-horses in America but was also an outstanding rider, he was accepted automatically as a "good chap."

The great day of the Calcutta Year was the day of the Viceroy's Cup Race, the cup being given annually by the reigning Viceroy.

The grandstand was filled with beautiful and important women from England, America—in fact, from all parts of the world—and to Craig it had a fascination and delight he had not expected.

Having once been accepted by the British as one of them, he was introduced to their hunting, which in India consisted of a pack of hounds reinforced with an odd terrier who set off in pursuit of jackal, elk, pig, hare, red deer, hyena, or whatever else was available to chase.

It was after he had proved himself in that field as well as on the race-course, and had taken up pig-sticking and Polo, that he found himself dining at Government House and in the Officers' Mess of the most important Regiments.

It was there that he had first heard a murmur of *The Great Game*, only very little, but enough to make him curious.

Because he had a retentive memory as well as an insatiable curiosity, he was able to put a remark made after dinner together with some disjointed conversation

in a Civil Servant's office, and it began to make a
pattern.

It was after the Viceroy had spoken of Randall Sare
that Craig had asked a few questions and received
somewhat ambiguous answers.

"Randall Sare—strange chap, brilliantly clever, I'm
told, but prefers to mix with the natives rather than
us."

At first Craig was naïve enough to think that "the
natives" meant Rajahs and Maharajahs, who entertained
lavishly in their Palaces and whose hospitality almost
any Englishman would accept.

Then he learnt from somebody else that Randall Sare
in various disguises spoke every language known in
India, and frequently vanished for months on end,
although where to and why, nobody seemed to be ready
to explain.

It was only when being quite by chance in Simla that
he met the man himself and began to understand and
admire him.

Not very tall, Randall Sare had one of those strange,
unforgettable faces which was, as it happened, easy to
disguise because he did not rely on the make-up that
any actor would have used, but on thought, and on a
lifetime's knowledge of the people amongst whom he
moved and whose personalities he often assumed instead of his own.

Because Craig found it impossible to forget him, he
had deliberately sought him out on his second journey
to India, and found as he expected that he was not only
one of the most interesting men he had ever met, but
was also a mine of information on all the subjects which
no-one else had ever discussed with him.

The Indian castes and the creeds of men who were
merely an enigma to the Western Powers were subjects
that Craig found irresistible, and which to Randall Sare
were the breath of life.

It was then that Craig began to understand how men

like Sare could love a country as another man could love a woman.

India was not only a teeming continent which, when it had been conquered, had to be organised and made respectable and civilised by the social standards of Cheltenham, but there was also a marvellously complex way of life that hid beneath its surface secrets which had inspired some of the greatest religions in the world.

Because at the age of twenty-four Craig was prepared to sit at the feet and become a pupil of a man who he was astute enough to realise was a giant amongst other men, he learnt from Randall Sare in the short time they were together more than other men learnt or even touched the fringe of in a whole lifetime.

It was three years ago, on his third visit to India, that Randall Sare told him he was going to Tibet.

"Why?" Craig had asked bluntly.

"I am convinced," Randall Sare replied, "that the Russians are absorbing one after another the Khans of Central Asia and are aiming to control the whole of the Northern Frontier of India."

"It cannot be possible!"

"They are already building a Railway across Siberia to the Far East," Sare went on, "and I am told they are also building a Railway in Turkestan, and..."

He paused for a moment.

"... planning the annexation of Tibet."

"I thought no-one was allowed into that country," Craig remarked.

"I think it would be difficult to stop Russia if they were determined," Sare replied, "and if that is what they intend, that is what they will do."

"How can we prevent it?"

Randall Sare smiled, and it gave him an attraction that was all his own.

"That is what I am going to find out."

When he said good-bye, Craig knew it would be a long time before he would see him again, if ever.

Now, if the Marquis was to be believed, Sare had not only returned to Europe but had disappeared in Monte Carlo.

It seemed incredible first that Sare should leave India without the Foreign Office being informed of it, and secondly that he should have stopped in a place that was known as the most frivolous, extravagant, and wicked in the whole of Europe.

Bishops and Clergy of every denomination thundered continually against the wickedness that prevailed in the "City of gambling."

Yet, the Casino at Monte Carlo was patronised by almost every Crowned Head, and the threat of "hell fire for sinners" went unheeded.

There could be only one explanation as to why Sare had come here—that he was unable to reach England and had had no alternative.

'I have to find him—I must!' Craig thought.

Perturbed by his own thoughts, he was so absent-minded at luncheon that his very attractive hostess reproached him for neglecting her, and the lady on his other side said very much the same thing.

Their rebukes immediately reminded Craig that he was not acting the part that was expected of him.

So, excusing himself as having a slight headache, he set out to be his gay, inconsequential, and amusing self, which when the meal ended left the two women more in love with him than they were already.

He had an invitation to play tennis, but he had already had a game with the Professional early in the morning, when, on finding it hard to sleep, he had turned to the comforting male solace of hard exercise.

"You must enter the Lawn Tennis Championships, Sir," the Pro. said when, after three hard sets, Craig won comparatively easily.

Craig knew that this Championship had been initiated three years previously, and he had in fact thought of entering for the Cup in the Men's Singles, which was presented by the Prince of Monaco.

Then he decided that he had other, more interesting and more important things to do than to collect trophies, and besides, he preferred to take his exercise without an audience.

Nevertheless, he enjoyed playing a game at which he had distinguished himself in America, and he booked the Professional to play with him every morning while he was in Monte Carlo.

However, when he was free after luncheon he had no intention of playing anything until he had talked to Father Augustin.

Therefore, as he had the day before, he walked down the hill to the Chapel of St. Dévoté, entering the quiet, incense-filled Church to find that there were just a few more worshippers than there had been yesterday.

After the noise and brilliance of the Hotel, the dimness of the Chapel, which always seemed to be filled with sunshine, made him aware of a peace which came from the faith which it had enshrined for so long and was like a cool hand on his forehead.

He stood for a moment to compose his thoughts and, although he was hardly aware of it, to make quite sure there was no-one present in the Church who might recognise him.

Then he walked quietly towards the Confessional and knew as he pushed aside the curtain that Father Augustin was waiting for him.

He knelt down, and automatically the Priest said the familiar Latin words which began every confession.

Then as he said "Amen" Craig asked:

"Have you any news for me, Father?"

"A little, my son, but you have not given me much time."

"But you have heard something?"

"I have heard that the man you seek," Father Augustin

replied, and wisely did not mention his name, "was hiding in a certain place in the town two weeks ago."

"He is not ill or wounded?"

"There was no reference to that," the Priest replied, "but it was understood that he was in hiding. The place where he was staying is used only by those who are avoiding the Police, or who have other reasons for not wishing to be seen."

"He is there now?" Craig asked eagerly.

Then he knew as he asked the question that the reply would be disappointing.

"From what I have been able to ascertain," the Priest replied, "he has gone."

"Have you found out where?"

"That is what I am trying to do," Father Augustin said, "but you will understand that it is not easy to make enquiries in that particular place, where men deliberately hide and whose identities are always secret."

"I understand," Craig said, "but please, Father, because it is of the utmost importance, find out more."

"I am trying, my son, I assure you I am trying," Father Augustin replied, "but it is not easy. If I appear too eager, it will inevitably mean that doors will be closed which might otherwise remain open."

Craig knew that this was only too true, and all he could say was:

"I am deeply grateful, Father. This man is of great importance to humanity, and somehow with your help I have to save him."

"I can only rely on God," Father Augustin replied, "and I have prayed for His help."

"Then please continue to do so."

There was a little pause. Then he added:

"I have something which may help to loosen the tongues of those who know the answers to our questions. Where shall I leave it?"

There was silence for a moment, then Father Augustin replied:

"There is a wreath in front of the effigy of St. Dévoté."

There was no need for him to say more, and Craig asked:

"When shall I come again?"

"Tomorrow I shall be hearing confessions a little later, so I shall be here just when it is growing dark."

"That will be helpful," Craig said.

He waited until Father Augustin said the blessing in Latin, and when he rose from his knees he pulled aside the curtain of the Confessional.

As he did so he saw that there were more people in the Church than there had been when he came in, and when he glanced at them he saw with a sudden leap of excitement that kneeling only a little way from him was the Countess Aloya.

Her clasped hands were resting on the top of the *prie-Dieu* at which she was praying, and her head was thrown back a little, her eyes raised to the lamp burning in front of the sanctuary.

She was obviously completely unaware of him, at least that was what she appeared to be, and yet, because he was so conscious of her, Craig thought it would be a mistake to walk past her and out of the Church.

Instead, he stepped across the narrow aisle and sat down in a seat next to hers.

He did not kneel but bent forward and put his hand over his eyes as if he were praying.

He was wondering what he should say to her, when, without moving, she said in a voice so low that he could only just hear her:

"Please...do not...speak to...me! There is...somebody...watching."

Another man might have stared at her in astonishment, or even expostulated, but Craig had been trained in a school where one unwary movement, one slip of the tongue, could mean, if not certain death, discovery.

For a moment he did not move; then, as if his prayer were over, he rose from his seat and, without even looking at the Countess, genuflected in the aisle, then walked deliberately slowly to where the wax effigy of St. Dévoté, to whom the Chapel was dedicated, lay against the north wall.

St. Dévoté, the Patron Saint of Monaco, was born in Corsica in 283 A.D. Her parents were pagan, but her Christian name brought her the new faith.

In the great persecution she was tortured, but she endured it, praying and smiling. As she died, her soul flew up to Heaven in the form of a dove.

The same dove piloted the barque which carried her body to Monaco, where it settled on a rock, and there the Chapel dedicated to her was ultimately built.

Few people who came to Monte Carlo to worship the green tables in the Casino knew of the Chapel, but, as he did in everything with which he had any contact, Craig learnt the history and stored it away in his mind.

He stood for a moment looking at the wax figure of a very young girl with a dove resting on her head.

Then he saw, as he had expected, that there was a wreath laid in front of it, obviously commemorating the death of somebody who believed that the Saint would pray in Heaven for those who had died on earth.

The green vine leaves, the faded pink and white carnations, and the ribbon which tied the wreath at its base were all too familiar even to be noticed.

Craig knelt as if in reverence before the Patron Saint of the Chapel, then slipped an envelope beneath the wreath so quickly that it was doubtful if anybody watching him would have been aware of his action.

Then he rose to his feet and deliberately moved very slowly down the Church.

As he had expected, while he was engaged in looking at the statue of St. Dévoté and leaving a considerable amount of francs for Father Augustin, the Countess had left.

He was sure that it had been a move on her part so that those whom she had said were watching would not see him, or if they had done so, they would have been aware only of his back.

It was something he would have thought of himself, but he was surprised that the Countess had been so astute.

At the door of the Church he lingered again, picking up some books of prayer, flicking over the pages, and pretending to read a leaflet which gave the times of the Services.

Only when he was quite certain that the Countess had driven away, if she had come by carriage, or was out of sight if she had walked, did he leave the Chapel.

He now had a great deal to think about.

It was obvious last night when she had left him so hastily that she must have heard the Russian servant come into the room behind her.

He imagined now that either the maid, which would have been usual, had accompanied her to the Church, or perhaps she had another bodyguard of some sort.

It was so intriguing that Craig found it impossible to think of anything else for the rest of the afternoon.

It was only when he had puzzled over what had been said and found himself wondering how soon he could see the Countess again that he remembered that the Grand Duke Boris was giving a party that evening and had been determined to invite her with Lord Neasdon.

As by this time it was after four o'clock, Craig was certain that the Grand Duke would be in the Casino.

The place was filling up as it inevitably did before dinner, and he walked quickly into the *Salle Touzet* and was relieved to see, as he expected, the Grand Duke sitting at the Baccarat-table, playing with what to any other man would have been a fortune.

As Craig watched, speaking to one or two of the spectators whom he knew, the Grand Duke lost the pile of notes and gold in front of him and rose to his feet without any expression of annoyance or disappointment on his handsome face.

Then as he moved away from the table he saw Craig and put out his hand.

"Come and have a drink with me, Craig," he said. "I need it."

Craig was too wise to commiserate with him over his losses, knowing it was something a gambler hated more than anything else, just as they thought it unlucky to be congratulated on their wins.

"It is rather early for me to drink," he replied. "I am keeping myself for your party tonight, if it is still taking place."

"Of course it is taking place," the Grand Duke said, "and Zsi-Zsi has asked all your special friends to meet you, although I expect most of them already know that you are here amongst us."

"You make me sound as if like Lucifer I dropped from the sky," Craig said with a smile.

"A good simile," the Grand Duke joked. "I think the mere fact that you are so rich, Craig, brings out the devil in those who know you, and especially in the women who love you."

"I disagree," Craig replied, "but never mind, and thank you in anticipation of tonight. Have you persuaded Neasdon to accept your invitation?"

He thought it would be a mistake to sound too eager. At the same time, he had to know.

The Grand Duke laughed.

"He jumped at it like a hungry salmon. I have never invited him before, and I am damned if I would do so now, unless I had a good reason for it."

"Is he actually bringing the Countess?"

"He said so, but the strange thing is that he sounded so sure he would do so that I had the feeling her opinion would not be asked."

"Obviously," Craig said with a cynical note in his

voice, "Neasdon has some hidden charms of which we are not aware."

"If he has, all I can say is that I am a bad judge of men and women," the Grand Duke replied, "which is something I never imagined I would be. Anyway, tonight you shall see her for yourself and how she clings to Neasdon. Believe it or not, I have never seen her talking to anybody else since she has been here, and it seems to me extraordinary."

Craig agreed with him, but because he thought it would be a mistake to talk too much about the Countess, he changed the conversation to other subjects, then made the excuse that he had an appointment and went back to the Hotel.

In his own Suite, he resisted an impulse to go out onto the balcony which adjoined that of the Countess.

Firstly, he knew he had no wish for any of his staff to be aware that he had even entered the empty bedroom, and secondly, he suspected that if the Countess was in her Suite, her Russian maid might be with her.

But why she should be frightened of her maid, and why it had been so important that he should not speak to her in the Chapel or appear to know her, was a mystery.

They were questions to which he could find no answer, and when he was dressing for dinner he had the feeling that he was on the verge of an exciting adventure, and one that seemed so unpredictable that he had no idea of what the outcome might be.

Because it was a feeling he had not had for some time, but which he had known in the past and therefore recognised, Craig felt as if there was a new pulsation of power flowing through him.

It was something he had always felt when he was in danger or when he was engaged on some of the strange missions with which he had been entrusted by the Marquis.

Because it was so utterly different from his life both

in New York and in London as a rich, carefree young
man, he cherished and enjoyed the challenges which
these missions gave him.

He knew now that if he was to be successful he
would need all the mysterious, mystic power which he
had always called on in an emergency.

He had not forgotten that he wished to know more
about the Russian yachts, and on returning from the
Casino, before he went upstairs to his Suite, he had
gone to the Manager's Office.

The Manager of the Hôtel de Paris was one of the
best-informed men in the whole of the Principality.

It was his business not only to be aware of the
background of every person who stayed in the Hotel,
but, because it was so closely allied with the Casino,
the habitués of the green tables also came under his
surveillance.

If there was one thing the authorities detested it was
a scandal or a suicide, and every possible precaution
was taken to see that anything that could reflect badly
upon the reputation of Monte Carlo as a whole must be
prevented from taking place.

If unfortunately that was impossible, then what occurred
must be swept out of sight as quickly and as discreetly
as possible.

Monsieur Bleuet was therefore a man of discretion,
besides having a sharp and intelligent brain which
missed very little.

Because it was almost certain that to *Monsieur* Bleuet,
Craig was exactly what he appeared—a wealthy American in search of amusement—Craig knew he must
phrase what he had to say as carefully as possible.

"I hope, *Monsieur* Vandervelt," the Manager said,
"that you are comfortable. Is there anything I can do for
you?"

"I came to tell you that I am very comfortable," Craig
answered, "and it was exceedingly kind of you to let me

have the same Suite that I had last year and the year before that."

Monsieur Bleuet smiled.

"We try always, *Monsieur,* to make our favourite clients feel at home, and to do that it is important that they occupy the same rooms they have used before and have if possible the same room-service."

"I appreciate that," Craig said, "but I also want to ask you what you know about the two Russian yachts in the harbour."

He smiled as he added:

"It may sound merely as curiosity, but as it happens I am anxious, if they are new, to compare them with my own yacht, which I like to think is more advanced than any other vessel afloat."

"I have always heard, *Monsieur* Vandervelt, that *The Mermaid* is the envy of every yachtsman in the harbour, and quite exceptional as regards its engine, its steering, and the new gadgets you have yourself installed."

Craig smiled complacently and knew that what *Monsieur* Bleuet was saying was what he might have expected him to know.

"I went over the Duke of Westminster's yacht last year," he replied, "and I know it does not compare with *The Mermaid.* The same applies to Mr. Pierpont Morgan's boat, which is old, and it is time he bought a new one."

Monsieur Bleuet laughed.

"It is something he can certainly afford."

"I suppose when one gets older, one becomes attached to one's possessions," Craig remarked. "I can understand that, as I am sure you can, when it concerns something like a painting, but for me, where yachts and motor-cars are concerned, the newer the better."

Monsieur Bleuet laughed again.

"I might almost say the same, *Monsieur,* in the case of *les femmes!*"

"Now that is a different subject altogether," Craig said, "but we were speaking of the Russian yachts."

"Yes, of course," the Manager agreed. "But I regret to say that I have never been aboard either of them, and in fact I do not know anybody who has."

"Do you mean to say that their owners do not entertain?"

"Their *owner, Monsieur.*"

"Only one?"

"Yes. Baron Strogoloff is his name, and he is an invalid."

"Oh, that explains everything!"

"Not exactly," the Manager said. "The Baron has some affliction of the legs, I understand, which necessitates his being always in a wheel-chair. He is pushed round the deck of his yacht, and he also comes to the Casino."

"To gamble?"

The Manager shook his head.

"No. They tell me he is fond of music, so he attends the Concerts and the Operas that take place in the Theatre."

"He does not gamble?"

"*Monsieur le Baron* has not yet entered the *Salle Touzet,* which you will understand is very sad for us since he is, I believe, amazingly rich."

"And when he leaves, he will take it all with him!"

Craig laughed before he added:

"That of course is a tragedy, but he must be very eccentric to need two yachts."

"*Monsieur le Baron* uses one himself, and the other is for his guests and those who wait on him."

"That is certainly luxury," Craig remarked. "And what are his guests like?"

"You will hardly credit this, *Monsieur,*" the Manager replied, "but in Monte Carlo, of all places, they stay on board and never come ashore."

"I do not believe it!" Craig exclaimed. "It seems incredible!"

"That is what we all feel," the Manager said, "and

our discussions about the Baron take up a great deal of time when we meet officially."

"I am quite sure about that," Craig said with a smile. "And what does Prince Albert think about it?"

"We have not yet had the privilege of discussing it with His Royal Highness," the Manager answered, "but now that you mention it, perhaps he, and he alone, could persuade the Baron to be a little more sociable."

"I doubt it," Craig said. "These Russians are always unpredictable, and you can thank goodness you have people like the charming and very extravagant Grand Duke Boris."

"There I agree with you, *Monsier* Vandervelt, we are very, very lucky. As the Grand Duke Boris was saying to me only yesterday, when he goes back to Russia he counts the days until he can return to us, and what he refers to as his 'home away from home.'"

The complacency in the Manager's voice told Craig how much the Russian Grand Duke contributed to the huge profits the Casino was making every year.

Because such details interested him, he was well aware that the shareholders were becoming millionaires, and the other resorts were grinding their teeth in fury at the success achieved by Monaco.

They talked for a little longer, but Craig deliberately did not mention the Countess.

Then, because he knew it would please the Manager and even increase his own prestige, he spoke of his delight in finding so many distinguished visitors in Monte Carlo, including Prince Radziwell, who had brought his own polo-ponies, the Duke of Montrose, and the beautiful Duchess of Marlborough, who was an American.

The Manager had something interesting to say about each one of them, but Craig, having learnt what he had come to find out, was not listening.

When he reached his own Suite he stood for a long

time at the window, looking at the two Russian yachts side by side in the harbour below.

* * *

The Grand Duke's Villa was a dream of Oriental magnificence, a mixture of Russian taste which ran to cupolas and domes and an endless profusion of gold.

It also combined every possible Western comfort, which involved huge over-padded sofas and armchairs, velvet hangings, and paintings which any connoisseur of art would have given his right arm to possess.

Each Oriental rug on the floor was a poem in needle-work, and the gold ornaments which decorated the dinner-table were priceless not only in their antiquity but because they were ornamented with the most magnificent precious stones that the Siberian mines could produce.

There were orchids everywhere, and yet, because his guests were so glamorous, they were not overshadowed by their surroundings.

As usual before one of his parties, the Grand Duke gave a dinner-party for about fifty of his personal friends, and then acquaintances arrived afterwards from midnight until dawn.

Looking down the long table, with the gold plate off which they were to eat, and with crystal glasses which shone like diamonds and were emblazoned with the Grand Duke's insignia, Craig was aware that neither the Countess nor Neasdon was there.

It was what he had expected, but nevertheless he was disappointed. He had wanted to look at her, perhaps to reaffirm that she was as beautiful as she had appeared the night before.

It seemed incredible that he had not seen her during the day, except for when she had been praying in the Church, and he wondered where she hid herself when she was not with Neasdon.

It was then, as he looked more closely at the other

guests, that he realised the Grand Duke had finally made up his mind into which category she belonged.

The other men were all of great importance, aristocrats to their fingertips, and, Craig thought a little cynically, with the exception of himself they were entirely European or Russian, and the women were extremely beautifully dressed but undoubtedly belonged to the *demi-Monde*.

This was not to say that they were not delightful companions in public as well as in private.

Because of their profession, they had manners as beautiful as their faces, and it was an unwritten law that they never embarrassed their protectors by trying to meet their families.

Craig knew from past experience that their behaviour at the gaming-tables was exemplary, and they never created scenes as Society Ladies were sometimes prone to do.

As might have been expected, the Cocottes wore the most superb jewellery. Their gowns, which came from the most famous Houses in Paris, the majority designed by Frederick Worth, would have graced any Royal Palace.

But even in Monte Carlo, where from a social point of view everything was far more lax than anywhere else, *les femmes de joie* never attempted to cross the dividing line between the *Monde* and the *demi-Monde*.

The only additions to the famous Cocottes like La Belle Otero and Gaby Delys at the party were a few women of blue blood who had, for love, thrown away their position in Society.

Craig recognised a Marchioness who had run away from a drunken and brutal husband to live in what the world called "sin" with a French *Duc* who already had a wife and a large number of children, whom he left in a *Château* in the country and seldom saw.

There was also the daughter of a very well-known British Earl who had been twice divorced and was still

lovely and attractive enough to be considering taking a
third husband, who was sitting beside her, gazing
adoringly into her eyes and obviously completely
uninterested in anybody else in the room.

It all seemed somewhat familiar, a scene Craig had
witnessed a dozen times before, but which he enjoyed
aesthetically and would have enjoyed even more if a
new face in the shape of the Countess Aloya Zladamir
had been there.

Then he told himself that he must wait in patience
until dinner was over and the Grand Duke's other
guests arrived, and he forced himself to be pleasant to
his dinner-companions.

This was not a very difficult task, as they had been
trained in a hard school to amuse any man they were
with and to make him find them desirable.

As was usual in France, the ladies and gentlemen all
left the Dining-Room together.

When they walked into the large Salon where they
had been before dinner and which opened onto another, equally spacious one, where the furniture had been
cleared away so that they could dance, Craig saw the
Countess.

She was standing at an open window looking out onto
the garden, which was lit with a thousand small candles
fluttering in the evening breeze, and huge Chinese
lanterns glowing golden in the branches of the trees.

There was the scent of mimosa, which was in flower,
and Craig, seeing the Countess's profile against the sky,
thought it would be impossible for any woman to look
so lovely.

In fact, she seemed part of the night itself.

He had wondered, after her dramatic appearance last
night, if she could equal the sensation her black gown
had caused in the Dining-Room of the Hôtel de Paris.

Now he thought that she was in fact even more
spectacular in a gown that was of silver like the moon-

light outside and seemed to cling to her slim figure, except where the skirt billowed out round her feet.

Because it shone from the moonlight on one side of the Countess and in the light from the chandeliers on the other, she seemed almost to be enveloped in running water, like a nymph from the sea, without human substance.

He did not approach her but just stood looking at her. As she turned her face towards the Grand Duke as he advanced across the room to greet her, he saw that her only jewel tonight was a huge diamond star which she wore on top of her head and which seemed to melt into the shining silver of her hair.

As she curtseyed to the Grand Duke, he thought it would be impossible for a woman to be more graceful.

Then the Grand Duke was affably welcoming Lord Neasdon, and there was no doubt that the Englishman was extremely gratified.

There was a band of twenty violins already playing in the next Salon, and to Craig's mind it seemed to make the whole scene dream-like and without reality.

There was also, he knew, another room in which there were the inevitable green tables, where the Grand Duke's guests could lose their money at every known game of chance without having to go to the Casino.

As he might have expected, the female guests were already eagerly luring their partners to the table where the Roulette-wheel was spinning, or to another where *trente et quarante* was a quick way to win or lose.

It was accepted that a gentleman gave half his winnings to the lady who accompanied him, besides giving her enough to play herself, should she wish to do so.

The Grand Duke had moved away from Lord Neasdon to greet other guests who were now arriving in large numbers, and the Countess was once again looking out the window while Lord Neasdon talked to her.

Craig decided that if he was going to make her

acquaintance formally, he would have to take the matter into his own hands.

This was made easy by the fact that he saw that Zsi-Zsi, who was acting as hostess during the evening, was for the moment standing alone.

Although she was known to be living with the Grand Duke and was always with him when he was in Monte Carlo, while his wife remained in Russia, Zsi-Zsi, because she had been married to a respectable French *Comte*, was accepted by quite a number of Society hostesses.

It was therefore possible for Zsi-Zsi still to be there when the Grand Duke had wished to invite only the *crème de la crème* to his party.

Craig did not question that the Grand Duke had finally decided the status of the Countess, and Zsi-Zsi had arranged the party accordingly.

He walked over to her, took her arm, and said to her quietly:

"You have made me curious about the newcomer, so the least you can do is introduce me to her."

"I think it would be a mistake, Craig," Zsi-Zsi replied. "She is quite obviously tied up with Lord Neasdon, and there are several women here tonight who have begged me to ensure that they have an opportunity to be with you, including the one who was on your right at dinner."

"I still wish to meet the Countess."

Zsi-Zsi shrugged her shoulders.

"Very well, if you insist, but do not blame me if you get a 'set down' such as poor Boris received, although he tried to keep it a secret from me!"

Craig's eyes twinkled as he remembered what the Grand Duke had said to him, but he merely said:

"I will risk it, and if my morale is damaged, I can always come to you for consolation."

"Which you are quite certain I will give you," Zsi-Zsi said mockingly.

As they were talking, Craig deliberately moved her

across the Salon towards where the Countess and Lord Neasdon were standing.

Now, as they reached them, the Countess turned her head from her contemplation of the garden and looked at Zsi-Zsi in a way that Craig thought was almost as if she were shy.

Then he told himself that it was ridiculous to think such a thing, and it must just be a clever trick which would undoubtedly endear her to an older woman and certainly to any man.

"How nice to see you, Countess," Zsi-Zsi gushed, "and, Lord Neasdon, His Imperial Highness is so delighted you could come this evening. He has been wanting to make your acquaintance for a long time."

"You are very kind, *Madame*," Lord Neasdon replied.

"And now as you are our guest for the first time," Zsi-Zsi said, "I insist that you open the Ball with me. The band is playing '*The Blue Danube*,' and what could be a more delightful dance with which to start our acquaintance?"

As Zsi-Zsi smiled up into Lord Neasdon's face, it would have been impossible for any man to refuse her such a request, but diplomatically Lord Neasdon hesitated and glanced at the Countess.

"*Tiens!* I forgot!" Zsi-Zsi exclaimed in her bird-like voice. "*Madame la Comtesse*, allow me to introduce to you Mr. Craig Vandervelt, who will look after you while I dance with the charming Lord Neasdon."

She paused to add impressively:

"Mr. Vandervelt is American, but as he is so very rich, we forgive him for choosing to live in such a far-off part of the world."

She laughed as she spoke, and it was like the joyous twittering of a songbird.

Then without saying any more, she drew Lord Neasdon by the hand into the next room.

Craig moved two paces nearer to the Countess and stood looking at her.

She did not speak and turned her face towards the garden.

"I have been waiting for this moment!" he said in his deep voice. "And because we have a lot to say to each other and I have no wish to be disturbed, shall we go outside?"

Chapter Four

For a moment Craig thought the Countess was going to refuse. Then she looked over her shoulder nervously, and he knew she was wondering if Lord Neasdon was watching her.

However, he had already vanished into the adjoining Salon, and, as if she felt released from some restraint which Craig could not understand, she walked quickly through the open French window into the garden.

There were not many people moving across the lawn, and under the trees Craig deliberately put his hand under the Countess's elbow and guided her to where there were fewer lights.

Having been in the Grand Duke's garden several times before, he knew there were seats made comfortable with silk cushions, and there were also small arbours which, covered with climbing vines, were places where those who wished could be private and unobserved.

They walked without speaking. Then as he turned towards one of the arbours which was only faintly lit by lanterns hanging from an adjacent tree, he feared at first that the Countess would protest.

But as if he read her thoughts he knew she was aware, as he was, that in the arbour they would not be seen, and she allowed him to pilot her there.

As Craig expected, the seat inside was covered with

soft cushions, and as they sat down he looked back the way they had come and saw that they were alone in this part of the garden where there were no fairy-lights.

He turned to sit sideways on the seat, with his arm along the back of it, and said:

"Now at last I can talk to you as I am very eager to do."

He spoke in a voice which most women found irresistibly beguiling, but the Countess did not look at him and only stared ahead. He could just see the outline of her straight little nose.

"What do you . . . want to talk . . . about?" she asked, and there was a quiver in her voice.

"About you," Craig replied, "but it is difficult to know where to begin."

"I do not . . . think we have . . . anything to say to . . . each other."

"I have a great deal to say," he argued, "but first I want to know why you are frightened and of whom."

He knew that she stiffened, then she said quickly:

"Please . . . I think we should . . . go back. I am sure . . . Lord Neasdon will want to . . . dance with . . . me."

"He has only just begun to dance with our hostess," Craig replied, "and as she is undoubtedly the most alluring woman here, with the exception of yourself, I do not think he will be in any hurry to change partners."

If he thought he was being reassuring, he was mistaken, for the Countess appeared to be even more tense than before, and he saw that her fingers in her long white gloves were clasped together, twining and intertwining with one another.

Craig bent a little nearer. Then he said very quietly:

"Let me help you. If you are in trouble, I will get you out of it, and I promise I will free you from being afraid as you are now."

"No-one . . . can do . . . that."

He could barely hear the words, and yet they were spoken.

"Why not?"

She did not answer, and after a moment he said:

"I am aware that there is something wrong—very, very wrong. You are the most beautiful woman in the whole of Monte Carlo. Everybody is eager to meet you, every man is at your feet, and yet you are being menaced by some fear, and that is something I must bring to an end."

As his voice died away, the Countess, clenching and unclenching her hands, said pleadingly:

"Please . . . do not talk to me like this . . . I want help . . . desperately . . . but I cannot ask . . . you for it . . . nor anybody else."

"And yet I believe I am the only person who can help you."

She turned her face farther away from him, and he went on:

"You and I have both been in India. We know that strange things can happen there about which the Western World knows little, and that thought is used to enable two people to have an inner knowledge of each other, however many miles they are apart."

She did not speak, but he knew a little quiver passed through her, and he said:

"I know you need me, and I know that I am the one person who would be able to help you. I think you know it too."

Now she looked at him and replied almost passionately:

"How can . . . you talk to me . . . like this? How are you . . . able to . . . understand?"

"You know the answer to that," Craig said. "There is no need for us to waste time in proving it to each other."

"But . . . how can I be . . . sure? You are a man I have . . . never seen . . . before."

"And yet you warned me that it was dangerous to

speak to you this afternoon in Church," Craig said.
"Why should you do that if you did not already think of
me as being far from a total stranger?"

"I... I do not know... anything," the Countess replied.
"I am... frightened... terribly frightened... and yet I
dare not... trust you."

There was a frantic note in her voice, and Craig
deliberately waited a moment before he replied very
quietly:

"Do not listen to your brain, listen to your instinct,
as you would if you were in India and the same Guru
was teaching us."

She drew in her breath. Then just as he thought she
was about to confide in him, she said in a whisper:

"Suppose... somebody is... listening?"

"Here?" Craig enquired. "I think it is very unlikely,
but if there is somebody watching you, tell me why."

"I... I cannot do... that," the Countess said with a
little sob, "but they are watching... they are always
watching... and although I cannot always... see
them... I know they are there."

"Who are they? And why?"

Even as he asked the questions, he knew perceptively that she was not going to answer him, and that her
fear was rising in her, seeping through her body and
into her mind so that it was impossible for her to think
clearly.

"Now listen to me," he said in a low voice. "I
understand your difficulties better than you think I do.
What I want you to remember is that I am here, and I
can and will help you as nobody else in the world can
do."

She did not speak but looked away again, and he
went on:

"Your room connects with mine, and what I am going
to do when I get back to the Hotel is to unlock the
communicating door on my side. If you want me at any
moment, slide a piece of paper under the door from

your side, and I will open the door between us without anyone being aware of it."

He knew she was listening attentively to what he was saying, and he went on:

"Or, if you wish, we can talk on the balcony, but only when you feel it is safe."

She looked at him fleetingly for a moment. Then she said in a whisper:

"Thank you . . . I shall remember . . . but please . . . do not come to the Church again in the afternoon . . . they might . . . realise that our rooms are . . . near to each other's."

"I understand," Craig answered, "but if you will tell me who 'they' are, it might be easier for me to help you."

As if his question agitated her almost unbearably, she said quickly:

"No . . . no . . . I cannot stay . . . I dare not . . . please . . . forget we have . . . talked together like this."

"I think the truth is that it is I who talked," Craig said with a smile. "But at least you know I am here, and if you are afraid, then I am prepared to tackle anyone or anything to wipe the tears from your eyes."

Even in the dim light he could see a little smile that was somehow pathetic. Then she rose to her feet.

"I must go back . . . I am sure the dance is . . . over."

"Walk slowly and casually," Craig said. "If, as you fear, someone is watching, if you hurry they will think that you have something to hide."

He saw her eyes widen, then as she stepped from the arbour she said in a voice that was different from the one she had been using:

"How delightful it must be to have a garden like this and to know that almost all the year round it is full of flowers!"

Craig knew she was speaking as if somebody might overhear her, and he replied lightly:

"In my opinion, the Côte d'Azur is never lovelier

than when the mimosa trees are golden and the first hibiscus comes into bloom."

He deliberately moved slowly and knew the Countess took her pace from him.

Only as they got back to the lights thrown from the windows of the Villa did he see that she was very pale, and at the same time in her glittering silver gown and with the star on her silver hair she looked ethereal and hardly human.

Now they were moving amongst the other people returning from the garden into the house, and as they walked in through a French window, Craig saw Lord Neasdon and Zsi-Zsi coming from the other Salon, where they had been dancing.

He sensed that at the sight of Lord Neasdon the Countess seemed to shudder, and he had the feeling, although he was not sure why, that she recoiled from him and instinctively moved closer to himself.

"We have had the most delightful dance," Zsi-Zsi said in her attractive voice. "His Lordship is a very good dancer."

"Surely that is unusual for an Englishman?" Craig remarked. "I hope you will introduce me, as we have not yet met."

"*Oo-la-la!* How remiss of me!" Zsi-Zsi exclaimed. "Lord Neasdon, this is Craig Vandervelt, a very charming American who honours us with his presence here in Monte Carlo nearly every year, and we women look forward to his arrival with palpitating hearts."

Lord Neasdon held out his hand.

"How do you do!" he said rather heavily. "I have heard of you, although we have never met."

"I think you work in the Foreign Office with a relative of mine, the Marquis of Lansdowne."

"He is a relative of yours?" Lord Neasdon asked in surprise.

"A distant cousin."

"I had no idea!"

"I see him from time to time," Craig answered, "but I live in America when I am at home, which is not very often."

Zsi-Zsi laughed.

"I can tell you that Craig is an inveterate traveller who goes round and round the world like a meteor, if that is the right description."

"You must find it very interesting," Lord Neasdon said.

As he spoke it was obvious that he was not at all interested in the conversation, and his eyes were on the Countess. Craig was aware that she was looking at him with an expression he could not understand.

It seemed almost as if she was pleading with him, and at the same time he had the feeling that she was trying to attract him but did not really know how to do so.

There followed an uncomfortable silence when nobody could think of anything else to say, until Craig bowed to the Countess.

"I hope I may have the pleasure of dancing with you later this evening," he said. "May I say it has been delightful meeting you."

Then, without waiting for a reply, he moved to Zsi-Zsi's side and said:

"Let me congratulate an old friend whose party is, as usual, perfection, and why should I expect it to be anything else?"

"That is very nicely said, *mon cher*," Zsi-Zsi replied, slipping her arm through his and drawing him away, leaving Lord Neasdon and the Countess alone.

When they were out of ear-shot, Zsi-Zsi said:

"*Oo-la-la!* I hope you are grateful. Never have I met a more boring man who can talk only of himself."

"I *am* grateful."

"That lovely woman! What can she see in him?" Zsi-Zsi asked. "He has nothing interesting to say, he dances like an elephant, and is so conceited that he believed me when I said he was a good dancer."

"Suppose you dance with me?" Craig said. "Then you can forget Neasdon."

"I would love it later," Zsi-Zsi replied, "but first I must see if there is anything Boris wants, and greet some new arrivals."

She moved away, and as she did so Craig was aware that Lord Neasdon was taking the Countess into the garden.

It suddenly struck him that if she had been afraid their conversation would be overheard, there was no reason why he should not listen to theirs.

The Band was playing a spirited dance which had brought onto the dance-floor almost all the guests except those sitting at the card-tables.

Casually, as if he were enjoying the night air, Craig walked out under the trees and saw Lord Neasdon and the Countess moving down the path lit with fairy-lights to the arbours on the other side of the garden from where he had taken her.

He watched them until he saw with satisfaction that they moved into an arbour which was surrounded by bushes and lit by several Chinese lanterns in the overhanging trees.

Only as they disappeared out of view did he move swiftly in the direction of the shrubs, and, walking quietly through them, he went to the back of the arbour in which they were now sitting.

As he reached it, he heard Lord Neasdon say:

"You are enjoying yourself?"

"Very much," the Countess replied. "It is very kind of you to bring me to such a . . . delightful party."

"The Grand Duke Boris gives them very frequently when he is in Monte Carlo."

"He is very distinguished."

"I believe a number of women find him so," Lord Neasdon said somewhat contemptuously.

"It is . . . strange," the Countess said a little tentatively, "that there should be so many English people at the party when I thought the English were angry with the Russians."

"Why should you think that?"

"I heard . . . although it may be wrong . . . that there is . . . friction between the Russians and the English . . . concerning India."

There was silence, almost as if Lord Neasdon was thinking what he should say. Then he replied:

"You must not believe all you hear."

"But it is true, is it not, that the Russians have made the British Government . . . very angry?"

"I do not know what you have heard," Lord Neasdon said, "but there is always a lot of tittle-tattle if there is any movement of troops, and if a few shots are fired on the Frontier it becomes a 'battle.'"

There was a little silence. Then the Countess said:

"You do not . . . think there could be . . . war between our . . . two nations? That would be . . . terrible!"

"There is no fear of that," Lord Neasdon said, "and I assure you the British have the whole situation very well in hand."

"You mean they will not . . . allow there to be a war, even if Russia should . . . wish it?"

Lord Neasdon laughed unpleasantly.

"The English can stand up to the Russians, and if there are a few scuffles between us on the Northwest Frontier, they would not defeat us."

"You are quite . . . sure of . . . that?"

"Very, very sure."

The Countess gave a little sigh.

"That means that the British have lots of troops in India to prevent any Russian . . . infiltration into . . . Afghanistan."

She spoke as if she was afraid of the idea, and Lord Neasdon said:

"Now do not worry your pretty head, Aloya. I promise

you there will be no war, but even if there is one, I will look after you and protect you."

"That might be . . . difficult if our . . . countries are . . . enemies."

"I shall never be your enemy," he said. "Let me show you how well I will look after you."

He must have put his arm round the Countess, for Craig, listening, heard her give a little scream as she said:

"No . . . no . . . please, you must not do that . . . here! It would be very . . . indiscreet."

"Nobody can see us," Lord Neasdon objected, "and you know quite well you are driving me mad! You promised you would let me love you when we knew each other better, and I think it is time you began to keep your promise."

"We . . . have known . . . each other such a . . . little time," the Countess said in a voice that sounded terrified.

"Long enough for me to know that I want you and love you!" Lord Neasdon said. "Why should you be faithful to this husband of yours who allows you to wander about the world alone instead of looking after you as he should do?"

"He is still . . . my husband, and I am . . . fond of him."

"If he was fond of you he would look after you properly," Lord Neasdon said firmly. "But I am here, and you have told me you find me interesting and attractive, while I find you adorable and very, very desirable."

He paused, and when she did not speak he added:

"Let me come to your room tonight and show you how much you mean to me and how happy we could be together."

"Oh . . . no . . . not tonight," the Countess said hastily. "It is . . . too soon, much . . . too soon."

There was a frantic, desperate note in her voice as she added:

"You know I like to be with you, I like to talk to you and listen to you. You are so interesting, and you can teach me so much about the world . . . a world of which I know very . . . little."

"A world in which you shine brilliantly!" Lord Neasdon said. "There is no woman in the whole of Monte Carlo to equal you, and I am very proud of you."

He spoke in a complacent manner which made Craig feel that he wanted to hit him as he went on:

"Now that the Grand Duke has asked us here tonight, we shall have many invitations together, and I think I can introduce you to people you would otherwise not meet, and whom you will find very interesting."

"I am quite . . . content to be with . . . you," the Countess said in a small voice. "You talk to me of . . . all the things I . . . want to know."

"I want to talk about ourselves," Lord Neasdon said, "and quite frankly, Aloya, it does not particularly concern me whether our countrymen prance about on the Northwest Frontier or try to invade Tibet when all I want is to invade your bedroom."

There was a little silence. Then the Countess said:

"That might be just . . . as difficult as . . . invading Tibet!"

"I am a very determined man."

"I keep . . . thinking of . . . my husband."

"Then forget him!"

"I try . . . but it is . . . difficult."

"Not for me."

The Countess gave a little laugh which Craig was certain was forced.

"Am I . . . really like . . . Tibet?"

"Of course you are," Lord Neasdon said, "mysterious, unknown, and impenetrable, except of course to me!"

"That is very complimentary, but perhaps the . . . barriers which will keep out the Russians will also prove . . . impenetrable to you."

"That is for you to say, but I am confident that

whatever barriers and obstacles there are, I shall be able to sweep them away. Let me kiss you now and show you how easily they can vanish when one is in love."

"No . . . no . . . this is not the . . . right place! I would be very . . . embarrassed to go back into the Salon looking . . . dishevelled."

Lord Neasdon did not reply, and somehow Craig was aware that the Countess had risen to her feet.

"We shall be . . . talked about," she said, "if we stay here for too long, and that would be . . . bad for your reputation as . . . well as . . . mine. After all . . . you are a very important and . . . distinguished member of the . . . British Foreign Office."

"I am glad you think so," Lord Neasdon replied, "and perhaps you are right. We can talk about ourselves later when we return to the Hotel."

"That would be a . . . mistake!" the Countess said quickly. "If you came into my room, my maid . . . might talk, and my husband is very . . . jealous."

"Damn and blast him!" Lord Neasdon said with more feeling in his voice than there had been before.

Craig was aware that they were now out of the arbour and moving back towards the Villa, their voices gradually fading into the distance until he could hear them no more.

He stood where he was behind the arbour, thinking it would be a mistake to move until they were completely out of sight.

He knew now that the Marquis had been right in thinking that the Countess was a Russian spy who was attempting to obtain information from Lord Neasdon.

It had been a mistake on his part to mention Tibet. At the same time, Craig was aware that the Countess's efforts were extremely amateurish and very obvious to any man who was not puffed up with his own conceit.

Lord Neasdon must surely be aware of what was happening, and yet Craig had the feeling that he was so

naïve, and perhaps in a way so blinded by desire, that
he was oblivious of the dangers he was in and of those
who were using the Countess as a tool.

As he moved slowly and by a different route back into
the garden and then to the Villa, he knew that whatever
the Countess was doing, she was not doing it willingly.

He was in fact quite certain that the Russians who
were making her act as a spy on their behalf had
ordered her to take Lord Neasdon as her lover, and she
was fighting desperately not to do so.

He had listened closely to every intonation in her
voice while she was speaking to Lord Neasdon.

She was not only afraid, as she had confessed to
being when she was with him, but twisting and turning
with the desperate agility of a small animal to extricate
herself from the situation in which she found herself.

When he went over it step by step, Craig thought it
had been clever of the Russians in the first place to find
anybody so spectacular and so unusually beautiful to
work in a place where beautiful women of every class
abounded.

However, it was obvious that this was her first assignment, and Craig was willing to wager a very large
sum of money that she had taken it only because she
had been forced to do so.

Therefore, he had to discover why she was so frightened of her Russian masters that she had to obey them,
and secondly how he could help her personally as well
as prevent her from obtaining information from Lord
Neasdon which the Foreign Office had been afraid he
might be indiscreet enough to disclose.

It seemed to Craig absolutely incredible that in his
position Lord Neasdon should not realise that it was
unthinkable for him to take a Russian mistress at this
particular moment, when the reports from India were
so serious.

And yet he supposed that Neasdon, having had all his
experience in the Diplomatic Service in European Cap-

itals, had had little contact with Russians or knowledge of their aspirations in the East.

At the moment, it was in fact known only to a few people that Russia might be contemplating an invasion of Tibet, which was perturbing men of authority in India and the heads of the Foreign Office in London.

Yet, according to the Marquis, Neasdon had learnt enough for it to be important that on that subject, if on nothing else, he must keep his mouth shut.

Craig was quite certain that the fact that he had mentioned Tibet at all would be immediately repeated by the Countess to whoever was taking her reports back to a higher authority.

It was then that it suddenly struck him that Baron Strogoloff might be playing some part in this strange situation.

It was certainly a mystery that there should be two of his yachts in Monte Carlo, and that his guests, if he had any, never came ashore, and he came only to attend the Theatre.

"One thing is obvious," Craig said to himself. "I have somehow to make the acquaintance of the Baron."

Then as he reached the lighted windows of the Villa, he walked in smiling, determined to assume once more the guise of an American "playboy" as he went to find Zsi-Zsi and dance with her.

* * *

The following morning, having played four strenuous sets of tennis and seen his latest motor-car, which he was confident would win first prize in the *Concours d'Élégance*, Craig strolled onto the terrace below the Casino before luncheon.

Every head was turned in his direction, hands were held out to him in greeting, and he completed almost a Royal progress before he saw Lord Neasdon and the Countess seated at a table.

They were looking rather gloomy, and he thought,

although he could not be sure, that as he walked up to them there was a sudden light in the Countess's strange and beautiful eyes.

"Good-morning, *Madame!*" he said, sweeping his yachting-cap from his head. "Good-morning, Neasdon! Did you enjoy the party last night?"

"Very much," Lord Neasdon replied. "The Grand Duke lived up to his reputation of being an excellent host."

"I did not stay very late," Craig said. "I went on to another party, which was actually not so amusing."

The truth was that he had left immediately after he had danced with Zsi-Zsi, and on arrival at the Hôtel de Paris had waited in the adjoining room to the Countess's in case she should need him.

Whatever the difficulties, she had obviously persuaded Lord Neasdon to leave her alone that night, and the only voice he heard in her room was that of her Russian maid.

Craig had opened the communicating door on his side quite easily without invoking the aid of a servant.

There were few doors that stayed locked to him after the years in which he had undertaken missions for the Marquis, and silently, with hardly a creak, the door had surrendered to his expert hands.

Once it was open, he could hear quite clearly everything that was said in the next room.

He knew only a smattering of Russian, finding it a very difficult language, but he had learnt enough to know that the maid, with what he thought was an impertinent presumption, was asking the Countess questions about the evening, and she was answering in monosyllables.

Only when she presumably was undressed and ready for bed had the maid left her, saying good-night and closing the outer door noisily behind her.

It was then that Craig had debated whether he

should knock and tell the Countess he was there, but he quickly decided it would be a mistake.

Because she was so frightened, so sure she was being watched, the Russians might easily be tricking her into a false sense of security when they were actually still keeping her under observation.

He therefore waited for an hour in case she slipped a piece of paper under the door, but when she did not do so, he put the door on his side very quietly back into place and went to bed.

Now as he stood at their table, there was really nothing Lord Neasdon could do except say:

"Do sit down! Would you like a drink?"

"That is very kind of you," Craig answered, "but I must not stay long. I have promised to meet some friends, but they are not here yet."

As Lord Neasdon called a waiter and asked for a glass of sherry, Craig turned towards the Countess and enquired conversationally:

"Did you enjoy yourself last night?"

"It was a lovely party," the Countess replied, "and it was very, very kind of Lord Neasdon to take me with him."

"You are lucky I know so many people in Monte Carlo," Lord Neasdon replied; then he said to Craig: "I have promised the Countess that I shall be able to take her to quite a number of parties because, as you know only too well, Vandervelt, there are half-a-dozen taking place nearly every night."

"Yes, indeed," Craig agreed, "although some of them are doubtless extremely boring."

"That is what I have found," Lord Neasdon agreed, "but one can always pick and choose."

"Yes, of course."

The sherry was put down beside him and he took a sip before he said:

"There seem to be a dozen more ships here than

there were yesterday. Have you been aboard the Russian yachts?"

Craig asked the question of the Countess without seeming to have any particular reason for doing so.

Then as he saw a sudden shocked expression in her eyes, he knew that he had put his finger unerringly on something he should have been aware of before.

There was a perceptible pause before she answered: "No, no . . . I have not," but he knew that she was lying.

After lunching with his friends and taking one of them on a drive, Craig went to the Chapel of St. Dévoté after it was dark.

He entered the Church tentatively, just in case he was too early and the Countess was there. But there was no sign of her, and he walked quickly to the Confessional, sure that in the darkness relieved only by the candles in front of the effigies of the Saints, he would be unobserved.

Father Augustin was waiting for him and said as soon as he knelt down:

"I have some news for you, my son."

"I would be greatly relieved to hear it, Father."

"I am afraid it will not be what you wish to hear."

"Tell me!"

"The man you seek left his lodgings because he was afraid. I could not find out why, or where he was going, but he had somewhere to go."

Father Augustin paused for a moment. Then he said:

"My informant thinks he was either misled into a belief that his new hiding-place would be better than the old, or else it was a trap. Anyway, before he could reach his destination, two men apprehended him and took him to the harbour."

Craig stiffened, then knew exactly what he was going to hear.

"He was taken aboard the Russian yacht, *The Tsarevitch*, which is lying beside *The Tsarina*."

Craig sighed.

"Thank you, Father. I am more grateful than I can say in words."

"I am already grateful to you, my son, for your gratitude yesterday."

"Which I will express even more fully as I leave."

"Thank you. If I can help you again, you have only to come here at this time."

"You have never failed me, Father, and I need your prayers as I have never needed them before."

"You know they are yours."

The Priest blessed him, and Craig felt as if the sincerity of it remained with him as he went back to the Hotel.

He was well aware that not only would he need Father Augustin's prayers and the help of God, but the power of every religion with which he had ever associated himself, if he was to save Randall Sare from the Russians.

He was quite certain that they would stop at nothing to extract from him the information they needed so vitally, and the stories of the tortures they used on prisoners were not only horrifying but, as Craig was aware, not exaggerated.

As he dressed for dinner with the help of his Valet, he was thinking frantically that it was surprising that having taken him prisoner they had not already left Monte Carlo for Russia.

The only explanation he could think of was that they were expecting to obtain more information on Tibet from Neasdon.

They would not be aware that what he knew was very little, but even a little, added to what Randall Sare could tell them, would give them a great advantage in their position, which up until now had been ambiguous.

"I have so little time," Craig said to himself, not realising that he had spoken aloud until his Valet replied:

"You're not late, Sir, and anyway, few people are punctual in Monte Carlo."

Craig suddenly made up his mind.

"Go and find out what is on at the Theatre tonight!" he ordered, and his Valet hurried from the room to obey him.

He came back to say that there was an Opera, *Faust*, and Bellini was performing in it.

Because the singer in question was very popular, Craig was quite sure that the Baron would be present.

He therefore sent the Valet back to engage a Box and find out, without appearing to be too curious, who was in each of the other Boxes.

The man was away so long that Craig was just wondering impatiently whether he should go down to dinner and join his friends, when he appeared.

"They're very busy downstairs, Sir, but I found out what you wanted to know."

He handed Craig a slip of paper on which was written a number of names of distinguished people, headed by Prince Albert of Monaco.

Craig was only looking for one, and when he saw it he smiled.

"Thank you," he said to his manservant, then left the room.

The interior of the Theatre of Monte Carlo was pseudo-Gothic, as was the blue dome overhead, with golden friezes, golden frescoes, golden shields, golden goddesses, naked golden boys, and golden Nubian slaves holding golden candelabra.

It was said that when Marie Blanc, wife of the man who had made the Casino at Monte Carlo a success in the first place, saw it, she said acidly:

"All this vulgar display of golden gilt will only serve to remind the customers how much they have lost at the tables."

Nevertheless, the Theatre had been a success since its inception in 1879, when Sarah Bernhardt had recited at the Gala opening.

Craig was therefore not surprised to find it packed

when, accompanied by his friends with whom he had dined, he entered his Box just before the curtain rose.

He thought that the Opera was brilliantly done, but he was really only interested in watching the man sitting alone in the next Box.

He did not have to be told that it was Baron Strogoloff, for he was sitting in a wheel-chair, in which he had been half-propelled, half-carried to a position from which he could see the stage most comfortably.

The Baron looked like a large, overgrown goblin, and Craig, imagining him sitting with the Countess, thought they would be a perfect example of "Beauty and the Beast."

If he had gone on the stage just as he was, the Baron would have conveyed the horror that the Beast evoked in everybody he met, without the need of make-up or "props."

Watching him, Craig noticed his claw-like hands with their large joints, the cruelty of his down-turned mouth, and the sharpness of his dark eyes, which never left the stage.

Bellini may have sung brilliantly, but Craig never heard a note. He was concentrating all his powers of intuition and perception on the Baron.

When the intermission came and his friends moved out of the Box to talk to other people, Craig walked the few steps to the Box next to his and opened the door.

Immediately a man sitting just inside, who had been out of sight, rose to his feet as if to bar his way, but quickly Craig passed him and went up to the Baron to say:

"May I introduce myself? I am Craig Vandervelt, and my yacht, *The Mermaid*, is in the harbour a few moorings away from your yacht, *The Tsarina*. As one sea-loving man to another, I am very eager to have a word with you."

He knew as he spoke that the Baron was surprised, but then he said in tolerably good English:

"I have noticed your yacht, Mr. Vandervelt. I hear it is new."

"Very new," Craig answered, "and as I have invented a new type of engine and some special lighting to be used at night, which I believe has never been installed in a sea-going vessel before, you can imagine how curious I am to know if yours can beat me in respect of any new ideas."

He was speaking with a slightly exaggerated American accent, which was at any other time indiscernible.

He also affected an eagerness and a slightly boastful bravado which he was certain the Baron would not miss.

There was a little pause. Then the Baron asked:

"What other new ideas have you incorporated in your yacht?"

Craig reeled off a number of items which he thought would interest and intrigue any other yachtsman, and finished by saying:

"I am hoping that the American Navy will adopt some of these inventions."

"This all sounds very interesting, Mr. Vandervelt," the Baron said at length.

"What I am going to ask, Sir, although it may sound a little pushing," Craig said with a deprecating laugh, "is whether you would like to come aboard *The Mermaid* and then show me *The Tsarina*. To tell you the truth, I have never been aboard a Russian ship."

"You will find it very old-fashioned," the Baron said drily. "Russians are not very receptive to new ideas."

"That is not your reputation now, Sir," Craig replied, "either personally or as a country. We in America have been told that Russia is surging ahead when it comes to ships and guns, and it is about time we looked to our reputation! After all, we invented the Clipper!"

"That is true," the Baron agreed. "Well, Mr. Vandervelt, I shall be pleased to welcome you aboard *The Tsarina* tomorrow."

"What I suggest, Baron," Craig said eagerly, "is that you have luncheon with me on *The Mermaid* and afterwards show me *The Tsarina*."

"I am pleased to accept your invitation, Mr. Vandervelt," the Baron replied. "You will not object if I bring two of my friends with me?"

"No, of course not," Craig said with a smile. "The more the merrier."

He was quite certain from the note in the Baron's voice that the men he brought with him would be technicians who could copy anything that interested them.

Now the Orchestra returned and the Conductor reappeared to a burst of applause.

"That is a date, Sir!" Craig said, rising and holding out his hand. "I will expect you at one o'clock, and I am mighty glad to have made your acquaintance."

He shook the Baron's hand heartily and returned to his own Box.

As he did so, he was conscious that once again his luck had not failed him, and as he had touched the Baron's hand with his, he could understand only too well why the Countess was afraid.

Chapter Five

On leaving the Theatre with his party, they inevitably went to the Casino, and walked through the public part of it before going into the *Salle Touzet*, where Craig was hoping he would find the Countess.

Already the room was filled with gamblers, and as his party dispersed to the various different tables, he had a word with the Grand Duke and several other friends before he caught sight of the Countess.

Once again she was spectacular, wearing a gown of peacock blue, which made both her skin and her hair seem dazzling and which ended round her feet in a swirl of feathers.

There was no ornamentation except one huge aquamarine, hung on a slender chain round her neck.

The effect was sensational, and even in a room filled with beautiful women she seemed to stand out as if she were a light in a dark sky.

She was sitting at a table alone with Lord Neasdon, and, as might have been expected, he was talking while she listened.

Because Craig thought it was a mistake to approach her too obviously, he went to the Roulette-table nearest to where they were sitting and pretended to watch the gamblers and occasionally staking on a number.

He kept turning over in his mind the puzzle as to

why she was so afraid, but if, as he suspected, she was under orders from the Baron, it was not so surprising.

Because she seemed so fragile, so ethereal, it was somehow impossible to imagine her co-operating with a beast like Baron Strogoloff. Yet, there was no doubt that she was spying for the Russians.

If it was the Baron who had taken Randall Sare prisoner, then it was quite obvious that the whole of his problem in Monte Carlo emanated from him.

Like a vast spider, Craig thought, he was spinning his web round those he had captured to entwine them like flies, and it would be incredibly difficult for them to escape.

He was suddenly aware that because he had been so pre-occupied with his thoughts, the money he had put on number nine, which was a number he often favoured, had accumulated twice without his being aware of it, and now the *Croupier* was looking at him enquiringly as to whether he would take his gains or let the number run for a third time.

Almost as if he asked fortune for a sign as to whether he would win or lose a very much more complicated game than the one in front of him, Craig indicated that his gains were to remain where they were.

The *Croupier* picked up the small round ball, spun it, and said without any expression in his voice:

"*Mesdames et Monsieurs. Rien ne va plus!*"

Several greedy hands reached out in a last desperate effort to believe that fate and fortune would smile on them. Then there was a dull click as the ball came to rest.

The *Croupier* said, still in his expressionless tones:

"*Neuf, noir et impair,*" and Craig felt sure he would be successful in the greater issue too.

He picked up what he had won amongst the envious glances of those sitting at the table, and walked to the cash-desk to change the gold coins into notes, which he placed in the inside pocket of his tail-coat.

Then slowly, casually, he moved as if a magnet drew him back towards the Countess, debating whether he would speak to her, and if he did so what he would say.

He stopped on the other side of the same Roulette-table, and now he was aware that Lord Neasdon was leaning forward, speaking urgently and undoubtedly in a more animated way than was usual.

One of the things Craig had learnt when he was carrying out previous missions for the Marquis was lip-reading.

He had taken lessons from a very experienced teacher in New York, thinking it might at some time be useful, although at that moment there had been no necessity for it.

He had almost forgotten that it was something at which, when his lessons were finished, he had become exceptionally proficient.

Almost without realising it, he found that he could understand what Lord Neasdon was saying, and he moved a little farther round the table so that he could see him practically full face.

"Stop playing games with me, Aloya! My patience is exhausted, and I will no longer be put off with promises of a tomorrow that never comes."

The Countess's lips moved, and although Craig was aware that it must have been difficult for Lord Neasdon to hear what she was saying, he knew that she replied:

"I . . . I do not know what to say . . . please . . . could you not . . . come to my . . . room and perhaps . . . talk to me?"

"Talk? Who wants to talk?" Lord Neasdon asked aggressively. "I want you, Aloya, and you are driving me mad! You said yourself that we were made for each other! It is inevitable that you must be mine."

"I . . . I hoped," the Countess said, and her lips were trembling, "that you would be . . . kind to me."

"Kind?" Lord Neasdon asked. "Of course I want to be kind to you, but as a man I also want you, and I have played your game long enough. Either let me love you tonight, or I will realise I am just being made a fool of, and will leave Monte Carlo tomorrow."

The Countess gave a little cry which Craig knew was one of fear.

"Oh, no . . . you must . . . not do that! I want you to stay . . . you must stay!"

There was a complacent smile on Lord Neasdon's face as he said:

"Then what are we arguing about, my dear? I will make you very happy, and tomorrow we will go to Cartier and I will buy you something beautiful to commemorate the beginning of what I know will be a long and very exciting relationship."

The way he spoke, the expression in his eyes, and the smile on his lips made Craig feel a sudden fury which brought the blood throbbing into his head.

Only the rigid self-control which he had exercised over the years prevented him from going to the table and knocking Lord Neasdon down.

Then, surprised by the violence of his feelings, Craig suddenly knew that he was in love as he had never been in love before!

Because it was so amazing, he could not for the moment credit that he was not imagining it.

He knew that he wanted to protect the Countess not only from Lord Neasdon but from everything that was frightening her and making her tremble.

Never in his long experience with women who had pursued him, and with whom he had been infatuated to the point of being a most ardent lover, had he felt as he felt now.

What was so astonishing was that it was for a woman whom he should have regarded with contempt as a spy for the Russians and a danger to everything for which he had fought and risked his life in the past.

"I love her!" he said to himself in wonderment, and knew it was true.

There was nothing he could do until the situation became clearer than it was at the moment. But before he could rescue her from a brute like the Baron, he must first prevent Lord Neasdon from doing what he intended tonight.

Almost as if he was being guided, he knew the answer to the first step, if nothing else.

He walked towards the table, and as he reached it he said in a deliberately light tone:

"I thought I should find you here, but I wish you had been with me at the tables a few minutes ago when my lucky number came up three times running."

As he spoke with a smile, he realised that the Countess was looking up at him with an undoubted expression of relief in her strange eyes, while Lord Neasdon was obviously finding it difficult not to show resentment at his intrusion.

"I suppose," Craig went on, "I must celebrate my win in the usual manner. Will you have a glass of champagne with me?"

"We have some already," Lord Neasdon said in quite a surly tone.

"Oh, so you have!" Craig exclaimed, looking at the wine-cooler beside his chair. "So perhaps I should find our host of last night, who I see at the other side of the room, and thank him for a most enjoyable evening."

"I should do that," Lord Neasdon said.

Craig made as if to leave the table, then he turned back.

"By the way, Countess," he said, "I am hoping you will not be disturbed tonight."

"Disturbed?" she asked in a hesitating little voice, speaking for the first time since he had joined them.

"I have just heard that the Rajah of Pudakota is giving a party in his Suite at the Hôtel de Paris. I do not know which floor you are on, but the Rajah's parties are usually very noisy."

"I am . . . on the . . . third floor."

"I have a feeling, although I hope I am wrong," Craig went on, "that is the same floor as the Rajah's."

He paused for a moment. Then he said with feigned anger:

"I cannot think why people give parties in the Hotel where they are staying. They have no consideration for their fellow-guests. If I am at all disturbed, I am going to make a very strong protest to the Manager tomorrow morning, and I hope, Countess, you will do the same."

"Y-yes . . . I will . . . if I am . . . disturbed."

"I do not imagine His Highness will have a Band," Craig continued, "but there will undoubtedly be people coming and going half the night, and talking at the tops of their voices in the corridors as if nobody else exists."

"It sounds . . . very . . . disturbing," the Countess said faintly.

"It will be, I assure you," Craig said grimly, "but I am afraid there is nothing we can do about it until it happens."

"No . . . of course not."

He turned to the sullen nobleman and added:

"You are lucky, Neasdon, to be at L'Hermitage. Next time I come to Monte Carlo, I think I shall try it. The trouble with the Hôtel de Paris is that it is too popular."

He did not wait for Lord Neasdon to reply, but smiled at the Countess as he said:

"Good-night, but I am afraid I am being optimistic in thinking we have any chance of it being anything but a bad one."

He laughed as if at his own joke, then moved away, crossing the room to where he could see the Grand Duke smoking a large cigar and talking to Zsi-Zsi.

He could only pray that after what he had said, Lord Neasdon would be too nervous to force his way into the Countess's room, and at least for tonight she would be undisturbed.

He talked to the Grand Duke and Zsi-Zsi for some

time, deliberately standing with his back to the two
people he had just left.

Then, as if he felt in need of air, he went out onto the
terrace, thinking the night air would cool his brain as
well as his body.

He walked to the stone balustrade to look down at
the harbour.

He could see the lights of the two Russian yachts
very clearly, and he could also see *The Mermaid* some
moorings away from them.

The moonlight invested the promontory, the Palace
above it, and the sea shimmering away to the horizon
with an enchantment that was like music that lifted the
heart.

There was the scent of mimosa and night-scented
stock, while the stars seemed to gleam, Craig thought,
like the Countess's eyes.

He knew that their beauty was like the feelings
within his heart, which he still questioned because they
were so improbable and unpredictable.

But he knew irrefutably that what he felt was love,
and although it was not in the least like anything he had
felt before, his instinct recognised it, and it was something
he could not deny.

"She is beautiful and desirable as a woman, and that
is all I feel about her," he tried to tell himself, but he
knew he was lying.

The feelings surging within him were as intimate and
genuine as the power he knew he could call on in an
emergency, which had guided him ever since he had
first been aware of it long ago in India.

He knew it was the same power that Randall Sare
believed in, and almost without being aware of it he
sent out his thoughts and vibrations to the man he now
knew was a prisoner on one of the yachts he could see
below him.

As he had said to the Countess, the transference of

thought was something in which every Indian believed
and which they were taught by their Gurus.

Now that he knew where Sare was, he was aware that
he could reach him, sustain him, give him hope, and,
by a miracle, be able to rescue him.

"Help me," he pleaded. "You have been in this game
longer than I have, and you must tell me what to do."

He knew as he spoke the words in his mind and sent
them speeding out into the night that they came from
the Life Force within him and that he would surely get
some response.

Then as he waited, almost as if there was a voice from
Heaven, he knew the answer. It was there in his mind,
as if somebody was telling him what he should do, and
all that remained was to carry out his instructions.

Just for a moment Craig felt as if the very air round
him was filled with invisible wings, and that while he
could not see or hear them, every instinct in his body
was acutely aware of them.

Then as he tried to grasp at what he was feeling, they
were gone, but the plan was still there and that was all
that mattered.

He had had the same experience before when he had
been in a tight corner, and on one occasion on the very
edge of destruction, but not so vividly or so completely
as now in reaching Randall Sare, who had responded.

He stood on the terrace for a long time thinking,
until, aware that his body was feeling the chill of the
night, he went back into the overheated Gaming-Room.

He saw as he entered that the table at which the
Countess and Lord Neasdon had been sitting was now
empty, and as his anxiety for her returned, he felt his
fists clench at the thought that Neasdon might be
forcing himself upon her against her will.

He found it impossible to stay any longer in the
Casino and moved without hurrying down the room,
stopping at table after table so that he could be seen
speaking to a man here, a lovely lady there. Then

finally and unobtrusively he faded away without any-body being particularly aware of it.

He walked across the Square where fairy-lights were twinkling, then up the steps and through the brilliantly lighted door of the Hôtel de Paris.

He went up to his own floor, finding it quiet and with nobody in sight. He hoped that the Countess had not allowed Lord Neasdon to escort her to the door of her Suite, in which case he would have been aware that there was no party taking place on that floor.

Craig went into his own rooms, and, because his Valet was waiting for him, he undressed as he always did with his help.

Then, when he was wearing a long dark robe, he settled himself in a comfortable chair with the latest edition of *The Menton and Monte Carlo News*.

This was a newspaper which was first published in 1897. From a modest four pages it had developed into twenty-eight or more and was now the main source of information on the social life, sports, and entertainment of the Principality.

It also listed the new arrivals at the Hotels or Villas at which they were staying.

As he turned over the pages, his Valet said:

"I see, Sir, a lot more important guests arrived today."

Craig made a sound of annoyance.

"There are too many people here already," he said, "and I think it might be more comfortable and certainly quieter aboard *The Mermaid*.

The Valet looked depressed, and Craig was aware that both the men he had brought with him preferred it when their master was ashore, finding the unpredictability of the sea something which inevitably interfered with their duties.

Then as the Valet was tidying the room he added:

"Pack my clothes first thing tomorrow morning in

case I decide to run down the coast for a day or so. If I
change my mind, they can always be unpacked."

"Very good, Sir," the Valet replied in a voice that
conveyed no enthusiasm at the idea.

Craig waited until he was alone, then he put down
the newspaper, rose, locked the door of his bedroom
which led into the passage, and opened the door into
his Sitting-Room.

He passed through it and into the empty room on the
other side. Switching on only one light, he crossed to
the door which communicated with the Countess's Suite.

As he put out his hand to open the door he had just
unlocked, he knew that he was holding his breath in
case he should hear Lord Neasdon's voice, then mocked
at himself.

In the past he had not only never felt jealous about a
woman, but he had laughed at the men who suffered in
that way.

Yet, he knew that if he heard Neasdon with the
Countess he would, whatever the consequences, throw
him violently out of her room and save her, as he knew
she wished to be saved.

As the door opened there was only silence. Then
with a leap of his heart he saw something white beneath
the door.

He bent down and picked up the piece of paper and
saw written in a writing which he knew expressed her
personality:

"Please, I must speak to you."

As he read the words he felt not only relief but a
feeling of indescribable happiness because she wanted
and needed him.

Quickly and skilfully, with the instrument he had
concealed in the pocket of his robe, he managed to
open the door, and as he heard the lock click out of
place, he knocked very gently.

Instantly, so that he knew she must have been waiting for him, she pulled it open.

There was only one light in her room, and silhouetted against it she seemed to Craig like a vision that had always been in his imagination and, although he had not been aware of it, in a special shrine in his heart.

She was wearing a white negligé which flowed softly round her, and her hair was loose, falling pale silver so that it seemed to be part of the moonlight over her shoulders and down her back almost to her waist.

For a moment they just stood staring at each other as if they had met across eternity and found each other after a very long time.

Then—and afterwards, Craig could never remember how it happened—either she or he moved, his arms were round her, and her face was hidden against his shoulder.

He could feel she was trembling as he held her, and he knew it was the most perfect thing that had ever happened to him and was what he had sought but never found.

There was no need for words, for their closeness told them that all they needed was to be together.

Then the Countess said in a whisper that was barely audible:

"Help me ... please ... help me ... I do not know ... what to do ... and I am so desperately afraid!"

As she spoke he could feel the fear surging through her, and her whole body was trembling almost uncontrollably.

He tightened his arms, knowing instinctively that the strength of them was what she needed, and said very quietly:

"I am here and there is no need for you to be frightened."

He heard the Countess draw in her breath, and he went on:

"I think you would be happier and more sure that

no-one could hear what you have to tell me if you come into my Sitting-Room."

She raised her head then, and looked towards the outer door, and he thought he had never seen such terror in any woman's eyes, and that if it cost him his life he would somehow save her as she had asked him to do.

She made no reply, and he pulled her gently through the door he had just opened, closing it behind them.

He drew her across the empty room and into his Sitting-Room, where there were shaded lights, flowers, and his personal things scattered round, which made it somehow seem a haven of security.

He did not take his arm from her, but drew her towards a comfortable sofa. Then before he sat down he looked down at her, thinking how lovely she was, and at the same time, with her hair falling over her shoulders, she looked very young, little more than a girl.

She looked up at him and he felt that she was questioning whether she was right to be where she was and close to him, but he knew it was something she could not help.

"I told you to trust me," he said very gently, "and now there is a very good reason why you should do so."

He did not wait for her to ask what it was, but added:

"I love you! I was aware of it just now when I saw what was happening in the Casino, and because I love you I swear I will save you and you shall never again be as frightened as you are now."

She made an inarticulate little sound and her eyes filled with tears. Slowly Craig bent his head and very gently his lips found hers.

He kissed her because he could not help himself. At the same time, while he loved her he did not desire her passionately, but somehow spiritually, because she was part of the vibrations he had felt outside the Casino and the power he had evoked within himself on her behalf as well as from Randall Sare.

Then as he felt her lips quiver beneath his and he found they were innocent, inexperienced, and very soft, his kiss became more insistent, more demanding, and he pulled her still closer to him.

As he did so he was aware that this kiss was different from any other he had ever given or received in the past.

He could not explain it, he knew only that she had walked into his heart, she was a part of him, and now and for all time she was his.

Only when he felt they were one with the stars and the moon, and at the same time enveloped by a glory that was not of this world, did he raise his head, and she said in a whisper he could barely hear:

"I love...you! I did not...know I...loved you...and yet I have...thought about...you ever since we...first met."

"You thought of me—in what way?" Craig asked in a voice that was very deep.

"I knew you were the...only person I could trust when...everything else was...horrifying and...evil."

"And now you know that what you felt was love."

"I love you...I love...you...and I ought not to bring you into this...ghastly situation, which is...very dangerous...but there is no-one...else to whom I can...turn."

"You must tell me all about it, my darling," Craig said, "but first I must kiss you again, and because we love each other we will find a solution to your problem. I know it!"

He kissed her until he was aware that she had forgotten her fear and what she was feeling was something very different. As her body quivered against his, he knew it was from the rapture of love, and the sensations which he gave her were ones she had never experienced before.

Then as he drew her down onto the sofa, he said in a voice which was strangely unsteady:

"There is one thing I must know before anything else—are you really married?"

"No . . . no . . . it was just . . . part of the . . . disguise."

His relief made him feel as if the whole room were suddenly lit with a celestial light, and he said, as if he must make certain of the truth:

"And you have never been kissed?"

"Only . . . by you."

"My darling, I was sure of it when I touched your lips, and now I understand why, if no man has possessed you, you could not allow Neasdon to touch you."

The Countess gave a little cry.

"You . . . saved me . . . tonight. He was too . . . afraid to come upstairs when you said there was a . . . party on this floor, but . . . they will be . . . very angry . . . because they told me . . ."

She stopped, and as if she was afraid to say any more she hid her face against Craig's shoulder.

"They told you what?" he asked. "And I know now who you are speaking of—the Russians!"

The shudder that ran through her confirmed his words, and she said after a moment:

"If I do not . . . allow Lord Neasdon to . . . become my . . . lover . . . they have said that they will take Papa away to Russia . . . and I shall never . . . see him again."

Craig stiffened. Then he said:

"Your father? You cannot be Randall Sare's daughter!"

As he spoke, he thought he had been very obtuse not to have realised this before.

Aloya raised her head.

"You . . . know Papa?"

"Of course I know him, although I have only just learnt that the reason for his disappearance is that the Russians have him aboard the Baron's yacht."

She turned to him questioningly. Then she asked:

"H-how can you . . . know this? How can you be . . . aware of it . . . when it is not known to . . . anybody else in Monte Carlo?"

Craig's arms tightened round her as he said:

"There are a lot of explanations to be made, but first I want to hear about everything that has happened to you. Then I will explain why I am here."

"It is a reason that . . . concerns Papa?"

"Yes."

She gave a little cry.

"Now I know why I was so sure that . . . you would help me. I felt sure there was something about you that was different from . . . anyone else!"

Her eyes were shining as she said:

"Papa has always told me to trust in my intuition, and he was right."

"Of course he was right," Craig said, "and that is why I felt that you were not what you pretended to be."

She gave a little sigh, and he said:

"It is hard to express how glad I am that you are not the Countess Aloya Zladamir."

"It was the name they gave me," Aloya said, "because it sounded impressive, and they thought Lord Neasdon would find it easier to spend his time with a married woman than with a young girl, because of course as a girl I should have a proper Chaperone."

"I understand their reasoning, although I suppose it was the Baron who thought out the somewhat complicated plot."

"Y-yes . . . the . . . Baron! He is . . . wicked . . . evil! If Satan is a man . . . then he is the Baron!" Aloya said passionately.

"Were you with your father when he was captured by them?"

As if she knew she must tell him the whole story, Aloya put her head on Craig's shoulder. At the same time, she drew a little closer to him and his arms tightened round her.

Because he could not help himself, he kissed her forehead. Then he said:

"Start from the beginning. I had no idea, nor has

anybody in England, that Randall Sare is a married man."

"He kept it a secret because he thought that those who trusted him would find it hard to continue to do so if he had a wife who was what they thought of as a Russian."

Craig asked her to explain, and she said:

"Mama is actually Georgian, and my grandfather, Prince Volvershi, was very important in Georgia before it was annexed by the Russians."

Craig knew only too well how this had happened, but he did not interrupt, and Aloya went on:

"Mama fell in love with Papa when he came to Georgia, intending to move from there into Afghanistan, to find out what was being planned for rousing the tribesmen against the British."

She smiled as she said:

"He loved Mama the moment he saw her, and they knew that nobody else would ever be of any importance to either of them."

"That is how I feel about you."

"And it is the way I love you," Aloya answered. "I have always prayed that I would find a man to whom I could belong, and Mama knew as soon as she saw Papa that he had always been in her dreams."

Craig kissed her forehead again, but he knew he must hear the whole story, and Aloya continued:

"In spite of my grandfather's opposition, they were married very quietly and secretly, because as Papa explained, the Foreign Office in England and those who trusted him in India would not understand that the nationality of his wife would not interfere with his work for them."

She made a little gesture with her hands before she said:

"No-one who comes from Georgia thinks of themselves as Russian, although we dare not say so if they are listening."

"I know that."

"Because Mama had no wish to spoil Papa's life, which he loved, and in which he was so useful to those with whom he worked, she never interfered."

She paused before she went on:

"After I was born at home in Georgia, we joined him whenever it was possible, sometimes in strange places on the plains of India, sometimes in the foothills of the Himalayas, or in dak bungalows where we would go for days, sometimes weeks, without seeing anybody."

Craig understood now where Randall Sare had been many of the times when he had disappeared and no-one had any news of him.

"Then Papa would have another assignment," Aloya said, "or a message from those in authority, and usually he would send us home, or we would go to one of the big towns like Bombay or Calcutta, and live there very quietly so that nobody paid any attention to us or had any idea that we even existed."

"A very strange life!" Craig remarked.

"Fortunately, we had plenty of money, and Papa was insistent that I should be well educated and have the very best Teachers available. When he was at home, he taught me his own beliefs, and that is the only reason why I have not been more frantic about him than I am at the moment . . . but time is running out."

"What do you mean by that?" Craig asked.

"I think you will understand where most people would not," Aloya said, "but when we were captured by the Russians here in Monte Carlo . . ."

"Wait a minute!" Craig interrupted. "You are going too fast. First of all, why was he going home? He told me he would never return to England."

"Oh . . . of course . . . I forgot to tell you," Aloya said. "Mama . . . died! She had not been well for some time, but I managed with difficulty to send for Papa, and he was there to say . . . good-bye to her."

Her voice trembled for a moment. Then she said, and it was very moving:

"Mama knew he was coming, and she hung on when she might otherwise have died . . . until he actually appeared."

She turned her face against Craig's neck, and he knew she was crying as she said:

"She . . . just had . . . time to tell Papa how much she . . . loved him . . . and how happy he had . . . made her . . . then her spirit slipped away . . . and there was only her . . . body left behind."

Craig held Aloya very closely as he said:

"I know that describes what happened, but she must be still near you, to tell you that you can trust me."

"Of course she is . . . and near Papa . . . and although he would not . . . mind dying . . . I cannot . . . lose him."

"It would be a loss to the whole world," Craig said. "But tell me why he was going back to England."

"It was . . . because he could not . . . leave me alone in India, and although I begged him not to do so, he decided to take me to his sister, with whom he has always kept in touch. He thought she would not only look after me but would introduce me to English Society."

Aloya paused before she said:

"He decided it was quite straightforward, until he realised that the Russians were determined, because he had returned from Tibet, either to capture . . . or to kill him."

"You were not in Tibet with him?" Craig asked incredulously.

"We only went as far as Gyangtse, just inside the country. We had a house there while Papa went wandering about, finding out from the Monasteries, and of course in Lhasa, what the British wanted to know."

Aloya paused for a moment before she said:

"When Mama died in Gyangtse, there was nothing Papa could do but go home."

"Which of course was quite right where you were concerned."

"I do not think so, but I always do what Papa wants."

"What I cannot understand is why you left the ship at Nice and came here," Craig said.

"We went on board in disguise," Aloya said. "In fact, Papa was a Turk, and nobody questioned for a moment that he was anything other than he appeared to be."

"And you?"

"I was his wife! I wore a *yashmak* and a *burnous*, which as you are aware are very concealing. One can be fat, thin, pretty, or ugly, and nobody would be any the wiser."

"A very good thing, as you are so very lovely, my darling."

Aloya drew in her breath.

"I want you to . . . think that."

"I will tell you exactly what I think when you have finished your story. Why did you get off the ship in the South of France?"

"We were quite certain that no-one on board had the slightest idea that Papa was not the Turk he pretended to be, but when we stopped at Naples for new passengers to come on board, among them were two men whom Papa recognised, and he thought he recognised him too."

Craig heard the fear in her voice as she went on:

"However, it was not until we reached Nice that he was sure they intended to kill him. We slipped ashore the moment the ship docked, leaving behind practically everything we possessed so that they would not be suspicious until after the ship had left the harbour."

Craig saw the reasoning behind this, and Aloya went on:

"Papa did not know where we could be safe in Nice, but there was a place he knew in Monte Carlo, so we went there."

She gave a little sigh as she added:

"It was rather scruffy and uncomfortable. I went out shopping for our food, and although I did not see anybody about who seemed in the least suspicious,

Papa's instinct told him that he must not take any risks."

Craig knew they must have been hiding in the place where Father Augustin had first made enquiries.

"Why did you leave?" he asked.

"It was very unfortunate," Aloya replied, "but a man who was also in hiding came to this particular place, and Papa recognised him as an informer who would give information to anybody who was willing to pay for it, and it was therefore too dangerous for us to stay."

"So you moved," Craig said, "and that was disastrous."

"How do you know?" Aloya enquired. "What happened was that we left where we were really safe, and Papa instructed me to walk on the other side of the street from him."

Craig realised that this must have been when he was seen by one of the British Agents.

"He turned the corner along a street," Aloya said, "and there were two men waiting for him, who seized him, and he had no chance to escape from them."

"What did you do?"

"What could I do?" she asked. "I did not have time to reason it out. I just ran to Papa to be with him, for whatever happened we would be together."

The way she spoke was very moving, and Craig said:

"I understand, and so they took both you and your father to the Baron."

"It was . . . terrifying," Aloya said. "They started to question Papa, and when he refused to tell them anything they wanted, they said they would take him back to Russia and . . . torture him until he . . . told them what they . . . wanted to know."

Craig knew from the way she spoke how terrifying it had been.

"Then Papa said he would tell them some of the things they wanted to know if they would let me go free."

She gave a deep sigh.

"That was a great mistake. The Baron looked at me as if he saw me for the first time, and I knew by the expression in his eyes that he thought I might be useful to them."

"So it was the Baron who thought up the idea that you should seduce Lord Neasdon into revealing his secrets about Tibet?"

"He told me he was very, very important to the Foreign Office and would know the British plans if the Russians should invade that country."

"So they dressed you up in spectacular fashion!"

"They told me exactly what I was to do," Aloya said with a shudder.

"And your clothes?"

"A French designer over whom they apparently had some hold was brought to the yacht and instructed to make me look outstanding so that it would be impossible for Lord Neasdon not to notice me."

"But surely he was not expected to speak to you on sight?" Craig asked, feeling it was somehow out of character, considering Neasdon's impression of his own importance.

"Oh, no," Aloya cried, "they were far too clever for that! They found out all about him. His mother, of whom he is very fond, was leaving for America the day before he arrived here, and by some method of their own they obtained a letter she had written."

She paused and then went on:

"I think it was to be a friend of hers in Monte Carlo, and they forged her handwriting in a letter they wrote in her name to Lord Neasdon, begging him when he arrived in Monte Carlo to be kind to the daughter of somebody to whom she owed a great debt of gratitude."

"That was you, I presume?"

"Of course, and because of the urgency with which the letter was written, Lord Neasdon called on me within a few hours of his arrival."

"And was obviously bowled over by your beauty!" Craig said cynically.

"I had to tell him how much he impressed me and how wonderful I thought he was," Aloya said in a low voice, "and I knew all the time I was talking to him that my maid, who of course is their spy, listened at the door to make sure I did not say . . . anything that might make him . . . suspicious."

She made a little sound of despair as she said:

"I did not dare to do that . . . because they had told me that if I did not do exactly as they . . . wanted, they would . . . kill Papa immediately after they had extracted his secrets from him."

"Is that what they have been doing in the meantime?" Craig asked anxiously.

"No, Papa has been too clever for them," Aloya replied. "He played for time while they were arranging my clothes and the Baron was lending me the jewels I wore, which of course are his. Then, when they began to question him seriously, he went into a trance."

"A trance?" Craig exclaimed.

"It is something he learnt to do in India, and he can render himself completely unconscious so that it is impossible to wake him. But naturally the trance only lasts for a certain time."

"How long?" Craig asked, knowing it was of vital importance.

"Unless he is to die for lack of food and water," Aloya said in a voice that trembled, "he has . . . to come back to . . . consciousness . . . tomorrow!"

Craig knew then that this was why he had been aware perceptively that the sands of time were running out and that he had to do something quickly.

He was not only afraid for Aloya, but in some special way Randall Sare had made him aware that there was no more time.

"The Russians do not know this," he said, "so why

did they say you had to take Lord Neasdon as your lover tonight?"

"They are waiting for Papa to regain consciousness and for me to give them results. Then they intend to take both of us away, and if I have nothing to tell them . . . I think they will . . . torture me in front of Papa to make him speak."

Craig thought this was very likely, and he said angrily:

"I swear to you, my darling, that shall not happen as long as I am alive."

"Can you . . . save Papa . . . and me?"

"I swear I will do so," he said, "and I know you will believe me as no-one else would when I tell you that tonight when I was on the terrace outside the Casino, I was told either by your father or some other force what I have to do."

He saw Aloya look up at him, and the expression in her eyes told him that she not only believed him but knew he would succeed.

Then, as if there was no more to say, his lips were on hers, and he kissed her masterfully, possessively, and passionately, as if she were not a shy young girl but a woman whom he loved more than anything else in the whole world.

Chapter Six

Craig woke with a feeling of happiness which for the moment made him forget the difficult, dangerous task which lay ahead.

All he could think of was his love for Aloya, how last night he had held her in his arms and known that she was everything he needed to make himself complete, and that he was the most fortunate man in the whole world.

Having travelled in so many lands and having done so many strange things in his life, he was aware that she was unique not only in her astounding beauty but in the intelligence of her mind, her quickness of thought, and most of all her intuition and perception, which was the same as his own.

Her beauty, he now realised, came from her mixture of blood, in which she combined the fair skin of her English forebears with the mystical beauty of her Russian eyes.

It was this ancestry which had added the strange silver sheen to her hair, which Craig realised he had occasionally seen before on Russian women, whose hair however had been black.

He also knew—and he was certain that it was something Aloya believed, as her father did—that when two people loved each other overwhelmingly and were in fact the spiritual counterpart of each other, their children had a beauty that was created by love itself.

He knew better than most men the difficulties Randall Sare must have encountered when he had been forced because of his work to keep his marriage a secret from everybody.

Craig was sure that it was not only because the authorities would have been shocked at his marrying a woman who was ostensibly Russian, but also because his enemies might, as they were doing now, use his wife and family as a weapon against him.

It was still hard to credit that Aloya and her mother had travelled over the bitterly cold, treacherous, and extremely dangerous Pass which connected India with Tibet.

But he had known that Gyangtse, the first town inside the forbidden territory, was a Trading-Post, and therefore they would not have aroused as much interest or hostility as they would have done farther into the country.

Then in the dim light as the dawn crept up the sky, Craig thought that only Randall Sare would have felt it obligatory to leave his wife and daughter in such a strange place and go off into the blue, disguised so cleverly that he must have convinced everybody he met that he was neither a spy nor an enemy.

This might be comparatively easy in India or other countries in the East, but the people of Tibet had a perception equal to his own.

Some of the older Monks in the great Monasteries could use what the uninitiated thought was clairvoyance or magic, but which in fact was a supernormal power, to find the truth.

Craig could understand how Sare, bereft of his wife, whom he had loved so deeply, and encumbered with a very beautiful daughter, had known that the only possible thing he could do was to take her to England and safety.

And yet, because of his reputation and because to the

Russians he was a marked man, they were both now in a situation which Craig knew was so dangerous and so desperate that one false step could destroy them both.

The thought of losing Aloya was like a thousand daggers striking at his heart, and he made up his mind quite calmly and positively that if she died, he would die with her.

"I would have bet my entire fortune," he told himself with a twist of his lips, "that no woman could ever have made me feel as I feel now, but I know now that every word the poets ever wrote about love and every note the musicians played was true."

Then he forced himself not to think of the emotions surging within his heart, but to concentrate his brain and his whole being on what lay ahead.

Last night when he had taken Aloya to the door of her bedroom he had said:

"From this moment leave everything in my hands. Trust me, pray, and send out the vibrations which we both know will be received by your father."

"Will you be doing... that?" Aloya asked.

"You know I will," Craig replied. "I shall be telling him to be prepared, and I know he will understand."

As he spoke he thought there was no other woman in the whole world to whom he could say such things.

He had then held her close in his arms and kissed her passionately and demandingly until they were both breathless, with their hearts beating frantically against each other's.

"I love you," Craig said hoarsely, "and love will always win."

"You are... sure of... that?"

"Look at me!" he commanded masterfully.

She did as he told her, and he thought no woman could look more lovely or more desirable, and their need of each other was like the air they breathed and the sunshine which came from the sky.

Then as her eyes were held by his he saw the fear,

the worry, and the anxiety being replaced by a rapture which ran through him like little streaks of lightning, and he knew she was feeling the same.

Because there were no words to express what they were both feeling, he kissed her again, and since words were superfluous, without saying any more, he shut the doors between them and went to his own room.

Now he was going over step by step in his mind exactly what must be done, trying to make every detail foolproof as he had been taught to do in the past, anticipating the worst and being prepared for it, obeying the golden rule, which was never to take an unnecessary chance.

Nobody who saw him a little later walking through the Hôtel de Paris to the Tennis Courts which were behind it and in front of L'Hermitage would have guessed that he had anything on his mind but the joy of Spring and an anticipation of hard exercise to sweep away the excesses of the night before.

The Pro. was waiting for him, and as usual Craig managed to beat him in the last set, and they arranged to play again the following morning.

After he had put on his thick woollen sweater he walked not back to the Hôtel de Paris but to L'Hermitage, and passing through the glass door he went to the Reception Desk.

"Is Lord Neasdon down yet?" he asked. "I would like to have a word with him."

The Receptionist smiled at him in recognition.

"Good-morning, Mr. Vandervelt. His Lordship is in the Breakfast-Room. Shall I tell him you are here?"

"I will speak to him myself," Craig replied.

He walked into the Breakfast-Room, thinking it was typically English of Lord Neasdon to breakfast downstairs rather than in his own Suite.

There were only a few other people in the room, and a glance showed him that Lord Neasdon was sitting at a table in the window, reading the newspaper.

Craig walked to his table, and only when he had stood for a second waiting did Lord Neasdon raise his head.

"Good-morning, Vandervelt," he said in a not particularly effusive tone. "You are very early."

"I am sorry to disturb you," Craig replied, "but I am hoping that you will join me for luncheon today aboard my yacht, *The Mermaid*. I am having a small party, and I am very anxious for both you and the Countess to see my new yacht."

He knew as he finished speaking that Lord Neasdon was wondering how he could refuse because he disliked him, but before he could say anything Craig went on:

"I have already sent a note to the Countess, and I hope you will bring her with you in my motor-car, which will be outside the Hôtel de Paris at one o'clock."

There was really nothing Lord Neasdon could do in the circumstances but accept, and as he did so, somewhat ungraciously, Craig said:

"That is splendid! I shall look forward to seeing you. Good-bye until then, and perhaps we might take a turn out to sea after luncheon if the weather is as good as it is now."

He was gone before Lord Neasdon could think of a reply, and there was a smile of satisfaction on his lips as he walked back to his Hotel.

Because he thought it would be a mistake for him not to do everything he normally did, he spent the next two hours in his Sitting-Room, writing letters while his secretary paid bills, until soon after noon he walked onto the terrace.

The usual friends were congregated there, and he found Zsi-Zsi and the Grand Duke entertaining a number of people.

He joined them and received several invitations, which he accepted, until at exactly half-past-twelve he left the terrace and was driven in his car down to the harbour.

His secretary had already carried out his instructions to alert *The Mermaid,* and as he came aboard the Captain said:

"Everything's prepared, Sir, and I hope it's to your liking. The Chef complained that it was rather short notice, but I don't think you will be disappointed in the menu."

"I am sure I will not be," Craig replied. "And now, Captain, I want a word with you, so we will go into the Saloon."

The Saloon, which was painted pale green and had very attractive chintz furniture-covers which matched the curtains, was a novelty in the yachting-world, which up to now had kept strictly to the traditional polished mahogany panelling and leather chairs.

Having shut the door, the Captain stood waiting for his orders, which Craig gave him slowly and clearly, making absolutely certain that they were understood.

Only after he had finished speaking did the Captain give a little gasp and say:

"It seems almost incredible, Sir!"

"I agree with you," Craig said, "but when I engaged you, Captain, I went very carefully into your background, and I know you have been through some traumatic experiences of your own, and carried out your orders with a heroism which should have been rewarded."

The Captain looked almost bashful.

"It's very kind of you to say so, Sir."

"You will understand, after what I have told you," Craig said, "that this is the reason I chose an Englishman to command my yacht, although I am in fact an American."

"That's a compliment I greatly appreciate," the Captain replied.

"Then brief your men, Captain, and let there be absolutely no mistakes. The timing has to be done to a split second."

"I understand, Sir."

He saluted smartly, and Craig was aware that there was a look of admiration in his eyes which had never been there before.

It amused him to think how in the past while the Captain had been prepared to command his ship and obey his orders to the letter, it had always been at the back of his mind that it was a pity he was an American.

It was something he had met before with the English, and when he was engaged on some desperate mission on their behalf, he had often longed to damn their impertinence for daring to think that because he belonged to another nation he was not only slightly inferior but less intelligent than they were.

However, there was no time for personal retrospect.

Instead, Craig went from the Saloon into the smaller room adjacent to it, which was where they were to eat.

This room was also decorated in green, but the seats and the chairs and curtains were not of chintz, but of an emerald-green velvet which was echoed in the leaves of the camelias which decorated the table.

The centre-piece was a silver galleon made in Venice in the Sixteenth Century, and the rest of the silver was early Georgian. Craig wondered if his guests would appreciate the time and thought he had given to the furnishings of *The Mermaid*.

Because he could afford it, he wanted everything to be superlative of its kind as well as in excellent taste, and he had only to look at the very fine oil-paintings of ships which decorated the walls to know that there was no yacht afloat that carried such treasures.

In the silver ice-buckets were champagnes and wines of excellent vintages from the finest vineyards in France.

As Craig stood looking at them, his head steward came in, looking exceedingly smart in his silver-buttoned white cut-away coat.

Craig gave him his orders, which, like those he had given to the Captain, were concise, clear, and impossible to misunderstand.

Then, when the steward, who had been with him for some years in his other yachts, showed that he understood what was required, Craig moved back into the Saloon.

Exactly at the time expected, Baron Strogoloff was pushed aboard in his wheel-chair, to be welcomed by Craig's secretary, Mr. Cavendish, at the top of the gangway, and brought from there into the Saloon.

He was followed by two stalwart-looking Russians, hard-faced men but dressed impeccably in yachting-clothes, in which they appeared somewhat out-of-place and ill-at-ease.

One glance at them before he greeted the Baron told Craig that they were exactly what he had expected them to be, technicians who would take note of everything that they saw, and make sure the information was relayed to the yachts of the Russian Navy.

Smiling and speaking affably, he held out his hand to the Baron, saying:

"I am delighted to see you, Baron, and I have so much to show you after luncheon."

The Baron's wheel-chair was placed at the far end of the Saloon, and after Craig had shaken hands with his two attendants and asked them to sit down, the stewards immediately carried round glasses of vodka.

The Russians swilled them down their throats in one gulp, and the glasses were immediately refilled, as Craig sat down beside the Baron to say with an air of boyish eagerness:

"How do you like my scheme of decoration?"

"It is certainly unusual, Mr. Vandervelt," the Baron replied in a guttural voice.

"I thought you would think so. I cannot tell you how hard the builders tried to argue with me and persuade me to be more traditional."

"I see you have some fine paintings."

"I agree with you, and it would be a disaster if we were sunk at sea, but I do not think that will happen."

"The sea can always be a risk to anyone," the Baron said pompously.

Craig laughed.

"And so can a great many other things in life."

His secretary opened the Saloon door.

"The Countess Aloya Zladamir, Sir, and Lord Neasdon!"

Craig got to his feet.

"Can I say how pleased I am to see you, Countess," he asked, "and looking more lovely than Spring itself? I have a surprise for you, because I think you told me you have not met your compatriot, Baron Strogoloff, whom I have persuaded also to be my guest."

He knew as he took Aloya's hand in his that she was frightened. At the same time, with what he knew was a clever piece of acting, she replied:

"No, I have never met the Baron, but I have admired the beautiful yacht he owns."

She walked across the room to shake hands with him, and Craig turned to Lord Neasdon to say:

"Welcome aboard, My Lord!"

He then introduced him to the Baron's two attendants, who had risen rather awkwardly to their feet as the Countess had entered the cabin.

Aloya was standing by the Baron, who was glaring at her, and yet Craig knew perceptively that, fortified by her trust and belief in him, she was not afraid as she might have been.

As he joined her she exclaimed with exactly the right inflection in her voice:

"What a charming cabin, and so different from what I expected!"

"That is what I want to hear," Craig said, "and the Baron has already said that he admires my paintings."

"They are lovely, quite lovely!" Aloya cried. "I hope we shall be able to see the whole of your yacht before we leave."

"Of course," Craig replied. "The State-Rooms are very unusual, at least the American magazines seem to

think so. There is hardly one in which photographs of
my yacht have not appeared."

"I shall so look forward to seeing everything."

Aloya was looking so lovely that Craig knew he had to
be careful not to reveal both his admiration and his love
when he looked at her.

It would be a mistake, he knew, to underestimate the
Baron in any way, and as if what he was thinking
communicated itself to Aloya, she moved towards Lord
Neasdon and slipped her arm through his.

"What do you think of it?" she asked.

As she spoke she turned her eyes upwards in a way
which made Craig long to snatch her into his arms and
forbid her ever to look at another man.

But he knew she was only carrying out his instructions, and Lord Neasdon said heavily:

"I suppose these paintings are originals and not
reproductions?"

"You insult me!" Craig replied lightly.

"I am sure there is . . . nothing about Mr. Vandervelt
which is not . . . original."

As Aloya spoke she refused a glass of vodka and
accepted one of champagne.

Lord Neasdon looked surprised at the smaller glass,
saying:

"I do not believe I have ever drunk vodka."

"You must try it," Craig answered. "It is the traditional
Russian drink when you are eating caviar, and as the
Baron will tell you, it stimulates the entire system."

"Well, I suppose I must be daring," Lord Neasdon
said in a voice which showed it was the last thing he
was likely to be.

He picked up the glass and was about to sip it when
Aloya gave a little cry.

"No, no! That is not the right way to drink vodka. You
must pour it down your throat in one gulp. Am I not
right, Baron?"

"That is right," the Baron agreed.

He sat glowering from under his bushy eye-brows, and Craig had the feeling that he was slightly disconcerted at meeting her and was not quite sure what he should do about it.

The glasses of vodka were filled and refilled before luncheon was announced.

Then the Baron's wheel-chair was pushed into the smaller Saloon next door and he was seated on Craig's left, while Aloya sat on his right, with Lord Neasdon next to her.

The two Russians had been placed one beside the Baron and the other at the far end of the table. They sat down awkwardly, making no effort to speak, but proceeded as the meal progressed to eat and drink everything that was put in front of them.

The Captain had been right when he said the Chef had made a great effort.

Although the food was delicious, Craig had to force himself to eat, but he was aware that because she was afraid, Aloya's throat was constricted and it was almost impossible for her to swallow anything.

However, she was clever enough to appear to be eating while playing about with the food on her plate, only pushing what was left to one side just before the plates were removed for the next course.

Lord Neasdon, perfectly at his ease, ate heartily, but Craig knew that his guest not only disliked him as a man but was also envious of his possessions, and it was hard for him to respond effusively when Aloya praised everything, including the camelias which decorated the table and the silver galleon in the centre of it.

"I am a collector of ships," Craig explained, "and because I am fond of the sea, I have a great many ancient models in silver and gold, and some with precious stones."

"How exciting!" Aloya exclaimed. "I would love to see them."

"I hope one day I will be able to show them to you."

He spoke without any depth of feeling in his voice, but his heart told him that the day would come when he would not only show Aloya his treasures but she would share them with him.

Then, because he was determined to allay any suspicions the Baron might have that this was not a perfectly ordinary luncheon-party, he set out to be amusing and witty about Monte Carlo and his travels to other places in the world.

The way he talked made it impossible for anybody not to laugh, and he was aware that the Baron relaxed a little as he drank a great deal, and his eyes did not seem quite so hard and suspicious, and even his hands seemed a little less claw-like.

As if he wished to assert himself, Lord Neasdon told a long and rather boring story of an encounter with robbers in one of the high Passes in Switzerland.

When he finished, Craig capped it with a tale of being pursued by pirates off the coast of Malaya.

"I was fortunate," he said, "that at that time my yacht was considerably faster than their craft, otherwise I doubt if I should be here telling the tale."

"It sounds very frightening!" Aloya said.

"When one is in danger," Craig replied, "one often has a feeling of exhilaration."

"Why is that?" she asked.

"Because one is pitting one's brains and one's strength against another human being, and if the odds are equal, it becomes a challenge to one's personality."

"And if the . . . odds are not . . . equal?"

She spoke in a low voice, and Craig knew what she was thinking.

"One has to rely on the unexpected, or perhaps on a power greater than one's self, which is always available if we know how to look for it."

As he saw the expression in her eyes change, he knew that she understood what he was telling her, and because once again she was acting on his instructions, she turned to Lord Neasdon to ask:

"Have you ever felt that?"

"I have always relied on myself and my brain," he replied pompously, "and that is why we British have been victorious in many different fields."

"Of course," Craig replied. "At the same time, you are not doing so well at the moment against the Boers."

He could not help the jibe, but as he saw Lord Neasdon stiffen, he had no wish to antagonise him, so he added quickly:

"But we are not going to talk politics today. This is a happy occasion, and as you are in fact my first party aboard *The Mermaid*, I want you to drink a special toast wishing her success and a safe harbour wherever she journeys."

"Of course we must do that!" Aloya cried, clapping her hands.

As Craig was speaking, the stewards had brought in fresh glasses, and while one man passed them round to the guests, the other carried a decanter in each hand.

"This is the most famous wine in Europe in which to drink a toast," Craig explained. "It is Tokay, which you all know comes from Hungary and is highly esteemed by the Austrians, as I am sure the Baron is aware."

"Yes, indeed," the Baron agreed, "but I do not think I have ever drunk Tokay."

"Then this is the first time for you, and the first luncheon-party aboard *The Mermaid*, and the first time I have ever had such a beautiful guest as the Countess."

Aloya looked shy and blushed, and Craig knew that at the moment she was not acting.

The steward filled the glasses, then as if he could not be left out Lord Neasdon said:

"I will propose the toast! To *The Mermaid*, to its owner, and of course to somebody who is more beautiful and more alluring than any mermaid or siren to be found in the sea!"

Looking at Aloya, he raised his glass, and as she smiled at him he drank down the Tokay, saying as he did so:

"No heel-taps!"

It was echoed with pleasure as the Russians obeyed him, and the glasses of Tokay disappeared down their throats at the same speed as the vodka had.

"That was a very nice toast," Aloya said, who had only sipped her drink.

"Thank you," Lord Neasdon said. "I knew it would please you."

He spoke in an intimate, possessive manner which made Craig tighten his lips. Then as a steward started to refill the glasses, he said to the Baron:

"You have not told me, Baron, and it is something I would like to know, why you have brought two yachts with you to Monte Carlo."

The Baron hesitated, as if he was thinking up some good explanation, and as he did so there was a sudden clatter as one of the Russians fell forward onto the table, his forehead coming to rest on a saucer and the coffee in his cup slowly pouring out onto the white cloth.

The Baron turned his head angrily and said something sharply to the man next to him, which Craig, even with his limited knowledge of Russian, knew was a rebuke for a disgusting example of drunkenness.

But as he spoke the other Russian collapsed too, and because his face was turned towards the Baron, he fell sideways, and before anyone could realise what was happening he had slipped under the table.

The Baron looked absolutely furious, then as he opened his lips to speak, Craig said very quietly:

"Do not blame them, Baron, the Tokay they drank contained a drug which works instantly. They will sleep for the next three hours, then be left with nothing more than a very unpleasant headache."

The Baron stiffened and his fingers clenched slowly into his palm.

"As your two 'friends,' as you term them, are unable to enjoy the rest of your visit here," Craig went on, "I suggest their place be taken by another guest on your yacht, Mr. Randall Sare."

"I refuse, I absolutely refuse!" the Baron replied.

"Very well," Craig said. "If you will not send for him I will take *The Mermaid* out to sea, and there will be a most unfortunate accident, on which the two Russians who are here with you as your bodyguards will not be able to report coherently in any detail."

He paused before he added:

"A wheel-chair can so easily slip overboard."

There was a long silence. Then the Baron said surlily:

"Very well, I will send for Randall Sare, but you will get little sense out of him."

"That is my concern," Craig replied.

He must have rung a bell as he finished speaking, for a steward came into the room carrying a blotter on which was a piece of writing-paper engraved with the name of the yacht, an ink-well, and a pen.

"You will write," Craig said as it was set down in front of the Baron, "telling whoever is in command of *The Tsarevich* to bring Randall Sare here in my motor-car, which is waiting at your gangway. One man can help him, or two if necessary, and although it is only a very short distance, the car will make it unnecessary for him to make the effort to walk if he is not fit enough to do so."

The Baron's lips were tight with fury, but he wrote in a scrawling hand on the writing-paper and signed it with his name.

Then he put down the pen and Craig picked up the paper and handed it to Aloya.

"See that the Baron has written exactly what I said

and that there are no hidden instructions of which we are not aware."

She read it very carefully. Then she said:

"I think it is all right."

Craig took it from her and said to the Baron:

"If by some forethought you have left instructions that if Randall Sare should be sent for, or in any other way taken from the prison in which you have incarcerated him, he is to be killed, let me make it quite clear that if he does not come here alive, then your life will be forfeited for his."

"You would not dare . . . !" the Baron exclaimed furiously.

"I would not bet on that," Craig replied very quietly, and it seemed to Aloya, watching him, as if he somehow grew larger and exuded a power which menaced the Russian.

For a moment the eyes of the two men met as if in conflict, then the Baron looked away first and said gruffly:

"Sare will come, but we will get him sooner or later, Vandervelt, and you!"

"I should imagine it is a very outside chance," Craig replied lightly.

He called the steward back into the room, handed him the note, which he had put into an envelope, and without waiting for any further instructions the steward left.

Craig rose from the table.

"I suggest, as it is rather depressing to sit here with your two unconscious countrymen, Baron, that we move into the Saloon, which will be more comfortable. I am sure you would like a glass of brandy with which to finish the meal and perhaps take away the taste of Tokay."

As he spoke he glanced at the Russian whose head still lay on the table, then as Aloya rose, Lord Neasdon said as if he could no longer contain himself:

"I demand an explanation as to why I was not told that this sort of thing was going to happen!"

"The only explanation I am prepared to give will be in a report to your superior at the Foreign Office, and I hope for your sake he listens sympathetically."

The warning note in his voice made Lord Neasdon go pale, and when they had moved into the Saloon he threw himself down petulantly in a chair, as if he could not bear to look at his host or Aloya.

He picked up a newspaper, and it was only after he had been pretending to read it for several minutes that he realised it was upside-down.

The Baron was silent, and Craig knew he was thinking desperately of how he could avenge himself for what was an unexpected coup.

However, Craig was primarily concerned with Aloya, and as if she knew what he wanted she walked down the Saloon, looking at the paintings, discussing them with him, and inspecting the books on the large shelf in the corner.

After what seemed a long time but was actually quicker than Craig had dreamt possible, his secretary opened the door to say:

"The car has arrived, Mr. Vandervelt."

Without speaking, Craig walked to the door, where he could see Randall Sare stepping out from the car.

There was one Russian already on the Quay waiting to help him and another following.

They each took his arm as he walked the few steps towards the gangplank, and Craig knew it was not only to be of assistance but also to keep him prisoner in case he should try to escape from them.

When they reached the gangplank there was room only for one person to move up at a time, and one Russian walked ahead, with Sare sandwiched between him and his colleague.

He stepped aboard, and as he did so a sailor who had been standing to attention put his arm round his neck to pull him backwards, and Craig moved forward with a swiftness that came from years of practice and pulled Sare out of the way of the man behind him.

He was fumbling for the gun that was in his pocket, but he was too late.

Before he could get hold of it, he was in the vise-like grip of two sailors, and both the Russians were carried quickly out of sight, while Craig drew Randall Sare into the Saloon.

He put his arm round him protectively, and as he did so he realised that he was very thin, almost emaciated.

He saw too that there was a look on his face which meant he had not completely readjusted himself to life and was still dazed from being in the spiritual world into which his trance had taken him.

Then as they entered the Saloon and somebody shut the door behind them, Aloya gave a cry of happiness.

"Papa!"

She threw her arms round her father, and he smiled at her and it was as if the clouds moved away from his eyes.

"Are you all right, my darling?"

Randall Sare's voice was low and very hoarse.

"I should be asking that of you, Papa," Aloya said, tears running down her cheeks.

"I am all right," Randall Sare replied, "but still a little bewildered."

Craig helped him into a chair.

"Sit down," he said, "and I will bring you a glass of champagne, but what is more important, I know, is that you require food."

"Yes, you must be very hungry," Aloya said.

Even as she spoke a steward brought in a bowl of soup on a silver tray and set it down beside him.

"Light and nourishing," Craig said with a note of laughter in his voice. "I remember you told me that a long time ago, and I have not forgotten."

"You have a good memory, Craig," Randall Sare said, "and I received your message last night."

"I thought you would."

The two men's eyes met for a moment and they knew how closely attuned they were to each other.

Then as Aloya knelt at her father's feet, slowly, as if he knew it was a mistake to hurry, he sipped small spoonfuls of the warm soup.

Craig went back to stand in front of the Baron.

"I think, Baron," he said, "although it seems a pity that our acquaintance should end so abruptly, I should send you back to your yacht. My car is outside waiting to carry you there, and your friends will be ready to escort you. The two other gentlemen, who are still asleep, will be left on the Quay and can be collected by your own men, or left to be picked up by the Police."

He saw the expression of anger on the Baron's face and added:

"Your bodyguards will leave behind them some offensive weapons which, may I point out, are not usually carried by gentlemen when they attend a luncheon-party."

Craig was aware that the Baron was now shaking with fury at the way he spoke, and his hands were clenched so tightly that his nails were digging into his palms.

But he was completely powerless, and that was more humiliating to a Russian than anything else.

Craig rang a bell, and as the door was opened instantly by his secretary, he said:

"Have the Baron conveyed to my car, and when he is actually inside it, allow the last two Russians to join him."

As his secretary advanced into the room, Craig said to the Baron:

"We are leaving now, but should you consider following *The Mermaid* with either or both of your yachts, I will save you the necessity by saying that our speed is about double yours, and there is no possible way you can catch up with us and, as you are eager to do, make yourself objectionable."

There was a provocative note in his voice as he continued:

"Go now, otherwise I might regret that I did not dispose of you when I had the chance. But you will live to fight another day, and that should be some satisfaction, even though Randall Sare's secrets remain in British hands."

Now as if he could no longer contain himself the Baron swore under his breath volubly and furiously in Russian.

Only Aloya understood, and she made a little murmur of protest.

Then at a signal from Craig the secretary moved the Russian swiftly from the Saloon and the door closed behind him.

There was the sound of engines starting up beneath, and it seemed only a moment later, although there must have been enough time to get the five Russians ashore, when there was the sound of the gangplank being brought on board and *The Mermaid* started to move out to sea.

It was then, as if he had been too angry until now to ask questions, that Lord Neasdon enquired:

"Where are we going? Where are you taking us?"

"We are going first to Nice," Craig replied, "and because I have no wish to spoil your holiday in the sun, I will put you ashore there."

He thought Lord Neasdon looked slightly apprehensive, and he said contemptuously:

"You need not be afraid, the Russians have no further use for you, and I am absolutely certain that by the time you return, their two yachts will no longer be in Monte Carlo harbour."

"They will not . . . follow us?" Aloya asked nervously.

"There is not a chance," Craig answered. "Those old-fashioned yachts take a long time to get up steam, and by the time they do we shall be miles away along the coast."

"I suppose it is unnecessary to ask where we are going," Randall Sare said.

"I am taking you to safety," Craig answered, "which was the first thing I was told to do. The second was to rescue Lord Neasdon, a new member of the Foreign Office, from the wiles of a Russian spy."

Aloya gave a little laugh, and Lord Neasdon said angrily:

"That is a lie!"

"I am afraid it is . . . true," Aloya replied. "I was . . . spying on you, but not very . . . effectively."

"I cannot believe it!" he said. "Do you mean to tell me you were simply trying to extract information when you said all those things to me?"

There was a stricken note in his voice which made Craig for the first time feel rather sorry for him.

"What I am going to suggest, Neasdon," he said, "is that we leave Sare and his daughter together and go on deck to look back and make quite sure the Russians do not have some fantastic new weapon of which we have not yet heard by which they can either follow or sink us."

He spoke laughingly, and he knew that what he said did not make Aloya in the least afraid, but Lord Neasdon looked worried as he rose from the chair in which he was sitting.

Then, as if there was nothing else he could say, he left the Saloon, followed by Craig.

They walked out on deck and Lord Neasdon muttered:

"I cannot believe it! It is incredible! I thought she cared for me."

"She was forced by the Russians to play the temptress,"

Craig said, "and when you have been in the game as long as I have, you will learn that one must never take chances."

"How was I to know? How was I to guess that she would deliberately spy on me and tell me all those lies?"

"She was trying to save her father. She told me how desperately sorry she was at having to deceive you, but Sare's life was at stake."

"Do you believe they would have killed him?"

"Yes, after they had tortured him."

"I did not know such things happened in the modern world!"

"In your new position in the Foreign Office," Craig said, "you will find things can be very different from anything you have experienced before in the comfortable Embassies of Europe."

"How do you know all this?" Lord Neasdon asked aggressively. "After all, you are American."

"Even Americans have their uses at times," Craig replied, "and incidentally, we never ask questions of one another, nor do we ever reveal what we are doing or have done, or from whom we receive our instructions."

He spoke sternly, like a School-Master to a young pupil, and Lord Neasdon looked abashed.

Craig walked onto the bridge, where the Captain was navigating the ship, and said:

"Show Lord Neasdon our latest gadgets, Captain. I know he will be interested."

"It'll be a pleasure, Sir!" the Captain replied, and there was nothing Lord Neasdon could do but pretend to show an interest that he was far from feeling.

Craig left him and went back to the Saloon, and as he joined Aloya and her father, she said:

"How can you have been so . . . wonderful . . . so marvellous as to have . . . saved us so cleverly! Papa and I do not know . . . how to . . . thank you."

"You can both thank me very easily and very adequately," Craig said.

They looked up at him, and he said to Randall Sare:

"I think you know that the sooner Aloya and I are married, the safer she will be!"

Chapter Seven

Craig watched Lord Neasdon being rowed ashore in the boat which had been summoned from the harbour by a signal.

Just before it arrived, he said quietly:

"When you write your report for the Foreign Office, if you say that you were aware from the very beginning that the Countess Aloya Zladamir was not what she appeared to be and you were curious to verify what you suspected to be the Russians' intentions, I shall not dispute it."

Lord Neasdon, who had been looking extremely depressed, seemed to become more alert. Then he replied:

"Do you mean that?"

"I mean it for two reasons," Craig replied. "First, because I can understand all too well what you felt for the Countess, and secondly, I would not wish to be instrumental in damaging what I am sure will be a brilliant career."

"That is very generous of you," Lord Neasdon said.

There was no time for more. The sailors were letting down the rope-ladder by which he was to descend into the boat, and he paused only to hold out his hand.

"Thank you, Vandervelt," he said, and there was no doubt that his gratitude was sincere.

Then as the row-boat moved away, Craig said to the Petty Officer standing beside him:

"Tell the Captain full speed ahead!"

As he spoke, Craig went below.

When he joined Randall Sare and Aloya in the cabin and said that the sooner she was married the safer she would be, Randall Sare's eyes had lit up for a moment.

Then, before he could speak, his head dropped on his chest and he murmured a little above a whisper:

"I—am so—tired."

Craig did not wait to argue. He knew that Randall Sare had been buoyed up to exert himself far too soon after coming out of the trance, and now exhaustion had set in.

He merely picked him up in his arms and carried him below as if he were a child, followed by Aloya.

The moment they appeared, Craig's Valets came hurrying from one of the cabins and he said to them:

"I want you to undress Mr. Sare and get him into bed as quickly as possible. Do not disturb him. He is asleep."

As he spoke he was aware that Randall Sare's head was on his shoulder and he was in a deep sleep from which it would be difficult for him to wake for a long time.

One of the Valets opened the door and Craig carried him into an extremely comfortable cabin, beautifully furnished and decorated, as were all the cabins in the yacht, with valuable paintings of ships.

He laid him down very gently on the bed, and as his second Valet joined them, he took Aloya by the arm and drew her from the cabin out into the passageway.

"Will Papa be . . . all right?" she asked.

"I promise you he will be, although he may sleep for twenty-four hours before becoming conscious. But he has had something to eat, and that is all that matters."

"And . . . you saved . . . him!" she said in a little voice that broke on the words.

He took her along the passage and into another cabin, which she realised was Craig's private Sitting-Room, where he could escape and be alone if he had guests who occupied the main Saloon.

In it was a desk, a sofa, two comfortable red leather armchairs, and a magnificent painting of a battle at sea between an English man-of-war and a Spanish galleon.

But Aloya had eyes only for the man who stood beside her, and she said, still in the broken little voice she had used before:

"How can I . . . thank you for . . . saving us? How can I . . . tell you what it means to . . . know that . . . Papa is no longer in that . . . evil man's hands?"

"I will show you how you can thank me," Craig answered.

He put his arms round Aloya and drew her to the sofa, and as they sat down his lips were on hers.

He kissed her passionately, demandingly, as if he was still afraid of losing her.

To Aloya it was as if she had been taken from the depths of Hell into the celestial light of Heaven.

She could hardly believe that there was no longer any reason to be afraid that her father would be tortured and killed and she herself would be left in the hands of his murderers.

But for the moment it was difficult to think of anybody but Craig, the sensations he evoked in her, and the wonder of his kisses.

Only when he raised his head, and looked down into her face to see in her a new beauty springing from her happiness, did she manage to say:

"I . . . love you . . . I love you . . . I want to kneel at your feet and . . . thank you for being . . . so wonderful. There are . . . no words to tell you what I . . . feel."

"Your lips express that far better with kisses," Craig answered, and even to himself his voice sounded strange, deep, and unsteady.

He knew that never in the long list of his love-affairs had he felt as he was feeling now.

It was not only that he desired Aloya as a woman and her beauty thrilled him, but he felt that they were so closely attuned to each other that their vibrations linked them as one person, and it was difficult to think that even marriage could bring them any closer than they were already.

As if his thoughts conveyed themselves to Aloya, she said:

"Did you really mean . . . as you told Papa . . . that we should be . . . married?"

She spoke a little shyly and the colour rose in the magnolia whiteness of her cheeks.

"Of course I intend to marry you," Craig said, "but only, my darling, if you are willing to do so."

"Are you really asking me such an . . . absurd question?" she asked. "I can imagine nothing . . . more perfect than to be married to you, if you . . . really love me."

"I love you as I have never loved anybody before," Craig answered, "and this is true, Aloya, although you may find it hard to believe, I have never in my life said 'I love you' to any woman but you!"

"Is that . . . true?"

"I swear it is the truth, because I have never found anybody who is so completely perfect for me, and you knew just as I did that our vibrations linked us together long before you allowed yourself to love me."

She gave a little sound of happiness and hid her face against his neck.

He kissed her hair before he said:

"How can I have been so fortunate as to find you when I least expected it?"

As he spoke, Aloya gave a little laugh and asked:

"How could you . . . love me when you . . . thought I was . . . spying for the . . . Russians?"

"My instinct told me that you were not doing it willingly," Craig replied, "but even if you had been, I would still have loved you and been unable to escape from you."

She looked up at him, and suddenly the radiance in her face was replaced by a look of fear.

"Suppose," she said, "the Baron . . . carries out his threat and . . . kills both you and Papa?"

"He will not do that."

"How can you be so certain?"

"I will tell you later," Craig replied. "I want to talk about you and tell you how much I love you, and to hear you tell me that I am the only man you have ever loved."

"That is easy," Aloya replied, "because I did not know love could be . . . like this until I knew you . . . and found, even though I refused to acknowledge it, that you . . . were in my . . . dreams."

"As you were in mine."

Then he was kissing her again, kissing her until they were no longer on the yacht, but flying towards the sun, and the golden glory of it was in their hearts, in their bodies, and on their lips.

A century later, or so it seemed, there was a knock on the cabin door, and Craig took his arms from round Aloya and went to open it.

One of his Valets stood outside, and knowing that the man wished to speak to him, he went into the passage, closing the door behind him.

"Mr. Sare is all right?"

"He's still asleep, Sir, and we've made him comfortable. But those devils had slashed him with their knives and burnt him with cigar-ends!"

Craig's lips tightened. This was what he had expected the Russians would do when they were trying to find out whether Randall Sare's trance was feigned or real.

Because he knew that both his Valets were experienced in treating wounds, he asked:

"You have attended to him?"

"I've done what I can for the moment, Sir," the Valet

replied, "but the best thing he can do now is sleep, and every time he wakes I'll give him something nourishing to eat, so that he dozes off again."

Craig nodded and said:

"I am sure you two will take it in turns to sit with him."

"Of course, Sir."

The way the Valet spoke made it sound as though he was offended that even for a moment Craig should have thought they would do anything else.

"Thank you," he said. "You realise of course that I have no wish, unless it is absolutely necessary, to call in a Doctor. There might have to be explanations, which I would prefer not to give in this part of the world."

"Leave everything to me, Sir, and don't let the young lady worry about him."

"I will try," Craig replied.

As he spoke he knew that it would be a great mistake for Aloya to know how her father had been treated, but once again, because they were so closely attuned, when Craig went back into the cabin she asked:

"Is Papa all right? The Russians have not . . . harmed him?"

"He will be all right," Craig said soothingly. "My Valets are both trained in nursing a sick man and can do it very much more effectively than most Doctors."

"That means they have nursed you when you have been . . . injured on a mission . . . like Papa."

"I could never aspire to do the marvellous things your father has done," Craig answered. "I am only a humble pupil following along the path behind him."

"I know you are much more than that, from the way Papa spoke to you," Aloya said perceptively. "And if you had not saved him, I know they would have taken us back to Russia, and we would neither of us . . . ever have been . . . free again."

There was a note in her voice which told him she was

perilously near to tears, and Craig held her close against
him as he said:

"As your father's daughter, you know as well as I do
that once a mission has been successful, it is better
never to refer to it again, and certainly never to be
afraid of what has been prevented from happening. I
want you to forget all about it and concentrate only on
me."

"That is easy," Aloya said, "because I love you until
you fill the whole world, and there is . . . nothing else
but you . . . and you . . . and you!"

The way she spoke was very moving, and Craig could
only kiss her until there was nothing else for either of
them but the beat of their hearts, and a love which
could be expressed only by their lips.

Because Aloya was very happy and her love had
made her radiant, Craig was certain she would sleep
peacefully that night.

He, on the other hand, would have to spend several
hours writing a confidential report on what had happened,
which would go into the archives at the Foreign Office
and be seen by only two or three Senior Ministers who
were actively concerned with the problem of Russia's
encroachment on Tibet.

Later, as the afternoon came to a close and the sun
sank, having finished a very English tea in the Saloon,
Aloya said:

"I suppose you realise I have nothing to wear except
for the clothes I stand up in? I am only hoping that one
of your Valets may be able to provide me with a
tooth-brush."

Craig smiled.

"Come and see your cabin," he said. "I think when I
designed it I must have been thinking of you."

She gave him an entrancing smile and he could not
help adding:

"Once we are married, you will share my cabin,
which is larger, but it needs a feminine touch."

She looked shy, and he thought the blush that swept over her face was the loveliest thing he had ever seen, and she slipped her hand into his as he took her to the cabin which was opposite his Sitting-Room.

As he opened the door she saw that the walls were Nile blue in colour and the bed was draped with coral curtains, which the Egyptians used in many of their Temples.

"It is lovely!" Aloya exclaimed.

Without speaking, Craig opened one of the panelled walls, which concealed a large cupboard, and she saw to her astonishment that all the gowns which the Russians had provided her with to entice Lord Neasdon were hanging there.

She gave a cry of amazement, then looked at Craig for an explanation, and he said:

"You underestimate my powers of organisation! I thought it was poetic justice that, having been provided by the Russians with such an expensive and elaborate trousseau for their own ends, you should continue to use it until I can buy you, as I intend to do, the most beautiful clothes any woman ever possessed."

"But . . . how did you manage to get . . . hold of them?" Aloya asked.

"Before I left the Hotel," Craig explained, "I instructed my two Valets to go to your room and pack everything that was there."

"But . . . surely Olga—my Russian maid—tried to . . . stop them?"

Craig gave a little laugh.

"I believe she spoke very volubly on the subject," he replied, "but my men silenced her."

He saw on Aloya's face an expression that was almost one of horror, and he added quickly:

"They did not harm her. They merely gagged her and tied her up, so that she was obliged to watch them taking away your things! On my instructions they left the Baron's jewellery behind, heaping it into her lap so

that there could be no question of her later accusing
them of theft."

He spoke with such a note of amusement in his voice
that Aloya could not help laughing.

"I can hardly believe it!" she said. "Olga was a
very . . . frightening . . . overbearing woman."

"I imagine it may be some time before she is discovered
by the chambermaids, probably just about this time of
the day."

Aloya gave another little laugh and put her arms
round his neck.

"How can you think of everything?" she asked. "I
shall always be frightened that you will find me inade-
quate as a wife and certainly as a housewife."

Craig's arms tightened about her.

"You are everything I have ever dreamed of, and that
is the only thing that matters."

He kissed her until a sudden movement of the ship
made them sway on their feet, and he said:

"I want you, my darling, to make yourself beautiful
for me, although I think it is impossible for you to look
any lovelier than you do at the moment. But in half-an-
hour's time I shall know I was mistaken!"

"In half-an-hour!" Aloya exclaimed. "I need all that
time in which to change, so leave me quickly."

She was laughing, and because she looked so adorable Craig kissed her again until she pushed him away
and shut the door behind him.

As he went to his own cabin he knew that never in
his whole life had he been so happy, while every nerve
in his body seemed to glow as if with an electric spark.

When Aloya joined him upstairs in the Saloon, night
had fallen and the stars were coming out in the sky.

The sea was calm, and the lights from the yacht were
reflected in the water, while the lights along the coast-
line made a picture that was so beautiful that Craig
thought it would always remain in his mind.

But when Aloya came into the Saloon he knew that

she was lovelier to him than any view he had ever seen in his life, lovelier than the snows on the peaks of the Himalayas, the sun rising over the desert, or even the moonlight on the Taj Mahal.

Almost as if India had been in Aloya's mind when she was dressing, she was wearing a gown that was not unlike a *sari*, draped over one shoulder and gathered round the waist.

As if the designer had tried to capture the mysterious depths of her eyes, the material was of a very deep mauve, embroidered with silver and ornamented with stones like amethysts.

It was a lovely gown, but Craig had eyes only for the translucence of Aloya's skin, the silver of her hair, and the light of her eyes, which told him far better than any words how much she loved him.

They stood for a moment looking at each other, then she ran across the cabin as if only in his arms could she be safe and secure.

"You look very beautiful, my darling," he said.

"That is what I wanted you to say," she answered.

They had so much to talk about at dinner that they sat for a long time at the table after the stewards had left them. Then Craig drew her from the Saloon out onto the deck and they stood together looking up at the stars.

"How could I have been so stupid as to think for a moment that God and the Power in which we both believe would not save Papa and me?" Aloya asked in a small voice.

There was a pause. Then she went on:

"I am ashamed now that I was so frightened . . . and yet there seemed to be no way out . . . no chance of survival until I . . . found you."

Craig remembered how when he had listened to her talking to Lord Neasdon, she had seemed like a small animal caught in a trap and trying vainly to escape from it.

Because it hurt him to remember how anxious he too had been when he was unable to solve the problem of Aloya or to find Randall Sare, he put his arms round her protectively and looked up at the stars to say:

"We must have faith, and that is something the world needs—the faith that we are never really alone and the Power is always there if we choose to use it."

Aloya drew in her breath.

"You understand," she said, "and I thought there would never be another man in the world who would think as Papa does."

"We have so much to learn," Craig went on, "and because we will do it together, my darling, it will be more exciting for me than it has ever been before to explore the unknown and find the secrets of the Universe, which are hidden except to a chosen few."

"And you are one of them," Aloya said softly.

Because he was afraid that she might get cold, he took her below and said:

"Tomorrow we shall be in Marseilles, and I want you now to go to sleep and not worry about anything."

She looked up at him, and he knew she was longing to ask questions, but unlike most women, because she guessed that he wanted to keep his plans secret, she was silent.

Then she said softly:

"I must say good-night to Papa."

"Of course," Craig answered.

He opened the door of the cabin in which her father lay sleeping, and as soon as they appeared the second Valet, who was on duty, went outside to leave them alone.

Although in the dim light Randall Sare looked pale and emaciated, the expression on his face was one of peace, and Craig knew that he was sleeping naturally.

Aloya stood looking at her father for a moment, then she went down on her knees beside him.

Softly, as if she knew he could hear her in the dream-world into which he had gone, she said:

"We are safe, Papa, and I am thanking God and Craig for saving us. I am happy, far happier than I have ever been in my whole life, since now we need no longer be afraid."

The way she spoke was very moving.

Then she hid her face in her hands and Craig knew that her prayers were too private even for him to hear.

He waited until she rose from her knees, and he thought as she did so that she had such a spiritual look of rapture and joy on her face that it must have been the way in which St. Dévoté had looked when her soul had flown up to Heaven in the shape of a dove.

As he thought of the Saint, he sent up a little prayer of thankfulness for the help which Father Augustin had given him.

He knew that the very large sum of money which he had instructed his secretary to leave for Father Augustin before he joined the yacht would be of inestimable benefit, not only for the poor of Monte Carlo but for all those who were hiding there for some reason and went in fear of their lives, as Randall Sare had done.

Then he took Aloya to her cabin and kissed her good-night, and only when the door was shut behind him did he find that his whole body was throbbing with the emotions she had aroused in him.

He knew that unlike all other women with whom he had been intrigued and infatuated, she stimulated his mind.

More important, his soul combined with hers until they reached out together towards the spiritual that was beyond the comprehension of ordinary people, who had no idea that the things that interested and aroused them actually existed.

'I have found what many men seek but which always remains out of reach,' Craig thought before he fell asleep.

* * *

The following morning Aloya woke knowing that she had slept deeply, and her dreams had been so happy that she found it hard to come back to consciousness.

She was sensible enough to realise that since this was the first time for many nights that she had slept without fear, she felt different both mentally and physically from what she had felt for a long time.

Then she became aware that the engines were no longer throbbing under her, and knew they must be in harbour.

She rose, went to a port-hole, and pulled back the coral-pink curtains that covered it. Seeing the Quay, she knew that they must have reached Marseilles while she was still asleep.

Because she felt it was urgent to see Craig to make sure he was there, she started to dress, wondering what time it was.

She was in fact astonished when she learnt that it was already almost noon, and she had slept for nearly fourteen hours.

'Craig understood that that was what I needed,' she thought. 'He thinks of everything! How can any man be so wonderful?'

She rang the bell, and when one of Craig's Valets appeared, she asked first:

"How is my father this morning?"

"He's had a good night, Miss," the Valet replied. "He woke twice and I gave him some soup which I'd kept hot through the night, and he drank it and went back to sleep again."

"He is sleeping now?"

"Like a baby, Miss. Don't worry about him. I'll fetch your coffee."

The Valet disappeared before she could ask him about Craig, and while she waited she wondered if he was as eager to see her as she was to see him.

When the Valet returned with the coffee, she managed to say:

"Does Mr. Vandervelt know I am awake?"

"The master's gone ashore, Miss," the Valet replied, "but he'll be back soon, and he said if you asked for him he wouldn't be very long."

Aloya therefore dressed herself in one of the pretty gowns which the French designer had proudly told her would be the talk of Monte Carlo.

She remembered how she had hated the idea then of strange people staring at her and also being humiliated and ashamed that she was being decked out in order to attract a man so that she could extract from him information that was required by the Russians.

"If you do not learn from him what we wish to know," the Baron had said bluntly, "we will take your father away immediately and you will never see him again."

Aloya had given a little cry of horror, and he had added:

"It is up to you. Make this man your lover. A woman can extract anything she wishes to know from a man once they are in bed."

"How can you expect . . . me to do anything so . . . horrible . . . so despicable?" Aloya had faltered.

The Baron had merely looked at her in a way which made her feel as if she were a slave, naked in the Market-Place, and he was assessing her price.

She had known only too well that when they tortured her father for the information they required of him, there would be nothing she could do to save him.

Therefore, her only hope had been to play for time and pray for some miracle that would enable them to escape from the Russians before they were taken away from Monte Carlo.

She had therefore set out to attract Lord Neasdon as the Russians had told her to do, playing on his vanity and telling him how attractive she thought him, but being afraid that it was only a question of days before she had to become his mistress.

Every word she uttered, every moment she was with him, had made her feel as though she wallowed in the filth of the gutter, and yet there had been no other way in which she could save her father.

It had seemed like a light from Heaven, or rather the Arch Angel Michael, when Craig had appeared, and her instinct had told her she could trust him even while she was afraid to do so.

"One word to anybody outside," the Baron had said, "one cry for help, and your father dies!"

But her instinct had told her that Craig could save her. She had known even in the first few minutes when he had spoken to her on the balcony that he was different from any other man she had ever met.

There was something within her which reached out towards him and made her feel that they vibrated to each other and were close in a manner that she had known before only when she was with her father.

But while she prayed that he could save them, her mind warned her that one unwary step, one indiscreet word, and she would have signed her father's death-warrant.

At night when she tried to sleep, she had thought of the Power that her father had told her was always there, and she tried to believe him.

At the same time, she had been terrified that she might do something wrong because she was so inexperienced.

Then the miracle had occurred and Craig had defeated the Baron and outwitted the men who had guarded her father both by night and by day. He had been so clever that even now it was hard to believe it had happened without bloodshed and without anybody being injured.

"I love him!" Aloya had said in her heart. "Please, God, make him love me."

Her intelligence told her that there must have been

many women in Craig's life. He was so handsome, so attractive, and Lord Neasdon had told her enviously how rich he was.

But her instinct had told her that all that was of no importance, and they had something so precious, so sacred and unique, which they shared between them that nothing else was of any consequence.

She was waiting on deck when she saw a motor-car being driven along the Quay, and then Craig stepped out of it, followed by the Captain of the yacht.

As he came up the gangplank her first instinct was to hurl herself into his arms, but with a superhuman effort she stood waiting until he joined her.

They looked at each other and somehow there was no need for words. They were as close as if their lips were touching and a kiss joined them.

Craig did not speak. He only took Aloya by the hand and drew her into the Saloon.

Then he stood with a smile on his lips, looking at her, and she said almost childishly:

"I . . . I was waiting for . . . you."

"I thought you would be, but it took a little time, my darling, for us to be married."

She stared at him incredulously, and he said:

"In accordance with the law of France, we have been married by the Mayor of Marseilles, with the Captain acting as a very able proxy for you."

"I . . . I am . . . married to . . . you?"

Aloya's voice seemed to come from a very long way off.

"We are married!" Craig replied. "But because I know it will please you, I have been to the Russian Church to arrange for us to be married again later in the afternoon, in the faith to which your mother belonged."

Aloya gave a cry that was also a sob, and the tears were in her eyes as she said:

"How could you . . . do anything so . . . wonderful? It is something I want . . . more than . . . anything else."

Craig put his arms round her but did not kiss her, and merely said:

"I think both of us know that we have a faith to which all religions aspire, and the Power in which we both believe, my darling one, does not depend on any particular creed. At the same time, I want to see you as a bride, and I know you will feel that you are even more blessed than you are already if you hear the words spoken in your own Church."

Aloya drew in her breath.

"I . . . wanted that," she whispered.

Then Craig was kissing her freely, demandingly, and possessively.

It was only after luncheon that she said:

"It seems a somewhat banal question, but what would you wish me to wear?"

Craig laughed.

"I thought sooner or later you would become feminine enough to ask that! While there will be nobody present except two witnesses at the Ceremony, at which the Priest will hold the crowns over our heads, I suggest we celebrate our Wedding Day in a manner which we shall wish to remember and which undoubtedly will delight our children."

He waited for the little expression of shyness that he knew would come into her eyes, and the blush on her cheeks, before he laughed and said:

"A Frenchman always marries in full evening-dress, and that is what I intend to wear. But I would like you, my darling, to wear the silver gown in which you look like a shaft of moonlight, and which you wore at the Grand Duke's party."

He drew her close to him as he went on:

"It was there, unless I am mistaken, that you became aware that you could trust me, and I seemed different in your mind and in your heart from any other man you had known before."

"I . . . love you . . . and I know now that I . . . loved you then," Aloya replied, "but because it was so . . . strange . . . and because I have never known love before . . . I felt as if you had come from the stars to help me, and for the first time there was a light at the end of the long dark passage in which I was incarcerated."

"That is what we have found together," Craig said quietly, "the light that will never leave us, and which will be ours for all eternity."

* * *

When they knelt side by side in the small Russian Church with its hanging silver lamps and its walls covered with sacred Icons, Craig thought that the blessing of the Priest came in the form of a light.

It was the light that burnt from their souls and would reveal to them the wonders of the Universe because it was so much a part of their love.

Because the Service had been very moving and for the time being the sanctity of it swept away their passion, they drove back to the yacht in silence, and Aloya knew that in becoming Craig's wife she had reached a harbour of safety that she had never thought would be hers.

They stepped on board to find the Saloon decorated with white lilies, and when Aloya saw a huge white wedding-cake on the dining-table, it was impossible not to laugh and feel as if the whole atmosphere were ringing with wedding-bells.

"We are married! We are really married!" she cried.

"I will make you sure of that, my darling," Craig said in a low voice.

They drank champagne with the Officers, who toasted them and wished them good health, and after they had given the crew a generous ration of rum, the cake was cut and sent to their quarters.

When Craig had ordered a bouquet for Aloya, he also ordered a wreath of small lilies to encircle her head which was covered with a lace veil.

After the Officers had gone, they sat for a while in the Saloon, then without speaking, since words were unnecessary, they moved down below just as *The Mermaid* slipped her moorings and moved out to sea.

"Where are we going?" Aloya asked.

"I do not want to stay in harbour, feeling that there are people all around us," Craig answered. "There is a little bay not far along the coast, where we will anchor for the night, and there we will be very quiet, with only the stars above us and the soft lap of the sea below."

"It sounds . . . very romantic," she whispered.

"This is what it will be, my darling," Craig promised.

He led her not to her cabin but to his, and here again she saw there were white lilies beside the bed, and huge jars of them on the floor where they could not spill over.

As she looked up at Craig in gratitude, she thought that only he could have organised their wedding so beautifully, and although it was so quiet and secret, it was being celebrated in a manner which neither she nor he would ever forget.

Very gently he took the wreath and veil from her head, and as she looked up at him with eyes that seemed to be filled with stars, he said:

"This is your Wedding Day, my darling, and because I love you, and because I know you are very young and innocent, I would not do anything that would spoil our happiness or make you feel afraid."

Aloya gave a little laugh of sheer joy.

"How could I be afraid of you?" she asked. "I understand what you are saying to me, and I am very ignorant of love because I have always lived in such strange places with Papa and Mama. But I have dreamt of it, and I know that you are the man who has filled my dreams, and we have been . . . together in other . . . lives."

"I love you!" Craig said. "I love you so much that it is hard for me to understand how one small person could completely change me overnight, and arouse in me emotional sensations I had no idea I was capable of feeling."

"If I can give you something . . . new and . . . different from anybody else, that would be the most . . . wonderful thing that has ever . . . happened to me."

She put her head against his shoulder as she added:

"You are so handsome, besides being so kind and so clever and so vital, that I am afraid . . . after a little while . . . you may find me . . . boring."

"That would be impossible!" Craig said. "How could I be bored with myself, which is what you are, my adorable wife, not only because we have been joined by the Sacrament of Marriage, but because our bodies are one, as well as our minds, our hearts, and our souls."

Aloya put up her arms to him.

"We are married and we are one," she said, "but you are the bigger and more important part of us. I shall love you and worship you for the rest of my life."

"You must not say such things to me, my precious!" Craig protested. "At the same time, that is what I feel about you, and so even in that we think the same!"

They heard the anchor being dropped and then there was no longer the sound of footsteps overhead but only the quiet of the night and, as Craig had said, the lap of the sea against the ship.

As Craig was kissing her he undid her gown and lifted her onto the bed. She realised he had pulled back the curtains from the port-hole, and now there were not only the stars but the light from a young moon climbing up the sky.

She felt it was like the life that they were starting together, with a light of such beauty and glory to guide them that it was impossible to express it except by love.

Then Craig came to her and she felt his body against

hers, his heart beating on hers, and his hands touching her.

The moonlight not only covered them with its silver light but vibrated within them, and it was the power of Love that had been theirs in the past and would be theirs in the future and for all eternity.

* * *

It was three o'clock in the afternoon and the sun was very hot when Craig, after swimming in the sea, climbed back onto the yacht to join Aloya, who was resting under an awning.

He dressed himself in a towelling-robe that reached the ground, and put a towel round his neck, before he sat down beside her in a deck-chair.

"Do you feel cooler now, darling?" she asked.

"Much cooler."

"While you were swimming they told me that Papa awakened, had a good meal, and went back to sleep. But later he would like to see us both."

"We will talk to him when he wakes," Craig said, "but I hope it will not upset him when we leave Marseilles tonight by train."

Aloya gave an exclamation.

"We are . . . leaving tonight?"

"I want to take you to England," he replied, "first because the Foreign Office are desperately anxious to see your father and find out what he has to tell them, and secondly because as soon as this business is finished, I am taking you both to America."

Aloya looked at him a little anxiously and he said:

"I want you to meet my family, and because I think your father should disappear for a while, I cannot think of a better place for him to be than on my Ranch in Texas!"

Aloya's eyes widened but she did not speak, and he went on:

"As soon as he is strong enough, I am going to make

him write down a great many things he will publish later, which will be of inestimable value to the world, and it will keep him busy until, in his own words, he can 'get back to work.' "

Aloya gave a little sigh of happiness.

"You seem to have it all planned."

"I have a feeling that your father will agree with me that this is for the best."

"Suppose I disagree?" she asked provocatively.

"Then I shall kiss you, my beautiful darling, until you change your mind."

His eyes rested on her lips as he spoke, and she felt as if he were already kissing her, and, seeing the fire in his eyes, she felt a little tremor like a shaft of sunlight run through her.

She thought that they could never look at each other without feeling a response that was, she knew, the vibrations of love seeping through them.

Never had she imagined that love could be so wonderful or exciting, and at the same time so divine that she knew that everything they did was sanctified and part of God.

"I love you!" she said, and she knew it was what Craig wanted to hear.

Then, as if it suddenly struck her, she exclaimed:

"You said that Papa must get away secretly . . . but why? You do not think the Russians . . . might be . . . pursuing him?"

There was a touch of fear in her voice that Craig had heard before, and he covered her hand with his as he said:

"I thought you might ask that question sooner or later, and because I cannot bear that you should be afraid, my darling, there is something you should know."

"What is it?"

Craig picked up one of the newspapers which his secretary, Mr. Cavendish, had put on a low stool beside Aloya's chair when he had been swimming.

She knew he had been back to Marseilles to fetch them, but she had not shown any particular interest, feeling that she had no wish for the outside world to encroach on them while all her thoughts were concentrated on her husband and their happiness.

Now Craig opened the newspaper and, folding it, handed it to Aloya.

For a moment, because she felt it was vitally important to both of them and she was a little apprehensive, the black printed words seemed to swim in front of her eyes.

Then she read:

TRAGEDY IN MONTE CARLO

On Wednesday evening fire broke out on the Russian yacht The Tsarina, *which was anchored beside another Russian yacht,* The Tsarevitch, *in Monte Carlo harbour.*

It was nearly thirty minutes before fire-engines could reach the ship, and by that time the fire had gained a firm hold, and a large part of The Tsarina *was badly damaged.*

In the panic that ensued, the owner, Baron Strogoloff, was unfortunately not rescued from the flames, and when they were under control his body was found in the Saloon, where he had obviously fallen from his invalid-chair.

It is with deep regret that we announce the death of the Baron, a distinguished Russian nobleman. It was his first visit to Monte Carlo, and he was known to be a regular patron of the Theatre and a lover of music.

Several members of his crew received major burns and two of the Russian guests were taken to Hospital, where they are reported as being out of danger and as comfortable as possible.

Aloya read the report and gave a little gasp.
"The Baron is dead!"

"He will not be deeply mourned," Craig said quietly.

The way he spoke made Aloya look at him sharply.

"You were ... responsible for ... this?"

"I did not want you to be worried," he answered, "and go on feeling that the Baron was threatening your father or me. Whatever reports he intended to make on Randall Sare have, I imagine, been burned with him."

He continued with a note of sarcasm in his voice:

"If I am not mistaken, the Baron would wish to have had all the glory of having captured and imprisoned such a notable character, so very little of what has occurred will be known by the Secret Police, on whose orders he was acting."

"Is that ... true?" Aloya asked.

"I am sure of it," Craig answered. "I know the way they work, and when the Baron was forced to hand over your father, I was certain there would be consternation among his personnel and the bow of *The Tsarina* would be left unguarded. I therefore had one of my men go on board, and they were unaware of it."

"How did you manage that?"

Craig smiled.

"The Russians are inveterate talkers. They talk and talk about everything. I gambled on the fact that when the Baron sent for your father, they would be too busy talking about it to think of anything else."

"So while that was happening, your man climbed on board!"

"He is a brilliant electrician and also a very efficient underwater swimmer," Craig said. "I gave him ninety seconds to tamper with the electric wiring aboard the Russian yacht and render it exceedingly dangerous, but he told me proudly that he had taken only sixty. Then he swam back to *The Mermaid*, and nobody had the slightest idea he had ever been there."

Aloya put out her hands.

"You are so ... clever that you ... frighten me."

"Now you need not be frightened by anyone else," Craig said, "and we can do anything we want to do."

Aloya's eyes twinkled.

"I think, as it happens, it will be what . . . *you* want. How can I possibly oppose or argue with anybody as . . . brilliant as . . . you?"

Craig lifted her hand to his lips.

"I have the feeling that we shall argue and confront each other and stimulate each other's mind. It will be very exciting, but it will always end in the same way."

"With my giving in?" Aloya asked with a smile.

"No. In being aware that we both want the same thing," he replied. "This morning nothing matters except that we love each other. It is going to take me a lifetime, my precious darling, to tell you how much and how greatly I love you!"

He rose from his deck-chair as he spoke, and, putting out his hands, he pulled her to her feet.

"I am going below to dress," he said, "and I want you to come with me, firstly because I cannot bear you to be out of my sight, and secondly because I want to kiss you."

The way he spoke the last words told her that they meant a great deal more than what he actually said.

She looked at him with adoring eyes. Then she let him lead her along the deck and down below.

They went into their cabin and shut the door, and he took her in his arms.

"The last cloud has been swept away," he said, "and if I ever see you looking frightened again, I shall be very angry!"

"How could I be frightened of anything now that you and Papa are safe?" Aloya asked. "Oh, darling . . . darling Craig, will you promise me that whatever Papa wants to do in the future, you will stay with me? After all we have been through, I do not think that I could think of you in . . . danger and not . . . want to . . . die."

Craig did not answer. He only took her in his arms and kissed her.

Then as he felt her lips soft beneath his, and as he felt the fire that burnt within him evoke a flame within her, he lifted her in his arms and laid her down on the bed.

Then he was kissing her demandingly, passionately, fiercely, and the flames leapt higher and higher.

As they were carried up together into the sky, they knew that the divine fire of love burnt away not only fear but evil.

Now ahead of them was a happiness in which there was no fear, no danger, but only the ecstasy, the perfection, and the glory of Love.

ABOUT THE AUTHOR

BARBARA CARTLAND is the bestselling authoress in the world, according to the *Guinness Book of World Records*. She has sold over 200 million books and has beaten the world record for five years running, last year with 24 and the previous years with 24, 20, and 23.

She is also an historian, playwright, lecturer, political speaker and television personality, and has now written over 320 books.

She has also had many historical works published and has written four autobiographies as well as the biographies of her mother and that of her brother, Ronald Cartland, who was the first member of Parliament to be killed in the last war. This book has a preface by Sir Winston Churchill and has just been republished with an introduction by Sir Arthur Bryant.

Love at the Helm, a novel written with the help and inspiration of the late Earl Mountbatten of Burma, Uncle of His Royal Highness Prince Philip, is being sold for the Mountbatten Memorial Trust.

In 1978, Miss Cartland sang an Album of Love Songs with the Royal Philharmonic Orchestra.

She is unique in that she was #1 and #2 in the Dalton List of Bestsellers, and one week had four books in the top twenty.

In private life Barbara Cartland, who is a Dame of the Order of St. John of Jerusalem, Chairman of the St. John Council in Hertfordshire and Deputy President of the St. John Ambulance Brigade, has also fought for better conditions and salaries for midwives and nurses.

As President of the Royal College of Midwives (Hertfordshire Branch) she has been invested with the first badge of Office ever given in Great Britain, which was subscribed to by the midwives themselves.

Barbara Cartland is deeply interested in vitamin therapy and is President of the British National Association for Health. Her book, *The Magic of Honey*, has sold throughout the world and is translated into many languages.

She has a magazine "Barbara Cartland's World of Romance" now being published in the USA.